I0601433

Dragon Justice

Dragon Justice

Legion of Riders: Book Two

J.D. Hallowell

SMITHCRAFT PRESS

Smithcraft Press
110 San Paulo Circle
West Melbourne, FL 32904

ISBN 978-1-62927-026-5

Dragon Justice © 2018 by Joseph Delno Hallowell. All rights reserved. Printed in the United States of America. No part of this book may be used or reproduced in any manner whatsoever without written permission except in the case of brief quotations used in critical articles and reviews.

CONTENTS

DEDICATION

DRAGON JUSTICE IS dedicated to the memory of my friend and sometime editor, John Barker, whose help was invaluable in so many ways. Rest in peace, John. You are missed.

Acknowledgements

WHILE SPACE DOES not permit me to acknowledge everyone I owe a debt of gratitude to regarding this book, I am especially grateful to my wife, Jennie; my son, Connor; my brother, Jim; and my friends, John Barker, Matt DuPree, and Craig R. Lloyd-Smith; who have been endlessly patient, encouraging, and helpful. Special thanks are due to several authors who have given generously of either their general or specific advice and support, especially Michael J. Sullivan; Leeland Artra; Cheryl Matthynssens; Brian D. Anderson; T. Jackson King; Cheryllyn Dyess; G.W. Pomichter at the Hangin with Web Show; everyone at the Fantasy Sci-Fi Network; Jaimie Engle, whose tireless energy and enthusiasm along with the wealth of knowledge and insight that she shares so freely makes her a treasure; and last, but certainly not least, the incredible and inspiring Kerry Hall. Of course, my deepest gratitude is reserved for my readers and fans, without whom I am simply talking to myself.

PROLOGUE

"I'VE SEEN TO the patrols, Nassari," Nadia said as she entered the office, "however, we need to decide soon what we are going to do about replenishing the herd, or the dragons will be out of food before winter sets in."

"Out? Completely?" Nassari asked. "We only just brought in that lot from Trent. Surely we can't have used so many cattle in such a short time?"

"We had those animals brought in almost four months ago. Our dragons had only eaten lightly after flying here from Corice because the hunting is poor in this region. When the herd arrived, they devoured a fair portion of it immediately. Now, with the increase in their physical exertion flying patrols and running messages to and from the capital, they've eaten more than they normally would have, and most will need to do so again soon. Also, don't forget that two unbonded dragons decided to clutch here this past spring because they wanted their daughters to be bonded. Nothing eats like a baby dragon!"

"You're right, of course," Nassari replied. "And we'd better remember as well that both Wanda and Pina have said they wish to compete to mate this year, so that will give us two more clutches to deal with. I have no idea where we are going to find suitable candidates, but we will have to make sure we can at least feed them."

"Can we get Lord Johnston to send more cattle?" she asked.

"Oh, he'll send them, but at triple the price."

"Triple?" she nearly shouted.

"*What is upsetting you, Nadia?*" Pina asked her telepathically, ready to lend whatever assistance her bond-mate might need.

"It's nothing that need concern you, Dear," Nadia silently answered. "You were almost asleep, I'm sorry my thoughts disturbed you. You flew an early patrol; get some rest while you can."

"You flew that same patrol," the dragon replied. "Perhaps you should heed your own advice."

"As soon as I have finished with Legion business, I intend to take a hot bath and then have a nice nap. Don't worry about me, Pina. Get some sleep, and we will try to take a little time for ourselves later this afternoon."

"*We will see, Nadia…*" Pina let the thought trail off without further comment.

"Pina is alright, I take it?" Nassari asked.

"Yes, she's fine, just responding to my outburst. What in the world could we have done to so anger that nobleman from Trent that he has tripled his prices? I thought we dealt with him fairly."

"It wasn't us, Darling," Nassari replied. "That damnable local, Lord Bastian, intercepted the drovers on his land and demanded they pay a toll for the graze and water the cattle were using. They weren't on his land for more than three leagues, but he charged so much that Lord Johnston actually lost money on the sale. I offered to at least cover enough for him to break even, but he refused. He said that dragon riders have come to the aid of his family in the past without thought of recompense, and he would consider it a favor returned this time. However, good will only goes so far. The man can't afford to lose money like that, so he has to charge accordingly when making any future deals." He paused a moment before adding, "Lord Bastian lets nothing cross his land without lining his pockets."

"That one," Nadia said, as if she were speaking about something she needed to scrape off the bottom of her boot. "I have met him twice. On one occasion, I actually had to deal with him directly concerning the purchase of vegetables, and I would rather swim in a cesspool than do so again. Besides being totally lecherous, he is more miserly than all of the politicians in Corice combined."

Nassari opened his mouth to speak, but she didn't give him a chance before she continued. "I met our supply wagons at his estate to oversee the purchase of staples for the Fort. While we were there, one of his 'indentured' servants, slaves if you want to put a realistic label on the practice, dropped a jar of pickled goods. When the vessel broke, his lordship became enraged and began beating the man with that metal-ended walking stick. If I hadn't personally intervened, he would have clubbed the poor wretch unconscious. Then his foreman actually moved to lay his hands on me."

Nassari stood up at that bit of news and said, "I know that you are completely capable of taking care of yourself, but if he actually touched you, I will fly out there this minute and make challenge myself!"

Wanda didn't know exactly what caused Nassari's upset, but the dragon bellowed her outrage anyway.

Nadia held up her hand and said, "Calm down," then added, "both of you. When the man moved in my direction, he ran straight into Pina's tail. As he was picking himself up off the ground, she told him that whatever part of his body touched me she would take home as a trophy."

"Still," Nassari replied, "I may have to have words with those people. They may not respect Dragon Riders, but I'll make certain they at least fear us enough to be courteous."

"It might come to that," Nadia said, "and I certainly wouldn't mind instilling a bit of dread in that landholder, but the situation was dealt with. Of course, I had to pay for the broken container of goods to ensure no further harm fell on the man who dropped it. Bastian even took offense that I kept the man from his work long enough to heal the injuries from the beating. Pina is so upset about how he keeps and treats those people she absolutely refuses to return to the estate unless it is to remove him in favor of someone more benign. The only thing in the world the dragons hate as much as Roracks is slavery, and those indentured servants are nothing more than slaves."

They were both quiet for a moment before she asked, "Can't we get special dispensation from the crown to get our goods without paying that worthless cheat's extortion?"

"It's possible," he answered, "but that comes with problems as well." At her look of inquiry, he added, "The king of this country would very much like to make us part of his own military. He has tried on several occasions to do just that, and he continues to manipulate circumstances toward that end. If he were as clever as he is ambitious, fending off his efforts might prove more tiresome than it does now. However, every time we have to ask for special favors, he tries to slip in conditions that attempt to control us. The fewer such interventions we use, the better off we are."

Nassari walked to the small table by the door and poured them both coffee from a stoneware pitcher before returning to his desk and sitting back down.

"I'm afraid, Darling," he said, "we will have to deal with this situation ourselves. As for more cattle, we will have to buy steers from Bastian himself for the time being. They are somewhat scrawny compared to Johnston's stock, and more expensive by over half again as much, but still cheaper than paying the tolls to bring Johnston's animals in from Trent."

"I just wish there was more we could do…" She let her thought trail off.

"One thing at a time, my love," he responded. "We have to get our own house in order before we can go on a crusade."

CHAPTER 1

SIMON WOKE SUDDENLY; something wasn't right. He lay as still as possible hoping the feeling of dread would go away, wondering what was scaring him. Then he heard someone, or something, breathing. Whoever, or whatever, was standing right next to his bed, directly above him. He tried to call out for his mother, but his voice stuck in his throat, and only a hoarse croak came out that couldn't have carried to the door, let alone down the hall to the room his mother shared with two other women.

Simon was completely alone. He had reached the age of ten just after winter solstice, and, since he was beginning to show obvious signs of entering puberty even at his tender age, he had been moved out of the girls' room. There were no other boys in the quarters, so his weak cry for help would go unanswered because the other three beds in this small room—more a closet, really—were empty. His visitor would be undisturbed unless somebody happened to wander in, and the likelihood of that happening was small since it was against the rules for the servants to move about the house unbidden in the night.

A hand pressed down on his back between his shoulder blades.

"I know you're awake, little mouse."

The voice belonged to Broderick, the son of Lord Bastian, who owned the manor and the surrounding lands.

He tried to move, but Broderick, who was sixteen and larger than Simon, held him down firmly.

Simon opened his mouth, but before he could scream, Broderick laid a knife against his cheek and said, "Make one sound, little mouse, and I will cut your tongue loose and make you eat it."

He closed his mouth and wondered what cruel game Broderick had thought up this time. Broderick had always been malicious, ever since Simon and his mother had moved into the manor just over three years ago. Simon still carried scars from some of the times the older boy had lashed out at him for no reason other than his own sadistic pleasure, but he had never before attacked Simon in the night. Of course, Simon had only very recently been moved from the room he had shared with the girls.

A strange sort of sensation began at Simon's ankles. At first, it was like something crawling up the backs of his legs. Then he realized that it was his nightgown slowly being pulled up. The implication of this act was lost on the ten-year-old; at least until Broderick began to force Simon to move his legs into a position that would better accommodate the assault. Simon had heard of such things while listening to conversations of adults and older children, mostly sons of field hands who shared quarters outside the main house, but he had never thought much about it until this very instant.

The pain as Broderick consummated the act was awful. He could do nothing to stop the older boy, who was not only larger than him, but also didn't lower the knife from Simon's face. All he could do was hold still and endure the attack.

Finally, after some grunting and harsh words, Broderick withdrew, but remained kneeling behind him, and said, "You've been a good little mouse, so I will allow you to keep your tongue, for now. However, if you breathe a word about what has happened here tonight, I will not only see you punished as a liar, I will follow through on my threat to feed the thing to you."

He shifted his eyes to see Broderick's face. He could see that the older boy was watching him, waiting for something. Then he realized what it was Broderick wanted: he wanted to see Simon cry. Simon bit back the bitter tears that threatened to flow like water from a dam. He refused to give Broderick the satisfaction. After waiting for a few moments, Broderick simply shrugged his shoulders and got up from the bed. He adjusted his clothing and then looked back once before he turned and left without another word.

Simon didn't move for several minutes, knowing that when he did release the tension in his muscles it would also signal his body to release his pent-up tears. He wanted to be sure that Broderick wouldn't come back before allowing his legs to straighten and his stomach to come to rest on the bed. Then he cried silently for a long time.

CHAPTER 2

THE YOUNG BOY walked through the world as if he weren't really part of it. His mother seemed concerned that he appeared detached, but her questions on the matter went unanswered. He simply couldn't tell her anything. Broderick had broadened his threats over the next few nights to include not only Simon's mother but anyone he might be friends with as well.

He knew that he was an indentured servant. Since his father had died owing Lord Bastian money when Simon was seven, the full amount owed fell to him and his mother. Being indentured to Lord Bastian was as good as being owned outright. All such "servants" were required to not only work off their debt, but they also had to pay for their food and lodging. Since they could not leave the Lord's lands while they still owed money, they had no choice but to take lodging under Bastian's roofs and buy their food from his larders at ridiculously high prices that kept them from being freed from the original obligation. Even though he was only ten, Simon understood that the system was designed to keep the indentured servants from paying what they owed and leaving.

Running away meant that the Lord would have you tracked down and brought back. After a severe whipping, you would then be put back to work, and the bounty paid out for your return would be added to the outstanding balance. One man had run away three times. The last time Lord Bastian had ordered that the man's right foot be lopped off and the stump roughly cauterized. The poor fellow was now forced to hobble around the stables on a crudely made peg, helping the blacksmith.

Simon went through his day in a near daze, dreading the coming night. He feared running away, but he feared staying just as much.

He was helping the girls clean the kitchen. He had been assigned to clean the ashes from the pit beneath the stove, and that was where he found the little utility knife that had gone missing nearly two weeks before. Why no one had found it while doing this job up until now was a mystery in itself, but the only puzzle that interested Simon at the moment was how to keep himself safe from Broderick.

Looking at the knife, Simon felt as if Fate were dealing him an extra hide tile. He just stared at it for a long moment while he thought about how he would use something like this. He quickly rejected the idea that he could use the blade to kill his tormentor. He felt he might be within his rights, but he also knew that Lord Bastian would not see it that way and would retaliate against his mother as well as against him.

The knife was a tool, but what was the best way to use that tool?

Then, as if a light had suddenly gone on, he thought about going hunting with his father, about how they had used knives and other tools to help build shelters, make snares, and any number of other tasks. He had been young when his father died, but the man had taught him the basics of survival away from civilization. Suddenly, his lethargy lifted, and he felt reattached to the world around him. He had the beginnings of a plan! He knew that he would have to endure Broderick's attacks until he was ready, but even that could be done now that he also felt he could eventually escape.

He quickly shoved the knife into his short boot and walked carefully so that it wouldn't fall out and clatter to the floor. He wasn't sure what would happen if he got caught with the blade, but he was determined not to find out. Before he left the kitchen, he also managed to steal a bit of cured bacon and two biscuits. He made his way back to his room and hid everything, double wrapping the food in two pieces of cloth to prevent the smell from betraying its presence.

He went back to his chores and worked with renewed vigor. By finishing a task quickly, he would be assigned another, which would most likely take him to some other part of the house where he might find some new item that he could add to his growing list of "supplies." He was actually humming to himself by the time he finished work for the day.

He ate quickly and quietly, squirreling away anything that wouldn't spoil. He hid his bread and a piece of hard cheese inside his shirt before leaving the table and going to his room. Once inside, he put his newest acquisitions away with the rest. He noticed that his "hoard" was getting big enough that he might have to seek out a better hiding place soon. He decided he would look for a good place to stash his supplies when he chose his escape route. He would have to choose that route carefully because there were no windows in his room for him to climb out, and all of the doors leading outside could only be reached by passing the sleeping quarters of other residents of the house.

He had just settled into bed when he heard the door hinges creak: it was Broderick. Simon did just what he had thought about doing and lay there detached, thinking about running away, not the assault.

Broderick liked to taunt him, and this time was no different.

"Do you know why I call you my Little Mouse?" he asked.

Simon said nothing and gave no indication that he had even heard the question. Broderick went on as if it were simply a normal conversation, "I call you that because you are a mouse, and I am a cat. Have you ever seen a cat play with a mouse?"

Again Simon refused to engage and lay there trying to imagine scenes from his hunting trips with his father: the scenes kept turning into images of Broderick caught in a snare and Simon standing over him with a knife.

"A cat doesn't eat a mouse, you know. At least, not right away. A cat will toy with the mouse as long as the mouse tries to escape. As long as the mouse tries to save itself, it stays alive. When the mouse gives up, like you have, the cat begins to get bored and eventually kills the little thing. Then the cat will eat it. I have no intention of eating you, Little Mouse. I think I will, as the cat sometimes does, leave your headless corpse on someone's bed: perhaps your mother's."

That got the response that Broderick was looking for. Simon turned his head with real fire in his eyes and said, "If you don't leave my mother alone, I will kill you!"

The look in Broderick's eye went from disinterested to that of a feral dog watching a wounded animal. He suddenly lashed out and punched Simon hard just below the ribs on the right side. The pain was tremendous, and Broderick simply allowed his whole body weight to fall with his elbow digging into the same spot he had just battered.

He put his lips against Simon's ear in a parody of tenderness and whispered, "That's better, Little Mouse, I was beginning to get bored with you, but you have moved and piqued my interest again. Try and remember that the next time."

After Broderick left, Simon forced back the tears that tried to flow. He refused to cry, determined to turn that anger and frustration into the energy he needed to complete his plan to get away from his tormentor.

CHAPTER 3

THE NEXT MORNING Simon's mother woke him early.

"Hurry up," she said sweetly as he was wiping the sleep from his eyes. "Lord Bastian and his son are leaving today on business, and we have to help make ready for the trip."

Simon had forgotten all about this trip. It meant he would have nearly two weeks without Broderick's night time visits.

His mother mistook his smile for one of simple pleasure, something she hadn't seen for some time. She tousled his hair and said, "It's good to see you in such fine spirits; hope it lasts." Then she smiled warmly at him before adding, "Hurry and get to the kitchen, there's plenty to be taken to the stables and loaded, but if you're quick I can get you a bite to eat before you have to start carrying."

Simon rose out of bed gingerly and moved directly to the chamber pot. His back still hurt where Broderick had hit him, but there was no problem emptying his bladder and no visible trace of blood in his urine. His mother was a remarkably well-educated woman for her station in life. She had once been a healer's apprentice, and she took every opportunity to pass that knowledge, and her extensive herb lore, her only legacy, on to her son. He knew that Broderick had punched him in the kidney, and he knew how dangerous that could be.

Once in the kitchen, he ate hurriedly: since it was simply a bowl of porridge, he couldn't hide anything to add to his supplies. When he finished, he took up a load of foodstuffs and carried it out to where the small cargo wagon was waiting. There really wasn't much for him to load, and he was left to his own devices in the barn. Looking around, he noticed that a length of rope, about twenty-five feet of it, had been carelessly tossed aside. Simon made sure no one was watching before he grabbed the rope and hid behind a barrel of odds and ends near the blacksmith's forge. He hastily wrapped the rope around his waist, hiding it under his shirt. The rope was about as thick as his thumb and would be invaluable when he ran away.

He had just finished hiding the coil when Broderick said, from quite close by, "What are doing there, Little Mouse?"

At first, Simon thought that Broderick had seen him hide the rope and was certain that he would be severely punished. However, Broderick only moved very close and continued talking, taunting him.

"I'm only going to be gone about two weeks, Mouse; don't get used to the idea that you won't see me again. I've grown quite fond of our little games. When I get back, we can see if we can come up with something new and more interesting." Then he sneered and added in a low voice because others were approaching, "Meow."

Broderick then moved to join his father, who had just entered with the other travelers. The blacksmith, who came walking over from the direction of a side door, looked at Broderick with open contempt as the older boy walked toward his sire. The smith moved closer and stood by Simon, almost protectively.

"I wish those damn Dragon Riders at the old fort could be trusted," Lord Bastian intoned to his chief foreman. "I hate to make this kind of trip, but I can't take the chance that they won't take advantage of a servant. Damned Riders are calling for herd beasts, and I intend to get my money for my stock. Don't know why they had to settle here; we haven't needed them before, and we damn sure don't need them now. We've always been able to protect ourselves, even this close to Rorack territory."

The smith leaned over conspiratorially and whispered, "I've been told that he didn't complain so loudly when it was that Warrick fellow who was taking herd beasts for *his* Riders. Now that Warrick's gone and we have honest Riders who are willing to pay, the fat old bastard is going to soak them for every ounce he can get."

While he couldn't hear what was said, Bastian did notice the movement, focused on the smith and Simon, and spoke out angrily, "That's one of the house children. What's he doing out here? Doesn't he have chores inside?"

Bastian took a step toward Simon while tightening his grip on his walking stick. Broderick smiled, and Simon cringed. They had both seen Lord Bastian lash out with that cane at servants before.

The smith, however, was undaunted. He quickly stepped between Simon and Bastian and said, "He's doing exactly what I told him to do. I got him running errands for me this morning because that one-legged fellow you gave me can't handle the job." Then the smith puffed up and said irritably, "If you want all of this work done, I need an able-bodied man to help. All I get is your rejects. This boy can do twice as much work as any of them."

Simon could hardly believe his ears. He didn't understand why the smith was trying to save him from Bastian's wrath, and he didn't care, so long as he didn't get the beating that was almost sure to come otherwise.

"Liar," Broderick cried. "He was simply hiding behind that barrel when I found him. You were nowhere to be seen."

What happened next stunned Simon to his core.

"You're naming me liar," the smith growled dangerously. Then he looked at Lord Bastian and said, "I'm not one of your indentured slaves; you either put a leash on that pup, or find yourself a new smith!"

Simon had not even dared think that someone could stand up to Lord Bastian like that.

Broderick started to make a hot reply, but it ended in a yelp as his father poked him hard in the ribs with the metal handle of his walking stick.

"No need for all of this," Bastian stated flatly. "If the boy is working for you, fine; he now works in the smithy. Find him sleeping quarters out here in the barn. Damned waste having him take up one room by himself, anyway." Then he looked directly at Simon and added, "If I hear you aren't working hard enough, you'll go to the fields next."

His Lordship then turned back toward his foreman and continued on as if the whole incident had never happened.

Broderick, who looked as if someone had just taken his favorite toy, walked over and said in a low voice, "One day, smith," he made the title sound like an insult, "you will push your luck too far. You are not the only one in the all the lands who can do your job."

The big man was not impressed and retorted, "I may not be the only one, boy, but I'm the only one that will work here. If you have a problem with that, you're sixteen and old enough to make a proper challenge. Do it: your daddy can make another one that looks pretty much the same."

Broderick paled visibly when the smith mentioned challenge. According to law, anyone who had reached his sixteenth birthday could make a legal challenge to a duel. Also, anyone of that age could be held legally responsible for his words and deeds, and therefore, could be challenged. The law that governed such things in Horne was harsh, but it made for a more polite society. The implied threat from the smith was that if Broderick didn't make formal challenge, but continued to make insult, the smith would simply call him out as the law allowed. Since the smith was much larger and stronger than Broderick, and the boy was mostly a coward and a bully, he didn't want to push his luck any further.

Then the smith added, "Whatever is going on between you and this boy is over. Now, don't you have some flies you can pull the wings off of or something?"

Broderick simply turned and stomped off into the daylight outside the barn, trying to grind his anger into the ground as he went.

Simon turned and smiled up at the big man.

"Before you thank me, wait until you've done a day's work out here. You might just come to wish I'd kept out of this whole thing." Then he looked at Simon and shook his head. "Not much to you, though you're plenty tall enough. How old are you, about fourteen?"

"I'm only ten, Sir; my mother says I take after my father in my height."

"Ten? You are large for your age, but not much tone to you. I suppose you'll develop some muscle after working for me out here for a while." Then he held out his hand and said, "I'm Boron, not Sir."

Simon stared for a moment and then clasped the big man's wrist as he had seen his father and other men do. "I'm Simon," he replied.

Boron looked at him for another moment and smiled, "Now then, you don't have to tell me anything, but is there a reason you stole that length of rope you have wrapped around your waist, or are you just a packrat collecting odd bits and pieces?"

Simon shook his head; he was certain that no one had seen him take the rope.

"C'mon now, I'm not going to turn you over to his Lordship, or any such rot. But if you are going to steal, don't forget to look up when you're looking around. I was above you putting something in the loft. The man they gave me to help around here can't climb a ladder with that peg leg of his."

Boron's face became somber, and he added, "I didn't hear what that jackass was braying about when he thought it was just you and him, but I've got my suspicions. You can tell me, or not; it's up to you."

Simon opened his mouth to refuse to tell, and the whole story just sort of spilled out. He couldn't believe he was hearing himself talk about it. He had never thought he would have the courage to speak about it to anyone. He also thought that he would be too embarrassed, but somehow telling Boron just felt right, and he did owe the man for standing up for him.

Boron had stood quietly while the boy told his story. When Simon finished speaking, the big man put his hands on the barrel and leaned there for a moment collecting his thoughts. Simon could see the tension begin to build in Boron's arms, and then the head hoop suddenly bent and the staves splintered in the man's hands. The

smith looked down surprised at the damage: he had completely ruined the barrel without even realizing he was doing it.

Boron turned back to Simon and said, "It's good that you didn't
tell your mother this. If his Lordship finds out, he will most likely
kill you and anyone you might have told. Even I won't be able to
protect you if you speak of this to anyone else."

Simon was suddenly confused, and he said, "But I just watched
you all but challenge Broderick just a little while ago."

"It's one thing to scare a bully, son. It's quite another to kill a
man's only son, even in a fair fight, especially if the man has some
power like Bastian does. If it actually came down to Broderick making such insult that I'd be within my rights to challenge the twerp,
his Lordship would pay a suffrage price and have the boy striped,
but he wouldn't let me kill the little monster."

"I don't understand. Are you saying that Broderick can continue
to do as he pleases?"

"No!" Boron's answer was so fierce that Simon jumped. "I'm not
saying he will continue; I'm saying that directly confronting him
will do no good. His father won't accept it, and will try to stop the
tale from being told."

As Simon's expression became even more confused, Boron sat
down on a nearby bench and bid Simon join him. Then he explained,
"You see, lad, it comes down to the old man's immortality."

When Simon did a double take, Boron said, "Immortality is living forever, or at least for a very long time."

"I know what the word means; my mother has educated me pretty well. I just don't understand what that has to do with this."

"Most men want some measure of immortality. Some are lucky
enough to bond to a dragon and live for two or three thousand years,
or longer. The great men, like the Rider Corolan and his grandson
Delno, are written into sagas that will be retold for a long time to
come. The rest of us have to get our immortality by having children,
knowing that we live on through our offspring. Unfortunately, Lord
Bastian's immortality is Broderick." Boron said this as if he had just
bitten into something that tasted foul. "I wasn't necessarily correct

when I said Bastian could make another. It's not for lack of trying; from what I hear, he's randy enough, but he hasn't *gotten* on any woman but the one in his life. To me, it raises the question of whether or not Broderick is even his, but the boy is his only heir, and, therefore, he will protect not only him but his reputation, even if that means killing everyone who might know the story. I've only been here since the end of the Great War against Warrick – only a few months - but in that time, I've seen Bastian have men maimed and killed for less than this."

The two of them sat silently for a moment. Finally, Boron looked at Simon and said, "Look, son, you have every right to run away from here. Hell, if you could convince the authorities that your story is true, the law would see to it that Broderick is castrated, and then spends a few years working in the mines for his crime. However, it's your word against the word of a noble-born, with no real evidence to back you up." Boron shook his head sadly before continuing. "I'll make you a deal. You stay on with me here, and I'll see to it that Broderick can't get to you. In the meantime, I'll teach you what I can about the world you will be running out into, and how to defend yourself. Then, when you're ready, I'll make sure you have everything you need to get away."

He held out his hand to Simon to seal the deal. Simon hesitated for a moment, and then, realizing it was the best he was likely to get, he shook on it.

"Good, now go and get your stuff. There's a place up in the loft where you can make a bed, and you can pull the ladder up behind you while you sleep at night."

CHAPTER 4

THE NEXT TWO weeks were full of hard work, but Boron saw to it that Simon ate well and wasn't overtaxed in his chores. By the time Lord Bastian got back from his trip, Simon was already starting to feel at home working for the smith.

Neither Lord Bastian nor Broderick stopped at the barn upon their return. They simply left their horses and all of their gear to be handled by the stable boys and went directly to the main house. Then Simon had to help Boron check the animals' hooves, and re-pack the hardwood wheel bearings on the wagons. By the time they were finished, it was nearly dark and Simon was exhausted. He ate quickly and then climbed up into the loft and fell into bed, dozing off almost at once.

He sat bolt upright out of a sound sleep and remembered that he had not pulled up the ladder behind himself. He had just finished doing so when he saw someone about Broderick's size walk into the barn. He hung back in the shadows and watched as the figure walked directly to where the ladder should have been. Then he heard Broderick swear when he found the ladder gone. What happened next almost stunned him.

"What are you doing sneaking around out here at this hour?" Boron's voice demanded from somewhere in the darkness.

Broderick jumped nearly a foot in the air at the sound. "I – I am not sneaking around," Broderick stammered. "I am the son of the rightful Lord of this property, and I have the right to come and go as I please. Since you are nothing but a servant, I could ask you the same question."

"This is my work station. That forge may belong to your father, but everything else in here is mine. I have the right to protect my possessions from people sneaking around in the middle of the night."

"I told you that I am not sneaking," Broderick replied. "I couldn't sleep and decided to walk around. I thought I heard something in here, so I came in to see what it was."

Boron stepped closer to Broderick, and Simon could see the smith now. He was armed with a long knife he carried easily in his right hand. He didn't brandish the blade, but it was obvious that the young lordling was not comforted by the sight of the weapon.

"Are you threatening me?" Broderick asked somewhat defiantly.

Boron looked at the knife in his hand and replied, "If I was threatening you, boy, you wouldn't have to ask." Then he shook his head and added, "Go on, get yourself back to the main house before someone else *mistakes* you for a sneak thief, and you get hurt."

"I come and go as I please: you can't order me about."

"In my shop, I make the rules, and they apply to everyone. You don't like that, talk to your father about it, but do it in the main house where I don't have to listen to you prattle on."

Broderick was nearly spitting incoherently, but he also knew better than to push the issue. He turned and began to stomp out of the barn.

As a parting shot, Boron added, "See to it that you don't get restless and make any more late night visits out here. I'll be watching."

Broderick stopped as though he might turn and say something. Then he apparently reconsidered and resumed his march.

Without glancing up, Boron said, "Looks like you pulled that ladder up just in time. Make sure you don't forget again. See you in the morning, bright and early." Then the smith walked out of sight.

It was over an hour before Simon was able to get back to sleep.

Chapter 5

S IMON WAS AWAKENED by the sound of Boron banging his hand against one of the support pillars while calling his name. It wasn't even full light yet.

"C'mon lad, we've got work to do, and I want you to get some practice in before the day starts."

Simon wasn't sure what that meant, but he lowered the ladder and climbed down from the loft.

"Get yourself to the privy and do what needs doing," Boron said brusquely. "Then meet me behind the barn."

Simon quickly finished his physical necessities and went to meet the smith. He was quite surprised to find the man holding two swords.

Boron handed one of the blades to the boy, saying, "We don't have a lot of time this morning, but I'm going to show you some of the basics of defending yourself with a blade. As time progresses, we'll practice more, and, eventually, add another blade in the off hand. Later, if we have the time, we'll also work on using a shield for both defense and attack."

Once the startled lad had the sword in his hand, Boron made a quick attack. The strike was so fast and fierce that Simon could barely get his own blade up to block. The block was weak, though, and if the big man hadn't pulled the cut at the last second, even with the blunted blade, Simon would have been seriously injured.

Boron shook his head and said, "It's good that you got a block up in time, but you didn't put any power into it. If that had been a real attack, with a good sharp blade, you'd be dead. Now try it again…"

As his voice trailed off, he again swung his weapon, and this time, Simon managed to do a little better. So the lesson went on. Boron taught Simon several blocks and then worked on cuts. This first lesson lasted a little over an hour, and Simon was so exhausted he wondered, as he and Boron walked toward the kitchens to get breakfast, if he would have the strength to do his work.

As he dug into the plate that Boron had piled up with food for him, the smith spoke. "You can expect the same every morning from now on. That little bit of a run in with Broderick last night has convinced me that you will most likely need to know how to defend yourself, and you will need every bit of skill I can teach you. That bastard isn't one to leave this alone. He will come back. It won't be soon, but it will happen, and eventually one of us might have to kill him if you don't get clear of this first. I'm not bragging when I say that I'm a pretty good swordsman. I was good enough to be one of the palace elite when I was in the grand army of Horne. I've been teaching sword for a few years, and you have the makings of a good fighter if you put your mind to it."

"I will practice every chance I get," Simon promised.

"Good. We have to work hard, and you have to practice before anyone up at the main house is awake, so we'll want to keep training early. I'll see to it you get the extra food you will need for the increased physical labor you will be doing."

"Boron, why are you doing this for me? Not that I'm not grateful…"

Boron was silent for a long moment before responding, "What's been done to you is wrong. The one who did it should be punished, but that's impossible in our situation. So, the only way we have to punish him is to make sure he learns that he can't just do as he pleases anytime the whim strikes. Maybe someday he'll get what he deserves, but until then, I just can't sit back and let him continue as he would like."

CHAPTER 6

"DAMN! I'VE RUINED the piece." Simon spoke more to himself than to Boron, who was watching him hammer-weld a metal wagon tire.

"No, you haven't; we can still fix it. Just take your time, and do it the way I've shown you," Boron said patiently. "And watch your language; there're ladies present."

There were indeed ladies present. Several of the women servants had brought out all of the pans and other metal items that needed repair from the house. Simon's mother gave him a stern look for his use of profanity, but she couldn't quite hide the pride she felt in him for his elevated station working at the smith's side.

In the four months that had passed since he had moved his quarters, the boy had changed considerably. He was more than an inch taller, and he had gone from a scrawny preadolescent boy to a lean, well-muscled youth. He was much broader through the shoulders now, and the muscular definition of his chest and stomach was clearly visible as he worked shirtless over the forge.

Simon looked up sheepishly and smiled at the three women and two older girls who had come to the barn. As he gazed at the girls, whose sleeping quarters he used to share, he was dimly aware of the fact that they had also grown since he had moved to his new job.

The girls, both older than Simon by a couple of years, though he now looked several years beyond his tender age of ten, were more than *dimly aware* of their feelings. They giggled and playfully pushed each other in the boy's direction. In fact, they quickly became such a distraction that their mothers felt compelled to call them sharply to order and send them back the house.

Once all of the household items were set out for the smith, the other two women left as well. Simon's mother stayed for a moment watching her son finish the wagon tire under the smith's watchful eye. When the job was complete, she stepped forward and put her arms around the boy. Then she held him at arms' length and smiled.

"You're growing up so fast now; you've added height and weight," she said. "You're looking more and more like your father every time I see you; he was always taken for being older when he was a boy because of his size as well. I've known since you were very young you would take after him like this." She paused for a moment as she continued to look at him. Her voice broke slightly as she said, "He would be so proud of you, Simon."

Simon reached up with a callused hand and wiped away the tear that trickled slowly down his mother's face. "I have come a long way in short time, Mother. I am learning a trade, and soon I will be able to make enough to buy your freedom." Then he added in a low, fierce voice, "You have my word on it!"

She looked at him with a mixture of pride and awe, not sure how to respond to the oath he had just made. The smith's voice broke the spell.

"He's a fine lad, and he's growing into a fine young man," Boron said. "Soon he'll be trained well enough to take on a few of the small jobs that come in from the lesser farms, and the money he earns from those will be his own. With that, he'll be able to make good on that promise."

Then, remembering his manners, he wiped his hands on the cleanest rag he could find, held out his right hand, and added, "I've seen you around since I got here, but we've never been properly introduced: I'm Boron."

The woman hesitated for only a second before placing her hand in Boron's, as was customary for a man and woman shaking hands. "I'm Sheena, Simon's mother."

The two adults held the handshake for a little longer than etiquette called for before letting go almost reluctantly.

"I want to thank you for taking my son into your care. He would never have learned a valuable trade working in the house. Whether he can buy my freedom is not important, but if he can purchase his own and leave this estate, I will be at peace. I owe you a debt that I can never repay."

"You don't owe me a thing, Sheena. The boy works twice as hard as any full grown man they've given me, and he seems to just *know* when something is about to break, so we can fix it before it gets worse. That alone has saved me more time than having three more apprentices. No, he earns his keep; there's no doubt about that."

"Well," Sheena replied, "you have my thanks, anyway."

She then turned to Simon and tousled his hair before kissing him on the forehead. "Now I have to get back to my work before his Lordship finds me shirking my duties." With that, she smiled at Boron and started back toward the main house.

"Do you get any time to yourself?" Boron asked before she could take more than a couple of steps.

Sheena glanced back at him and replied, "I have some time after sunset when I might be able to take in the cool evening air." She smiled and added, "Of course I wouldn't feel safe walking around outside alone, after dark."

"Well, then," Boron shot back as she once again began walking away, "I'll look for you by the kitchen door; that is, if you think you'll be safe enough walking with me."

"I don't know; will I be safe walking in the dark with you?" she asked coyly.

"Only one way to find out for sure," he retorted.

Simon was amazed to hear his mother giggle as the two younger girls had earlier.

When Boron saw the boy staring openly at him, he said, "Let's get this tire heated so we can mount it on the wheel. We have enough time to get the wheel back on the wagon and still get some of this repair work done before supper."

Simon wanted to talk to Boron about what had transpired between the smith and his mother, but Boron seemed just as determined to finish everything in the shop well before dark, and the pace he set left no room for idle chat. As they sat down to eat, all thoughts of his mother were quickly pushed aside when Boron said, "We will start even earlier tomorrow. You've completed the basics for the sword that are set down in the army training regimen, and now it's time to start adding to what you've learned. If I end up sending you out on your own, I want to make sure you have more than just the bare bones of self-defense under your belt."

"I've completed the army training regimen?" Simon asked incredulously.

"The fundamentals, and only for the blade," Boron replied. "After four months of training hard for an hour and a half every day, I'd say you are trained at least as well as any of his majesty's troops who have completed basic fencing and moved on to regular duties. In fact, I'd say that when it comes to blade work, you're a damn sight better than most recruits."

Simon puffed up with pride, and Boron held up a restraining hand. "Don't get too full of yourself yet, boy. You've still got a lot to learn, and a lot of hard knocks ahead of you on the practice field before you will be ready to call yourself a warrior. Now finish your supper and go and get some sleep; we'll be starting earlier tomorrow."

"How much earlier?"

"Hmpfh," Boron snorted. "Let's just say that you won't have the excuse that the sun is in your eyes."

CHAPTER 7

"I'VE WRITTEN A letter to the governor. He's my former commander and a friend. I am at least going to get clarification of the laws concerning this debt slavery," Boron said.

"Don't do anything to get yourself in trouble," Sheena replied.

"I won't get into any trouble. In my case, it's Lord Bastian who owes me, not the other way around."

"Well, I thank you again for all that you have done, and all that you are doing for my son."

"I told you there is no need to thank me, Sheena," Boron stated flatly as he and Simon's mother walked in the thin moonlight. "The boy is strong, he does a good job, and he's good company when we're working. He's so big for his age that he's almost as capable as any man I've worked with and a sight better than any Bastian's sent to the smithy in the past. Add to that that he has a good attitude as well as an aptitude for the craft that the others all lacked, and it's a winning situation for both of us. He helps me, and I'm teaching him a valuable skill: it's a fair trade."

"Well, regardless of that, I'm happy to find that he is working for such a kind master. I was very worried when the foreman told me that he had been sent to labor in the smithy. He implied that Simon's new position would be little more than a beast of burden."

"I'm not his master," Boron protested. "I'm just a hired hand around here, no better than Simon or anyone else. I've got something to teach the boy, and he's a good worker. It's an equitable deal for both of us."

"That attitude, my good smith, is why I am so glad that my son is under your supervision." She quickly stood on her toes and kissed him lightly on the cheek before adding, "Thank you anyway: regardless of how well the arrangement works out for you, Simon is getting more than I could have hoped for him."

Though she couldn't see it in the dim light, Boron actually blushed. "I like the lad. Having him around doesn't make up for never having a son of my own, but it fills an empty spot I didn't even know was there."

"Why don't you have children, Boron? You're not that old, and you're certainly not too ugly to attract a wife."

His discomfort was clearly evident. "I had a family once: when I was much younger; a wife and daughter. She insisted on going off with me to an isolated post away from the capital. They both died of a fever that spread through the camp."

Sheena had to push hard to get her next words past the lump in her throat. "Boron, I'm sorry. I didn't mean to pry, and I didn't mean to bring up bad memories."

He stopped walking and took her hands in his and looked her in the eyes. "You couldn't have known. Besides, the same fever swept through Fallon and the other large cities that year and killed a lot of people there as well, so it might not have been any different if I had left them behind. At least this way, I was with them until the end, and they died knowing how much I loved them. Don't worry; the memories of my wife and little girl are good memories, and what happened to them has softened in my mind over time. I took no offense at your questions, and I didn't have to tell you if I didn't want to."

"Still, I talk too much when I'm nervous. I always have. Simon's father said he could always tell that I was 'in a state' by how much I jabbered on. I engage my mouth without any assistance from my mind and ask questions that are none of my business. Or I go on and on with no real point..."

"Kind of like you're doing now," he teased.

She looked at him and tried to be angry, but his smile was infectious, and she couldn't help but smile back. "Kind of like I'm doing now," she agreed.

They stared at each other for a long moment, and he bent forward and kissed her.

As the kiss ended he said, "I shouldn't have done that; I was much too forward, I'm sorry."

"You'll notice I didn't object," she replied. "Look, Boron, we're both adults who have been out in the world. I am a widow, not some giggly young girl who's never even held a boy's hand before. I'm not offended by one innocent kiss. However, curfew is approaching, so I need you to walk me back." She let go of his right hand but held his left as they turned and headed in the direction of the main house. As they walked, she added, "Besides, I rather liked it."

Deep in the shadow cast by one of the fruit trees that grew near the house, a figure scrutinized the couple's every move. Broderick waited until he was sure the smith wouldn't see him stepping out of hiding before heading for his own quarters. He didn't know how he might use what he had learned, but he would continue to watch: eventually some kind of opportunity would present itself.

Chapter 8

Even though Simon had done as Boron bade and had gone to bed shortly after supper, he was still surprised at how early it was when he looked at the sky as he entered the practice area behind the barn. There wasn't even a hint that dawn would approach any time soon.

"High summer is behind us and the days are getting noticeably shorter," Boron said gruffly, by way of greeting. "If we are to get in enough practice and still finish our daily work, we will have to start much earlier from now on. If your sleep is more important than learning what I have to teach you, speak up now."

The big man waited for a moment and then smiled slightly when Simon held his peace and stood ready for training.

"Good, I thought as much, but I wanted to be sure you understood before we start. Today, after we work with the blades, we'll begin empty-handed combat."

Saying that, Boron handed Simon two blades: one was the longer, curved blade he had been using, and the other was a blunted copy of the long knife that Simon had seen the smith carrying months earlier when the man had confronted Broderick that night in the barn.

"Now then," Boron instructed, "the two-bladed style substitutes a short blade for a shield. So, for the time being, think of the long blade as attack and the short as defense. Later, after you've got the basics, we'll work on using both blades for both purposes. The two-bladed style is popular with many men who are city guards. It has become so for several reasons. One is that most cities can't, or won't, buy shields for their guardsmen. However, it isn't just money that has brought about this style. In cramped quarters, the long knife is easier to wield than a bulky shield. Also, an opponent is less likely to get too close on the off side if he is afraid of being stabbed for his troubles."

Simon hung on every word. He wasn't sure why, but he had the unmistakable feeling that his training had just taken on a new urgency.

"And," Boron continued, "if you have to walk for hours on a long guard shift, the knife won't get nearly as heavy hanging on your belt as having a shield strapped to your arm. There are conditions where having a large shield is a definite advantage, such as when you are in the army facing a large enemy force, especially if they are using bows. But if you can master the basics of the two blades, you will also be able to use a shield fairly effectively. Learning the shield, however, doesn't give the mastery of using a blade in your off hand. Since we are not grooming you for military campaigns, I thought the two blades would serve you better."

Over an hour later, about the time that Simon thought his left arm might fall off from fending off Boron's attacks, the big man called a halt. The sun was just starting to lighten the far horizon.

"Now we'll start on empty-handed combat." Boron informed him.

By the time they were done and ready to eat breakfast, Simon felt as if he had already done a full day's work and could easily sleep through until the next morning. It was three weeks before he was sufficiently used to the new routine that he could do more in the evenings than fall exhausted into his bed and sleep the night away. He was, however, rapidly becoming a force to be reckoned with.

The work was mounting up as well as the training. There seemed to be no end to the broken and damaged tools and equipment, not only from the estate, but also from the surrounding farms that had no blacksmith in residence. Boron, as always, was true to his word and allowed Simon to keep the bulk of the money he was paid for doing outside work, only holding back the fifteen percent that went to Lord Bastian. The boy wasn't getting rich, but he was amassing a nice sum. He wouldn't have enough to buy their freedom this year, but by next fall, if all kept going as it was, he would be able to pay their debt, and he and his mother would be free.

As Simon mused on the prospect of leaving the estate, not alone as a runaway, but with his mother as free citizens, Broderick walked up to him.

"Eating well, Little Mouse?" Broderick said caustically.

Simon stood with his empty plate in his hand and replied, "Well enough."

He started to turn and walk away to clean his plate and return it to the kitchen, but Broderick grabbed him with his left hand by the left arm to restrain him. Broderick got a pleased look in his eye when he saw that Simon was startled. What the older boy didn't know, though, was that Simon was only startled because he realized that Broderick, although still a little taller than him, was soft and fleshy, and his impression of the stronger, older boy had been an illusion. That illusion was wiped away by Simon's sudden recognition of the effects of nearly six months of eating well and doing hard physical labor. He was amazed because he knew that, if he wanted to, especially with his new training, he could easily break Broderick's arm.

"I see that you still realize who is in charge, Little Mouse," Broderick sneered.

Simon turned to face his antagonist, and reached across his body with his right hand and grabbed the older boy's left in a painfully tight grip. Broderick immediately punched Simon in the stomach with his unoccupied fist. Simon, seeing the blow coming, simply tensed up his muscles, and the punch had no effect on him. It was Broderick's turn to be shocked. Not only did the punch not disable his victim as he had expected, he had swung so hard that he was now afraid he might have broken his own wrist.

With the pain and surprise clearly evident on his would-be tormentor's face, Simon stripped the older boy's hand off of his arm but kept his own grip firm, and said, "You once asked me if I had ever seen a cat play with a mouse. Now I am asking you: Have you ever seen a kitten try to play with a shrew? The kitten is obviously bigger, but the size of the attacker doesn't necessarily determine the outcome of the battle."

Then Simon let go of Broderick's left hand and added, "You might do well to remember that," before resuming his course to the kitchen.

As Broderick was, once again, left with no clear target on which to vent his unspent anger, he lashed out at the first person available as he stomped back toward the main house. His new victim was Ronny, a scrawny eight-year-old whose father owed Lord Bastian more money than he would ever be able to pay. The young boy yelped from both surprise and pain as Broderick knocked him down with a backhanded strike as the two passed near each other.

Simon's rage surged up, and he dropped his plate to the hard packed ground, not even caring that it broke into several pieces. He started to move toward his long-time tormentor when a restraining hand stopped him. He instinctively reacted as he had been training to do and ended up in a short wrestling match with Boron.

The smith quickly brought Simon under control and then said, "Let it go, lad. Now's not the time!"

Simon continued to try to get loose while he spoke, "He just hit that boy because he was mad at me! Ronny's not a half-wit, but he isn't loaded all the way to the top, either. He doesn't even know why he's been hit, and I won't have the poor boy suffer on my account."

"It's noble of you to want to protect the lad, son, but if you attack Broderick outright like this, when he's walking away from you, not only will his father have you striped until you can't stand, he'll move you to the far fields and probably dock my pay for teaching you self-defense. If all of that happens, where will you be with respect to earning yours and your mom's freedom?"

Simon stopped struggling, and his demeanor deflated somewhat. "You're right, of course. Thank you, Boron. If you hadn't stopped me, I would have done something extremely stupid."

"Well, Simon, it's not right to teach you how to fight if I'm not going to teach you when not to do so," Boron replied kindly. "Now, I think Ronny will be all right, but why don't you go and see if you can help him up and check on him anyway?" Then, almost as an afterthought, he added, "I'll pick up these pieces of plate and tell them I dropped it, so his Lordship doesn't add the replacement cost to your debt. When you're finished checking on the boy, meet me in the smithy: we've got a lot of work to do today."

CHAPTER 9

ONCE THE FALL harvest was done, the work in the smithy tapered off considerably. Simon found himself with more free time than he really knew how to handle, so he spent it practicing the moves that Boron had been teaching him. Just going through the motions without an opponent wasn't the same as actual training, but Boron called it "fighting an invisible enemy," and said that it would still set the techniques securely in his mind and muscles nearly as well as if he had a real person to spar with. Several other boys, including Ronny, had gathered to watch him. That was how Simon got caught on the practice pitch.

"What are you doing, Little Mouse?" Broderick said as he came around the corner of the barn.

Simon instinctively finished the empty handed move he was working on and came up in a fighting stance, ready for an attack. He and Broderick stood staring at each other for a moment.

Finally, Broderick called for an answer to his question. "I said what are you doing? Damn it, answer me."

"I'm exercising," Simon replied. "My work is done for the time being, and I can spend my free time as I see fit."

"You are an indentured servant; you have no free time! When your tasks are done, you are supposed to find new tasks to earn your keep and pay back the lawful debt that you owe to my father."

"Lawful debt?" Simon was unable to hold his tongue. "The debt owed to your father by my father was worked off by my mother soon after we arrived. If it weren't for the ridiculous rule that indentured servants can't leave the grounds, coupled with the criminally high prices that your father charges for food and lodging, my mother and I would no longer be obliged to stay here."

"Are you calling my father a criminal?" Broderick was nearly spitting with rage.

"No. Unfortunately, your father's practices are a legal means of getting around the law forbidding the outright owning of slaves. However, it is simply slavery under the guise of honest business. I have to live with it; I don't have to like it."

"So, you don't like it, huh boy?" Lord Bastian's voice rang out as he approached from the barn.

Boron was walking by the land owner's side. The look on the big man's face was a mixture of chagrin and anger. Simon wasn't sure whether the anger was for Bastian, Broderick, or himself, but he suspected it was a mixture of all three: he shouldn't have risen to the older boy's bait.

"I find it very interesting," Lord Bastian went on, "that you have so much free time that you can not only spend it on idle physical exercise, but you also have enough time left to spend in such deep contemplation of the economic situation you find yourself in. Most interesting that you come to the conclusion that I am to blame for the poor financial state in which your father left you."

Before Simon could respond to the insult to his father, Boron spoke up, "The boy is working for me. I give him free time as I see fit. Even with the free time, he still does more work around here than any two of your other indentured servants. He earns his rations and a damn sight more."

Bastian looked at the smith with open contempt and started to raise his cane. For a second everyone watching held their breath waiting to see how Boron would react to being struck by his Lordship.

Broderick nearly cheered and said, "I've been waiting for this for some time; hit him, Father!"

Boron looked at Bastian and said calmly, "That wouldn't be a good idea. You may be the Lord of this land, and I am just an employee, but I am a free man and have a right to defend myself."

"Your insolence has gone far enough, smith." Bastian was still enraged, but he wisely lowered his cane. "I have had all of you I am willing to take." He looked at Simon and said, "If the boy is as good at his job as you say, then why am I still paying your salary? Perhaps I should send you on your way and let the boy take over the smithy."

Boron looked at the ground thoughtfully for a moment. Simon could see the triumphant smile spreading across Broderick's face, and he desperately wanted to wipe the look away, preferably with a sanding cloth.

Boron looked directly into Bastian's eyes and said, "Fair enough. My contract says you owe me for two full years' service. That amount is to be paid in full if you terminate the employment early. I've worked for you for eleven months, since shortly after the end of the Dragon-Rorack War. So, if you'll just pay me for the thirteen months that you still owe me, I'll be on my way. Of course, I'll be taking all of my tools with me, so you will also have to resupply the smithy if you expect the boy to do his work. Once you've supplied him with tools, he'll probably be able to keep up until spring planting time comes and the shop gets busy again."

Bastian's eyes went wide, and he appeared to be at a loss for words. Simon was pleased to see the smug look on Broderick's face turn sour.

"You can't honestly expect me to pay you for thirteen months of work you haven't done?" Bastian sputtered.

"We have a legally binding contract. You set great store by such things when it's another man who is in debt to you. I expect you to live up to your end of that arrangement. I was on my way back to the capital when you waylaid me and offered me this deal. I didn't put that clause in the contract; you did. You were willing to do that because you needed a skilled craftsman, and I wouldn't take the job without a solid guarantee, and no one else would work for you under any circumstances."

"That's preposterous; I won't pay it."

"That's fine; we'll just have to take it to the local governor for arbitration, then. I believe he is housed in North Point, close to the old fort where the Dragon Riders stay. I'll warn you in advance, though, he's my old commanding officer and my mentor in His Majesty's Army, and he won't take kindly to someone trying to cheat a former soldier. Also, he frequently seeks the counsel of that Rider, Nassari, who is in charge of the fort itself, and from what I hear, he isn't exactly your best friend after the way you've charged for the herd beasts they've bought to feed the dragons. You may be nobly born, Lord Bastian, but I dare say I have enough friends in power to enforce a simple contract."

Bastian again raised his cane, but this time, he held it out between himself and Boron defensively, as if he were trying to ward off Boron's words the way he might ward off a physical blow.

"Very well," he said, "I won't pay you that much to be rid of you, but I won't have my indentured servants lounging about when they should be working off their honest debt. The boy will go to the fields!"

The look of absolute triumph from Broderick was almost too much for Simon, but Boron spoke quickly and intervened before he could make matters worse for himself. "The boy stays on working for me. There's six months invested in his training, and it'll do more good to have him here to help with the metal work come spring than having one more hand in the fields."

"That isn't for you to decide, smith!" Broderick shouted as he stepped closer to his father. He was rewarded for his efforts by a poke in the ribs from his father's cane.

"Very well, smith," Bastian replied, "but the boy is still to be punished for his insult to me. If he were sixteen, I'd have the right to challenge him to a duel for his earlier words."

"If he were sixteen, Lord Bastian, you'd be wise not to make such a challenge," Boron retorted. "How much is the debt owed by the boy and his mother?"

"What?" Bastian asked incredulously.

"How much do they owe you?" The smith repeated as if he were speaking to an idiot.

"I don't keep such figures in my head," Bastian answered.

"Nonsense, man. I have a good aptitude for working metal and a real gift for killing people; your greatest ability is being able to keep track of money. You once told me that you always know down to the last copper where every bit of the coin under your control is at all times. You know how much debt is owed; give me a figure."

"Very well. The boy and his mother collectively owe one hundred and thirteen full gold sovereigns." The land owner smiled, "Even you don't make enough to have that much money lying around, Boron."

"Fine," Boron replied, "How much for the boy?"

Bastian again smiled, warming to the game. "Well, as you have stated, the boy is now a skilled craftsman, so he is worth much more than a simple household servant." The lord made a show of doing the calculation in his head before continuing, "I would say that I would consider the boy's worth at this point to be ninety gold sovereigns."

Simon spoke up before Boron could respond. "So, that means that my mother could be free for twenty-three gold?"

Everyone was astounded that Simon had spoken up. Bastian sneered and said, "That's right, boy. That would leave your mother's debt at twenty-three." Then his voice took on a mocking tone, "Do you just happen to have twenty-three gold sovereigns in your purse? Oh, that's right; you're so poor you don't even have a purse."

"I have twenty-three gold," Boron spoke up. "I'll pay the mother's share."

"That figures," Broderick stated flatly. "You may as well pay her share, after all of the "sharing" she's done with you in the last few weeks." Then, at the look he got from the smith, the lordling went on, "Oh, did you think that you were the only one capable of watching from the darkness, smith? I've seen you and that whore on your nightly "walks": I know what the two of you do on that blanket under the stars."

Simon might not have been old enough to truly understand about complex adult relationships, but he still understood what the word "whore" meant. Though he moved toward Broderick quickly, he was still two steps behind the big man.

Boron snatched the lord's son off the ground by the front of his shirt and said, "You sneaking around in the night and spying on people doesn't surprise me, boy, but if you call that woman a whore one more time, I'll make formal challenge, and there won't be a damn thing your daddy can do about it." Then he set Broderick down so hard that the boy's legs gave way, and he fell on his rump.

Bastian gave his son a hard look as a warning to stay out of this affair before turning back to the smith. "As the debt holder, I have the right to hold both of the indentured individuals until the full debt is paid. Accepting partial payment might make me appear weak to others who owe me money, and lead them to believe that they, too, can get away with not paying their full share. Therefore, I believe I deserve some extra consideration for taking such a chance. I will release the woman for forty gold, and thirty lashes to her son for his insolence."

Boron nearly grabbed the land owner but got control of himself. "Thirty lashes? Are you so enraged that you are willing to kill a boy who you have claimed owes you ninety gold sovereigns? Strong men have died from thirty lashes: the boy is only ten years old."

Before Bastian could say anything, Simon responded, "Twenty-five gold, and ten lashes." He could barely believe he was the one who was speaking. He had seen men whipped before and knew that even ten lashes was serious, so he went on before his courage failed him. "You get your money, I get the punishment, and I will still be able to work afterward."

Boron looked at Simon and said, "You're not doing this; there's got to be another way."

"The boy will be punished either way this goes, Boron," Bastian assured him. "What we are deciding now is how much money it will take to mitigate his insult to me." He turned and gave Simon a purely predatory smile. "I'm not totally unsympathetic, forty-five gold and twenty-five lashes."

"If you insist on this course, Bastian," there was no hint of either civility or compromise in Boron's tone, "I will take this whole matter to Governor Sellers. He may accept some reasonable punishment for the insult, but I know the man well enough to know he will certainly not be happy if he finds that you have cheated the boy and his mother, and he will not look kindly on you for excessive punishment for such a small grievance. I suggest you rethink your position and be reasonable."

Bastian thought about it for a moment and then shook his head. "You are right, your friends are powerful and could make trouble. Therefore, I will accept thirty-five gold, and the boy gets twenty lashes."

Before Boron could respond Simon once again spoke up. "Thirty gold and fifteen lashes and the deal is done." He stood defiantly, looking Lord Bastian in the eye as if his position in life had suddenly been raised to that of the lord's equal.

"Done!" the man shouted before anyone could intervene. "Now, then," he turned to the smith. "Let's have a look at the money, so that we know this little scene hasn't been played out merely for the entertainment of those watching."

Simon started to move out toward the barn to get his stash, which came to less than twenty gold, but Boron motioned him to stay where he was. Then the big man untied a cloth belt that was hidden under his trousers and started counting out coins from those in the pouches sewn into it. When he had counted out thirty gold coins, he put the belt, now considerably lighter, but not empty, back around his waist and tied it into place.

Bastian took the money and then said, "Well then, there's only one part of the bargain left." He turned to Broderick and said, "Take the boy to the beam."

Broderick started to move toward Simon, but Simon glared at him and said, "I don't need you to lead the way, Kitten. I know where the post is, and I honor my debts. I can walk without any assistance."

He then turned and walked in the direction of the whipping post while his Lordship called for the estate foreman to bring his whip.

The whipping beam was made up of two thick timbers set deeply into the ground about eight feet apart with a heavy crossbar on top; the structure was a little more than seven feet high, and two rough cord restraints hung from rings bolted into the top bar two feet in from either end.

The foreman, a man almost as tall as Boron, but not nearly as broad or well-muscled, grabbed Simon roughly. He raised the youth's right hand to the rope.

Boron grabbed the man's arm and said. "There's no need to be rough with the boy; he isn't struggling."

"Stay out of this, smith. Punishment is my job, your job is shoeing horses; maybe you'd best be off to it." Then he looked at Simon and added, "Sometimes I lose count, and have to start over."

Boron grabbed the front of the man's jerkin with his left hand while his right hand reached for the foreman's own belt knife. In less than a second, the foreman was slammed against one of the posts, and the tip of his own blade was pressed to his throat.

"You're a sadist, Bill Weaver," Boron growled dangerously. "I can't stop you from enjoying your work, but I promise you this: I won't lose count of the strokes. If that whip falls on this boys flesh one time more than it's supposed to, or you hit him anywhere other than his back, it'll be the last mistake you ever make!"

The foreman was so shaken he lost control of his bladder. As the wet spot spread across his pants, Boron looked down and said, "I see we have an understanding," before letting the man go and turning to Simon. He didn't, however, return Weaver's knife to him.

"Step up here and put your hands through the loops, son," Boron said sadly. As Simon did as he was told, the smith pulled the loops tight and then took a piece of leather out of his pocket. He folded the leather and put it into Simon's mouth and said, "Bite down on this; it will keep you from breaking your teeth when the whip strikes."

As Simon waited for the first stroke to fall, he noticed that Broderick had moved around to where he could look Simon in the eye. It was just like in his old room: Broderick wanted to see the pain on his victim's face and see the tears. The first stroke was like a red-hot brand as Simon felt the braided leather rip into the flesh on the side of his neck and his back.

As if from a distance he heard Boron's voice shout, "Careful, Weaver, that was too damn close to his face, and I know that you know exactly where that whip is falling. You're too damn good with that thing to make mistakes."

"Sometimes they flinch and lose an eye or an ear," the foreman replied sarcastically.

"Yeah, well I promise you this: you'll lose two of any body part he loses. Keep those strokes on his back and away from his head!"

The next stroke fell squarely on his back, but it was still searing agony. Broderick was thoroughly enjoying the show. Simon looked at him with hatred in his eyes and actually managed to smile. The next stroke very nearly broke his resolve. He steeled himself and then simply disconnected from what was going on. It was very similar to when he would detach from Broderick's torments in his old room. He was dimly aware that Broderick realized what he was doing and wasn't happy about it. That brought him a great deal of satisfaction despite the pain from the blows. Then he had no time to consider his former tormentor's mood as he had to slip deeper into the state to keep from being overwhelmed by the agony. He lost count of the strokes.

The next thing he was aware of was that he was being carried. Despite his height, his buttocks were sitting on someone's forearm and his head was resting on the person's shoulder, the way a parent might carry a sleeping child to bed. He figured it must be Boron holding him since the only other person tall enough to carry him in that manner was Weaver, and Simon knew he would get no such compassion from the foreman. He could also hear a woman crying and realized it was his mother. He wanted to tell her that it was all right because she was now free, but he was unable to raise his head

and do so before he passed out. His last thought before the black-
ness took him was that at least Broderick hadn't gotten the satisfaction of seeing him cry.

Chapter 10

THE FIRST THING Simon became aware of as he woke was the pain in his back. The second thing was his full bladder. The third was two people, a man and woman, whispering to each other.

"What about appealing directly to the Dragon Riders? Perhaps they will intercede on our behalf," the woman's voice said.

"Some say the Dragon Riders are great, fair-minded men who swoop to the rescue of innocents and sweep away injustices. Others say they are no more than thieves, helping themselves to whatever they please. I have noticed that they are men, and, like other men, have to get their own houses in order before they can assist anyone else," the man's voice responded. "They flew in months ago, close to four months after the Great Dragon-Rorack War. They brought wagon loads of supplies with them, but it wasn't enough. They have used almost all of their resources just getting the place set up and are now hard-pressed to make it through the winter with what they have left. From what I've heard, many of them have had to fly off to distant lands for the time being to relieve some of the burden on the fort. We can't expect them to come here and interfere in what is legally the collection of an honest debt, especially when they have their own survival to worry about. We're on our own until Bastian breaks the law in such a way that it will stand up in court."

"Breaks the law!" she almost shouted. "Doing this to a ten-year-old boy isn't breaking the law?"

"Unfortunately, no, it's not."

Simon opened his eyes and looked around. He was lying on a cot in a room that was easily five or six paces by eight to ten paces. The people with him were, as he had surmised, his mother and Boron. A fire in the hearth on the far side of the room cast dancing shadows on the walls. At least two lamps were burning, and when he listened for it, he could hear the sound of night insects somewhere outside.

He decided to risk trying to rise. He had been positioned on his stomach and he could feel bandages on his back. Bringing his arms under himself to push up off of the cot brought the pain of his injuries back to the forefront of his concerns. His mother was facing the smith and had her back to him, so it was Boron who first noticed his stirrings.

Boron pointed in Simon's direction and said, "I see the subject of our conversation has finally woken up."

Sheena turned and moved quickly to help her son rise. "I was so worried about you," she said with tears in her eyes. "I did everything I knew how to do for your wounds."

As Simon managed to get into a sitting position, his mother began to cry outright.

He put his left arm around her and pulled her into an awkward embrace. He favored his right arm because moving it aggravated the injuries on his right shoulder and neck: apparently Weaver's strokes had done more damage to one side than the other. "Don't cry, Mother. It's all right now. You're free, and I'll be fine in no time."

His words only made her sob more, and he looked to Boron in confusion.

"She's been very worried about you, Simon," Boron explained, "and proud of your actions. That was a very brave thing you did. Most grown men wouldn't have shown that kind of courage."

Sheena brought herself under control and said, "You should never have done such a thing. If you had simply stopped talking and apologized you would have gotten off with nothing more than five lashes and a few gold added to our debt." Then her eyes once again teared, and she added in a sobbing voice, "You could have died!"

Simon hugged her to him and held her for as long as he could until his aching bladder became too urgent. "I need to go to the privy," he said trying to extricate himself from her embrace.

Instead of allowing him to go, his mother brought him a chamber pot and then she and Boron busied themselves with setting out supper to give him some measure of privacy. Once he finished, and washed his hands and face at the nearby basin, he gingerly moved to join them at the table.

"Well," he said as he carefully lowered himself onto a stool that had no back to aggravate his injuries, "I don't know how much I'll be able to do, but I told his Lordship I would still be able to work."

Boron smiled, and his mother shook her head. "You will do no such thing until those scores are healed," Sheena said flatly.

"How long do you think you've been sleeping?" Boron asked.

The implication of the question wasn't lost on Simon: he might only be a ten-year-old boy, but he certainly wasn't stupid. "I assumed this was the evening of the same day," he replied. "How long have I been out?"

"Three days," Boron responded. "Mostly that was due to the herbs your mother used to dose the water she poured into you so you wouldn't feel the pain, but enough of it was from the injuries themselves that we were plenty worried. I made Weaver keep the strokes on your back, but he knows how to use that whip of his. He nearly flayed you alive. Some of those cuts went almost to the bone."

"I will personally rip that man's eyes out the next time I find him away from the estate!" Sheena said with such vehemence that Simon physically flinched. Realizing her words had upset him, she covered the boy's hand with her own and smiled with all of the love that a mother can put into such a gesture. Then she said, "Your stew is getting cold, Dear. Eat, you need to build your strength back up, and that takes food as well as rest."

"Do as your mother says," Boron spoke up. Then, to Sheena, he added, "And don't you worry about Bill Weaver. I humiliated the man in front of everyone by making him wet his britches. He told me that I'm a dead man."

Both Sheena and Simon were suddenly concerned, but the big man just smiled and said, "Now, then, I don't want either one of you to go fretting about me. Bill Weaver is a sadist and bully, not a warrior. He doesn't have the guts to challenge me outright; more's the pity. If he musters the courage to act on the threat, he'll come at me from behind, most likely in the dark. Then he'll find that there was a reason I was a member of the Elite Guard assigned to protect nobles from assassination. I'll deal with him when the time comes, and it will legally be self-defense." Then he looked at the food and shook his head, "Now eat, both of you. It's a fine stew, and you both need the nourishment."

As Simon picked up his spoon, he remembered what the smith had said to the landowner: "I have good aptitude for working metal and a real gift for killing people", and he realized that Boron hadn't just been bragging to keep the negotiations going. Then the boy stuck a spoon full of the stew in his mouth and all thoughts, other than his empty stomach and the flavor of the rich food, were pushed to the back of his mind for the duration of the meal.

After he finished eating, Simon found that he was as tired as if he had done a full day's work and a double practice session. His mother removed his bandages and put an herbal preparation on his wounds.

"The herbs will soothe the pain and help reduce the scarring," she told him as she began redressing the scores.

Then she lightly rubbed the backs of his legs and hummed to him while he drifted off to sleep.

She left Simon sleeping and walked back to the table. Her eyes were moist and she said, "If I hadn't spurned Lord Bastian's advances when we first arrived, none of this would have happened."

Boron visibly tightened at those words and replied softly, "If you had, you simply would have delayed the inevitable. That fat pig may be lecherous, but he doesn't do his thinking between his legs when it comes to business. You and the boy might have been kept a bit more comfortably, but you'd still be his slave."

"I know that, but it's hard not to think about with what has been done to Simon. I just want to protect him."

As Sheena sat down, Boron whispered, "So when do we tell the boy about us?"

"I'd like to wait until his wounds have healed," she replied. "He's had enough shock to deal with for the time being."

"Well, we need to explain ourselves soon. He's a smart lad, smarter than a lot of adults I know. It won't be long before he figures it out for himself." As his voice trailed off, he added, "If he hasn't already…"

Sheena just smiled and slipped her hand into his.

CHAPTER 11

S IMON SPENT THE next four days recuperating in the smith's quarters, which was a large, converted outbuilding near the main barn. His mother was forced to move off of estate property once Simon was back on his feet, and even Boron couldn't persuade Lord Bastian to allow her to stay until Simon's wounds completely healed. The smith did, however, find her a position with the new healer in the nearby village. He didn't really need a housekeeper, but he took her on because of her prior training: she wasn't a physician but her knowledge meant she could also help him with the storage and preparation of his herbal remedies.

Boron had been right. Simon was no one's fool: he knew there was more to the relationship between his mother and the smith than just looking out for him.

"Are you and my mother lovers?" he asked as Boron handed him his weapons on the first day he resumed training after two weeks of healing.

The smith wasn't surprised by the question. He looked at the boy while he considered his answer carefully. "Your mother and I have become very close. We are working into our relationship slowly to be sure of our feelings. We believe we are falling in love, so yes." Then Boron stared hard at him for a moment and added, "Anything else is a personal matter between me and her, and none of your business."

"I don't want details," Simon responded, "I just want to know that my mother is happy. She has been through a lot and deserves a bit of happiness in her life."

That stopped the big man in his tracks. He shook his head and smiled. "You really are a remarkable young man, Simon. Here I thought you might be getting a little jealous: that's actually a natural reaction when a new man moves into the picture in a family like yours. Instead of thinking of yourself, though, as most boys your age would, your concern is for your mother's happiness. I am truly proud to know you, son."

Then, without warning, he stepped back and swung his blade around in a vicious attack. When Simon blocked the strike and countered with an equally ferocious volley of his own, Boron laughed outright and said, "A remarkable lad, indeed." Then the pair continued the sparring match.

After exchanging several series of blows, Boron called a halt. "You're distracted, Simon. What's got your attention?"

"I can't shake the feeling that I'm being watched."

"That's because you are being watched," Boron said so quietly that his words barely carried across the scant few feet between them. "Look toward the far edge of the barn wall, your *friend* Broderick is standing in the shadows watching every move we make."

To his credit, Simon didn't stare at the place that Boron had indicated. However, he could see the dim shape of his former tormentor out of the corner of his eye, highlighted by the predawn light on the horizon.

Simon shook his head and said in a low whisper, "It looks as though we are found out. I suppose his Lordship will put a stop to our practice."

"I don't think it will be a problem," Boron replied. "The fact that I have been training you ceased to be a secret the day you were caught exercising. His Lordship and I had words about it, and he has agreed that so long as it doesn't affect your work he won't get involved. Let Broderick have a look-see; maybe it will help him to remember not to cause you any more trouble."

Simon stared up at the smith with wide eyes. "How did you manage to convince his Lordship of that?"

"Oh, I mentioned that I sent a letter to my old commander. You know, the current governor of this territory. And I might have also mentioned that I got some clarification concerning the indenture laws. The way the law was explained to me, the debt owner can only require the indentured servant to work twelve hours a day, and can only require you to work six days a week. Also, you were closer to right than you knew: while he can compel you to stay on the grounds, he can only charge fair market value for food and lodging. His Lordship has decided that what you do on your own time really is your business."

A dawning light of triumph suddenly appeared in Simon's eyes, and Boron quickly held up his hand for the boy's full attention. "Before you go getting any ideas about suing for your freedom, you need to know everything. Lord Bastian has been cheating you, and that has come to a stop. But I only have so much power to help you. The governor may be an old friend and comrade, but he has only limited authority when it comes to enforcing the law against the nobility, and the nobles can always petition the Council of Lords, which is the governing body directly beneath the King in Horne. They don't have a lot of power, and the King can overrule them, but that doesn't happen often in matters like this. Also, a noble can seek intervention from the King himself, who can interpret the law as he sees fit."

Simon had been educated to some extent, but he was almost completely ignorant of the politics of his homeland.

"Now, before I left the service, I would have had many noble-born friends who might back me against a minor Lord such as Bastian. But I didn't leave the army under the best of circumstances." At Simon's astonished look, he shook his head and added, "I wasn't discharged for cowardice or anything of the sort."

Boron sighed and motioned Simon to a wooden bench near the barn. "Sit down over here. I might as well tell you the full story."

Once they were seated, he continued his narration. "I was sent to the front to help with the war against the Roracks. It was desperate times, and His Majesty felt he should send at least some of his best troops to help hold the beast-men at bay. My men and I were directly under the command of the man who is now governor. A friend of mine, an enlisted man I had known since basic training, was under the command of a noble-born twit who shouldn't have been in the army, much less commanding elite troops. The idiot got a bunch of the soldiers in his command killed due to his own stupidity and need for glory, and my friend got into an argument with him about it. The argument got physical, and the officer was hurt badly enough that he had to be sent back to the capital on a medical evacuation wagon: this all happened just before the Dragon Riders showed up, so magical healers were in short supply. Word came in that he died on the trip, and my friend was to be sent back for trial. The whole thing might have been swept under the rug: officers die in combat occasionally; especially stupid officers. However, this particular man was the younger son of the King's first cousin, who is also his most favored advisor."

"So what does that have to do with you?" Simon asked. "You can't be held accountable for another man's actions."

"That's true enough, as far as it goes, but you can be held responsible if the man gets away on your watch. My friend knew he would be tried and executed, so he ran away. I was assigned to take a group of men and track him down and return him to the capital. Now, I may not have looked as hard as I could have - it's hard enough to track an experienced man when you don't have to worry about Roracks ambushing you at every bend in the road - but the accusation was made that my group let the man get away on purpose because we were his friends. I was in command, so I took full responsibility for my unit's failure. I was removed from command as soon as the war was over and given meaningless tasks for a couple of months while waiting for a final decision about my own fate. In the end, I made a deal that I would resign with no pension if my men were sent back to their duties with nothing held against them. That's why I was willing to take this position after I was put out of the army rather than rush back to the capital. I still have friends in Fallon, but so does that dead officer's father, and he has the king's ear as well."

"That doesn't sound fair," Simon responded, and then he looked Boron in the eye. "Did you let the man get away on purpose?"

Boron shook his head, "I might have let the man get away, but it wasn't on purpose, and I certainly didn't condone what he did to that young officer. As I said, if the man had died on the field, even if it was because the men in his command let it happen, it could have been swept aside as occurs from time to time. However, while a good thumping off the field is one thing, beating someone to death out in front of forty or so witnesses is another, and can do more to damage overall morale than letting the matter go. Remember, though, we were a small detachment of men deep in enemy territory. This all took place a couple of weeks before that Rider – Delno – brought that grand army of men and dragons to Horne and put paid to Warrick and the beast-men. I might have overlooked some sign of our quarry while watching for signs of those bloodthirsty creatures. My main concern was keeping the men in my command alive, or at least not throwing their lives away for nothing. Was it fair that they wanted to try me for that? I can't say for sure, but I can say this: the concept of fair play doesn't usually work its way too far into either the military or politics, and this situation was all about both."

Boron took a break and just looked at Simon for a long moment before continuing, "What all of this means to you is that while I do have some pull with the local governor, my boasts of friends in high places aren't as certain as they were in times past. As long as neither side pushes this too far, we won't have to find out if the nobles in the capital will side with me or with Bastian. You won't be able to sue for your freedom, but he will back off in your case to prevent the authorities from looking too deeply into his concerns. You won't get back what he's already cheated you out of, but it is now possible for you to work off that debt and be free of this place."

The two sat for a long time and simply watched the sun come up over the horizon.

CHAPTER 12

DESPITE THE WINTER chill in the air, Simon was sweating. He and Boron had just finished nearly three hours of practice, and both were quite pleased with the session.

"Winter solstice is two weeks past, and you can already tell the days are getting longer, Simon," Boron said as they walked back toward the barn. "Soon we won't have to get up so early to practice because the light will last longer into the evening. Now go and get yourself cleaned up and dried off, and I'll meet you for breakfast."

Simon headed in the direction of the rain barrel. He didn't relish the idea of breaking the top crust of ice and splashing the frigid water on his body, but he didn't have time to heat water for a proper wash before meeting the smith at the kitchen, so he simply gritted his chattering teeth and did what he had to do.

As Simon approached the kitchen, wearing the new tunic and britches his mother had given to Boron to deliver to him, he was brought up short by the sound of Broderick's voice.

"Going somewhere, Little Mouse?"

He looked around quickly to make a hasty reply, but the older boy wasn't close. Again the voice spoke. "I can always find you, Little Mouse; anywhere you go, I'll be right there."

He hadn't even seen Broderick sneaking around at his morning practice sessions for over a month. It suddenly occurred to him why that was so: Broderick wasn't speaking to Simon, the bastard had found someone else to focus his attention on, and he had simply happened along to hear this. Rounding the corner of the building that housed the workers' kitchen, he found Broderick towering menacingly over Ronny. The young boy looked terrified.

"You don't have to be afraid of him, Ronny; he's just a coward, a bully, and a **pervert**." Simon emphasized the last word with such hatred that Broderick actually flinched slightly.

He recovered quickly and took a step toward Simon. Simon dropped into a fighting stance, hoping that the older boy would attack. Boron had once told him that, no matter how large or fierce your opponent was, if you could break his knee he'd drop down to your level and could be dealt with. Broderick was still a couple of inches taller, but Simon was ready, and consequences be damned.

Broderick looked Simon in the eye, and what he saw in his former victim's gaze told him that attacking the boy would be extremely dangerous, if not outright suicidal. He moved back just a bit and said, "You need to remember your place, boy. I am the son of the lord of this estate and you are an indentured servant. I could have you flogged to death for laying hands on me."

"No, Little Kitten," Simon responded, "your father could have me flogged to death; you would be dead and unable to enjoy the spectacle." Then he relaxed out of his stance and added, "I might actually find that it's worth it, considering your crimes against me and this boy. You need to remember that. You will stay away from Ronny, and any other boys on this estate, or I will see to it that your crimes are brought to public attention." Simon knew he had just stepped onto very thin ice, but he couldn't just sit idly by while Broderick used another boy as he pleased.

Broderick was visibly shaken by the threat, but he recovered quickly. "Careful, little boy, you'll find that situations such as this can shift quickly. It's entirely possible that you will find yourself on the wrong end of the foreman's whip if you make such accusations without a great deal of proof." Then he added, "Also, do not think for one moment that your mother is beyond my reach just because she is now living in the village and sleeping with that traitor."

Broderick smiled broadly at Simon's reaction to him calling Boron a traitor. "Oh, the big oaf didn't tell you about being thrown out of the military? Well, I can assure you that it's true. You see, I have friends also, and I know that he let a murderer go; the murderer killed a nobleman. I'm afraid your large friend's boasts of having connections in the capital may not be as real as he would like the rest of us to believe. So you would do well to mind your own business; unless of course, you would like me to tell my father all about the smith's military indiscretions."

Recovering his demeanor, Simon replied, "Boron can take care of himself. His military record may not be general knowledge, but it's certainly no secret, so you tell your father whatever you like. I told you once that if you ever tried to harm my mother I would kill you; that is still true, and if it costs me my life, so be it. I won't be bullied by you, Broderick, and I won't ignore your *indiscretions* either. So you had best go back to the main house and leave Ronny alone; I will be watching you."

Broderick snorted with disdain and said, "We will see, boy, we will see." Then he simply walked away.

Simon turned to Ronny and laid his hand on the boy's shoulder. "You need to stay close to your father, Ronny; especially at night."

The youngster looked up at him and replied, "I'm not allowed to stay in the men's quarters. I have to sleep in the children's room." He lowered his voice and gaze before adding, "That's when he comes for me."

The estate rules forbade children to be housed with their parents to make it more difficult for the parents to take the children and run off during the night.

Just then Boron stepped around the corner. He looked at the two boys for a long time. Simon could tell the man was nearly shaking with unspent rage and, therefore, knew that Boron had been listening to the exchange with Broderick.

Boron turned Ronny toward the workers' tables and said, "Go and find your father, son," before gently pushing him in the right direction. Then he looked back to Simon. "We can't seem to get you clear of this, can we?"

Simon started to protest, but Boron held up a hand to silence him. "I don't fault you for confronting the bastard." Then he smiled before continuing, "Tell the truth, I'd have been a bit disappointed in you if you hadn't intervened. That being said, though, it does make our situation a little harder to deal with. If that cretin goes to his father and embellishes on my military discharge, his father just might get into his head to make our lives harder and see how far this will go."

"I stuck my foot in it again, Boron, I'm sorry."

"Don't say that," Boron said sharply. "It's not wrong to stand up for what's right. You did the best you could do under the circumstances, and you stood up for someone who isn't able to protect himself. I'm proud of you."

At the compliment, Simon straightened a bit and smiled.

"Now, we just have to play the tiles we've been dealt. Hopefully, a way out of all this will present itself before one of has to kill Broderick; otherwise, we might both have to leave as fugitives." He drew a deep breath and sighed before switching subjects, "Let's just get some breakfast for now, and then we can start on that wagon that needs fixing."

"I don't have much an appetite after what's happened," Simon replied.

"I can believe that, but you just did three hours of hard physical work, and you have twelve more in front of you. You won't make it through the day if you don't eat. Oh, I almost forgot. Your mother told me that today is your birthday. She sent you some more clothes, and I put something in there from me as well."

Simon took the bundle that the smith handed him. It was obviously a pair of britches and a tunic, but he could feel something hard and heavy wrapped inside them. When he unrolled the bundle, he found a large, well-made dagger in a leather sheath. The knife wasn't as long as the blade he used in practice, but it was sharp and perfectly balanced.

"You didn't have to do this," Simon said, smiling broadly.

"I know I didn't have to; that's kind of the point of giving presents, isn't it? Now off to breakfast; there's work to be done." He playfully shoved Simon toward the kitchen door.

Chapter 13

Simon woke in a cold sweat and instinctively reached for the dagger he kept near his pillow. Rolling out of bed rather than simply rising straight up, he ended in a crouched position, ready to defend himself. Glancing quickly around, he could see well enough to know that no one was immediately threatening him, so he took a second to be sure of his position. The ladder was pulled up, as was the rope that Boron had hung months ago and insisted he climb to get to his bed: he said it would help make him stronger in ways no other exercises could. It had been over a month since his last confrontation with Broderick, and though the Lord's son wasn't one to forget or forgive, he had not made it up into the loft, if he was even here at all.

Moving to the edge of the upper floor, he surveyed the rest of the barn. Not finding anyone lurking in the shadows, but still not able to shake off the feeling that something was wrong, he tossed the loose end of the rope over the edge and lowered himself down. After making a more thorough inspection of the inside of the building, he moved to the door and slipped outside. Again he found no reason for his abrupt awakening.

He was about to go back to bed when he noticed a very dim light coming through the cracks in the door of the small equipment shed that was used as quarters by the children of the field hands. The only child in residence at the moment was Ronny. Sudden comprehension of what that light most likely meant nearly caused him to be physically ill. He took only a second to force himself not to vomit and then set off across the open space at a run.

He could hear a struggle going on inside the shed, and Broderick's harsh voice, though he was whispering, was clearly audible. "Hold still, you little fool. The more you struggle, the more I will hurt you!"

Somewhere in the back of his mind, Simon knew that barging in would cause him more trouble than he had ever been in before. The voice of caution told him that the time had not yet come when he could confront the rapist with impunity. But it was a very small voice, and easily ignored. He put his shoulder to the flimsy door and shoved.

Broderick stopped in the middle of fighting to remove Ronny's trousers and turned. At first, the expression on his face was that of a small child caught doing something he knew he shouldn't. The expression turned to a mixture of hatred and disgust as he realized who had caught him.

"Come to watch, Little Mouse, or are you more interested in joining the fun?" Broderick said. The contempt in his words was so intense it was almost visible.

"I told you I wouldn't allow you to hurt this boy again!" Simon replied with equal disdain. "I told you I would be watching."

Ronny got up and moved to the wall away from the two antagonists, and stood there petrified.

"Then now is the time you die of curiosity, Little Mouse." Saying this, Broderick grabbed a spade that was hanging on the wall, and, in the same fluid motion, swung the shortened shovel at Simon's head.

Months of training paid off. Simon dropped below the arc of his attacker's swing and kicked out. He was pleased to feel the older boy's knee give way, though he chided himself because he had lost his grip on his dagger. Broderick started to scream in agony, but his breath was knocked from his body as he fell hard against a wooden crate. As he hit the box, he let go of the spade, and it clattered to the packed dirt floor at Simon's feet while the older boy came to rest face down.

Still winded, Broderick tried to scramble forward and retrieve his weapon, but Simon was faster. Picking up the spade before it could again be wielded against him, he was surprised to find himself using the tool. He swung it around in a wide arc and hit the lordling on the side of the head with the flat surface. Broderick pitched sideways and landed in a heap at Ronny's feet.

Simon looked the young boy in the eye and said, "Run, Ronny! Run and hide!"

The boy didn't need to be told twice. He jumped over Broderick, scooted past Simon, and ran out the door.

Simon took stock of the situation. He knew that tonight was the night he would leave the estate. All other options were gone: if he stayed he would die for what he had done. He also realized that, whether he got away or was tracked down and killed, Broderick would continue to do as he pleased with Ronny, and any other children of the indentured servants, unless something was done to stop him. He could see that the older boy was still breathing, and he briefly considered simply cutting his throat. He even retrieved his dagger for the purpose. However, kneeling next to the boy, he just couldn't bring himself to do it. While he could have killed Broderick in a fight, doing so now felt too much like murder to him.

Knowing he needed to do something, he grabbed some cord and began tying Broderick up while he pondered his next move. He noticed that the boy's britches were unfastened and had slipped down nearly to his knees during the brief struggle: seeing this, inspiration struck. He bound Broderick hand and foot, very securely; then gagged him as well.

As he finished with the gag, the older boy's eyes opened. Simon could see the terror in them as realization of his position came over him.

"I know that your father will have me flogged to death for what I've done so far, so, since I am to die anyway, I am also going to ensure that you never again do to anyone what you have done to me and Ronny."

Saying this, Simon picked up his dagger, and with his free hand, reached toward Broderick's groin. The full impact of what Simon was about to do motivated Broderick to try and fight against his bonds. He twisted and bucked, as well as trying to scream against the rags stuffed and tied into his mouth. Blood appeared where the cords cut into his wrists and ankles, but it was no use; Simon had trussed him up so well that his struggles barely hindered the act. Simon castrated him just the way he had seen the men castrate the young bulls that were to be raised as steers for beef. All Broderick could do was lay tense against his bonds and cry.

Simon wasn't sure why, but he felt absolutely no pleasure in what he was doing. As many times as he had imagined watching Broderick cry as he tormented him, the reality just left him cold. He wasn't interested in revenge. He simply knew that he must leave, and he refused to abandon this monster to continue to prey on the innocent once he was gone. When he finished, he even had no problem resisting the urge to put the parts where the older boy would have to look at them. He simply grabbed the dirty blanket from the floor and shoved it tightly into Broderick's groin to staunch the flow of blood. Then he got up, and, without a backward glance, extinguished the small lamp before leaving his former rapist alone in the dark.

Half expecting to see men coming toward him from the other buildings, he surveyed the area before running back to the barn. Apparently Ronny hadn't raised an alarm. It was well known among the other servants that Ronny's father would drink any alcohol he could steal, and Simon had seen that the man was staggering noticeably as he headed off to bed after supper. If Ronny had run to his father, it was likely the man was so drunk the boy couldn't wake him. Counting himself lucky, and knowing that the luck wouldn't last forever, he quickly climbed the rope to the loft and gathered his things. He lowered the ladder so that he could take the extra rope that had been tied to the rafter.

The smith kept paper and charcoal for sketching plans of different projects; he used a bit of that to write a quick letter to the big man telling him what had happened, saying that he felt it was best not to have any further contact with anyone he cared for now, as doing so would drag them into his crime and at least make them guilty of aiding a criminal. He thanked Boron for everything he had done for him, and asked him to tell his mother goodbye and that he loved her. Then he asked that he also give her the coins he was leaving for her. Once the letter was finished, he hid it and half of his money amongst Boron's tools where only the smith would find them. Then he slipped off into the night

He briefly considered taking a horse, but rejected the idea because doing so would take time and make noise. He had several hours of darkness, and he intended to be long gone by the time the rest of the estate awoke and discovered what he had done. Besides, stealing a horse would be one more thing added to his list of offenses, and he had never been trained to ride a horse, anyway.

The road to the village led east and he stayed on it, jogging along at an easy pace for over an hour. Instead of going to the village, though, when the road turned north in the direction of the small settlement, he left the path and continued east, toward the mountains, straight into Rorack territory. It was a grave risk, but the mountains were less than a day's travel if he could keep up the pace. Not even Lord Bastian would be able to pay enough money to entice men to follow him there. He made sure he left enough spoor that it was clear he had not run to his mother. If Bastian burned off his anger chasing him away from the village, he would be less likely to lash out at her to get his revenge. As dawn became a dim promise of coming day, he veered a bit south, hoping that he could reach the river there; Boron had once told him that Roracks were unable to swim and couldn't cross deep water without some sort of bridge. Not that Roracks were his chief concern, but he couldn't help thinking of them because of his chosen course. He had no real need to worry about them, at least, not yet.

Chapter 14

BASTIAN HAD BEEN quick to mount up with a group of men and go after Simon once Broderick had been found, but it was nearly mid-morning before they set out. Bill Weaver was left in charge of the estate, but he had no real authority over Boron. The smith ran to his shop and gathered his weapons. He found Simon's letter and the little bundle of coins hidden with his sword. After reading the letter, he realized that Simon might just be able to hide from the landowner, and Sheena would then be in real danger, so he decided to go to the village instead of going after the boy. He prayed he had made the right decision as he saddled his own horse to leave.

Weaver was waiting just outside the barn as Boron led the horse into the sunlight. "Where do you think you're going, smith?" he asked in a tone that left no doubt the question was an accusation.

"Get out of my way, Weaver, I don't answer to you," Boron responded.

The foreman, having not noticed the sword hanging from the horse's saddle, drew his knife and advanced while motioning two other men forward to help him. As the others joined him, he said, "His Lordship has left strict orders that you are not to leave the estate. If you insist on trying, we'll be more than happy to stop you."

Placing his hand on the horse, Boron said without emotion,

"That only leaves one question to be answered then."

Weaver snorted and asked, "What's that?"

Pulling his sword and long knife, the big man replied, "Which of you dies first?" He looked at the other two men, who were suddenly wide-eyed with fear and said, "Have you two made arrangements to have your final draw sent to your next of kin? If not, I'd advise you to stand aside."

Neither man moved, but the one on Weaver's left said, "We don't want to fight with you Boron, but we've got our orders. If we let you leave, we'll lose our jobs."

"If you try to stop me, you'll lose your lives."

"Enough of this," Weaver shouted, sheathing his knife and pulling his whip from his belt. "Get away from that horse and go back to your work station, smith. You've got 'til the count of three. One…"

"Don't tax your brain trying to count, Weaver," Boron said, and then shouted, "Three!" He swatted the horse on the rump with the flat of his short blade.

The animal bolted straight at the foreman. Weaver and the man who had spoken were both knocked down: the other farmhand managed to avoid the horse and, seeing that he was the only one still standing against an armed and determined opponent, he turned and ran away. Boron ignored the other lackey and advanced on Weaver so quickly that the man didn't have time to recover. Putting his weapons on the ground and grabbing Weaver's wrist in one hand and the whip in the other, Boron disarmed him and then hauled him to his feet. The other flunky wisely stayed where he had fallen.

Boron once again took the foreman's belt knife and then said in a low, dangerous voice, "I'm leaving, Weaver. If you try to stop me again, I'll kill you." Then he dropped the man's knife on the ground at his feet and stepped back over his own blades, saying, "Now, you can either make a try for that knife and die, or you can walk away and live. Make your choice quick or I'll be happy to decide for you."

Weaver hesitated for only a second before stepping farther away from the weapon. "Go ahead and leave," he said almost hysterically.

"You go and help that little bastard. You'll share his fate when he's caught, and I'll enjoy watching you swing on the end of a rope."

Boron started to open his mouth to make a reply, but changed his mind. He had already wasted enough time with this jackass. He whistled and his horse trotted back to him. Retrieving his sword and long knife, he mounted up and rode out. As he reached the main gate, he stopped and hung the foreman's whip high on the arch, well out of easy reach before turning his horse onto the road and coaxing the animal into a trot.

CHAPTER 15

A S THE MOUNTAINS loomed larger with each passing step, Simon could also see the river coming out of the cleft between two peaks. He had been keeping up the same pace since leaving the estate, and he wasn't sure how much longer he could continue.

Just about the time he thought his legs would fail him completely, he reached the point where the river met the plain and spread out, wide and shallow. He dropped down to his knees at the edge of the shore and dipped water up to his mouth with his hands while he scanned the terrain; Boron had once told him that good soldiers never lay down and drink directly from a stream, but bring the water up to their mouths so that they can stay alert for danger while quenching their thirst. The river was fed by melting snow as well as underground sources, so it was cold and refreshing. When he had slaked his thirst, he filled the waterskin he had neglected to fill in order to save time and weight while getting away from the estate.

Simon knew from listening to the other men at the estate that once he crossed to the south of the river he would, technically, be out of Bastian's province. However, he also knew that men who had gotten this far before had still been hauled back and flogged for running away. The lord might not have been popular with the other nobles, but no one would bother with a complaint for exceeding his boundaries to bring back a runaway debtor, especially one who had done what Simon had. Still, though, as he crossed the river it simply felt good to know that he had made it beyond Bastian's boundaries.

Once he reached the far side, he looked back the way he had come and could dimly make out several specks in the distance. It was more than an hour past noon and the sun was still high. He couldn't see the shapes clearly yet, but he was sure they were riders looking for him, and they weren't even an hour behind. He turned east and ran toward the mountains as fast as his legs would carry him.

The ground beneath his feet quickly changed from sand to pebbles, then to broken shale. Soon he was picking his way through large boulders and broken trees that had been carried by spring floods. Minutes later, he found himself scrambling amongst the shale to get up a steep hill. At the top, his hands cut and bleeding, he looked back and saw that the men on horses had just crossed the river and turned to follow him at full gallop. He climbed higher. By the time the horses began to balk at the steep hill and treacherous loose rock, he was over a hundred feet above them. There were six riders, and he could clearly see Lord Bastian glaring up at him. He could feel the hatred in the man's gaze.

Bastian spurred his mount, and the horse redoubled its effort to climb but lost its footing. Both man and animal tumbled, taking two others down with them. They slid nearly forty feet before the ground leveled enough that they came to a stop. Bastian's horse tried to rise, but its left front leg was obviously broken. The other two horses got up and retreated down the hill. Bastian and one of his men were bleeding from several cuts on their faces and hands and one man, who had ended up under one of the horses, wasn't moving at all.

Simon reflexively checked his purchase while he watched. He was somewhat sheltered by the rocks and in no immediate danger of falling. He still had his pack, including his water, and he still had the rope, but the treacherous path he had been following up the incline had petered out to the point that a mountain goat would have chosen an alternate route. If he had to, he would continue to climb, but doing so would be risking a fall even more serious than the one he had just witnessed. He was amazed that Bastian, middle-aged, fat, and out of condition, hadn't been killed.

Bastian drew his sword and dispatched the horse that had broken its leg before shouting up at Simon. "This has gone quite far enough, boy! You've mutilated my son, stolen from me, and now caused the death of one of my men and a good horse. Come down here this instant."

"If I come down," Simon yelled back, "I'll be killed. I think I'd rather stay up here." He cast about wildly, looking for hand and foot holds to continue climbing. There were two big rocks, quite close together, almost touching, about twenty feet farther up, and it looked as though there might be a trail of sorts on the other side. If he could just get there, he might be able to move past them and continue climbing.

"I won't tell you all will be forgiven, boy," Bastian responded. "But I will tell you this. You have nowhere to go. I won't stop hunting you as long as you live. You have us below you and beast-men's territory above." He paused for a moment to let that sink in, thinking Simon did not know where he was heading. "Now then, I will promise you this: your death will be much quicker at my hands than it will be at the hands of the Roracks. They will tear the flesh from your body and eat it while you are still alive, and they will keep you alive for as long as they can."

"The beast-men will have to catch me first. If they catch me, they eat me alive; if you catch me, you will have your foreman flay the flesh from my body and leave me to the vultures. If I keep running, I at least have a chance to stay ahead of both possibilities, however slim that chance may be." Simon pulled his rope off of his shoulder and picked up a rock that was nearly as big as his head.

"Really boy, do you think you can avoid both them and me for long? I will see you dead for your crimes, I assure you. If you will listen to reason and come down, I promise to make it quick and painless."

"I somehow doubt your sincerity, Lord Bastian. I've seen your mercy before: in fact, I still bear scars from the last time you bargained with me." He quickly began tying the rope securely around the rock.

"That was different, boy. There'll be no bargaining your way out of your rightful punishment this time. You committed an unprovoked attack on my son and rendered him unable to father children. I can never forgive that, and even your friend, the smith, hasn't enough connections to help you now."

"Well, Lord Bastian, I wouldn't worry too much about Broderick not being able to father children. He didn't have much interest in women anyway: he preferred young boys, or didn't you wonder what he was doing out in that shed in the middle of the night?" He finished tying the rope to the rock and stood up.

"He was in that shed because you lured him there," Bastian screamed. "Once you had incapacitated him from ambush, you cut him like a spring pig, and I'll see you suffer for that." The man then signaled to the other men who hadn't fallen.

"That shed is the sleeping quarters for the only other boy on the estate," Simon stated as he judged the distance to the two boulders he needed to reach. "Broderick was attempting to rape that boy when I interrupted him. He attacked me, and I subdued him. I castrated him because I knew he would only go back after the other boy once I was gone if I didn't."

"Liar!" Bastian yelled while he motioned more fiercely to one of the men still on horseback farther up the hill.

Before Simon could use the rock he had tied to the rope, an arrow narrowly missed his leg. He ducked back behind what cover he had. Then he gathered several fist-sized stones and threw them at the archer's horse. He hated attacking the animal, but he couldn't risk exposing himself for more than a second and the horse was a bigger target. His first two throws missed, but the third projectile hit the animal's neck, and it reared. The horse lost his footing in the loose shale, and his rider screamed as he was crushed beneath his mount and dragged down the hill.

"Get him," Bastian yelled at the two men remaining in their saddles. They tried to coax their mounts further up the treacherous incline, but the horses were too spooked to attempt the climb, so the men dismounted and began inching their way toward him. Both men were much heavier than Simon, so they couldn't move upward as fast as he had, but they were making steady progress.

Simon stood and spun the improvised bolo around his head several times. They thought he was going to use it as a weapon and ducked down as flat as possible in the shale. He let it fly, and the rope sailed neatly over the two boulders. When he pulled it taut, the large rock was too big to slide back through the space. While Simon began to pull himself hand-over-hand up the steepest part of the slope, Bastian shouted orders for the men to increase their efforts to catch him, while cursing them for their failure to do so. Another arrow, this one fired by the man who had survived the first fall, went wide of its mark. Simon climbed behind the cover of the two boulders and pulled his rope up after him before the others could use it as he had done.

On the other side of the cover, he found a little path. There were enough hand and foot holds for him to clamber up another fifty feet to a ledge. On the ledge, he found a small boulder about the size of his torso. He looked down to see if his pursuers had given up, only to find that they were actually nearing the easier part of the trail. He positioned himself behind the rock and shoved with all of his might. At first, nothing happened. He could hear the men making the last leg of the climb to get him. Then the rock began to move. It slid a few inches before catching again. He was beginning to think he would be taken when he felt the large stone shift upward as he pushed with all of the strength of his legs. It rolled over the obstacle in its way and off the ledge.

The man closest to the top was the first to be hit. Then he and the rock knocked the second man off the incline, and all three continued down the slope picking up speed and more debris as they went. At first, the horrible sound of the two men shrieking could be heard clearly, but that was drowned out in just a few seconds by the calamitous noise of the avalanche that he had started. The roar of the falling shale and other detritus as it swept downward seemed to go on for a long time. Finally, after the last echoes of the slide faded away, Simon looked over the edge. All he could see where Lord Bastian had been standing was a massive dust cloud.

He sat down on the ledge and picked up a handful of pebbles and began to toss them idly, one by one, into the dust. When he had gone to bed the night before, he had been an indentured servant and a smith's apprentice with real prospects in life. It was less than two hours past noon the following day, and he was guilty of castrating one nobleman and killing another, as well as killing the five commoners accompanying the second. There would be no pardoning of these crimes. He didn't know where he would go, but he had to get as far away from Horne, and everyone he had ever known and loved, as soon as possible. He tossed the last stone he was holding and then turned and continued up toward the top of the ridge.

CHAPTER 16

THE REST OF the climb had been difficult, and the ridge of this mountain was too narrow and rocky for him stop for more than enough time to catch his breath and move on. The downward climb was not quite as dangerous, but he was still completely exhausted when he reached the bottom. He wanted to do nothing more than lay down and sleep although there was close to an hour of light left to the day. However, it was cold, and he would need shelter if he expected to last until morning.

At the bottom of the slope, he found a large stream and again drank his fill. He ate a little of the hard rations he had brought with him and wished there had been time to raid the kitchen before he left the estate. Once the water had swelled the dried food in his stomach, he felt a bit better. He cast about in the now-failing light for anything that would work as temporary quarters for the night. About twenty yards east of the stream, he saw a rock outcropping and made his way to it.

He found a space in the middle of the rocks that was sheltered on three sides, about chest high, just a bit over two feet wide and deep enough for a tall man to lie down comfortably. Not too far up the next incline, above the high water mark, the desolate terrain grudgingly gave purchase to small conifers and a few deciduous trees. The trees got taller and thicker the farther up he looked. Simon knew this spot was in the floodplain of the stream, but he also knew that the spring thaw was still weeks away, and freezing to death was the immediate concern. He put his things down and moved off to gather firewood.

His clothes were still too damp from the sweat of his earlier exertions to keep him warm, and the light was failing more rapidly than he had anticipated. His estimate had been based on what he had observed in the flat lands. Once he had descended into this valley, the surrounding peaks had obscured what little sun remained and cast the entire place into an eerie twilight, and it was getting noticeably darker by the moment. The shadows among the rocks and dead wood of the floodway made him imagine that he saw monsters at every turn. Boron's descriptions of Roracks rang in his head, and he began to panic.

He had faced much so far, escaping the estate without losing his nerve, but his current situation was the last straw. He was actually beginning to cry with fear before he slammed his closed fist into his own thigh and said out loud, "Stop acting like a frightened child! Use your head before you injure yourself running from shadows. You've been alone in the dark before, Simon, and you will be again. Your biggest concern right now is panic. If you don't get a hold of yourself, you'll die of cold long before you are found by beast-men, or anything else."

He straightened his shoulders and cast about with all his senses to see if anything, man or beast, could possibly have seen or heard him. He had always been able to tell intuitively when he was being watched, and could sense nothing near him now. He also doubted that a group of fully grown Roracks would bother waiting to ambush a young boy, regardless of how big that boy was, or even a lone grown man for that matter. If any were close, they would simply charge forth and grab him. His feelings told him that he was completely alone, so he finished gathering deadwood and returned to his campsite.

He built a small fire at the back of the niche. While his senses told him that no one was watching, he knew that fire could be seen from a long way off in the darkness; he decided it would be wise to keep it small and hidden. He put some water into the little earthenware bowl he had brought and set it almost directly in the fire. Then he put some dried meat into the water. The water would soften the meat and the broth would help to warm him from the inside. Again, he wished there had been time to get a few things from the kitchen before leaving. The food would be better with some salt and herbs added to it.

Once the soup was set to cook, Simon laid out his bedding. Boron had told him that the soldiers always slept on top of their thickest blanket and covered themselves with their thinnest. The cold air could certainly siphon off your body heat, but the cold ground could pull it away much faster. After his meal had come to a full boil, he set it aside and added fuel to the fire. Then he placed a half a dozen large rocks in the fire before eating. The rocks would hold the heat, and could be placed in his bed to keep him warm long after the fire had died to embers.

CHAPTER 17

Boron watched Sheena go to the window and look out; he had long since lost count of how many times she had done so. He desperately wanted to go after Simon, but he also knew that doing so would leave her undefended. If Bastian didn't find Simon, he would turn his attention here to the house where Simon's mother now lived, and take his anger out on the woman. As the town's only physician, her employer might have enough pull the at local magistrate's office to get a guard for his property if push came to shove, but Bastian wouldn't give him time to seek such protection if he took it in his mind to vent his rage on Sheena.

The healer, Roland Fine, watched with patience. He was well over fifty and had been studying human behavior long enough to know that nothing anyone could say or do would dissuade the woman from pacing and checking the window for some sign of her son. He knew that she hoped the boy would come to her, while fearing that doing so would result in his capture.

"Damn it!" Boron exclaimed. "Even when I was a soldier I never liked waiting like this. I want to go after the boy, but if I do, Bastian will follow me. Simon would come to me if I caught up to him, but then we'd both be caught. He'd be tried for what he's done, and I'd be tried for aiding his escape."

"I wish I had known all of the story before now," Sheena said flatly. She was quite angry that Boron and Simon had conspired to keep it from her.

"It wouldn't have done you any good, and Bastian would have had all three of us killed if he had found out we knew. The fewer people you tell a secret to, the easier it is to keep it a secret."

"It shouldn't have been a secret," she argued.

"In this case, I have to agree with Boron, my dear." Roland interjected before Sheena's emotions got the better of her. "He is absolutely right: if Lord Bastian had any idea that you knew about his son's crimes, he would have had you killed and buried where no one would ever find the grave. Your son was trying to protect his mother, and Boron was only trying to protect you both."

"I know," she said sadly. "But I'm his mother, and he's only a little boy. If I had protected him in the first place, none of this would have happened."

"You were a slave, Sheena," Boron replied. "Regardless of what the nobles call it, it's still slavery. You had no choice but to follow the rules and move your son into the boys' quarters by himself where Broderick could prey on him. If you hadn't, you would have been whipped for disobeying. Families are separated at night, so they will find it harder to escape together. That helps keep them from even trying; which means that Bastian can then save money he'd otherwise have to use for more guards. Every rule on that estate is designed to do one of two things: either to increase Bastian's profits or to keep his slaves in line so that he can increase his profits. Nothing else matters, and that bastard son of his has always been given a free hand to torment the workers as he pleases as long as it doesn't interfere with the first rule of the estate, which is to ensure that all aspects of the estate are profitable."

Sheena opened her mouth to speak but closed it as they all heard the sound of horses and men outside the healer's home. Boron moved to the window to see who had arrived. On one horse was Lord Bastian himself, though he looked more like he had been dragged here rather than having ridden. His head was crudely bandaged, he was covered with scratches, his clothing was dusty and torn, and his right arm was in a sling.

Accompanying Bastian were Bill Weaver and four other men. Boron recognized two of them as the men who had tried to help Weaver in his failed attempt to restrain him that morning.

"Weaver, take your men and search the house. If that little murderer doubled back, he'll be hiding here." They could all hear the landowner clearly.

The men dismounted and the foreman motioned them toward the front door. Boron, his weapons clearly visible on his belt, opened the door and stepped onto the porch before anyone could mount the steps.

"What's this about, Bastian?" he asked.

"You know damn well what this is about, Boron Samuels. I am searching for the fugitive, Simon Harding. I have reason to believe that he has doubled back and is hiding here with the full knowledge of his mother, Sheena Harding."

"When we find the boy," Weaver spoke up, "I'm going to personally put the rope around your neck, smith."

The healer stepped forward and said, "Lord Bastian, you are not on your lands. You have no legal right to ride up here and force me to submit to such a search of my home." Bastian started to speak up, but the physician cut him off and continued, "However, in the interest of getting this matter settled quickly and quietly, I will allow you to search my house, provided that you understand that I will hold you personally responsible for any damages that your ruffians do to my property. If that is not acceptable to you, then I suggest that you go and get the local constable before someone gets injured here." As he finished speaking, he turned enough that everyone could see that he, too, was wearing a sword on his belt.

"You had best step aside, old man," Weaver said before Bastian could reply. "I wouldn't want the town's only healer to find himself in need of medical attention."

"I know you, Mister Weaver," he replied, still being polite. "I have stitched and bandaged your victims several times. You seem to delight in picking fights with men who are either too drunk or too weak to adequately defend themselves. So, let me assure you that I am neither. I may be an elderly man by your standard, but I am not from Horne. I come from Corice; Larimar to be specific. Men in my homeland typically live to be one hundred and ten or older. Since I have not yet reached my fifty-eighth birthday, I am not considered to be that old."

"I don't give a damn where you come from, *old man*. Get out of my way if you don't want to get hurt."

"Very well, Mister Weaver...," the physician began, still being polite.

The foreman stepped forward and put his foot on the first step.

"As I was saying," the physician raised his voice as he stepped ahead of Boron to block the way. "Very well, Mister Weaver. If you insist on continuing this course, you should know this: I have been practicing the art of the sword since before you were born. If you take one more step onto my property without permission, I will, regrettably, have to cut you down like a cur dog."

While his words were courteous, there was no hint of compromise in Roland's eyes. Weaver stepped back in confusion and looked to his lord for direction.

Bastian was nearly beside himself with rage, but he realized that neither his bluster nor his nobility would prevail. "Very well, healer," he snapped, "I will pay for any damages. However, if we find the boy, I will see you charged with aiding a criminal."

"As it should be," he responded. "Two of your men may search. They will leave their weapons outside, and I will accompany them. They may look under all of the beds and into every nook, cranny, and cubby, but I will catalog everything they damage and present you with the bill."

The look of disgust on Bastian's face was clear, but he turned to Weaver and said sharply, "Do as he says!"

As Weaver and another man hung their weapons on the hitching post and accompanied the physician inside, Bastian looked to Boron. "Your contract is terminated. If I catch you on my lands, I will have you flogged for trespassing."

"That's funny; I was going to have you arrested for ordering your men to imprison me," Boron shot back.

"That's preposterous: I have a right to order my servants not to leave my lands, especially with what happened this day."

"You have the right under the law to order your indentured servants to stay on your lands, but I am now and have always been a free man. I have the right to come and go as I please and even the events of this morning don't change that. I'm sure the governor will agree, especially now that you have made an illegal search of another free man's home."

"Even if you get that over-the-hill infantryman to agree, I will simply appeal that decision to the Council of Lords. You can't win."

"I can if what I am trying to do is make sure that you don't get to enjoy the money you save by not paying my salary. You can't deny that it will take a great deal of time and gold to fight this if I do go to the governor."

Bastian stared at Boron with a blank expression and the big man knew he was doing the calculations in his head. After a moment, the landowner asked, "Very well, what do you want?"

Boron motioned toward the lord's men and inclined his head to indicate he wanted them sent away for privacy.

"You, men," Bastian called for their attention. "Move away so that the smith and I can have a private conversation."

Once they were alone, Boron looked at him and said, "Call off the search for Simon!"

Bastian couldn't believe his ears. He actually began to laugh. "You can't be serious. What in the world would make you believe that I would do such a thing? That little bastard has mutilated my son, killed four of my best men and nearly killed me, not to mention the four horses I lost. No, I'm afraid, Boron, that you have taken leave of your senses."

"This is no bargaining session, Lord Bastian. You've pushed me to the point that I will have what I've asked for, or I will leave for the Old Fort this very night. While I am making my charges against you, I will also see if I can't get the governor to go over your books.

I know the man doesn't like you. You know very well that he feels that you collaborated with the enemy during the war by simply letting Warrick feed his dragons on your herds as well as doing nothing to hinder the movement of Roracks on your lands. With my testimony, he will have all he needs to examine your accounts to see if you are cheating your indentured servants. Of course, if he finds that you have been less than fair in your dealings with the government concerning the sale of livestock, the Council of Lords may not be so favorably disposed toward you either."

At first, Boron thought that Bastian was so enraged that he would suffer some type of stroke. The former soldier held his ground while the man got control of himself. Realizing that the smith would not back down, Bastian finally nodded.

"Very well, Boron. You have my word that the search will be nothing more than a sham to keep up appearances in front of my servants. However, the boy must never return to Horne. I will not remove the bounty I have placed on him, nor will I ignore any aid he is given by you or anyone else, and I will have people watching you and his mother closely. If he returns, or is returned, to Horne for any reason, he will be tried and punished for his crimes." He paused and took a breath before continuing. "Now then, my feelings toward you remain the same: stay off of my lands or I will carry through on my threat to have you flogged."

"Done, provided I can return once to collect my personal belongings," Boron replied.

"Very well," Bastian said acidly. "You may return tomorrow for your possessions. Then I will have nothing more to do with you unless I can prove that you helped that young criminal escape."

Boron simply nodded and walked back to Sheena.

Bastian turned to his men and shouted, "Get the others. There is no point in continuing this farce. If the boy were here, they wouldn't have let us search the place. I'm tired and in great pain. I want to return home and tend my wounds. We can send riders out to where he was last seen at first light. With any luck, the Roracks will find him first."

As Weaver and the other man came out of the house and joined their master, Sheena asked, "What has just happened?"

"I'll tell you inside," Boron replied and led her through the door.

Chapter 18

THE NEXT MORNING Simon was so stiff and sore he could hardly move. His hands ached to the point that he wanted to do nothing more than sit and cry. He chided himself for his depression and told himself that he had best get used to it because it wasn't likely to get much better in the near future. He reached out and pulled the last two rocks out of the warm ashes and used them before he got out of his bed. The heat on his low back and legs as he moved the rocks to get the best effect from them helped. It wasn't long before his aching bladder became more urgent than his other pains. He rose and headed downhill to the stream. Normally he wouldn't foul the water he needed to use for drinking and cooking, but the stream was swift and some dim memory from hunting with his father told him that he would be better off letting the water carry his spoor away. Then he moved upstream to wash and fill his bowl.

While moving about, he looked for game trails and found none. He wasn't the hunter that his father had been, but he had plenty of common sense even if he had very little actual knowledge of the surrounding country and the animals that inhabited it. Not finding signs of animals was both good and bad. It was bad because his supplies were meager, to say the least. It was good because it meant that no prey animals frequented the area, so predators weren't likely to come looking for them.

His first thought this morning was to skip breakfast to save his resources, but he decided that the cold had taken its toll. He need-ed the energy, so he ate a small meal. While eating, he decided to make camp in this spot for a time to try and better prepare himself to cross the beast-men's territory. Spring melt would most likely inundate the site, and summer storms could bring flash floods - which was the most likely cause for this area being swept barren. However, spring was still several weeks in the future and summer was so far off that, in his current survival situation, he couldn't even bring himself to think about it.

His immediate concern was improving his shelter. Even with the fire and hot rocks, he had not slept comfortably. He spent the morn-ing gathering dead branches that were too large for him to break up into firewood. Then he arranged them over the shelter to make a roof. By using the wet clay from the stream bank, he was able to turn the niche into a nice little cave of sorts. He left a smoke hole at the back, so that his fire would vent, and then he dug under the rocks near his fire pit to create a small drain so the shelter wouldn't fill with water if it rained.

He moved up the east slope and gathered conifer boughs to cush-ion his bed. While returning with his third bundle, he saw an ani-mal moving toward the stream. The animal was nearly as large as a small dog; he estimated its weight to be close to two stone. It was striped and had markings on its face like a bandit's mask. The crea-ture moved slowly and appeared to be in some pain, as if it were very old. He stalked closer and could see that the poor animal's eyes were also clouded over with age. Simon drew his knife. He wasn't sure if this animal would be good to eat, but he reasoned it would be easy prey, and therefore, worth the effort. He crept closer, wait-ing until the beast was fully engrossed in drinking before he lunged.

Whether the animal's hearing was still good or some other in-stinct had warned it of his presence was unclear, but his knife missed the mark, and the little monster turned faster than he would have thought possible and sank its teeth painfully into his right arm while rolling over and clawing madly with all four legs, ripping long, shallow furrows in his chest and abdomen. At this point, Simon wanted nothing more than to let go of the thing and leave it alone, but the beast would have none of it. It let go of his right arm and made a curious-sounding growl before going directly for his head. He managed to get his hand up and save his face, but it bit down viciously on his left hand and wouldn't let go while it simultaneously hung on to him with its front legs while clawing madly with its hind feet. Unable to get away from his 'prey', Simon brought his knife around and stabbed the creature in the back. He was rewarded by a lessening of the onslaught as the animal's back legs ceased to work - apparently he had hit it in the spine. It continued to hold his hand in its mouth while trying to get its front claws into his eyes. Simon pulled his knife from the beast's back and sliced across its neck. A gout of warm blood sprayed onto his neck and right shoulder as he severed an artery, but the beast still hung on, growling, for several moments until enough of its blood drained to render it unconscious.

Simon was too shocked and tired from the fight to feel much pleasure in his victory. He rolled away from the corpse and crawled to the water. His wounds burned like fire and he stripped out of his clothes and bathed the lacerations thoroughly. Then he washed the blood, both his and the creature's, out of his clothing and arranged the fabric on a large flat rock to dry before turning to his hard-won prize.

The creature's back legs were larger than its front and ended in clawed feet as he expected. However, the smaller front legs ended in what appeared to be hands, complete with opposable thumbs. Simon wondered if this was a naturally occurring creature, or something magically concocted. He'd never seen the like of it, though he had to admit that what he didn't know about the world at large could fill volumes. He dimly remembered his father describing something similar living in the foothills, but decided that, if it were naturally occurring, it certainly must be related to some type of demon by the way it fought. He briefly considered just burying the thing and being done with it, but he examined his reflection in the water and saw that he looked rather like a large cat had defecated on him and tried to cover it up. He was scratched from his cheek-bones all the way down to his waist. Some of the scores were still oozing blood. He had fought too hard for this prize to simply throw it away.

Shivering with cold, Simon gutted the creature and tossed the entrails into the water. Finger fish greedily picked at the feast he had thrown them. He then removed the hands and feet to facilitate skinning the carcass. Once he had removed everything but the head, he set the meat in the stream to cool while he washed once again before gathering his clothes. Carrying the corpse and his other things, he moved back to his camp and built a fire with the remainder of his supply of wood.

Looking over his clothing, he realized that the creature had done more damage to his tunic than he had first thought. There were long rips in it, and he had no sewing kit to make repairs. Fortunately, he had another, but he would have to be more careful in the future. He had no fur to keep him warm, and damn little body fat, for that matter.

He left the shelter long enough to find three long sticks, two of them forked. First, he drove the forked sticks into the ground on either side of the fire. Then, after removing the beast's head and fur, he spitted the carcass on the straight stick and placed it to roast over the coals. While the meat cooked, he scraped the hide until there was no trace of fat or meat left on it. Once he had done that, he took it outside, spread the skin out over a depression in the ground so that it formed something like a bowl. He cracked the skull and scooped the contents out onto the hide and added enough of his own urine to make a paste of the brains, which he worked into the hide thoroughly. After setting that aside to cure, he put on his clothes and cut off a piece of the roasted meat. It was fatty and had an odd taste, but it wasn't unpalatable. It was extremely tough, like the living creature from which it came.

Once he had eaten a bit, and ensured that his wounds, though painful, weren't serious, he decided to gather more wood for his fire. While doing so, he thought about his situation. His first attempt at "hunting" had shown him just how inadequate he was against something with real natural weaponry. The only thing he had that gave him any advantage at all was his brain, and if he didn't start using it, he would surely perish. He needed something that would be deadly, and keep him out of range of a counter-attack. The first thing that came to mind was a bow, but he quickly rejected that idea. He was no archer, and he hadn't the first clue about how to make a real bow and arrows. He bent down and picked up a stick about four feet long. It had the remnants of roots on one end, and must have been a sapling before it was torn from the ground and carried here by floodwaters. He picked it up thinking to use it as firewood, but once it was in his hand, he noticed how straight and narrow it was and an idea occurred to him.

He and Boron had talked a great deal during their many hours together, and while ranged combat had not been something Simon had practiced, Boron had told him of a curious weapon used by the dark-skinned men of the far south for hunting. The smith had described a throwing stick used to add power and range when hurling a javelin. From Boron's descriptions, the weapon and technique were fairly simple, and could be readily mastered with a bit of practice. Looking at the spear-sized stick in his hand, he decided to give it a try. After making sure he had enough firewood for the coming night, he began looking about for more javelins and a piece of tree limb with a natural bend that could be used as a throwing stick.

Later that day, as the sun dropped beyond the mountain to the west, he remade his bed, reasoning that with the pine boughs working as insulation, he could use the thicker blanket to cover himself. Once his bed was finished, he cut the remainder of the meat into long strips and speared them on the spit and set them to dry over the embers of the fire. He used some strands from the frayed end of the rope he had cut from the rafter in the barn and did his best to repair his damaged tunic and pants. It wouldn't win any awards for craftsmanship, but he was able to make the clothing serviceable again.

Then he began working on his newest tool. The piece of tree branch he had found was a little wider than two of his fingers and about the right length. It was oddly flattened and had a knot on one end that would make a good place to rest the javelin against. It was slightly curved and Simon had soaked it in the stream all afternoon to soften it. Now he increased the curve by bending it slightly in the middle and then held it near the embers until it began to dry and hold the new shape. He wedged the piece with rocks to prevent it from straightening out and left it near the fire pit to finish drying.

Next he cut the root ends off of the six dead saplings he had gathered to use as projectiles, and then, after stripping the bark, cut them all to a uniform length of about four feet. He had spent a great deal of time hunting for these sticks. They had to be long and straight and not much bigger in diameter than his thumb. After inspecting each of them one last time to be sure that there were no hidden weaknesses, he used a rough flat stone to sharpen them.

He had helped the women of the house make glue several times and thought he could duplicate the process if he could get the raw animal products, preferably hide and sinew, but even fish would work. If he did, he could find feathers and fletch the javelins, and perhaps make some sort of points for them – maybe bone. For now, though, he felt that the pointed sticks would be enough to allow him to feed himself if he could master the technique of throwing them accurately.

He pulled the two forked sticks out of the ground and moved his improvised drying rack farther from the fire pit before putting more wood on the glowing embers. He needed the fire both for the warmth and for the light. Once the fuel was burning, he picked up his throwing stick and examined it. He fitted the end of one of his javelins against the knot of the stick and it wobbled quite a bit. He used his dagger to carefully carve the notch deeper and wider, testing often until the projectile set solidly. Then he spent nearly an hour trying and retrying different ways of gripping the piece before setting about working the actual handle end of it.

By the time Simon was satisfied with his throwing stick, it was quite late. He added a little more wood to his fire and then put the stones into the pit to heat. The inside of his shelter was so warm that he doubted he would need them, but he reasoned that it never hurt to be prepared. As he settled down into bed, his thoughts turned to his mother. He didn't understand why this was happening now; he had been in worse shape the night before, but he had fallen asleep almost immediately. Tonight, however, he was suddenly overcome with homesickness; he cried himself to sleep.

Chapter 19

SIMON CLIMBED OUT of bed in the predawn gloom and moved to the stream. He was still sore from his injuries and exertions, but didn't let that bother him this morning. He was eager to start practicing with his new weapon.

Once he had attended to bodily functions, he put the rough-cured skin of the animal in the water and weighted it with rocks to wash out the urine and brains. It wasn't very thick hide, and there wasn't much of it, even ignoring the large hole in the middle where he had stabbed the creature. However, having no idea how long it would be before he would again see a town or any other sign of civilization, he refused to waste any resource.

He gathered some wet clay and made several targets. They were simply unbaked discs of mud about the size of a dinner plate. Setting them out at different ranges, starting at about ten paces, and as far away as twenty-five, he returned to his shelter and gathered up his throwing stick and javelins. Stuffing two pieces of the dried meat in his mouth, he moved into position to make his first attempt at hitting the targets.

He found it a bit awkward to use the throwing stick initially, and his shots went wide. He finished chewing his breakfast and tried again. After several more throws, he had actually hit the closest target. Encouraged by his success, he continued practicing until the sun was above the ridge to the east and his throwing arm was sore. He had achieved a fair measure of accuracy out to about fifteen paces. Beyond that, his power was still good, but his javelins tended to drift off the mark.

Knowing that if he continued to practice with a sore arm he would train himself to do it wrong, he decided to spend the rest of the day looking for edible plants and medicinal herbs higher along the slope. He took three of the javelins with him just in case, but he saw no game while he explored his surroundings. He did, however, find some edible berries, as well as some moss that could be crushed and boiled to produce a soothing balm for his injuries. All in all, he felt it had been a productive day.

On the fourth day in camp, after retrieving the small piece of rawhide from the stream, he managed to spear two fairly large fish. He was certainly glad he had, since the meat he had cooked and dried was all but gone, and he had found only small amounts of berries and other edible vegetation. Besides, he was getting quite tired of that meat anyway. He longed for a bit of pork or beef, but any change was welcome.

He saved the fish heads and bones and, with a fire-baked pan he had made of clay from the stream bed, he was able to produce a small amount of glue. Using feathers found in the woods while foraging, he fletched his javelins. While doing so changed the characteristics of the missiles, he was able to compensate readily enough, and it improved his accuracy a great deal. By the end of practice on the seventh day, he could easily hit the farthest targets he set out - about twenty-five paces away.

On his eighth morning, he saw more fish and decided to try his luck at spearing a few. He quickly fetched one of his javelins and returned. When he did, he noticed that the rock where he normally put his feet when he was washing or gathering water was almost submerged. The water level had risen in the last day or so. That meant that the spring thaws had started early, and he might have to move his camp sooner than expected. He found a nearly straight stick and jammed it in the stream bed, then piled stones around it to ensure it stayed stable. He then cut a notch in it at the water line. He hoped that by measuring the amount of rise each day, he would be able to accurately judge how long before he would have to quit the site and move on. With no tent, it would be hard to give up the shelter and the security of his little stone dwelling.

The next morning the water was about a hand above the notch on the stick. He marked it again and decided to forage farther up the slope, rather than try for more fish. That way he could range farther to look for a new campsite on higher ground.

He had found an actual game trail and was following it when the feeling came over him. Though he wasn't sure why he suddenly felt danger, he heeded his instinct and found cover, trying not to make a sound as he waited to see what had spooked him. The sound of movement in the brush made him hold his breath. He waited as it got louder. That much noise had to be either several smaller animals or one large one. Four large bipedal creatures came into view along the trail, and it was instantly apparent that these were Roracks. Their hides were jet black and rough textured, just the way that Boron had described. They had wide noses, jagged teeth, and nasty claws on the ends of their fingers. Three of them were completely naked—and the fourth, who appeared to be leading the group— wore an animal skin on its shoulders and some sort of rough necklace that was decorated with bones. The leader carried a crude wooden spear, and two of the others bore large clubs that were nothing more than roughly broken tree limbs; the fourth was empty handed.

The beast-men stopped and sniffed the air curiously. Simon almost bolted when the leader made a loud barking noise. The other three seemed to understand what the bark meant and looked back the way they had come. Then all four of them moved off, quickly disappearing into the brush as if it had all been a mirage.

Simon realized he had been holding his breath the whole time the beast-men had been in sight and slowly, making no noise, let the air escape from his lungs. Then he just stayed right where he was for nearly a quarter of an hour, partly to ensure that the Roracks wouldn't return and find him in the open, but also because it took that long for his breathing to return to normal and his legs to stop shaking enough for him to walk. When he felt he could move without stumbling, he carefully picked his way among the trees and rocks back to his camp. By the time he returned to his shelter, it was well past noon. The valley would be in shadow before long. He decided to make a cold camp and then leave this place in the morning. He used the time until full dark to pack everything except his blankets.

Chapter 20

S IMON HAD NOT slept well. With no fire, it was almost freezing, even inside the shelter, and he had been awakened several times by dreams of being hunted by the beast-men. So when he woke the last time, still before dawn, he simply decided to give up on sleep and get an early start. After eating a cold breakfast, he quickly packed his blankets and set out into the pre-dawn chill. He briefly thought about trying to remove any signs of his camp, but rejected that plan, reasoning that it would be better to spend the time putting more distance between him and any evidence of his presence.

By the time he carefully picked his way to the top of the eastern slope of the small valley, the sun was already high enough to cast good light. He exercised extra caution, wanting to be sure that he would have ample time to hide at any hint of approaching danger.

At the top of the ridge, he could see for many miles in each direction. He discovered that the ridges were nothing more than the arms of a large mountain whose peak was nearly due north. There were several valleys between the ridges and all of them had water flowing through them. He rested for only a few moments on the crest before continuing his trek.

As he neared the top of the second ridge, shortly after noon, he heard a sound that made his blood run cold. It was the same barking sound that the lead Rorack had made the day before. He started to turn away, but the next sound, even louder and more frightening, caused him to stop short. That sound had obviously been made by something extremely large, and it was quickly followed by a higher pitched scream of anger and pain that was abruptly cut short. He wasn't sure how he knew, but he was certain that something had just killed the beast-man he had heard seconds before.

Though terrified, he was unable to keep himself from moving toward the sounds of battle. He just had to see what creature could put a stop to one of those monsters as easily as he might step on an insect. He was about to pull himself over a rock outcropping at the top to have a look when a bright light came from just the other side. Simon could feel the heat of an intense fire, and several more Roracks screamed. Again the cries died suddenly rather than trailing away.

Realization swept over him. He had heard that dragons and Roracks were natural enemies and would kill each other if they got the chance. He had also heard that wild dragons could be dangerous to humans as well, so he hesitated for a moment. Then there was another cry of pain, but this was no beast-man. It wasn't exactly human, but it had a quality to it that struck a chord deep inside him. It had to be the dragon. Whether it would turn on him or not, to ignore that cry would be no different than to ignore the cry of any person in dire need. He quickly fitted a javelin to his throwing stick and climbed to the top of the rock.

What he saw on the other side of the ridge made him pause involuntarily. There were seven beast-men still standing. The leader he had seen yesterday had stabbed a blue-green dragon below and to the left of the neck with a rough-made spear that was little more than a sharpened log about eight feet long, and was trying with all of its might to drive the two-inch diameter lance in deeper. Simon took only a second to size up the situation before throwing the javelin directly at the large Rorack, desperately hoping that it wasn't too late for the dragon. The missile flew straight and penetrated all the way through the monster's chest from one side to the other. It looked down and pivoted its head from left to right examining the object that now stuck out of either side of its body, but it appeared to be more surprised than in pain. It did, however, lose its grip on its own spear. The respite gave the dragon time enough to lash out and knock the beast-man close to five yards away. The creature struggled briefly and then went still.

Two of the remaining six Roracks looked in the direction that the deadly projectile had come from and, seeing Simon, charged toward him. Boron had once told him that in the heat of battle, time can appear to slow down, and the beast-men seemed to be running at him in slow motion. The smith had explained that the effect was caused by physical changes that happened in the body under stress, and by narrowing your focus too much. He had said that the way to counter it was to widen your perspective; otherwise, it could get you killed. Simon, his first time in actual combat, forgot to widen his perceptions and nearly lost his life.

He managed to fit another javelin to the throwing stick and launch it, but he was momentarily confused as to why he seemed to be moving as slowly as the two beast-men. He saw, in vivid detail, the projectile hit its mark and take down the target, but he couldn't move fast enough to either fit another to the throwing stick, or even get up a reasonable block in time to prevent the second assailant from hitting him across the side of the face with its clawed hand. Simon was knocked several feet to his right, and he fell down the slope onto a curiously rounded rock. There was a bright flash as the wind was knocked from his body by the impact, and he felt strangely disconnected from his own body for just a second or two. He closed his eyes, and he could still see a reddish light, as well as feel the searing heat of the dragon's deadly breath, so he knew she was again using that fearsome weapon on her attackers. He laid there for several more seconds to let his senses return to normal.

When the heat eased, he opened his eyes and looked back over his shoulder in time to see the beast-man who had hit him raise a crude club over its head to make a two-handed swing. Just as he thought he would die, something the size of a small tree whizzed over his back, and the Rorack disappeared with a thud and a grunt.

He noted that the passage of time was returning to something close to normal as he watched the beast-man's club spin, at first slowly, but with increasing speed, as it flew into the nearby brush after being knocked from the monster's hands. Simon looked around and realized that the dragon had used her tail as a weapon, saving his life.

As he rose, he took stock of the situation. The dragon hadn't been idle while he was being knocked senseless. Two of the remaining Roracks had been burned to a crisp by her last blast of fire, and the remaining two, smoldering, but alive, were in full retreat. The beast-man who had tried to kill him a moment before began to rise awkwardly, and Simon surprised even himself by pulling his knife and quickly diving onto the creature and shoving the blade hilt-deep into it just where the base of its skull joined the back of its neck. The monster died before it had the chance to either attack or run away.

The dragon stirred behind him. An old tale about wild dragons killing and eating humans briefly surfaced in his thoughts, but he put it out of his mind. If she wished to attack him, she would have done so by now, and he was more worried about the blood running from the wounds on his face. Also, his chest smarted where he must have abraded it when he was knocked down.

"I thank you, human, for helping me, though I fear you came too late to save my life." The dragon's voice was definitely feminine, and actually quite pleasant.

Simon turned to her and responded, "Too late? Are you wounded that badly?"

As he asked the question, he looked her over; he could see the numerous large wounds that the beast-men had inflicted, and the spear still embedded in the front of her shoulder.

"There must be something we can do to stop the bleeding and heal you. You'll be all right!" The last was, though he wasn't sure why, as much a plea as it was a reassurance.

The dragon chuckled and smiled, though the smile was almost a grimace of pain. "No, young human, I am afraid the beast men employed poison on the makeshift lance that pierced my flesh, and that I will soon pass to shadow. If I had not been so exhausted from my journey and then laying my last egg, my scales would not have been slack, and the attack wouldn't have penetrated. However, it did, and I am dying. I wish it were not so, because that will leave you to care for my daughter with no guidance, but that is the way of it."

Simon was completely confused. He looked around and saw no other dragon in evidence. "Your daughter? I don't see her. Is she close? And why am I to care for her?" He paused to quell the panic he felt creeping up his spine. His voice broke as he asked, "How am I to care for her?"

The dragon laughed out loud, which caused her more pain, and said, "You are nearly standing on her. She is inside the egg that you landed on when you were knocked down." She smiled at him and added, "I perceive that you are not very old by human standards. You are very brave for one so young."

The compliment was completely lost on Simon. He stared at what he now realized was a dragon egg. It was a little less in length than a man's height, and roughly the diameter of a rain barrel, perhaps just a bit more.

"I don't know anything about dragons," he pleaded. "How can I care for her? I can barely care for myself."

"You will find a way, young human," the dragon replied softly. "Now, I am fading fast. I must pass on my lineage to my daughter while I still have the strength to do so. Please stand to one side and don't interrupt."

Simon moved away from the egg and was stunned by his unwillingness to do so. He felt an intense impulse to protect the unhatched baby inside the shell. He actually had to fight down the urge to get between the mother and the unborn dragon-child. Then a voice that he knew was coming from inside his head, but which originated inside the shell itself said, *Do not worry, no harm will come to me. This must be done, and then we will be together for all time.*

It took nearly half an hour for the dragon to pass on her lineage to her unborn daughter. During that time, Simon busied himself with retrieving his javelins and scouting to make sure the last two Roracks weren't circling back for another attack. He found one of them where it had succumbed to its burns and fallen. It was barely breathing, and Simon dispatched it with one thrust of his knife. He was surprised at himself for doing so. It wasn't simply an act of mercy; there was just something about these monsters that made it feel right to eliminate them from the world. Though he searched for nearly a quarter of an hour, he found no further sign of the last beast-man.

The dragon looked up as he approached her. "It is good you have returned."

Simon could see that she was noticeably weaker. "Perhaps if I pull that spear from your body you will feel a little better," he observed.

"No, young human, though I appreciate that you wish to ease my suffering, that spear is lodged in an artery: pulling it would cause me to bleed to death much faster. Now listen, I still have something to tell you and there isn't much time."

Simon gave the dragon his full attention.

"My daughter will free herself from her shell soon, perhaps this very day. I was interrupted twice before when attempting to lay her egg, so she has matured longer inside my body than a young dragon usually does. This last time I was too far along in the process and that is why the beast-men were able to catch me on the ground." She paused while a spasm wracked her body. "You must find a way to move the egg in case more beast-men come. If they find my body, they will be a long time scavenging from it, and that will give you more time to get away. But if they find you here, they will take great delight in killing both of you. The beast-men are not very intelligent, but they are extremely cunning, and they have an instinctive hatred of my kind, and they easily extend that loathing onto any found associating with dragons."

Another spasm of pain washed over her and she waited for it to subside before continuing. "My mother, many times removed, was one of the first dragons ever born. She was also one of the leaders in the dragons' fight to be free of the mages who made and tried to enslave them. I have passed that lineage on to my daughter, who is the first lineage holder of our line to bond with a human. It is her duty to live and bear more daughters to carry on that long lineage, and I implore you to do your best to help her with that task."

Simon had only made one other oath in his young life—to see his mother released from her bondage. He had fulfilled that pledge and felt free to make another. "You have my word that I will do everything in my power to help her."

The dragon nodded and said, "Good. The first thing you will need to do when you are clear of this place is find food for her. She will be unable to hunt for several weeks, but will need a tremendous amount of meat to sustain her growth. Fresh meat is best, but she will eat whatever you can find. There are fewer Roracks to the south. I don't know where you were going, but I would recommend that you head in that direction. To the west is the land called Horne; there are human habitations and many herd beasts there."

Simon spoke up quickly, "I can not return to Horne; if I do my life will be forfeit, and your daughter will be on her own."

The dragon looked at him curiously and then said, "I don't know what one so young could have done to warrant a death sentence, but if that is the case, then you need to head southeast. The bond between dragon and human is so strong that if one of you dies, the other will lose all will to live."

Simon had heard such before and now, thinking about the unhatched dragon, he believed it. "We will head south and east, as you have suggested."

Again the dragon nodded, "Fine. Now, there is one last thing I can do to help you. Stay where you are and do not interfere. No harm will come to her or you." Saying this, the dragon turned to the egg and began to breathe a small intense jet of flame on the shell.

Simon was alarmed and made to step forward to protect the little dragon, but that voice once again sounded in his head. "*No! Do not try to intervene, I am in no danger."* Then, almost as if giggling, the voice continued, *"Wait and see what comes of this."*

When the dragon finished, she turned back to Simon. "I have used my flame and magic to etch a Dragon Blade for you. It is my reward for your bravery, and your oath to help my daughter." The dragon looked back at the shell for a moment and then said, "How curious; instead of one blade, there are two. I don't believe there have ever been two blades etched onto a single shell before now."

Simon looked at the egg and could clearly see the two blades outlined there. One was a long curved blade like the one Boron had taught him to use, similar to, but shorter than, a scimitar. The other was clearly a long knife for his off hand.

He looked back to the dragon to ask some of the many questions he had on his mind and realized that she wouldn't last much longer. The exertion of etching the blades onto the shell had used up nearly all of the strength she had left.

"The blades will come away clean when she breaks free from her shell. They are indestructible, and will never dull." Then she lowered her head and said, "It is time for you to go."

Simon shook his head, "I don't want to leave you here to die alone. There must be something I can do."

"There is. You can take my daughter away from here before the lone beast-man that got away finds more of his kind and returns. There is no force on earth, magical or mundane, that can stop my death now, and I am only managing to stave off the shadow by sheer force of will." As Simon continued to stare and shake his head, she added, "My kind believe that we will be reborn after we pass to shadow. Remember me, but do not grieve. Who's to say? We may meet again in the future." She chuckled once more. "Of course, if we do, I won't remember this past life so we won't know each other, but it's still comforting to know that such a meeting might occur."

Then, gathering the last of her waning strength, she once again raised her head, and added, "You have done much for me thus far. Now honor my wishes and go! Do not stay and watch me die; I prefer to be alone for that."

Simon turned to the egg without another word. Realizing that he would not be able to lift the vessel, he began rolling it gently down the hill. When the terrain steepened, he had to move to the other side of the egg to prevent it from rolling uncontrolled. As he did so, he looked back. The mother dragon was stubbornly holding her head up, refusing to lie down and seek her peace until the two of them were out of sight.

Getting to the bottom of the hill was exhausting. It took all of his strength to keep the egg from simply tumbling down unchecked. The trip took a little more than a quarter of an hour. Simon was soaked with sweat and covered with dirt by the time they reached the flood channel. His wounds hurt worse because of the grit and sweat in them. He stopped and sat down once the ground leveled out.

Immediately the egg started rocking madly. He could feel the little dragon's panic. She felt an intense need to be free of the confining shell. Suddenly a crack appeared on the surface. Soon more cracks opened up. Then, as if an explosion had occurred inside, the egg broke into dozens of pieces.

The dragon wasn't one specific color as her mother had been. She was red along the entire dorsal surface of her body. The leading edges of her wings were the color of her back. The color faded to orange on her sides, and her belly and wing membranes were yellow.

She sat upright, somewhat shakily, and raised her wings. Then she reached skyward with her head and let out a strange, high-pitched, undulating cry. The sound sent shivers up and down Simon's spine, and he knew that she was keening for her mother's death.

CHAPTER 21

H E COULD FEEL the grief the little dragon felt for her mother, and he grieved with her. However, that emotion was rapidly replaced by a more urgent need. Food! Waves of hunger began to assail him as if he had been physically attacked. He was nearly incapacitated by the onslaught. He needed to find meat, now!

His thoughts turned to the dead Roracks he had left up the hill.

"I would rather die of hunger than eat those foul creatures." It was as if she were shouting inside his head.

"I'm sorry," he shouted back both mentally and aloud. "But your hunger has me nearly doubled over in pain and unable to think straight!"

He was rewarded by a lessening of the intensity. "I am also sorry, I will do my best to protect you from my feelings. But I must eat soon!"

Just then a fish jumped; trying to feed on airborne insects. Simon grabbed up one of his javelins and ran to the water's edge. His first stab missed, but his second hit its mark, and he dragged back a fish roughly as long as his arm. The dragon was almost dancing in anticipation as he brought the fish to her. He started to pull his dagger to gut it...

"What are doing?' she pleaded. "Just give it to me, I have teeth."

Simon shrugged and threw the fish in her direction.

It took her only a little more time to devour the thing than it took him to throw it. He waited to see if it would be enough but, judging from the hunger pangs, it would take a great deal more to satiate her. As she watched with a mixture of annoyance and anticipation, he returned to the stream—a small river, actually—to try for more food.

Fortunately for him, there were quite a few fish attempting to feed on the insects that were trying to get a head start on spring mating. After the second one, he stopped going back up the bank and simply threw the fish as he caught them. By the fifth one, she had become quite adept at catching them in mid-air. Most of the catch were smaller than the first had been, so it took the better part of the remainder of the afternoon to fill her belly. Once full, she laid down on the bank and almost immediately went to sleep.

Simon briefly considered building some type of shelter for the night, but rejected the idea. Their position here on the river-bank was much too exposed, and since her hunger would again surge to the forefront when she woke up, he decided to spend the remaining hour or so of light obtaining more food.

When he could no longer see the fish because of the darkness, he got his blankets out of his pack and spread them next to the dragon. It suddenly struck him that he didn't even have a name for her yet. He laid down huddling against her for warmth and fell asleep thinking about it.

The next thing Simon was aware of was that he was standing on the side of a mountain watching clouds swirl in the reddish light. Then he noticed that he was standing next to the dragon.

"Welcome to the Dream State, Simon," she said.

"You can speak actual words? How come you haven't done so earlier?"

"I can speak actual words here because this is a collective psychic realm maintained by the dragons. Our physical bodies are still asleep, not here."

"So, this is just a dream?"

"No, not *just* a dream. Here we can communicate as we would while awake. Our conscious thoughts are in play, not just our sub-conscious ones. However, while we are here our bodies can still get the rest we need."

He started to ask a question, but she shushed him. "I have much to tell you before we wake, and if you interrupt me with questions, it will take a long time indeed."

She then proceeded to tell him her lineage. It took some time, though he surmised that time passed differently in the Dream State. He watched other dragons, most fully grown, soar among the clouds while he listened intently to her. When she finished the history of her line, she said, "I am Sienna, and I am your bond-mate."

Her last sentence was filled with such love and devotion that tears trickled down his cheeks and he put his arms around her neck and hugged her fiercely, trying to convey as much love back to her as she had to him.

Finally, she gently pulled away and said, "We have been here all night: it will be light in an hour, and we must return to the waking world." At the look in his eyes, she added, "Do not worry, Dearest One, I will be with you. I will always be with you."

The Dream State faded to black, and he came fully awake. Sienna was right there beside him, and he snuggled tighter against her. She stretched out her neck and laid her head on his chest. He didn't go back to sleep; he simply lay very still and took comfort in her presence until the ridge to the east was silhouetted in the predawn light.

CHAPTER 22

A S SIMON RETURNED from the stream, he remembered the Dragon Blades and looked among the shards of the egg. Sure enough, there were the two blades he had seen etched into the shell by the dragon. The blades felt strange to him; not wrong, just strange. Almost as if they would come alive in his hands. He couldn't resist making a few practice swings with them.

"If you could tear yourself away from your dancing," Sienna said in his mind, "I would really like to get some food."

He hadn't meant to get caught up in blade practice, but the sword and long knife, even without proper hilts and grips, felt so natural in his hands that he had gotten lost in the forms as he sliced the air and battled invisible opponents.

"I apologize, Sienna, I didn't mean to neglect you. I left seven fish on the bank there behind you. While you eat those, I will try and spear some more."

She turned and actually pounced on the small pile of fish. They were gone before he could get a javelin and make it to the water. It took over an hour to get sufficient fish to sate her appetite enough that he could take a break. She had eaten enough food to satisfy several grown men.

"I hope that meal will hold you for a while. We need to move on. We are not nearly far enough away from where the battle took place yesterday for my taste," Simon said.

"I am not full, but I do admit that moving away from this place would be wise. I feel very exposed here," Sienna replied.

"Yes, I was thinking that we might follow this river south. Fish seem abundant in this water, and we need to go in that direction anyway." Watching her waddle clumsily to the river to drink, he added, "I think it would be much easier than heading directly east over the mountains, and probably safer as well."

As she stepped into the water, she replied, "I agree, the water is not uncomfortable. We could even swim if you would like."

"Not uncomfortable? I had my hands in that water for a short time when I washed a few minutes ago and they are still numb from the cold," he responded incredulously.

"I do not find it too cold; you must be more sensitive to temperature than I," she stated curiously.

"Apparently so; if I submerged my body in that water for very long, I would probably die," he responded.

She turned and looked at him. "You are not making a joke; you really believe that you might die from swimming in this. Dragons are capable of living well in a wide range of temperatures. Apparently, the range for humans is a bit narrower."

"Apparently," he agreed.

"Then I will swim, and you must stay on the bank of the river. I am less awkward in the water and will be better able to keep up with you that way."

Simon was struck by how reasonable she was for a newborn. *Are all dragons born with such good common sense?* he asked.

She gave him the mental equivalent of a smile for the compliment and replied, "Lineage holders do get more from their mothers than other newly born dragons. Also, I believe that the bond between us helps as well."

Simon didn't know how to respond to her line of thought, so he changed the subject back to their travel plans. "If you are ready to travel, we should leave," he said. "Let me stow these Dragon Blades in my pack and we can get started. Your mother said that if the beast-men returned, they would be a long time scavenging her body."

At Sienna's growl he quickly added, "I don't like leaving her body to those monsters any more than you do, but, since she chose to make such a sacrifice, it would be wrong of us not to honor her wishes and use the extra time she has given us to our advantage."

The little dragon's mood softened and she said, "You are right, of course. It would seem that when it comes to those foul creatures, you have more common sense than I do."

Simon shouldered his pack and pointed downstream to indicate that he was ready, and they should begin their journey.

He walked for nearly an hour, trying not only to keep to the rocks to avoid leaving a visible trail, but also to remain within sight of her at all times in case she needed help. She was good to her word, though, and swam along well. The river widened and was swelled by numerous streams and springs as it flowed. Still, they were making pretty good time when they came to the first obstacle a little less than two leagues downstream. A rock slide at a bend in the river had completely covered the path on this side.

"Perhaps you could swim to the other side and continue from there," she suggested.

"I'm not a strong swimmer to begin with, and we still have the temperature of the water to consider. The sun will not be up high enough above the ridge to warm this valley for at least another hour, so even if I don't stay in the water long, my wet clothes will still cause me to be dangerously chilled until I can get dry. That would mean stopping to build a fire, unless you can use your fire to…"

"No good," she interrupted him, "I don't have fire yet. Dragons don't usually begin to breathe fire until they are about a year old."

"Well, that's good to know; I'd hate to have found that out in an emergency."

"*I am sorry you are disappointed.*" She was a bit perturbed at his tone.

"I didn't mean it like that. I simply meant that I had thought you were born with the ability—like your mother, only smaller. If I had continued with that assumption and relied on you to breathe fire at an enemy, or for emergency warmth, it would have caused a problem. Knowing that the ability will take time to appear is helpful."

"Well, my love, if you had been given more instructions, you'd have known. It's not your fault or mine, nor can it be blamed on she who was my mother. Our situation is what it is, and we just have to do our best to deal with it. Now, I am still hungry, so you find a way over those rocks, and I will attempt to catch some more of these fish. I don't know if I am capable of doing so at this point, but it will give me something to occupy my time while I wait for you."

Simon was amused with her reasoning and wished her luck as he began to carefully work his way over the slide. As he picked his way among the debris, he kept his attention partially focused on Sienna in case she ran into trouble. The fact that her first few attempts to catch a fish weren't successful didn't dampen her spirits, but by the time he could clearly see the far edge of the slide, about ten minutes later, she was in a rather bad mood.

"I wouldn't worry too much, Sienna," he told her, "you'll get the technique in time."

"That's all well and good, but I am starving," She said peevishly. "If I do not get food soon, I will not be able to continue traveling."

"*I will fish for you when I reach the far side of these rocks,*" he replied. "*Wait a minute…*" His thought trailed off as he spotted something that looked out of place and moved toward it to investigate.

Several moments passed before he spoke again. "Sienna, how would you feel about a bit of real meat?"

"If you do not have real meat, don't ask such a question," she said angrily.

"I have stumbled upon several wild pigs that were killed in this rock slide. Apparently, they were rooting near the river and undermined the bank, and died when they couldn't get out of the way," he replied. "I am attempting to free one of the carcasses now. Be patient and you will soon have your fill."

The little dragon was prancing on the bank when he finally dragged the pig from the rocks and other debris. She didn't even wait for him to get completely out of the way before digging into the animal's belly. She finished the entrails in just a few moments then turned her attention to the actual meat. Simon was impressed as she effortlessly ripped loose one of the front legs and ate it bones and all. The ribs were no problem for her and she moved to the hind quarter in short order.

When she had devoured half the pig and showed no sign of slowing down, he asked, "Are you going to save a small bit of that for me? The meat is still quite fresh, and I could use some of it myself."

"You did say there were several of the animals?" She didn't look up from her meal as she spoke.

Simon chuckled. "Yes, I did say that there were several animals. I will retrieve them while you eat your fill, but I am going to get some of the meat. If I don't eat, I will not have the strength to forage for you," he teased. She was so engrossed in her food that his sarcasm was lost on her.

The first pig was completely gone by the time he returned, and he was astounded to find that she was still hungry enough to eat the entrails of the second carcass. Then she moved just a few feet away and went to sleep as if she were a drunkard passing out from too much ale. He could actually see the meal pressing outward against her hide.

Simon figured that if he dug a pit and built a good fire, he would be able to set some meat to roast when he returned with another pig. He knew that there were four more that he could easily see, all a little smaller than the first two, and bringing them all back could supply his Bond-mate for a couple of days, and perhaps give him time to find more food for her.

It took the rest of the day to retrieve all of the pigs - digging through the debris he had found two more buried - and then set up a suitable camp. He made a small lean-to of sorts by laying branches against a large rock and then covering the structure with conifer boughs. He roasted enough meat to last him through the next day and then, by firelight, set enough for several more days to smoke and dry.

The next morning he again woke before the dragon. Leaving her to sleep, he went to the river and attended to bodily functions before rekindling his fire. Then he took out the Dragon Blades and examined them again. They needed to have guards and hilts made, but they were otherwise perfect in every detail. He couldn't resist taking a practice swing at a log the diameter of his calf. The blade neatly cleaved it in two.

He returned to his fire and set some water close to the heat. He cleaned the blade and then went through his pack while he waited for the water to boil. He found the skin of the first animal he had killed and busied himself with sewing the hole in the hide. He punched the holes with his dagger and used more fibers from his rope as thread. When he finished, he returned the hide to his pack.

"*I'm hungry,*" Sienna *said* sleepily.

"I'm beginning to think that you will always be hungry no matter how much food I stuff into you." He retrieved his hot water and took a small sip.

"I must eat to grow. How else do you expect me to attain the same size as she who was my mother? If I don't grow, I will not be able to carry you in flight."

Simon was about to take another sip and stopped with the cup halfway to his mouth. "Carry me in flight? I hadn't thought about that. When will you be big enough for us to fly together?"

"Not for several months, I'm afraid, and not at all if I don't get enough food."

Simon laughed out loud.

"I'm glad you find that amusing. You promised to bring more of that meat and I don't see it," she accused.

"I gutted all of the animals to keep them from spoiling as much as possible: I thought you would want the entrails so I put them all in a pile over there," he pointed toward the spot where she could find the stuff. "The carcasses I put in the river to keep them cool. I figured you would prefer not to eat rotten meat."

"Well, dragons are not scavengers," she responded as she moved in the indicated direction, "but we have strong stomachs and can eat meat that is tainted if that is all we can get."

She fell on the pile of internal organs.

"I don't see how you can eat most of that stuff," Simon said, screwing up his face in disgust at the thought. "I can understand the liver and heart, but the gut itself?"

"The gut contains substances that are helpful to both my growth and my digestion that are not abundant in the meat. I could survive and even thrive without them, but I will eat it if it's available." She finished the soft portions of her meal and asked, "Where is the meat? I am still very hungry."

"I tied them up so the current wouldn't take them away if the river rose during the night. I will fetch you one of the carcasses. I don't want you to bite through the rope in your frenzy to get the meat."

He rose and went to the river. Returning with the remains of one of the pigs, he said, "I've noticed that you tend to sleep if you've gorged yourself, and I expect this morning will be no different."

"I am only doing what young dragons do. I'm sorry if that bothers you," she replied defensively.

"Don't be like that; it was just an observation. My question is this, though: would you mind if I explored a little while you sleep off your meal? I won't go too far."

"As long as you don't go far, I see no harm."

"Good. I figured we can stay here at least until the meat runs out. We are near enough to deep water that we can easily escape if any beast-men come along, because they can't swim. However, I would like to see if I can find a place above the high-water mark that is more sheltered. Also, I need to look for game trails, or you will be back to eating fish."

"Very well, I will try to maintain my awareness while I rest. If you find some place safer, we can move everything when you return."

Privately, he had his doubts about her remaining aware of anything once she had filled her belly, but he let it go. "If you think you will be full after that one pig, I will leave now," he said out loud.

She didn't *say* anything to him, but nodded in a surprisingly human-like gesture.

CHAPTER 23

THE BANKS HAD gotten steadily steeper as he moved south. After picking his way along the river for about an hour, he sat down near the north end of what appeared to be a canyon through which the river ran. He rested for nearly a quarter of an hour. He was beginning to doubt that he would find suitable high ground nearby, but he decided to look just a little further south anyway.

Once inside the canyon, he could see that the river turned somewhat westward. The near bank was elevated and steep, but climbable. The opposite side, however, could only be described as a cliff. The distance from the water's surface to the top of the precipice was easily fifty feet at its lowest point. From his position on the opposite shore, it looked to be smooth. The river itself widened into a small oxbow lake in the middle of the bend before continuing its course.

Right in the middle of the dog-leg on the far side, easily fifty yards from where he was standing, he could see a large sandbar that led up to an overhang. The shelf stood well above the point that he estimated to be the normal high water mark. It must have been carved out by flash floods during the summer rains. If he could find a way to move back and forth from the sheer sides of the eastern cliff to the bank on the west, he and Sienna could stay in this place for the next couple of months, provided he could find enough food for her. By then, he hoped, she would be able to hunt for herself.

Simon only pondered on his decision for a few moments. Then, dragging several logs to the water's edge, he used the short rope he had brought along to lash them together. Once he had a small raft made, he carefully stepped onto the logs to test the buoyancy. The makeshift raft held his weight fine, so long as he didn't rock the craft while he was standing on it. He found a dead sapling, about as big around as his wrist at its wider end and nearly twelve feet long, that had been washed down the river in the annual floods, and, hoping the pole was long enough, he knelt down and pushed off from the bank.

The surface of the water came over to the top of the pole in the middle of the little lake, but the water was fairly calm and he had no trouble at all reaching the overhang. Once there, he found that the sandbar made a good landing, and the shore rose several feet as the sand gave way to actual rock. The overhang itself was a half again the height of a tall man and the roof sloped downward as it receded until it met the stone floor about twenty feet back. He and Sienna would both be able to shelter here for several weeks even if she tripled her present size.

From his vantage point on top of the sandbar, he could see several game trails leading to the river's edge on the other shore. He could set snares on those to catch game and then finish the animals off with his javelins. The place appeared perfect for now. The sheer cliff would preclude being attacked from behind, and the deeper water would frustrate any beast-men who might approach from the river side.

Pushing off for the return trip, he realized that the only problem he was going to have would be his raft. It was nothing more than four logs tied together. It floated low in the water and was unwieldy, as well as very heavy. With Sienna's help, he could haul it up the shore enough to prevent it from becoming waterlogged, but the slight current caught it and made it difficult for him to maintain a straight course across the lake. By the time he reached the far side, he was also almost forty yards south of where he had wanted to come ashore. He pulled the raft as far out of the water as he could and tied it to a large dead tree, deciding to worry about that problem later. He turned and headed back to the north.

The sun was high in the sky, and Sienna was just stirring as he walked into camp. He fully expected her to ask for food, but she walked a little away from the lean-to and began flapping her wings wildly.

"*Are you going fly?*" he *asked* with great anticipation.

"No, I do not think I am ready for flight just yet, though I will be very soon. I am simply exercising my wing muscles."

She had said she wasn't trying to fly, but her feet left the ground. Simon was pelted with small bits of debris kicked up by the wind she was creating beneath her. Sienna was more surprised than he was when she looked down and realized that she was several feet in the air. As she looked down, she was so startled that she forgot to continue flapping, and she fell back hard, knocking herself flat as she hit.

Simon rushed forward, suddenly worried. "Are you all right?" he asked aloud, his voice full of concern.

"I think I bit the inside of my cheek," she replied, obviously upset with herself for falling.

"What happened? One second you were airborne, the next you were sprawled out on the ground."

"Noticed that, did you?" she answered sarcastically. "Did you also notice that I forgot to keep flapping my wings?"

He couldn't suppress the laughter that bubbled out.

"I'm happy that I have amused you. Perhaps you could flap your arms and show me the proper way of it."

While the comment had been designed to quiet him, he laughed all the harder. Sienna actually growled and turned her back on him. It took a moment for him to get himself under control.

"Don't be angry with me. I'm not laughing at your pain, but even you have to admit that it was funny."

"I don't *have* to admit anything," she said glaring at him. Then her countenance changed and she added, "Though I do suppose that, from your perspective, it was amusing." She actually chuckled. "I guess that I do have a bit to learn before I will be proficient at this."

"Well, I wouldn't worry about it too much," he replied. "I imagine that all flying creatures have little mishaps during their early attempts to get off the ground."

"I wasn't trying to get off the ground, if you will recall. But I do suspect that you are right, though this was still a painful lesson. I believe that my cheek is still bleeding."

Simon was suddenly worried. He had seen what Sienna's teeth were capable of, and wondered if it was possible for a dragon to do serious injury to herself in such a way; one of the horses on the estate was missing a large chunk of its tongue, and Boron had told him that the animal had bitten it off when it had fallen.

"Let me see your cheek," he said, forgetting in his concern to speak mentally.

"I am fine."

"Let me see it," he insisted. "I want to see how bad it is."

She started to object, but the look on his face made her change her mind. She opened her mouth to show him the injury. The first thing he noticed was that the array of teeth was extremely impressive despite the dragon's youth. However, he could see the cut and it was indeed still bleeding. The jagged laceration was as long as his outstretched hand, and though it wasn't gushing forth, the amount of blood still flowing worried him. He stared at it, wishing he knew more about the healing art. He concentrated on the cut and wanted it to heal. He wanted it to close over as if it had never happened. He wished that he had the power to simply take the cut away and make the pain stop.

As he stared, he noticed that the blood stopped flowing. He could feel energy moving from him to the wound and could actually see the wound beginning to close. He opened himself up more and could almost see the energy, and not just what flowed between him and the dragon, but what was flowing in the stream and from the earth itself. He felt the energy at his feet and allowed it to rush up through him and into the wound, which closed almost instantly.

The dragon balked and drew her head back sharply as if she had been stung. *"Careful, you almost cooked my mouth!"* She seemed less startled than he was.

It took several moments for Simon to recover enough to ask, *"What just happened?"*

"It appears," she responded as if not quite sure, "that you have managed to tap into the energy of the earth to heal me. I had to step back because you continued to let that energy flow once the cut was healed, and it became painful, as if I were being burned."

"How is that possible? I don't know how to work magic."

"I am not sure. The memories passed on to me are vague on this. Dragons know of such techniques, but we heal so rapidly that we rarely have need of the knowledge. It looks as though flying is not the only thing we have much to learn about."

"I hope we can learn it without hurting each other," he stated firmly.

"I suspect that it is simply a matter of control. However," she said, dismissing the whole incident, "I am very hungry and need to eat."

Simon shook his head, finding it hard to believe she could put such a thing out of her mind so easily. Then he smiled and, shrugging his shoulders, replied, *"I will fetch another of the pig carcasses for you. Then I will tell you what I found on my trip this morning."*

Simon got the meat, and she fell on it with great appetite. While she ate, he told her all that he had found down river.

"So, the only problem you have is how you will navigate the water," she said thoughtfully. "Perhaps we can work together on that. I am not bothered by the water temperature, and I am a strong swimmer. Maybe, if I push while you use the pole you made, together we will be able to overcome the problem of the current."

"That might just work. Between the two of us, we should be able to get me to and from the game trails to check the snares I intend to set."

"That sounds like a wonderful plan," she *said* sleepily. *"We should move our camp soon, perhaps tomorrow."* She barely managed to finish her thought before laying her head down and drifting off.

He smiled at her like an indulgent parent before turning and heading off to gather a bit of firewood. Sienna had eaten the entire pig he had retrieved, and he was hungry. Building a fire to cook over, he then set off to the river with one of his javelins to try for a fish or two for his own meal, hoping to save the pork he had smoked for later.

Surprisingly, he managed to spear each fish he tried for, not missing a single one. Engrossed in what he was doing and how well it was going, he had six fish before he realized he had taken much more than he could possibly eat, so he stopped and moved back to the fire to cook them.

After eating, he was so tired from the day's exertions that he fell asleep and only woke once, briefly, during the night. After checking to make sure that Sienna was all right, he settled back into slumber.

Again Simon found himself in that strange landscape of reddish light and shifting clouds. Sienna smiled at him and spoke. "I believe I have some answers to our earlier questions. I have been speaking to some of the other dragons here, and they have told me more about how that healing worked. Also, they have told me of other side effects of our bond that you should know about."

Simon sat attentively while she relayed what the others had told her. It wasn't hard to quell the urge to ask questions; this night he simply felt at ease sitting with her in the Dream State and would have been content to have no other interaction than the close proximity they shared; the knowledge she imparted was simply an added bonus.

The older dragons had not only told her how to gauge and control a healing, they had also told her how to look for and gather energy and to allow energy to pass through like a conduit rather than using up personal reserves. They had even given her some basic information about using the energy for both attack and defense, but they were somewhat vague on the last points. She passed it all on faithfully to Simon.

Finally, she ended by saying, "I have told you everything, and it is almost dawn. This information should help you when performing healing magic, which might be quite useful to us. However, the weather is not pleasant today, so we must wake and gather what we will need before the rain starts to fall. I will have to have more food, and you will need more firewood to keep you warm."

Once again, the Dream State faded to black, and he awoke in the physical world. He reluctantly moved from his bedding and climbed out of his lean-to. Once he had attended to his own needs, he got the remaining meat from the stream and set it out for her. Then, after coiling the wet rope and laying it inside the shelter to dry, he gathered more wood for the small fire he built just under the cover of the shelter.

She had the raw carcasses, and he had the rest of the fish he had caught the night before as well as a bit of smoked pig left from what he had set aside. The gray sky didn't let loose a downpour. Instead, a steady, cold, light rain fell. It wasn't enough to cause him to worry about flooding, but it was enough to soak him if he ventured out into it. Since he couldn't build a big enough fire to dry himself, he stayed inside his shelter for the remainder of the day.

He got the animal skin he had kept. Not knowing why he'd kept this pelt yet hadn't worried about the hides of the pigs he had butchered, he set about sewing the skin into a somewhat conical shape. By mid-afternoon, he had turned the thin hide into a fairly comfortable hat complete with flaps to cover his ears. Then, not even stopping to consider why he was doing so, he put the small bits of skin he had cut away from the hide while making his hat back into his pack. They were part of the prize of his first attempt to procure food for himself. That small article of clothing and those few scraps were the first real proof that he could hunt and take care of himself in the wild, and he was reluctant to part with any of it.

With the hat to keep his head and ears warm, and still bored, he turned his attention to his Dragon Blades. He uncoiled some of the rope and cut a length of about four feet. Then he unwound the individual strands of cord from each other until he had nine woven cords, each the diameter of a piece of string.

Sienna, though not bothered by the rain, poked her head in one end of the shelter and watched him work. She didn't ask what he was doing. She was merely looking for his company, and he was more than happy to have her close.

He held the longer blade between his knees and began winding the still damp cord around the tang, weaving it as he did so. He used all of his strength as he worked so that the cord stayed tight. When the cord was woven thickly enough on the tang, he tied the ends off and set it near the fire to dry, knowing that doing so would shrink the material and tighten the grip. There would be no guard to protect his hand in a fight, but the cord would allow him to hold the blade effectively if the need arose.

By the time he was finished with both blades, the dim gray light was beginning to fade. Sienna smiled and said, "It will be full dark soon. I am going to eat again and then sleep. I suggest that you do the same, my love. This weather will break during the night, and we will be able to move our camp in the morning."

"I believe you are right, dearest. Even without exerting myself today the cold has sapped my strength, and I am still tired. Eat, and I will see you in the morning."

CHAPTER 24

ONCE AGAIN, HE woke before Sienna did. As she had predicted, the rain clouds had dissipated during the night. He decided to wait to wake her until he had speared enough fish to take the edge off of her hunger, but he had no intentions of trying for enough to fill her belly completely. He wanted to move the camp, and a full baby dragon wasn't conducive to doing so.

The sun was still well behind the mountains but, oddly, he was able to see the fish well enough to get her breakfast. Once he had enough food to feed two or three large, hungry men, he then set about actually dismantling his shelter. This time, he reasoned, it would be more prudent to do what he could to erase the evidence of their presence before moving to a more permanent location, especially since the location was only a very few miles away. As defensible as the new camp would be, it would still be better not to be found at all.

While he was packing, Sienna woke and found the fish he had caught. She made short work of them and complained halfheartedly that she was still hungry.

"If you eat your fill, you will then go back to sleep. I want to move before that happens. When we get to the new camp, I will find more food for you."

"Very well. You finish packing, and I will stretch my wings."

Simon nodded and continued his work until he was suddenly distracted by her frantic bid for his attention.

"Simon, look at me, I'm flying!"

Simon looked up expecting to see her a few feet off the ground and found her gone from the shore.

"Up here, look!"

He tilted his head back and there she was, over a hundred feet above him and still climbing.

"Are you sure you should be flying so high this soon?" he asked with some concern.

"Of course I should be flying this high. Flying is what I'm made for. Besides, it's safer to fly this high rather than to fly lower." She was now well over three hundred feet up. "At this altitude, I have more time to recover if something goes wrong."

"Very well, Love, you know more about what you are doing than I do. I am going to find some pine boughs to brush away my tracks; then we can set out for our new camp. I will let you know when I am ready. I would prefer you to swim there rather than fly. You are less likely to be seen in the water than you are in the air. No sense advertising our new position right away."

She hesitated for a moment before responding. "Very well, you are right. When you are ready to leave, I will come down and swim."

It took about a half an hour to sweep the whole area clear of tracks. The beast-men, according to Boron, had good vision, and extraordinary hearing compared to a human, but their sense of smell was no better than that of men. Simon finished and moved onto the rocks near the shore where he could walk without leaving any trace of his passing. It was obvious that someone had cleared away the tracks from the sandy soil, but he hoped that sweeping the area would hinder any attempt to discern the direction they headed when they left.

"I am ready to move out, Sienna; if you could land in the water so as not to leave further signs of our presence, we can be on our way."

"*I'm coming, Simon,*" she *said* as she quickly dropped down from several hundred feet.

Seeing her plunge toward the water, he began to worry that she would injure herself when she hit. He was about to *say* something, but realized it was too late. She pulled out of her dive and tried to come down on the surface of the river on her belly, but her front legs dug in deeply, she upended and flipped completely over on her back before sinking like a stone. Simon almost dove into the water after her, but she bobbed to the surface like a cork.

"Hmm," she said as she snorted water out of her nose, "looks like I have a bit to learn about landing."

"I'm sure you'll get the hang of it; you did quite well considering that this was your first real flight." Simon didn't add that he personally would have called that "landing" a crash if he had been pressed to put a name to the procedure.

Sienna took his words as the encouragement they were meant to be and was quite pleased with herself.

The trip downriver took about an hour, and they easily found the raft that he had left tied to the dead tree. With the dragon pushing and him poling, they had no trouble keeping the craft on course. Once their few supplies were under the overhang, they went about securing firewood. It was quite easy working together. Simon would gather the wood and return it to the shore where Sienna would then ferry it across to the sand bar.

"You have a sizable store of wood now, and I am getting quite hungry," she stated, letting a good deal of her need come through in her message.

The sensation was intense, and he didn't argue. "Let me get a javelin, and I will get you more fish."

It took over two hours to spear enough fish for her, and once he had done so, as expected, she climbed under the overhang above the sandbar and went to sleep. While it was more difficult to navigate the water without her help, Simon decided to spend the rest of the afternoon trying to procure more food for Sienna. The number of fish available seemed to have increased, but he didn't want to leave anything to chance.

He went to each of the five game trails he had found and set rope snares on them. These traps were little more than a simple noose set on the path in such a way as to, hopefully, slip over the neck of any unsuspecting animal that might come along the trail on its way to get water. If the animal were ensnared, the noose would tighten and hold it until it either choked to death, or Simon could dispatch it.

Next he backtracked to the beginning of the canyon and gathered as much river grass as he could. He tied the grass into bundles which floated very well, and that gave him the beginnings of an idea. Then he took the bundles back to the oxbow lake and across to the sandbar and spread them to dry. The last thing he did before the light began to fail was spear more fish. Once he had enough fish for his own supper and breakfast, plus a large enough pile to take the edge off of Sienna's hunger when she woke, he built a fire.

After eating, he made a bed of river grass for himself. Then, using what was left of the tough, fibrous strands of flat grass, he began weaving a large basket which took the rest of the evening to finish. The basket was roughly an arms width at the top and tapered nearly to a point at the bottom. He had purposely woven it loosely so that it resembled a net more than a vessel. He had seen his father, in what now seemed like another lifetime, use a similar basket to catch fish by casting it into deep water and hauling it back quickly. Until his snares proved effective, fish were the most abundant food source, and the basket might allow him to catch more of them with less effort so that he could keep up with Sienna's appetite and still have time to care for himself. He had no idea of how long it would be before she would be capable of hunting, but if that landing earlier was any indication, it could be many weeks before she could do so without getting hurt.

CHAPTER 25

AFTER A GOOD night's sleep, Simon woke to the cold gray dawn. It wasn't raining, but the sky held enough of a threat that he decided not to wait for her to wake before starting his day. He had left the fish where the dragon could find them if she woke while he was gone. After eating the leftovers from his evening meal, he pushed his raft into the water and began the cumbersome chore of poling to the far bank.

Simon checked his snares but found nothing, though two of the five had been knocked askew. He reset the disturbed traps, taking greater care to better hide the cords this time. Then he set out for more of the tough river grass, using the rope to tow his raft from the shore back to the mouth of the canyon. The grass had flattened fibrous leaves with a segmented, hollow stem running up the center. The stem made it quite buoyant. He reasoned that, since it was light and floated better than the logs he was using, if he could tie bundles of it together he might be able to make a more efficient raft that didn't require all of his effort to move about.

The sun remained hidden behind the clouds and the cold air chilled him, but he worked diligently cutting grass and stacking it on the raft. By mid-morning he had stacked a fair amount of the material for transport, but his knife was getting dull from chopping through the tough strands.

"Simon! Where are you?"

The boy had not heard, or felt, Sienna so obviously frightened before. He started running back along the shore toward the shelter while inquiring as to the cause of her alarm.

"I am close, Sienna!" he reassured her. "What is wrong? Are there beast-men nearby?"

"No, no beast-men." Her tone softened and her anxiety was obviously fading. "I was dreaming of she who was my mother. The dream disturbed me greatly, and then I woke and found you gone. I'm afraid I panicked. I'm sorry."

Simon slowed to a walk and said, "There is no need to apologize, Love. You had a nightmare and needed me. I'm sorry I wasn't there for you. I am coming now."

"There is no reason to hurry now that I know where you are," she replied. "Finish what you were doing before you return. I can see that I have food, and I will eat what is here. There will be much rain later today, and I want to eat lightly and practice flying before that starts."

Simon stopped in his tracks. "If you are sure you are all right, Sienna, I would like to finish before I come back. Then I can try and catch you some more fish."

"I was hoping that you were bringing back some meat from your snares."

"Sorry, dear heart," he used a term of endearment his father had sometimes used for both he and his mother, "the snares were empty this morning. Perhaps they will provide food for us tomorrow."

"I'm sure they will…"

The dragon's words trailed off and Simon knew that she was eating the fish he had left for her. Once again he marveled at how easily she simply put aside the earlier disturbance and got on with the task at hand. A human child would probably have needed a parent to attend to such distress for some time.

He made his way back to his raft and spent about another hour gathering grass. He wasn't sure how much he would need, but he thought he had finally gathered enough, which was good since he had also dulled his blade to near uselessness.

Casting off from the shore, he found the return trip much easier than hauling the heavy raft upstream. He pushed the logs out into the middle of the river and let the current take them. He only had to guide the craft and let the water do the work.

While Sienna flew, he unloaded the grass, stacking it under the sheltering rock so that he could work with it once the rain started. Then he went to the water's edge to try for more fish. There were none near the surface to be speared; it seemed that the fish had gone deep to avoid the coming weather, so he tied a rope to his fishing basket, swung the basket around his head to get momentum, and cast it nearly fifteen feet out into the lake. It floated due to the buoyant nature of the grass, so when he hauled it back, it was empty.

Simon chastised himself for being so foolish. Of course the thing floated. He should have known that would happen; that particular property of the material was why he spent so much time gathering the stuff that morning. He looked around and found a large rock, a little bigger than his own fist, which he tied in place in the bottom of the basket. This time, it was heavier, and he was able to throw it out further, and it quickly sank. He waited a moment to let the mesh get to the bottom, and then he hauled it back in. He was actually a bit surprised to find two pan-sized fish in the clumsy net.

He spent the remainder of the morning and part of the afternoon fishing. It was back-breaking labor to cast the net and haul it repeatedly, but he was rewarded with a pile of fish large enough to feed the dragon and himself for the day. As he rubbed his sore shoulders, he hoped that the snares would yield something more substantial in the morning.

Just then Sienna made a soft "crash-landing" in the water nearby.

"My landings are getting better," she *said* as she waddled onto the sandbar toward the pile of fish.

"Yes, I see that," Simon *agreed*, though, other than her remaining upright, he hadn't noticed a tremendous difference since yesterday. Then he ran to the pile of fish before she could reach them. *"No, you don't,"* he *said*, laughing. *"I worked hard to get those, and I am going to take two of them for my own use before you devour the whole pile."*

He grabbed one of the creatures in each hand and quickly gutted them on the spot; dropping the entrails, which were laden with roe, back onto the pile for his Bond-mate.

"Very well," she responded. "You have worked hard to get the food. However, my requirements have increased. Flying takes a great deal of energy."

"Your requirements have increased? You were already eating more than enough to feed a dozen full grown men! I hope I can keep up with your appetite." He said, only half joking.

"Now that I am flying, I will soon be able to hunt for myself. I don't expect that you will have to feed me for much more than another couple of weeks."

The boy shook his head as he moved under the overhang. Just as he was about to reply, the sky opened up and distracted him with the sudden ferocity of the downpour. By the time he recovered and was ready to make a retort, Sienna was fully engrossed in her meal and nearly oblivious to all else. Shrugging his shoulders, he turned his attention to building a small fire to cook his own meal and to ward off the chill. When he had finished, he found Sienna curled up under the shelter sleeping as only a full baby dragon could. For all intents and purposes, he was again alone.

He began to think about his idea for a grass watercraft. At first, he had thought he might just weave the grass into a more manageable version of his log raft, so he began to lay the grass out in a long strip, overlapping the ends of individual strands to get the length he wanted. The strip was about eight feet from end to end, and he rolled it up into a kind of log about a hand in diameter and used fibers stripped from the leaves to tie it up so that it would retain that shape.

The stuff was coarse and sharp, and by the time he had two "logs" of about the same dimensions, he also had numerous cuts on his hands and fingers despite his heavy calluses. The cuts weren't deep but they hurt terribly and made it difficult to continue working. Simon decided to try and heal his hands the way he had healed Sienna's mouth. He thought about the energy he had used before and tried to feel it now. He was surprised to find that the rain itself released a great deal of energy as it fell from the clouds. He reached for that and then channeled it into his aching hands. The small cuts quickly healed, and he had to stop suddenly as his hands became uncomfortably hot.

He only allowed his amazement at the feat distract him for a moment before returning to his work. He laid the two grass logs side by side and tied the ends together. His knife was so dull that it would barely hack through the tough fibers so he grabbed up the smaller dragon blade and used it rather than take time away from the task to sharpen the steel. Not only did that blade cut easily through the stuff, but it showed no sign of wear after doing so.

Once the ends of the logs were tied together, he was about to tie them in the middle when sudden inspiration struck. He spread them apart at the center and they took the rough shape of a boat. When he released them they began to go back to their original straight lines: two round logs side by side. Simon moved to his firewood and selected a stick about two feet long and placed it between the logs to hold them apart. He put shorter sticks in about halfway between the middle and the ends. Then he went back to forming more of the grass into long bundles.

He made five more logs before adding anything to the boat. The third he placed down the middle and used several sticks driven into the sand to hold it up in the shape of a shallow keel. Then he tied the rest in place between the keel and the outermost logs. He had to make four more bundles because it took that many of them on each side, but when he was finished the boat looked like it would be quite serviceable.

It was late in the evening and full darkness had settled in, but Simon couldn't wait for first light to see if the craft would float. He would need it in the morning, and if any changes had to be made he would rather lose sleep and do it now. Turning the boat over on its keel, he hauled it to the water's edge. It wasn't quite as light as he had hoped, but it still weighed much less than his wooden raft. Then, realizing his hands were once again sore, he healed his fingers before shoving the craft into the lake. It floated well, so he climbed aboard. The craft felt spongy under his feet, but it stayed afloat, so he used his pole to move a bit out into the lake. The draft of the boat was much shallower than his raft and he had no problem with the current, although he quickly found that the pole was a bit unwieldy. He returned to the sandbar and pulled the boat all the way up to the shelter, deciding that he would look for a suitable piece of wood to make a paddle out of tomorrow. The vessel leaked a little, but he thought he could seal it by weaving more of the grass over the bottom.

Realizing he was soaked to the skin, he built the fire higher and removed his wet clothes. Simon was quite proud of himself. He was also glad he had discovered how to make his boat, even if it had been by accident. If he had simply continued to make the grass logs until he had enough for a raft, he would have tied them together that way and ended up with a lighter, but still clumsy means of transport. He was actually pleased that he had needed to stop and heal his hands, or he would never have taken the time to survey his work and get such an inspiration.

"I see you have finished your project," Sienna said as she came fully awake.

"I now have a boat I can navigate easily by myself," he replied with great pride in his accomplishment. "You usually sleep straight through the night; are you all right?"

"I heard you moving about and felt your discomfort from being wet and cold," she responded as she moved closer to share her body heat. "I am still very tired, and now that I know you are safe and well, I will go back to sleep."

Simon suddenly moved against her and hugged her fiercely. "*I love you, Sienna,*" was all he could think to *say.*

"*I love you, too,*" she *replied* sleepily as she drifted back into unconsciousness.

CHAPTER 26

THE NEXT MORNING it was still raining lightly, but when Simon looked out he was amazed to see that the tremendous agitation on the top of the ox-bow lake was caused not by the falling water droplets, but by hundreds, perhaps thousands, of fish moving frantically just below the surface. It seemed that there were so many of the creatures that he could almost walk across the lake on their backs without getting his feet wet.

Unsure of what was happening he called out to his bond-mate, *"Sienna! You have to wake up and see this!"*

"What is it, Dearest? What has you so excited?" she asked dreamily.

"The fish, something is happening with them. They're frantic. What could have them so upset?"

He had never heard of fish behaving like this, and he was worried that whatever was upsetting the animals would cause trouble for the two of them.

The dragon watched the water for a moment and then replied, "They are breeding. She who was my mother flew to this area trying to time her laying with this event. When the creatures are thusly involved, they are easy prey, and their abundant numbers can feed a hungry young dragon for quite some time. The breeding run usually lasts about a fortnight, sometimes a little longer." She thought for a moment and then added, "I suggest that you take the opportunity to cast your net and catch as many as you can."

"Why didn't you tell me about this sooner?"

"While much knowledge was passed on to me before I hatched, some of it needs to be nudged into my awareness before I actually realize that I know it," she replied as if this should be completely obvious. Then she added, "The weather is too foul to fly today, so I will try and catch some of these fish myself while **you use your net**." She spoke the last four words with great emphasis as a not-so-subtle hint that he should get started.

Simon quickly took care of his bodily needs, and then started casting his net out into the frenzied school of fish. As he did, he watched Sienna. She stood at the river's edge and thrust her neck into the water. Each time she brought her head back up, her mouth held several fish which she quickly gulped down. In less than an hour, she had eaten her fill, enough to feed an entire family for at least a week, and moved back to the overhang to sleep. Within two hours, Simon, now soaked by the rain, had enough fish to last the dragon at least two days, if not three. He moved back to the shelter and began gutting fish and setting them over an improvised rack near the fire to dry. One he set directly on the rocks that ringed the pit to cook for his morning meal.

Chapter 27

HE HAD EATEN and then spent the morning sharpening his knife. Then he set about carving a flat piece of driftwood into a paddle. Once he finished with that, because the rain was still falling, he settled back against the sleeping dragon and closed his eyes.

"Hello, my love," Sienna said as she looked at him. They were again perched on a cliff-side ledge in the Dream State. "I have been speaking with the other dragons here about our situation. They all agree that I am growing faster than normal due to the magic that passes so easily between us. Several of the older females, who knew my mother, have passed on many tips I will need to know when flying, especially hunting. I believe that what they have told me will greatly improve my landings. With a little luck, by the time the breeding run of the fish stops, I will be able to catch enough meat for both of us."

"That is good news," he responded with enthusiasm. "I was beginning to wonder if I would be capable of keeping up with your needs. I understand that you must eat to grow, but the more you grow, the more you eat. I have been working hard, but I'm still only one person."

"Well, you should find your burden lightened soon," she replied, a little hurt.

"I didn't mean that I resented the work, dear heart. I simply meant that I wasn't sure that I would be capable of keeping up with the task. It worried me greatly because I don't want to neglect you."

She bent her neck around and rubbed her head against him affectionately. "You would never neglect me, as I would never neglect you."

The pair settled down and Simon contented himself with just being with her while she communed with the other dragons. He became so lost in time that he didn't even notice that he had left the Dream State until he woke up next to her in their shelter.

His bladder was so full it ached, so he decided to attend to that first. As he walked to the water's edge where the current would carry his bodily waste away, he noticed, from the angle of the sun, that he and Sienna had slept through afternoon and night and it was now the morning of the following day. The next thing he noticed was that the fish were still quite agitated and their numbers didn't seem to have diminished in the slightest. In fact, he was fairly sure there were even more of them.

He was tempted, in the face of such plenty, to forego casting his net and trust that the food would be there. However, he remembered that Sienna had told him that the breeding run would only last two weeks and that she was not beyond eating meat that had turned if need be. He knew that any fish he caught today wouldn't keep for long, but if he could get ahead of her appetite for a few days, they would both be in better spirits.

While he was retrieving his net, she woke and moved to stretch and take care of her own bodily functions. He had a certain curiosity about her eliminations and had asked about it. It seemed that all waste was eliminated through one opening, but she had been somewhat vague when she answered his question. When it became necessary to do so the tube that carried the waste would be pushed slightly out of a long slit between the dragon's back legs and the waste then passed through the tube as a sticky paste similar to bird droppings, though in proportionately larger amounts.

Sienna noticed him watching and asked, "What is so fascinating about me eliminating waste? You do the same thing every morning, and then several times again during the day."

"Yes, but I don't do it the way you do. It is different and, therefore, makes me curious."

"Well, if it will satisfy your curiosity I will explain the process in more detail. A female dragon has two openings inside of the slit back near the hind legs. One opening is for breeding and laying eggs, the other is for elimination of waste. Adult dragons pass fairly large amounts of waste several times a year, usually soon after feeding. They pass very small amounts that accumulate from drinking and licking minerals on a more regular basis, though not daily. I pass more because I am eating a great deal more in proportion to my size than an adult dragon. The digestive system of a dragon is very efficient, and we digest more of the food we eat than other creatures do. No creature, however, is capable of digesting one hundred percent of the food it consumes."

"I see. I had wondered how that worked. I've heard of Dragon Riders staying for weeks as guests at some castle or other, and I was wondering why no one complained about the mess."

Sienna made a somewhat rude noise that he hadn't known she was capable of making, and responded, "We don't live amongst our droppings like some dumb beasts do. We're not uncivilized, you know. If an adult dragon were a guest and felt the need to eliminate she would fly off to a secluded location and do it, not simply pass the stuff right there for others to step in." The dragon actually rolled her eyes at the way the conversation was going.

"I'm sorry Sienna. I should have realized that. I didn't mean to imply that you weren't civilized. I was just curious."

"Apology accepted. Now that I have explained the process to you, perhaps you will afford me the same courtesy I show you and stop staring at me when I attend to my bodily needs."

Simon flushed with embarrassment and turned away and bent to the task of fishing to afford his partner a little privacy.

She finished and moved to the pile of dead fish already on the sandbar. After eating lightly, she said, "I am going to practice flying.

I think you should not do too much fishing. I will eat them if they spoil slightly, but a large pile of rotting fish will stink badly, which will not only offend us, but it could attract unwanted attention."

"You make a good point, dear heart, but I have found that it is much easier to stay ahead of your appetite than try and catch up if I get behind," he said, thinking of the times her hunger had nearly overwhelmed him.

"The memories passed on to me tell me the breeding run will last at least another fortnight, and I will be able to hunt by the time it ends, so please do not foul our living space with so many dead fish. I can't eat them all."

"Very well, I wanted to try my boat and paddle. I will put the net away and go check the snares."

"Fine, I will fly while you do that. Good luck." As she finished her thought, she launched herself skyward.

Simon immediately noticed, now that he was looking with a critical eye, that she had grown considerably in just the past couple of days. Also, not only was her power impressive, but her grace when taking off was a thing of beauty. He nearly forgot his own mission watching her fly. He shook his head to break the spell and, in spite of the light rain, hauled his boat to the water.

Again the boat leaked, but the buoyancy of the material kept it afloat just the same. He quickly learned that he needed to alternate sides with his paddle or he would go in large circles instead of a straight line. He aimed at one of his snares and made good progress toward it.

The first two snares were empty, although one had been disturbed. The third had a caught a doe. The animal had struggled to free herself, and thus had tightened the noose until she suffocated. He was so focused on the doe he almost missed the fawn hiding near its dead mother's body. He felt a slight pang of regret that he had killed the fawn's mother, but he squashed that emotion at once. This was survival—not just his, but also his Bond-mate's. Moving very slowly to avoid spooking the creature, he fitted a javelin to his throwing stick.

He waited to gut the animals until he returned to camp. Consequently, he'd had to make two trips, because the full weight of the doe and fawn plus his own weight was too much for his little boat. Sienna was grateful that he had brought the entrails, though. She ate that portion and nearly pounced on the carcasses, but he stopped her.

No matter how much she complained, he insisted she wait. He not only wanted some of the meat, but also intended to keep the hides. *"If you are so hungry that you cannot wait until I skin the animals, eat more fish. As you said, we need to use that pile up before they rot and foul our living space anyway,"* he told her. She then spent the next hour and a half sulking while he went about his task. Her mood lightened once he had finished and let her have the meat.

While she ate, he scraped the hides thoroughly and set about curing them.

"I don't understand," she said sleepily. "You went to so much trouble to get those hides, why are you fouling them?"

"I'm not fouling them. The hides must be cured or they will rot. I have no tanning chemicals other than urine and the brains of the animals themselves. It isn't my first choice, but it is all that is available. Once the urine and brains have soaked in and cured them for a day, I will put them in the water to wash the filth away. Then I will work them as they dry and they will be soft, supple, and will not decay."

"If you say so, Dearest. I have no knowledge of such things."

"Well, my knowledge is quite limited, but I remember my mother and father curing hides in this fashion before my father died," he said sadly.

Sienna had nearly fallen asleep, but she raised her head and said, "I'm sorry, Simon. I didn't mean to bring up painful memories."

"It's all right, Sienna. I like to remember my parents when my father was still alive, and we were all happy. I just can't seem to remember that without remembering what I lost when he died, and now that I'm on the run it pains me that I will most likely never see my mother again." He thought for a moment and then, as tears trickled down his cheeks he added, "I suppose I have no right to complain about that to you."

"I am saddened by the loss of she who was my mother, but such loss doesn't seem to affect dragons the way it does humans." She paused in thought for a while, and as she lay her head down, she said, "You will see your mother again, I promise you that."

Simon looked up in shock and was about to explain why that was impossible, but she had already fallen asleep.

Chapter 28

O VER THE NEXT three weeks, Simon's snares produced only one scrawny wild pig and three small rabbits: perhaps he wasn't the hunter his father had been. However, the breeding run of the fish held for the whole time, so neither of them went hungry, and Simon was able to find several sources of edible plants to augment his diet. He was also lucky enough to take two deer with his javelins. By the time the fishing petered out almost completely, Sienna, true to her word, was hunting and supplied the bulk of the meat they were eating, though she refused to carry the full carcasses back and wait for him to skin them.

In the last three weeks, she had grown so much that she was now bigger than any draft animal he had ever even heard about. When she had hatched, she wasn't much larger than a full-grown man. Now, her head covered most of his torso and he couldn't breathe if she laid it on his chest while they slept the way she had done when they were first bonded. She had told him that the older dragons in the Dream State said that she was nearly twice as big as an un-bonded dragon of her same age, and they speculated that her growth was not only augmented by the magical bond between her and Simon, but that their bond actually created a direct connection between the two partners and the energy of the earth itself.

Simon, too, observed that he was changing a bit. He had not been small before, but his height had increased by a good four inches, a fact that had been confirmed by Sienna. He had also noticed that he could handle heavier loads than he would have expected, and he tired less easily. In addition, he could see clearly at a greater distance than before, and his night vision had become extremely acute. He wasn't sure, since he had no one to test them, but he thought his reflexes were better as well.

"I am having to range farther and farther each day to find game, Dearest. I am afraid this area may be played out," Sienna said when she returned from her hunt later that day.

"Yes, I was thinking the same thing. I'm not the hunter my father was, but we know my snares will work if there is game to catch. I suspect that the beast-men don't take pains to manage their resources and that this area was nearly hunted out before we even arrived. That is the most likely reason we haven't been accosted by Roracks since you hatched. While I have a suspicion that dragons have amazingly good luck, I believe that if there were food animals to be hunted, those monsters would be here hunting them, and if there were Roracks anywhere near, we wouldn't have gone undetected this long," Simon replied.

"You are probably right. The beast-men would not tolerate a dragon in their territory if they even suspected she was here, and a young dragon would be even more enticing since I would be easier prey than an adult. I'm sure that if the monsters were near, they would have found us by now. Apparently, they have hunted this area out and moved on. Now we have to decide when we will do the same."

Simon looked around thoughtfully. It surprised him to find that he had actually come to think of this place as home. The overhang was still plenty large enough for the two of them, though she had to duck and keep her head down under it. He was also loath to leave the shelter of the deep water on one side and the steep cliff face on the other, but Sienna was right. The adult fish who had survived the breeding run and the dragon's predation had gone back to wherever they went between mating seasons. With no game in the area to feed her, she would have to find a more plentiful hunting ground soon.

"How much longer do think you will be able to find meat without moving on?" he asked aloud, and then added, "The spring thaws have apparently started and the water is rising, but I had estimated that we would be safe from high water for some time to come."

"We can leave sthoon. I sthpotted a large deer that isth very old not far from here thisth morning. It won't sthray far before tomorrow becausthe of histh age. I will find it and take it when I hunt again, if no other predatorsth finishth the creature off before then." She had begun to actually talk out loud in the last week, but her teeth seemed to have outgrown her mouth and caused her to lisp.

"Good; we will stay here at least until you have hunted tomorrow. That will give me a chance to finish the clothing I started making using those few skins I was able to preserve," he said somewhat testily. They were still at odds over her refusal to bring the whole animal back to be skinned when she hunted.

"I have told you, I will not carry that extra weight simply so that you may make me postpone my meal while you skin the animals."

"And I told you that my clothing is wearing thin crawling over these rocks looking for more food for you. I have neither fur nor your ability to withstand frigid temperatures. Spring may be nearly on us, but it is still cold, and the nights sometimes drop low enough to leave a sheet of ice on still water. If I do not have adequate clothing, I will die of exposure."

"I share my body heat with you when I am here, and since I am doing the hunting, you can stay in camp and sit near the fire. The animals I am able to find are mostly emaciated. They weigh over ten stone, but that is mostly because they have heavy bones. If I spend the extra energy to bring them back, I will have to hunt more to make up the loss. I am still growing."

Simon softened his stance and replied, "I know all of that, Dear Heart. You have explained it to me, and it does make sense. However, I cannot just go to the nearest town and buy more clothing at the moment. I am limited to what I can make. I'm sure a real leatherworker could have gotten more out of the skins I had than I was able to do. I know there was more waste material than I expected.

I am just worried that when we do reach a settlement, I will be naked and unable to enter a village to buy supplies."

"You aren't exactly naked, Simon. You have one pair of pants that is still nearly new, even if the legs are a bit short for you now. The other pair was only badly worn from the knees down and you have cut that off and used the material for patching your other clothes: those pants are short, but they still cover your posterior. While the one shirt you are wearing is almost more patches than original material, the other, though stained, is not threadbare. You will not have to go into a town wearing nothing but your own hide."

He shook his head and said, "I'm sure you are right, Sienna. I have told you what happened in Horne and why I can not go back there. The kingdom we will be going to borders my homeland and may not be opposed to sending me back if I am caught. I simply worry about attracting attention."

The dragon actually laughed out loud. When he looked at her as if she had taken leave of her senses, she shook her head and rose to her full height before saying, "*I do not believe that those who notice us will be staring because of how you are dressed.*"

Simon hadn't even given thought to the fact that he would be traveling with a dragon. To him, that had long ago lost its novelty. Being in the company of a dragon had become so mundane he had entirely forgotten that, while Riders traveled extensively, having a dragon visit a human settlement was still far from commonplace. If he and Sienna went to a village, her presence was sure to bring about unwanted scrutiny. He said as much to her, but she barely acknowledged his concern as she settled down to sleep off her morning meal.

Despite the fact that the water was still quite cold, Simon had taken to going about barefoot, mainly because even if the low boots he had originally owned had not now been woefully too small, they had been worn to uselessness on the rough rocks along the shores of the canyon. He had used some the thicker hide of the pig he had found in his snares to make the soles of a new pair of boots and then stitched some of the deer hide on as uppers. All he needed to do now was make holes for laces. With Sienna doing the majority of the hunting, he had a great deal more time on his hands. While absently fidgeting with the leaves of the river grass, he had discovered that he could easily strip it down to small fibers that could be woven into pliant, but very strong, cord. He now used the cord for several things, including stitching his clothing and making more snares: he figured that the stuff would make good laces for the boots, rawhide jerkin, and chaps he had made from the hides he had managed to procure.

He spent the remainder of the day working on his new clothing. The boots were a bit shapeless, but they fit well enough when he pulled the laces tight. The soles weren't as thick and hard as a real pair of shoes, but would still protect his feet from sharp rocks and sticks. The jerkin was a simple covering made in one piece, similar to a poncho. He laced the sides so that it could be tied shut to keep the cold out and his body heat in. Though it left his arms bare, it made a good windbreaker, too. The chaps were just two pieces of rawhide, one for each leg, attached to a belt of woven grass, and then tied in place above and below the knees. These leggings wouldn't provide for modesty without pants under them, but they would keep the rough terrain and the thorns that seemed to grow in abundance in this area from tearing his pants and his flesh while adding another layer of protection between the front of his legs and the cool air.

Finishing the clothing took much longer than he had expected. The darkness had fallen hours before, and he found he was quite cramped from sitting in one position while working. He decided to stretch out his muscles, relieve his distended bladder, and then go to sleep. Since Sienna would hunt and eat in the morning, he would have plenty of time to finish his preparations once the sun was up. He rose and stretched before moving off to take care of bodily needs.

He had just finished and decided to let the fire burn itself out when he heard a faint sound that made the blood run cold in his veins. He stood still as stone, straining to listen. There it was again, off in the night but echoing through the canyon: the harsh bark of a Rorack.

He almost screamed out loud but remembered to speak only mentally. *"Sienna, wake up! There are beast-men near!"*

The dragon nearly leaped to her feet, fully awake as if she had not been sleeping. *"Where are they?"* she *shouted* in his mind.

"I don't know for sure. I heard their cries in the darkness, but they are too far away to be seen."

As if speaking of them had elicited a response, the Rorack barked again. This time, it was closer, and it got answers from several others.

"It is hard to tell with the sound echoing off the rocks, but I believe they are still north of us, near the entrance to the canyon," she said as she moved to the dying fire and simply stepped on it, squashing out its light. She grimaced as the embers burned her slightly even through the small scales on the bottom of her foot.

Simon cast around for cover, even though he knew there really was none. "Let's move farther back under the overhang. Perhaps we won't be seen in the deeper shadows."

They both moved as far as they could back into the darkness. Simon had retrieved his javelins and he readied one in case they were spotted.

"Even if they don't see us," Sienna said, "it is likely they will smell us. We have been here for a long time and have left our scent everywhere. The beast-men don't have the well-developed sense of smell that many wild animals possess, but they aren't likely to miss the fact that a human and a dragon have been camping here for several weeks."

"It is good that the water has risen by more than two feet since we arrived," he responded. "That will make the middle of the river about five yards deep. According to Boron, the Roracks are unable to swim at all; they simply sink like stones."

"That is good, Dearest, but they do have enough intelligence to use projectiles. The creatures have even been known to make bows and arrows, and they often employ poison on them."

"Damn it," he whispered before switching back to strictly mental communication, "I should have been practicing the shielding that the older dragon explained to you in the Dream State. I was so worried about gathering materials to ensure that I wouldn't end up without clothing and other supplies, I simply put it out of my mind that I might not make it to civilization if I couldn't defend us. I'm sorry, Sienna; I have been very foolish."

"It's not your fault, Simon; we have both been lulled into a false sense of security by the peaceful nature of this place. I should have insisted that we move on as soon as I was able to hunt."

He shook his head to clear the depression that threatened to overwhelm him and then said, "Dear Heart, we can beat ourselves up over this until the beast-men fall upon us, but that won't help. We have both made mistakes and now we are hard pressed because of it. What we need to do is stay focused, and use our brains!"

Again they heard the harsh voice of a Rorack followed by the replies of his fellows. This time, the sound was even closer, making it obvious that the monsters had moved into the canyon.

"According to Boron they have extremely good hearing, but their eyesight and sense of smell are only slightly better than a human, if that good. Their night vision is probably no better than mine, and certainly not as good as yours. With your heat vision as well we are at an advantage there. If they have bows, we will simply do our best to shield ourselves until they run out of arrows; I'm sure that we can do so if we work together. We only need to protect ourselves until I have enough light to navigate the river. Then we will simply leave the beast-men standing on the far shore."

The moon was past full, but it still cast enough light for Simon to see the outlines of the Roracks as they moved along the bank. The creatures came into sharper focus as they stopped almost directly across from the sandbar and began barking and hooting. One of them stepped forward and looked in their direction, straining to see through the darkness under the overhang. The others watched intently as if waiting for a signal.

Simon reasoned that the beast-man looking directly at him must be the leader. While he couldn't make out fine detail, he could clearly see the broad shoulders and well-muscled chest of the fiend as it stood at the water's edge.

"I believe they know we are here, Dearest. They can't see us in the darkness, but they aren't making any move to leave either," Sienna reported unnecessarily.

Simon didn't respond. He gripped his throwing stick tightly and drew his arm back slowly. Then when he was sure of his target, he took a step while throwing a javelin at the beast-man. He might not have been practicing his shielding like he should have been, but he had been practicing with his javelins. He nearly lost his last javelin, because he had put so much power into the throw that it had gone completely through the deer and vanished into the brush. This target was denser than the yearling buck had been, so the javelin stayed in its body, but it did protrude more than a foot on the other side. The Rorack looked down at the object in the center of its chest as if it didn't comprehend the significance. Then it sank to its knees before falling face first into the river.

The others stepped forward and began to make a strange, almost mewling noise. The sound wasn't quite as harsh as the other cries Simon had heard up until now, but it still set his teeth on edge. One of the beast-men made that characteristic bark before standing and facing the shadow of the overhang. Suddenly it threw its head back and screamed in rage before running into the water at Simon and Sienna.

Simon began to fit another javelin to his throwing stick. He knew that the water was too deep to ford but, now that he saw the monster rushing at him like this, he found himself unable to simply trust that it was making an enraged suicidal charge. By the time he had the javelin ready the beast-man was chest deep and only hindered slightly by the water. It showed no sign of trying to swim; it simply continued to walk forward. There were five others, and two of them had entered the water as well. The other two were nearly waist deep when the first beast-man's head went under the surface.

The two stopped immediately and all five watched to see if their comrade either retreated or emerged from the water farther out. Both sides stood transfixed waiting to see what happened. To Simon, it felt as if the seconds were stretching into hours. He gripped his throwing stick so tightly that his ring and pinky fingers began to cramp. He ignored the pain from that and continued to wait, ready to launch another missile if needed.

Finally, the other Roracks moved out of the water and back up the bank. They once again began making that eerie mewling sound. After several more minutes, one of them barked and the others turned to that creature and made their own barking noises. Simon couldn't understand what was being said, if indeed the Roracks even possessed anything like real language. However, the difference in the tones was clear. The first bark obviously carried authority, and the others had acquiesced. He had hoped that by killing the leader, he would leave the rest disorganized. It appeared, though, that the monsters had a fairly clear social structure based on dominance, and the next in line simply took over when the leader died; the confusion of killing the chief would only last a few moments before the next in line assumed the rank. He had no idea how many he would have to kill before they would cease to be a cohesive pack.

"It seems that the loss of the two leaders has left them confused for the moment. They are making no move in our direction, and I can see no evidence that they are carrying any ranged weapons," Sienna reported. "I believe they still haven't been able to see us. They are watching intently, and they have most likely scented us, but they show no signs of agitation that I would expect if they had actually seen me."

Three of the Roracks simply squatted down as if resting. The remaining two stood with their faces turned toward the overhang.

"What do you think they are doing?" he asked.

"I'm not sure. They appear to have no clear idea of how to handle the situation, so they have hunkered down to wait. Perhaps they think that when dawn comes, and they can see their quarry, they will find a way to overcome the obstacles in their path."

"I was hoping they had given up and we might be able to slip away."

"I doubt that will happen, Dearest. What I know of these foul creatures tells me that they are not easily deterred. She who was my mother had fought them many times during her life and passed some of that knowledge on to me, though she didn't tell me all that she had learned because her time was so short. But simply giving up when they know their prey is so close is not in their nature."

"Well, I haven't given up either, and I have no intention of waiting until those monsters have fewer disadvantages. The light is not bright, but we can still see well enough to get under way. When I am ready to go, I want you to take off and fly high."

"I am not leaving you, Simon," she responded almost angrily. "Even if I would not be directly affected by what happens to you, I wouldn't simply fly off and leave you to face those foul beasts by yourself."

"Calm yourself, Dear Heart. I have no intention of facing them alone. When I am ready, you will show yourself just long enough to get airborne. While they are distracted, I will push off in my boat and head down river. I will then hug the canyon wall, keeping the deeper water between our enemies and me."

"I have seen this canyon from the air. The river narrows as it flows south. Just before the water leaves the canyon, it is less than twenty yards wide, and it becomes rough and flows over many rocks for nearly two hundred yards before it widens out as it flows onto a plain to the south. If the beast-men themselves don't get you, you are likely to be hurt, or worse, as you travel down those rapids."

"I know all of that; I have gone downriver that far hunting. The footing is unsure, and the opposite bank is steep. Even the Roracks will have to move slowly if they try and follow me. I have looked at the rapids, and I believe I can travel them if I keep to the center of the flow."

As he *spoke*, he worked quickly, tying his possessions into the boat for the trip. It only took a few minutes for him to finish the task. As he moved the boat to the south end of the overhang, Sienna tried again to talk him out of this plan.

"There must be a better way. It is possible that once they see us in the morning more of them will try and ford the river and thin their numbers." She sounded desperate, and Simon knew she was grasping at straws because she was worried about him.

"Roracks certainly aren't intelligent by human or dragon standards, but they aren't that stupid, Sienna. They have seen one of their group drown trying to get across the water; they won't do the same again. No, we will simply have to move on while we have the advantage of your superior vision." He had dragged his boat as far as he dared without a distraction. "The time has come. Go to the other end of the overhang before stepping out where you can be seen. Then make sure you have their full attention before you launch. As you fly up, head the other way. With the beast-men looking up and to the north, I will slip into the water in the shadows and head south. Once I am away, I will tell you, and you can then fly high and to the east to get out of their sight before doubling back to the river to find me. With a little luck, by the time the sun rises, we will have put many miles between us and them."

Sienna still didn't like it, but, since he was determined to go through with it whether she distracted the beast-men or not, she did as he asked. At his signal, she stepped out into the pale light and roared at her ancestral enemies. The Roracks were on their feet instantly. They forgot themselves momentarily and rushed into the river, only stopping when the cold water was up past their knees. The dragon suddenly crouched and launched herself skyward as they screamed in rage and waved their arms. One of them even threw a fist-sized rock. The rock missed, and as Simon silently told her he was ready, Sienna began flying north. The beast-men began to run after her along the far bank.

Simon slipped his boat into the water among the shadows of the cliff face. The boat moved easily as he began paddling. He had spent some time weaving more grass over the bottom and the craft no longer leaked. He was high and dry, and as he looked back over his shoulder, he saw that he was also rapidly leaving the beast-men, who were still running in the opposite direction in a vain attempt to keep up with the dragon, behind him. He bent to the task of paddling and increased his distance from his enemies.

Once he rounded the slight bend and the Roracks were completely out of sight, he informed Sienna that he was well away and she should turn east and get out of sight herself. She did as he requested and he began maneuvering the boat into the middle of the river in anticipation of entering the rapids. With the oxbow lake behind him, he could hear the water crashing over the rocks now and knew he would be in the thick of it soon.

He had scouted this stretch of river only once. There was a channel of sorts, right down the middle, but it was narrow and he had hoped to either portage around this stretch, or, at least, navigate it in daylight. Now that he could hear the sound and sense the power of the river, he began to doubt the sanity of this part of the plan. Just as he was about to turn toward the shore and continue on foot, he was nearly thrown from the boat as the craft hit a rock. The rapids were upon him, and it was too late to turn aside now.

By the time he hit the third rock, he began to wonder just how many more such collisions his boat could withstand. He knew that he hadn't practiced shielding, but he drew energy from the very water that was trying to destroy the vessel and reinforced the woven grass. He wasn't sure how long he could maintain the shield while he was distracted with trying to actually steer around the biggest obstacles. Again and again, the boat dipped into the water, and he and his gear were swamped. Several times he was nearly thrown end over end. Just when he was about to give up hope of getting through the rapids, the water suddenly smoothed out, and he found himself on a wider flat section of river. He looked back and could see the canyon walls on either side receding as the swift current carried him downstream.

He became aware that Sienna was nearly screaming in his mind, frantic to communicate with him.

"I am here, Sienna, all is well. I have made it through the rapids and am now looking for a good place to get ashore. I am wet, I am very cold, and I want to rest."

"I see you now," she said with great relief. "The beast-men were so angry they followed me a long way. I led them until they were out of the canyon to the north before heading east and losing them. When I doubled back and couldn't find you in the canyon, I nearly panicked. I hadn't expected that you would get so far in such a short time. I feared the rapids would be too much for your boat."

"They nearly were. I had to reinforce the boat with a shield, and even so, I believe that much of the weaving has been undone by the pounding it took." His teeth were chattering and he could barely feel the tips of his fingers and toes. In fact, he almost wished his extremities would go entirely numb so that he wouldn't feel the biting pain deep in his joints from the cold. "I'm afraid I won't make it much farther. I have to get to shore and get warm soon, but I am not sure I can hold the paddle."

He heard a soft splash to his right and she replied, "I am coming, my love. Sit still and I will push you to shore. There is a spot I saw on the eastern bank that is low, and the vegetation there should afford us some cover. You will be warm soon."

Sienna hooked the boat in the crook between her neck and shoulder and began to push it toward river's edge. She lifted her wings up and forward and then lowered them back into the water and pushed back as if she were flying. Using this method of propulsion, she was able to get the craft beached in just a few moments.

Once ashore, with Simon pulling and her pushing, they quickly hauled the boat up under the brush. Simon removed his clothing and, at Sienna's direction, lay across her front legs. Holding the boy's body off the ground, she curled her neck around him and then brought her wings up over him like a huge, leathery blanket. He was so cold that he was not just shivering, but shaking violently; his lips were blue, and he could barely stay conscious. The dragon drew in a huge breath of cold air and waited a few seconds for it to heat in her lungs. Then she put her snout into the living tent she had made with her wings and blew the warm air out through her nostrils. She continued this process until he stopped shuddering and drifted into a normal sleep.

Chapter 29

SIMON WAS IN his bedroom at the estate. He could feel Broderick's weight pinning his legs while the older boy held the covers over his head; not only holding him down but actually trying to suffocate him. Dimly he registered Broderick's voice, "The game is over, Little Mouse. Time for you to die!"

Simon began to struggle with all of his might. He managed to get one leg free and began kicking his attacker while trying to roll out from under the heavy blanket that held him pinned to the bed. His hands groped desperately for anything he could use as a weapon. He kicked again and was rewarded with the sound of pain while the pressure on his legs abated and the blanket was withdrawn. Broderick's voice sounded strangely feminine as he cried out.

"Ow! Sthimon, what are you doing? That hurt!" Sienna shouted as he thrashed violently and kicked her on the chin. She drew her head up and folded her wings back before he could become entangled in them.

Simon rolled away and sat up, ready to fight. He was dazed and didn't comprehend why he suddenly found himself kneeling naked on the ground surrounded by brush when he should be on the wooden floor of his room. Memories began to flood back to him. He knew that he had escaped his tormentor months ago. He remembered finding and bonding with Sienna. The dream had just been so vivid it had replaced all else, and he had once again been the scared little mouse tormented by that sadist.

Sienna gave him time to get his bearings before speaking to him. After a few moments, she tentatively asked, *"Are you back with me now, Dearest?"*

"Yes, I believe I am. I had a terrible nightmare. I dreamed I was a year younger and back in my room, and Broderick was trying to kill me."

At the mention of Simon's former antagonist she growled and bared her teeth. "If he were here, I would disembowel him and let him die slowly. You should have killed him when you had the chance."

"I thought about it. But as I told you, killing him while he was helpless felt too much like murder to me."

"I hope that you will not have a recurrence of this dream; you thrashed about so much I feared that you might injure yourself."

He looked at her and replied, "I hope so too, Dear Heart." Then he suddenly stood up, full of concern, and asked, "Did I hurt you while I was fighting in my sleep?"

"No, not really." Then she chuckled before adding, "It takes a great deal more than a little kick from a barefoot human to actually hurt a dragon of my size."

Simon was horrified that he had struck her, "I'm so sorry, Sienna. I would never harm you intentionally," he said out loud as he rushed forward to hug her. He was almost in tears as he spoke.

"Calm yourself, my love," she cooed in a soothing mental tone. "You were asleep and not aware of what you were doing. I may have a slight bruise on my chin, but there is no real harm done, and I don't blame you at all."

He hugged her more tightly and held on for several minutes, letting the comfort they took in each other wipe away the last remnants of the nightmare.

Finally, Sienna spoke, "We need to get moving soon. Your clothes are dry, and I need to hunt. Also, we are much too close to where we saw the beast-men last night for my comfort. I suggest that you make what repairs to your boat you can while I see if I can catch some breakfast for us both. Then we should move farther downriver. Once we have more distance between us and those monsters, we will look for a new camp site."

Besides the fact that she was right, Simon had been through so much in the last few hours that he was happy to let her take charge for the time being. After all, they were partners, and she was showing remarkably good sense.

"You're right, Sienna," he muttered aloud as he moved to retrieve his clothing. Then switching back to mental conversation, he added, *"See what you can find while I lay a fire and make what repairs I can to the boat."*

The dragon launched herself without another word. She felt hungry, but she was even more interested in circling the area a bit to be sure that their enemies hadn't doubled back and made their way out of this end of the canyon. It was unlikely they had gotten across the deep water, but she hadn't scouted that far south yet; there could be a ford not far ahead that he and she were unaware of.

By the time Sienna returned with the haunch of a pig for Simon, he was ready to go. He lit the fire and didn't wait for it to burn down before he started cooking the meat she had brought him: he sliced off pieces and held them in the fire speared on the end of his knife. When he had eaten his fill he gave the remainder of the haunch back to his partner and she bit easily through the thick bones to cut it into manageable chunks before swallowing the pieces whole. As she did that, he doused the fire and pushed the boat to the river's edge.

Once on the water, with her scouting ahead in the air, he spoke. "I believe that we should keep moving this time. While I would love to find a place we can call our own for weeks, even months, last night has shown me that we can not let our guard down while we are even close to the beast-men's territory. The sooner we have put this country behind us, the sooner I will be able to relax again."

"I agree, Simon. That is why I only took one of the four pigs I found this morning. I didn't want to be weighed down and need to sleep. If you can do it, I think we should simply keep moving most of the day without rest until the sun drops low in the sky. Once we find a campsite, I will hunt again and then we can do the same tomorrow. As long as you travel by water and I travel by air, we should be able to make a good distance each day."

"Providing the river doesn't turn west again, I agree with your plan. However, if the river moves more in the direction of Horne, or flows into another river that does, I will then have to move on foot to keep our southerly course. I will not go back to my homeland."

"What you left behind will catch up with you eventually, Dearest. Perhaps it would be just as well to turn west and get it over with. As you have told me, this lord's son will only send others to capture or kill you. It may be easier to confront this problem directly than let it sneak up on us in the night."

Simon was silent for so long that she thought he wasn't going to answer. Then he said, "You have a point, Sienna, but now is not the time to make such a confrontation. From what Boron taught me about the subject, Dragon Riders are treated courteously, but they aren't revered in Horne the way they are in some other countries. If we go back now, it would just be the word of a boy who happens to be bonded to a young dragon against the word of a nobleman. Broderick will take that title now that I've killed his father. When I return to deal with this, it will be as a Rider, on a fully mature dragon. Then I will seek out the Council of Riders and petition their support before confronting my enemies. Even that may not see Broderick further punished for his crimes. We may end up leaving in a hurry, still fugitives, after doing so. We will see. But for now, all of that is so far in the future I can't see it as real while our immediate survival is still our first concern."

"All right, Simon. I will follow your lead on this for now. I simply know that your dream this morning is one instance in what is becoming quite a history of disturbed sleep." She could feel Simon's confusion at her statement, so she continued before he could ply her with questions. "That is one of the reasons I have pulled you into the Dream State so often. I could feel your unrest and sense that you were disturbed by dreams of the past, mostly about your mother. I pulled you in with me so that your conscious mind would come forward and dispel the upset. You were sleeping so deeply this morning that I wasn't able to do so in time."

Again Simon took a long time to respond. "I understand your concern, Dear Heart, but I still feel that the time is not right to go back to Horne. I hadn't realized about the dreams; you should have told me. Maybe it would be best to allow me to experience some of those dreams. I have a feeling that this is something I must come to terms with whether I go back to my homeland or not. It's possible that allowing me to do so will help to purge them. I enjoy our time in the Dream State, but perhaps you should not be so quick to pull me in when I am dreaming of my past."

This time, it was Sienna's turn to take her time thinking before she made a reply. "Very well, but we are deeply bonded and your dreams affect me, too. I will try and let you work this through yourself, but I won't promise not to interfere at all."

Simon could think of nothing to say to her, so he let the matter drop. He kept the link fully open to maintain contact, but neither of them seemed interested in further conversation. They both had much to think about. He concentrated on navigating the water while she did the same in the air.

They didn't stop at all during the day. Simon didn't even stop to answer nature's call; he urinated over the side of the boat and kept moving, so when he finally put ashore to rest about an hour before full dark, he quickly used his paddle as a shovel to dig a latrine pit while Sienna flew off in search of game. By the time he had finished with his immediate concern and made camp, she had returned with a full belly and the carcass, minus the entrails, of a large pig.

"I have no objection to you salvaging what you can of that skin if you like," she said.

He rolled his eyes. "You know very well that I can't cure the hide while we are on the move, and I am much too tired for your teasing right now," he replied with mock severity.

Sienna chuckled as she settled down and lowered her head to sleep, leaving him with nothing more to say and no waking companion to say anything to. He shook his head and bent to the task of cutting himself enough meat for his supper and breakfast.

CHAPTER 30

DURING THE NIGHT, Simon had crawled onto Sienna's front legs to keep warm and that was where he woke. The dragon was still sleeping and he moved very carefully trying not to wake her. It didn't work.

She raised her head and asked, "Are you all right, Dearest?"

"Yes, I am fine. I simply woke early and decided to get on with the day." He made his way to the bushes as he spoke. "You should get some rest if you are still tired. The sun won't be fully up for at least another hour."

"No, I am awake now. We traveled twenty leagues or more yesterday, but according to the dragons I spoke with in the Dream State last night, at our current rate of progress it will still be two more days before we put the beast-men's territory well behind us. I want to move on as soon as we break camp."

"I agree; by starting earlier, we might be able to travel longer. The farther we are from those monsters, the better I will like it. Luck has been with us up until now, but that could change."

"Yes; it is only due to the Great War nearly two years ago that the creatures' numbers have been thinned enough to allow us such freedom of movement this close to the mountains. She who was my mother had been warned by others that laying here might be too dangerous, but for some unknown reason, she had felt compelled to do so. Perhaps, because of her age, she wasn't sure she could keep up with a hatchling's appetite, so she counted on the breeding fish to take the strain off of her. She had felt that I would be her last daughter and wanted to ensure that I got the best start possible."

"How old was your mother?" he *asked* as his curiosity got the better of him.

"She was over seven millennia old. She was one of the oldest dragons alive and had noticeably weakened with age. She only rose to mate this last time because she wanted one last daughter to pass our family's lineage to. Her age was the other deciding factor in coming here to clutch. She had come here in times long past, and it had always been safe enough, but, since she had been too old to join with the other unbonded females who fought in the Great War, she didn't realize that many of the scattered remnants of the beast-man army had been forced to move south to avoid the humans and dragons who still hunt them farther north. According to the other dragons, it is only by the best of luck that we have not seen more Roracks than we have."

"If you knew all of this, why didn't you warn me sooner? I would never have stayed so long in one place if I had been told of this," he said, somewhat angry that she had withheld such vital information.

"I didn't withhold the knowledge on purpose. I have been so worried about learning about flight and magic that I neglected to ask such questions until last night. So I didn't have the information to give until this morning," she replied defensively.

"I'm sorry, Sienna. I didn't mean to accuse you of neglect. We have both been so caught up in the here and now, simply trying to keep up with our own appetites, that we have been neglecting a source of great knowledge. We need to start thinking farther ahead than our next meal, or we are likely to end up on the menu." He was chiding himself as much as her.

"I did ask about the path ahead of us, and I have some answers if you would like to hear them."

"You have? That is good news. Let's hear it."

"Well, it isn't all good news, I'm afraid. This river does run into another, and we should reach that junction by day's end. That larger river runs south and more easterly still." As he brightened with that news, she shook her head and continued before his hopes were raised too high. "You will only be able to travel on that river for another day before it reaches a large waterfall. Beyond the falls, it again turns nearly due west and runs straight back to Horne. Once we reach the falls, you will be on foot. The falls themselves pretty much mark the southernmost extent of the beast-men's territory, though we will still need to be careful, because the creatures are not held in check by arbitrary boundaries, although they have not been known in the past to risk climbing down the steep eastern mountainsides into the lowlands beyond. It is still possible to run afoul of them south of that point, though that is a remote possibility at best due to the rugged terrain; they seem to prefer to continually try to move into the lands beyond the gentler slopes of the western foothills."

"At least we will get out of the Roracks' lands before I am reduced to walking; that's encouraging." He thought about it for a moment and then asked, "Could you ask about us flying together tonight?"

"I anticipated that," she replied. "I was told that while my growth has made me larger than most dragons twice my age, my wing muscles aren't ready to carry you in prolonged flight. It is one thing for me to carry a pig or deer a short distance before eating it, but I am not ready to carry a human at this point. Even though you are a young human and have more to grow, you are not exactly small by the standards of your species. However, the dragons I talked with have said that if my growth doesn't slow down, I should be capable of carrying your weight in less than a month."

Simon nodded his head and said, "Well then, there will be no choice. When I can no longer travel on the river, I will have to walk. It will be slower, but that is how it is. Now, however, I have finished my breakfast and you need to eat if we are to get an early start."

By the time he was ready to shove off, she had finished the meat and was preparing to launch into the sky. Simon felt a sudden unease and conveyed that feeling to Sienna. She didn't waste time asking what was wrong, but simply accepted that his inner sense was justified. Neither of them waited to see what had caused the sensation. He could feel the wind of her down strokes as his paddle bit deeply into the water.

Just then, they both heard the harsh commanding bark of a Rorack. It was not only on this side of the river, it was also very close. Not understanding why he felt the need to do so, Simon ducked. A crude spear sailed over his head as several beast-men screamed in rage. He fought down the impulse to turn and assess the situation and simply paddled harder while silently instructing Sienna to climb high and not waste time looking back. Then he erected a shield behind him and was pleased to hear something thud into it before dropping harmlessly into the water. Only when he estimated that he was well out of range of a spear or rock did he turn around and get a look. On the shore, still spitting with anger, were six large beast-men and eight smaller creatures that he took to be females of the species. He could see at least three of what he assumed to be young clinging to the females' necks. He didn't see any older offspring in evidence.

Sienna roared her hatred and he quickly *cautioned* her not to attack or even antagonize. He turned back and bent to the task of paddling the boat. He just wanted to put as much distance between himself and those fiends as he could. However, the beast-men had other ideas. They began to run along the shore following him. His boat moved easily and he was making good speed, but he was not putting any real distance between himself and his pursuers; they simply ran too fast for him to get away.

"They are keeping up with you, Love. Perhaps if I dived down and hit the leader hard enough…"

"No!" He shouted both mentally and aloud. "Those creatures were able to kill your mother even though she used her flame on them. If they managed to get their hands on you, you wouldn't stand a chance. There are too many for us to fight. We have no choice other than continue running away. They don't have any more ranged weapons, and they can't follow me into the water or they will drown.

I guess we'll see how long it takes for them to realize the futility of this chase and give up."

"Very well, my love, but I don't like it. Beast-men aren't known for giving up when they can still see their prey. It is likely they will follow us until we have nowhere left to go."

"If need be, Sienna, I can get out on the opposite shore and run away on foot. By the time they are able to find a crossing, we will be long gone."

"I hope you are right, Simon."

For the remainder of the morning, Simon, with his strength and stamina magically enhanced slightly due to his bond with the dragon, stayed in the middle of the river and, using the current to his advantage as well, set an exhausting pace. The females with young had fallen behind, but the rest showed no sign of slowing by mid-day. Simon was able to hold the pace until mid-afternoon. The remaining females had fallen back, but could still be seen in the distance. The males showed no hint of fatigue. The point where his original waterway joined with another, larger one was a barely noted milestone.

"There'll be no camping tonight," he told Sienna as the sun sank lower on the horizon. "These brutes have shown no sign of slowing, and I can't continue to paddle like I have been doing. I don't believe darkness will deter them, and if we simply put ashore on the opposite side of the river, they will raise such a fuss that any of their kindred over there will hear and come to investigate. I have no choice; I'm slacking my pace for now."

He stopped paddling completely and rose up on his knees to relieve his aching bladder. Then he leaned over the other side and used his cupped hands to get enough clean water to quench his thirst. The beast-men slowed to a walk. He realized that his rest period would give them a chance to do the same, but it couldn't be helped.

"How are you holding up, Dear Heart?" he asked.

"I am a bit hungry, but otherwise fine. The winds have been favorable, and I have spent most of the day soaring on the air currents.

Such flight isn't tiring at all. I could do this for many more hours if I need to."

"That's good news. I was afraid that such prolonged flight would exhaust you, if not harm you directly. Perhaps you should head west a bit and see about hunting."

"I would never leave you in a situation like this!" she said indignantly.

"Look at it logically, Sienna. There is nothing happening here, and won't be for some time to come. The Roracks seem to have put you out of their minds and are centered on finding a way to invite me to supper. If you head west and find a bit of game, you can eat lightly to replenish the energy you have used today, and when you come back, you will find that my 'companions' and I are in pretty much the same situation as when you left. You may as well take advantage of the stalemate while it lasts."

"It goes against my instincts to leave you like this…"

"It's not my first choice either, but this may yet come to a fight. If that happens, I will need you as rested as possible if we are to stand even a slim chance of getting through this with our lives. If you do not keep up your strength, you will be less effective when the time comes; now go and find food before your hunger becomes an issue." He hated ordering her about like this, but she herself had once commented that, when it came to the Roracks, he had more common sense than she.

"Very well, my love. You make a good point. However, I have no intention of going far. If there is no game close, I will go hungry before I get more than a few minutes flight from you."

Simon didn't argue with her. His boat was beginning to drift toward the Roracks, so he picked up his paddle and used it as a rudder to keep the craft in the middle of the river. He could almost feel the creatures' disappointment at his course correction. By the time he felt rested enough to begin paddling again, he also felt Sienna's sense of pride as she returned from the hunt.

"*Heads up, Love,*" she *said* as she strafed him. She dropped something and it splatted wetly into the boat about a half a yard in front of where he was kneeling.

He picked up the piece of meat she had dropped. It was about the size of both of his fists put together. Normally he liked his meat cooked, but his hunger outweighed any squeamishness and he began to devour the stuff.

"My thanks, Love. I hadn't even realized how hungry I was until I bit into this," he said as blood dripped down and off of his chin from the corner of his mouth.

"There would be more, but I wasn't sure how accurate I would be when I dropped it to you. I was afraid that if I accidently hit you with a larger piece that still contained the bone, you would be injured."

In spite of his situation, Simon began to laugh so hard he nearly choked on the meat he was trying to swallow.

"Have you gotten so tired you have taken leave of your senses?"

"No, I haven't lost my mind. It just struck me as funny that, considering my current circumstances, you are so worried that I might be injured by a piece of flying food."

Sienna giggled a little at his explanation herself before sobering and asking, "Have you given any thought to how we will escape our pursuers without having to resort to a fight?"

"No, I have been too preoccupied with the immediate concerns of bodily functions and hunger to give it much thought. I am still hoping they will give up the chase, though they show no inclination of doing so."

"Well, we need to think about it now. At the pace you have set all day, we will reach the waterfall before the sun rises in the morning."

At her words, the beginnings of an idea crept into the back of his mind. "Dear Heart, I have something to think about, but I need to concentrate on both it and keeping the boat from drifting too far toward our pursuers. You keep watch from the air, and let me know if you see any more trouble ahead, but I need to be undisturbed for a while."

"I won't be able to help if you don't let me know what you are thinking!"

"I won't keep you in the dark for long; just let me think for a bit."

"Very well, I will continue to scout ahead."

"I love you, Sienna. And thank you again for thinking to bring me food; it has not only quelled my hunger, but lifted my spirits."

"I always think of you, Simon. I love you, too."

He reached into the water to rinse the blood from his hands as he swallowed the last bite of meat. Then he grabbed up his paddle and began propelling the boat along with renewed vigor. All of the Roracks—the childless females had caught up with the males— made quite a show of pointing and hooting until the obvious leader pointed downstream and barked. They turned as one and picked up the pace to keep up with the boat.

Hours later, the Roracks continued to pace him, and his strength was once again waning. He had never felt so tired. He had woken early the previous morning, and even though dawn was still nearly two hours off, he hadn't had a real break. He had tried to summon energy from the river and use it to attack the beast-men, but his skills were woefully inadequate for the task. Not only did he not know the specifics of directing such an attack, but the creatures seemed naturally resistant to the energy. He did discover, however, that he could replenish some of his strength by drawing power from the world around him. It helped, but he needed to stop and rest.

"I have scouted ahead, my love, and the falls are near. The height of the falls is well over two hundred feet. There is no way you would survive going over that in your boat. The slopes on either side of the river are also extremely steep, and I can see no clear path down in the darkness. You only have a short time until you will have to make for the western shore."

"I have been giving some thought to what lies ahead of us, Dear Heart. If I simply stop at the falls and begin looking for a path down, the beast-men will do the same on the other side. They'll continue this game below the falls until we reach a point where the water becomes shallow enough for them to cross it."

"I have come to the same conclusion. Do you have any suggestions for how to deal with our problem?"

"I was thinking about what you said concerning flying. You can't fly long distances with my extra weight, but soaring is not as much strain on you. I was wondering if we could soar together if you didn't have the added strain of needing to launch upward."

"That might work!" she exclaimed. "Even with your other supplies, if you climb onto my neck, I should be able to launch off the cliff by the falls and glide far enough to lose the beast-men before I have to land. By the time those monsters find a way down the slopes, we should be long gone."

"That is what I am hoping. I see no reason why it shouldn't work. I will land near the edge of the falls on the far side of the river and get my pack. Even if the Roracks can figure a way to cross at the falls, we should be airborne before they get near us. Follow me, Sienna, and be ready to move quickly."

Simon could already hear the roaring of the rushing water as it plunged over the cliff ahead. The current was getting swifter and stronger, and it was becoming increasingly difficult to get the boat to do what he wanted. The time had come, so he angled toward the western bank and found a spot of shore to beach. Scrambling out of the craft, he took only a second to grab his pack and he headed right for the rocks at the precipice: Sienna had anticipated his intended launch point and awaited him there. Glancing across the water, he could see that, even though they probably didn't understand his plan, the Roracks had become agitated and redoubled their efforts to catch up. Not only were they upset about the possibility of losing their quarry, but they had apparently put the dragon out of their minds and the renewed sight of her so close pushed them to a reckless fevered pitch.

Sienna settled her chest to the wet rocks and instructed him to use her front leg as a step to climb up. The spot where her neck joined her body was somewhat dished, and seemed to be made for a rider to sit there. Simon looked for the beast-men and saw them picking their way over the rocks trying frantically to get across the river. He was pretty certain the center of the falls was too deep for them to ford, but he didn't want to wait long enough to find out for sure. Suddenly, the second one back lost its footing on the slick rocks and flailed out with its arms for balance. It desperately grabbed the Rorack ahead of it, and they both went over the falls. Any noise made this close to the rushing water was instantly lost in the din, and Simon watched in a kind of horrified fascination as the two appeared to scream silently before disappearing over the precipice. The rest of the beast-men hesitated.

Sienna didn't wait to see if they would continue or not. She bunched her muscles and *said, "Wrap your legs around tightly and hang on, Dearest. Here we go!"*

Simon wasn't sure what he had expected, but the sensation of flight was like nothing he had ever experienced before. There was a moment of sheer terror as he felt like they were falling, and then the air filled the dragon's wings and he could feel the sensation of the two of them soaring through the night. With his enhanced night vision, he could see the land far below in the dim light of the waning moon as Sienna caught an updraft and banked in a wide circle while she took full advantage of the lift to get as much altitude as possible. He watched in delighted horror as the plains below the mountain receded farther and farther. Finally, at what he estimated to be at least a thousand feet, she leveled out and began the glide southward. They soared for about a half an hour without speaking. During that time, Sienna found two more updrafts and managed to get to a height of nearly three thousand feet.

"If the wind currents hold, my love, we will put many miles behind us before we will have to land."

"I don't want you to overextend yourself, Sienna; if you feel the least bit fatigued, I want you to put down."

"This is not fatiguing. Soaring like this is not much work at all. I could do this for hours, days if necessary. The other dragons warned me that taking off with our combined weight could stress the sinews of my wing muscles. Since I didn't have to take off, there was no strain. I will be fine; do not worry. I can stay in the air until we have put the beast-men far behind us, and then I will look for a place where we both can rest."

Simon nearly fell when she touched down. He hadn't even realized that he had been sleeping.

"I tried to land as gently as I could, Dearest. I could have kept going for a while longer, but I was worried when you fell asleep that you might fall off."

Even though the sun was beginning to rise, he felt he could still rest for several hours. He slipped down to the soft grass, and, pillowing his head on his pack he closed his eyes.

"Thank you, Sienna: I am glad you were watching so closely. You should hunt quickly and then get some sleep yourself."

"I can wait to eat until you wake, Simon. We are safe for now, but this is unfamiliar territory. I won't leave you until you are able to keep watch. Sleep; I will doze and rouse you if there is any trouble."

CHAPTER 31

"DAMN!" SIMON SWORE as his shirt sleeve snagged yet again on still another thorn bush.

"What is troubling you, Love?"

"My shirt has now been torn to little more than a rag, my flesh is scored as if I had been whipped, and I am tired enough to sleep away the rest of the day even though the sun is barely past noon. I am hot, tired, sore, and hungry. I have so much gritty dirt inside my clothing that it feels as if I am wearing sanding cloth, and still there is no end to these thorn bushes in sight."

"I offered to fly you across this, but you refused. I can do nothing to help you if you insist on walking."

"We discussed this when we broke camp this morning. Until you have gotten confirmation from the other dragons that you are indeed large enough to carry me in normal flight, we can't risk injuring your wings. I have to continue walking for now, and you saying 'I told you so' doesn't help."

"I'm not saying 'I told you so.' I am merely reiterating that I could have flown you across this brush-choked dust bowl in two hours—maybe less—but since you insisted on walking, it is taking you more than a day, and you have to deal with those unpleasant thorns."

"Unpleasant? You, Sienna, are developing a real knack for understatement," he retorted.

The dragon didn't laugh, but her mental tone as she held her *silence* was so close as to make no real difference.

They had spent the entire first day after leaving the mountains resting where he had dropped exhausted to the ground. The next day, Sienna had been able to gorge herself so thoroughly that she had been nearly comatose for hours. When she finally woke up, they only moved a few miles until he found an old dead tree that had been carried down into the flatlands by the swollen river in some season past. He used the huge root ball as the backbone of a shelter. The flood plains were covered with rich soil, and game, both large and small, was abundant. While there were no flowing streams, Sienna could smell water just below the surface and simply dug a shallow well from which they drank.

Simon had been tempted to stay in that place longer, but spring was truly here, and the flood plain would soon be inundated by the rising waters from the snow melt; by the time they moved on, the land had become almost spongy and would soon have been completely under water. Also, he couldn't help but think of how they had been lulled into a false sense of security back in the canyon, and the new camp didn't have the natural defenses they had there. They resumed their travels after ten days.

Only a day's march later, the flood plain had given way to this forsaken waste. Once again Simon wondered, for the thousandth time, how a land could be so lush for so far and then suddenly turn to nothing but sandy soil and thorn bushes. He had been forced to don his chaps and jerkin to protect himself from the thorns, but that left his arms, which were bleeding from a score of new scratches, covered with nothing but a thin layer of cloth; and now that scant protection hung in tatters. Even Sienna, with her armored body, had complained about the brush when they had camped the night before.

The only thing worse than the thorn bushes was the sand. Because he had to wear his chaps and jerkin to protect his skin, and little air circulated through the brush, he was hot and sweaty. This made the sandy dust stick to him under his clothing. Moving through the brush caused his dust-covered hide to rub against the material and abrade every inch of him, especially his crotch and armpits.

They had been so happy to be out of the mountains, and Sienna had hunted so much well-fattened game, that she hadn't bothered going to the Dream State the whole time they had been camped on the flood plain. Instead, she had eaten herself into a stupor each day and slept as if nearly dead at night. She had not talked to any other dragons during that time. Simon admitted that her growth over the last week or so had been phenomenal, but without some confirmation from the older dragons that she was ready, he refused to entertain the idea of her carrying him. The night before, she had tried to get in touch with the dragons who had, unofficially, taken the job of teaching her. Unfortunately, all three of them were now completely involved in mating rituals of some kind and couldn't be contacted.

"Good news, Love," Sienna broke into his musings. "The brush thins out considerably less than a mile ahead of you, and there is a clear stream due south of where you are now. You will soon be able to wash and rest. Beyond the stream, it looks as though the brush continues to thin until it gives way completely to grassland a couple of miles beyond that point."

"Ow, argh!" He was about to thank her for the good news when a white-hot pain shot up his left leg as a particularly long thorn pierced the thin hide of his boot and was driven into his ankle just above the heel as he stepped down. He lifted his foot awkwardly and almost fell back into another thorn bush. While he was getting his balance and trying to find a safe place to sit and extract the thorn, Sienna landed hard, crushing the bushes on his right.

She surveyed the scene, ignoring the inconveniences of the thorns and said, "This has gone far enough. It is one thing for you to suffer scratches and abrasions to protect me, but that thorn is driven so deep into your leg that it nearly protrudes from the other side: you cannot walk on it. I am going to carry you out of this hellish brush, and your only choice is whether you do so as a proper Rider, or I pick you up bodily like a babe in arms."

He controlled his pain and responded, "I can heal this injury and make it out of here. You don't need to carry me."

She said nothing and simply reached out to grab him.

"All right!" he shouted out loud. "I will climb into place. I think it's best to wait to pull the thorn out until I can also wash the wound. Help me stand."

Once he was in position, she sank onto her haunches and launched. Simon's head whipped back uncomfortably from the acceleration, but he barely noticed over the exhilaration of flying. He almost forgot completely about the huge thorn in his ankle as he watched the ground, and those hated bushes, fall away. He was disappointed when the flight ended a few short moments later at the stream's edge.

He tried to remove his boot, but the thorn widened at the stem end, and he decided it would be less painful to pull it out first. He gritted his teeth and gripped the end of the offensive barb. Then, after taking a moment to muster his courage, he yanked it free. The pain of doing so was not as bad as the initial stab, but it was close. He removed his boot and stuck his foot and lower leg into the stream and let the cool water soothe him. Then he examined the wound before collecting energy and healing himself.

As he began removing his clothes, Sienna spoke up, "If you are all right, Dearest, I would like to hunt. I have been circling overhead since we broke camp this morning and I am hungry, so unless you want to move on right away, I will be gone for a while."

"I am fine now, Dear Heart, thanks to you. I have no intention of moving any farther from this spot than I must to gather firewood. First, however, I am going to slide my hot, sand-scoured hide into that mercifully cool water and bathe. I am also hungry, so if you would be kind enough to bring back a bit of meat for my meal, I will be so grateful that I will swear my undying love to you."

The dragon laughed out loud and said, "You have already sworn your undying love to me many times. However, since I have also sworn my undying love to you, I will bring you some meat, even though you have so little to offer in return."

Simon chuckled and continued to divest himself of his clothing while she beat down with her wings and headed off over the grassland on the other side of the stream. He had not been completely alone to bathe in many weeks. When they were in the mountains, the frigid temperature of the river had kept him from doing more than gingerly washing away the worst of the dirt. Since leaving the higher altitude, he hadn't been near enough to a sufficient body of water to submerge himself. He had been naked in past weeks, but always with Sienna near, so he hadn't really bothered to look and take stock of his body.

He hadn't lost any body fat, but he had gained a considerable amount of muscle since leaving Horne. His feet had continued to grow to the point that he would need new boots soon even if he hadn't planned on buying them anyway.

Then he looked at his chest. He understood about his dragon mark. It was the mark that was magically placed on a Rider at the point where the energy that bonded him to the dragon first touched his body. In Simon's case, it had been on his chest when he fell on Sienna's egg while fighting the Roracks that had attacked her mother. At the time, he had thought it was simply a minor abrasion. A long time had passed since he had last examined it closely, and he was surprised to find that it was now a perfect miniature picture of his Bondmate. Usually, it took many months for the mark to become so clear. The head of this dragon came up to his neck and would be visible if he wore a shirt that had an open collar, and the wings stretched along the nipple line from one side of his chest to the other, while the dragon's tail went all the way down and curved slightly at his waistline.

Then he noticed how much pubic hair he had grown. He was beginning to change into a young man when he left the estate, but the thatch between his legs was much denser than he thought was normal for a boy just entering puberty, and so was the stuff under his arms. He looked at his chest again and was somewhat disappointed at not finding any significant hair growth there.

He only took a few minutes to appraise his growth and maturity before getting back to the task at hand. He considered taking the time to heal all of the scratches and abrasions before bathing, but rejected the idea. The cool water would soothe the heat rash he was suffering from instantly and that was far more important at the moment. He placed his dragon blades at the edge of the bank within easy reach and slipped into the stream. The water was cool enough to be bracing, but not cold enough to be uncomfortable. He washed both his body and his clothes, then healed the sores that still bothered him. After that, he soaked for nearly half an hour before exiting the stream and building a fire. The fire had burned down enough to cook over by the time Sienna returned with a haunch of some grazing animal.

Later that night, Simon once again found himself staring at the changing hues of the Dream State from the vantage point of a cliff top where he and Sienna were situated. Several dragons circled overhead, and Sienna seemed to be concentrating on something besides him. He figured that she was talking with one or more other dragons and didn't interrupt. He sat down and rested his back against her; marveling at how solid everything felt here. He lost all track of time as he waited and watched the dragons soaring before she spoke to him.

"Good news, Love. Several older dragons have returned from spring mating flights and were willing to talk with me. One is even bonded, so she knows better how to instruct me in our situation. They all agree that, while I still have more to grow, since you are not a fully grown man, I should be able to carry you in flight, providing we don't over do it. We can easily fly in one morning as far as you could walk in three day's time. If we fly from morning until noon before stopping, we won't travel as long each day as we would if you were on foot, but our progress will still be much greater."

"That is good news. Did you get any other information from this bonded dragon? Are she and her Rider near us now?" he asked hopefully.

"They are not near. They are in a country called Iondar, while we are in the north of Trent. However, she did explain the basics of flying safely with your added weight, and she told me how to fashion safety straps out of rope so that I could instruct you in doing so. She also suggested that we continue south. She and her Rider will be making their way north soon, and it is possible that we may meet up and they will help us learn to work together as Dragon and Rider."

Simon was suddenly skeptical; he knew that most Riders had taken a vow to uphold the law. "Did you tell them that I am a wanted criminal in Horne?"

"No, my love, I didn't mention it. She and her Rider have been partners for a little more than five centuries, and she seems like a very nice person. Still, I thought we might meet them and see how nice they really are before I divulge too much information about our particular circumstances. I am not so trusting that I would simply tell them that there is likely to be a large a reward for returning you to Horne. After all, I am large enough now, and you know enough magic, that a small group of humans would be hard pressed to cause us any real trouble. However, another dragon with a fully trained rider, determined to return us to your homeland, could present a problem."

"Very well, we will continue south, and decide how much of the story to tell after we have met them both."

CHAPTER 32

S IMON FINISHED TYING himself into the improvised safety straps. After double checking everything he *said, "I am ready, Sienna."*

"Brace yourself to protect your neck, Love," she reminded him. She sank down in preparation for pushing off with her powerful hind legs and raised her wings for the down stroke before adding, *"Also, if anything happens, just remember to lie flat over my neck, and let me handle it. Don't try to help."*

The thrill of flight took away any shock he might otherwise have felt once they were airborne. His heart rate increased a bit, and he lost all sense of relation to the ground as the air rushed through his hair and he heard it whistling in his ears. He fervently hoped that he would never get so used to flying that it became mundane.

This time, Sienna didn't just climb a couple of hundred feet like she had yesterday. She continued to push herself upward as the ground receded. He was reminded of that first flight off of the cliff by the waterfall. Sienna had gained a great deal of altitude as well, but it had been dark and he had lost track of how high they had flown. This time, he could clearly see the distance to the ground and it delighted him. The wide stream he had bathed in was now little more than a sliver of silver ribbon as the dragon leveled out nearly three thousand feet up before she turned in the direction of the morning sun.

He was so preoccupied with the flight that he almost didn't ask why they had turned east instead of continuing directly south.

"I found out that we are less than ten leagues from a main, north/south trade road. That road goes all the way to Iondar. The bonded dragon, Leera, told me that we should follow that track, and she and her Rider will watch for us along it once they leave Iondar three days from now."

"That sounds like a good plan, and perhaps we will meet other travelers on the route as well. With any luck, we will find a caravan and be able to trade for some supplies. Since we are going to be flying, I will definitely need more clothing. I was so exhausted the last time that I forgot how cold it is up here."

"I am sorry about that. The winds at this altitude are with us and I can soar much of the way. If I flew lower where it is warmer, my wings would have to work much harder. It may be less comfortable, but you can lay your chest down on my neck to conserve some body heat."

"It's not bad yet, but if I start to shiver I will do that. Right now, I just want to reach that trade road."

About a half an hour later Simon could see the rutted roadway they were looking for. Sienna angled her flight downward as she turned south to follow the path. He was about to ask her to land for a bit when he realized that she had cut their altitude by half and it was no longer so uncomfortably cold, even with the wind still whipping past him. However, the dragon was now flapping her wings much more than before.

"I thought you needed to fly higher to soar and conserve your strength?" he asked. "I can stand the cold for a while longer."

"It isn't that, though I was going to ask how you were holding up. The wind up higher was blowing from west to east and I was riding that current, letting it push me forward. If I maintained that height, I would now be fighting a cross wind. I might be able to find a suitable air current up higher and continue to soar, but the higher we go, the colder it gets, so, for now, I have settled for being lower and using my muscles."

Sienna spent the next hour explaining about how the wind can blow in different directions at different heights, as well as how to find and ride thermals to keep soaring for hours. She was about to explain wind shear when she became alert to something else.

"What is it?" he asked.

"There is a lone wagon ahead of us, and several men on horseback who look to be chasing it. Something is not right. I am going to get a closer look."

Even with his magically enhanced vision, Simon couldn't see nearly as well as the dragon could, so all he could distinguish was that there was indeed a wagon and several riders. He couldn't see details yet, but he, like his partner, sensed that something was definitely wrong down there.

"It appears that the mounted men have weapons and are attempting to stop the wagon."

Simon strained to see better, but the drama was unfolding just beyond the effective range of his sight. He could, however, tell that one of the horses had gotten just ahead of the wagon.

"The man just used his sword to slice the draft animal's neck. It is slowing down considerably. We will be there in a moment. This isn't our fight; what do you want to do?"

"If those men are bandits, we would be wrong if we didn't interfere. Are they wearing uniforms?"

He felt rather than heard Sienna snort, "They are all dressed differently, and not much better than you are. I do not believe they are part of any military unit."

Simon could now see the men clearly. The one who had attacked the draft horse was dressed in dirt-covered cloth and rode a fine chestnut horse. He carried a long sword in his right hand with his scabbard strapped across the back of his saddle. His face was scruffy; more like he hadn't shaved than like he regularly wore a beard. The others were in similar shape, though their mounts weren't as fine as the first. Two of the other bandits had long bushy beards while the fourth, like the first, needed to use a razor.

He could only see one man on the seat of the wagon, but the vehicle was covered, so he had no idea if anyone else was inside. The man in the seat grabbed a wood ax and stood up as the wagon came to a halt. He looked scared but determined to stand his ground.

"We have to help him," he said. "Fly as low as you can when you go over them, and see if you can scare their horses into rearing. Then land and I will dismount."

"Is that low enough?" she *asked,* actually hitting one of the bandits with her back foot as she flew over, knocking the man to the ground hard. All four of the saddled horses reared, unseating one of the other riders. The two who remained in their saddles were hard pressed to keep their mounts from bolting.

The draft animal might have panicked as well if it hadn't already died from blood loss.

Sienna landed abruptly, and Simon untied the safety lines as fast as he could. By the time he had dismounted, the men had brought their horses under control, though barely so, and turned to face him. The man who had been thrown got unsteadily to his feet. The one Sienna had hit lay completely still face down in the dirt; there was a puddle of blood from the wounds that her claws had opened in his neck and head. She had used the same manner of attack on many prey animals since learning to hunt and found it just as effective in this instance.

The robber on the fine chestnut horse looked at Simon and recovered his composure. "You're just a boy!" he sneered. "I don't care what beasty you've brought along, I'm going to make you pay for killing my kinsman."

His bluster failed when Sienna roared. "If you attack my Bondmate I will tear you apart!"

Again the horses reared, and this time, neither man could control his mount. Both of them were thrown. The one on the chestnut landed clear, but the other, his foot tangled in the stirrup, could only scream as he was dragged northward along the road.

The first bandit who had been thrown dropped to his knees and begged for mercy, but the other unwisely rose with blade in hand

and tried to lunge at Simon. Sienna moved to intercede, but the boy had already drawn his weapons and reacted. He blocked a clumsy thrust with his short blade and sliced with the long one. The outlaw fell dead with his head barely still attached to his shoulders.

Simon stood staring at the corpse. He had killed men before, but not in personal combat, and felt sickened that he had done so now. The beast-men had been different; they were an abomination. But this was a man, another human being. He could feel the bile in the back of his throat, and turned away before dropping to his knees and vomiting. He spent several moments retching until there was nothing left to bring up. Then he knelt there for a while, unable to rise.

"Simon, are you going to be all right?" Sienna asked.

Her concern and the soft tone broke through and he replied, "I will be okay. I have never killed a man in such a personal manner before. I hope I never have to do so again."

"I understand, Dearest, but right now these people still need our help, and there is at least one bandit left alive who must be dealt with."

He hadn't even realized he had closed his eyes. He opened them now and slowly looked around. The brigand who had begged for his life was still on the ground cowering. The man who had driven the wagon was standing near the front wheel and he had been joined by a woman, a girl about thirteen years old, and a boy who was younger than Simon by two or three years.

He got up slowly and walked to the body of the man he had killed. He wiped his blade clean on the dead bandit's shirt before returning it to its rawhide sheath. Then he turned to the people standing by the wagon.

"I am Simon," he said, looking the man in the eye, "Bond-mate to Sienna." He pointed to the dragon with his left hand and held his right out to shake.

The man hesitated for a moment looking at the dragon before taking Simon's hand and saying, "I'm Rufus. This is my wife Cinda, and our children Tina and Martin."

Simon shook the woman's hand. She smiled, but stayed protectively in front of the children. Her boy tried to move around her and get a better look at Sienna, but Cinda held him back.

"You have nothing to fear from me," Sienna assured her.

Heartened by the dragon's kind tone, the bandit spoke up, "What are going to do with me?"

Sienna bent forward, very close to him, bared her teeth and said with a growl, "You, on the other hand, do have reason to be afraid."

The man whimpered, put his hands over his head, rolled into a fetal position on the road, and soiled himself.

"We'd be within our rights to kill him," Rufus said. "In Trent, the law concerning bandits is clear on that."

Simon looked at the wretch and shook his head. "While I'm sure he would have no compunctions about killing any one of us, or even all of us, I can't bring myself to sink to his level." Then he looked around and added, "Your horse is dead, and you won't go far without another. We can put this man to work burying his friends while we try and catch their mounts. With a little luck, one of them will take to harness well enough to get you on your way." Then he looked Rufus in the eye and asked, "Do you have a shovel he can dig with?"

Rufus stood with his mouth open for a moment before saying, "I can't leave this bandit here with my wife and children while I go off trying to catch spooked horses. I'm sorry Rider, I'll tie the man up and do the burying myself first."

"Really!" Sienna spoke up loudly. "Since it is me that the horses are running away from it is only logical that I stay here while you men catch the silly creatures. Your family will not be alone with this man. I will be watching him closely." She bent her head down so low that her mouth was nearly touching the man's ear before saying, "If he so much as looks at your wife or children with bad intent, I will end his life in an extremely painful and messy fashion."

To Simon's surprise, Cinda spoke up, "I'm sure that we will come to no harm if Sienna is watching, Rufus. And we do need to replace our horse."

The man looked at his wife for a moment before shrugging his shoulders and saying, "Very well, I suppose it will be all right. Martin, you can come with us." Then he dug around in the back of the wagon for a moment before returning with a shovel, which he dropped near the terrified bandit. He knelt down and said, "Drag 'em off the road and dig the hole. Remember, that dragon will be watching you."

They had walked about a quarter of a mile when they found the body of the bandit who had been dragged. Rufus shook his head and said, "I suppose we'll have to see this one in the ground too. Well, we'll collect the corpse after we get the horses. I'd rather strap it to a horse than carry it myself."

It took over three hours to track down and catch all of the animals. Then they had to stop and retrieve the body on the way back.

"These horses are yours by rights, Rider," Rufus said as they walked. "I didn't do anything to stop those bandits and would most likely be dead if you hadn't happened along. The law in Trent is clear: the horses, as well as any of the bandits' other possessions, belong to you."

"What am I going to do with them? Feed them to Sienna? Except for the chestnut, she could do better hunting for herself."

"You could sell them. There's a big gather going up at the ford a day's travel south of here. Local folks like me will be bringing all kinds of trade goods they've been growing and making all year, and the caravans will be there as well. I'm sure that even a Rider could use the coin those horses would bring, especially that chestnut."

"I'll think about it, Rufus. In the meantime, you still need an animal to pull your wagon."

"I'm just saying the animals are yours; I've no right to them. Those bandits didn't look as though their purses were heavy with coin. This kingdom doesn't offer a reward for dead bandits the way some others do. Selling those horses is likely to be the only compensation you're going to get."

"Well, since they belong to me," Simon replied, "would you mind if I hitched one of them to your wagon for the time being?"

Rufus smiled and shook his head. "You may be young, but you're a good man all the same, Simon."

When they reached the wagon, they found the one bandit left alive had been busy. With Sienna standing over him, he had dug feverishly and had a hole deep and wide enough to bury all three bodies. A quick inspection of the corpses before they were interred revealed that Rufus's suspicions were correct: the bandits had carried only two silver coins and several coppers between them, and their weapons were all dull and nearly as worthless as their clothing. Though it felt a little like grave robbing, Simon did as Rufus insisted and put the coins in his own pouch.

Simon picked the biggest of the three lesser animals and looked it over to see if it would take to harness. As Rufus spoke up to object, he said, "Your horse is dead and my Bond-mate needs to eat. Therefore, I will trade you this animal for that meat. You get the horse you need, and Sienna gets food without having to hunt. That seems fair to me."

Rufus looked at him for a moment and then, shaking his head he said, "I accept your bargain, Rider; otherwise, my family and I are stuck here. I also thank you."

They shook on the deal as Sienna dragged the dead animal off to eat in peace. Once she had finished eating a huge portion of it, she needed to sleep off the large meal, so they camped where they were until dawn the next day.

Chapter 33

S IMON OPTED TO ride in the wagon rather than fly. Sienna
had been a bit put off by this arrangement but acquiesced
when he pointed out that since Rufus had agreed to help take
the horses to be sold, the least he could do was ride in the wagon
with him. Since the bandit tied up in the back of the wagon hadn't
been willing to talk about his fellows, it was also entirely possible
that they might run into more brigands before reaching the ford. If
that happened, he would be on the ground ready and she could
swoop down and catch them off guard.

"I still can't believe you are only eleven," Rufus said as Simon
climbed up and took a place on the bench seat. "By your size I'd
have guessed that you were closer to fourteen or fifteen at least, and
I'd have believed it if you said you were a bit older. Also, your hands
look as though you're no stranger to hard work, not games and other activities of a boy your age."

"I was a blacksmith's apprentice before I bonded with Sienna,"
he replied. He had decided not to try and make up elaborate tales
about his past to hide his identity. The less he lied, the less chance
there would be of someone catching him out. This way he wouldn't
have to work hard at remembering what he'd said, and he didn't
have to give away any specific information either.

"A blacksmith's apprentice? Now that's not a trade I would expect one so young to take up. I suppose that you didn't get the chance

to learn much yet. Spent most of your time pumping the bellows, huh?"

"Actually, I have learned quite a bit. The shop was very busy, but small, and there was just me and smith; he had no one else, so he had to give me more instruction if we were to keep up. I can handle myself well enough to re-tire a wagon wheel, or shoe a horse, as well as fix most farm tools that get broken."

Rufus whistled, "It's not completely unheard of to find a boy your age apprenticing in a trade, but it is a bit unusual to meet one who's learned so much so young. Was the smith your father?"

"No," he said sadly. "My father died about four years ago. That left my mother and me very poor. The smith was kind enough to take me in and teach me. He wasn't my father, but we were good friends."

"Rufus!" Cinda chided from just behind them. "You've upset the young Rider with your prying." She shook her head and added, "And they say women are gossipy."

Rufus blushed. "I'm sorry, Rider. I talk too much, and I have a tendency to pry into things that are none of my business."

"It's all right, I took no offense," Simon responded, though privately he was glad Cinda had reined her husband in. "So, tell me more about this gather."

"Oh, it's the best time," Tina spoke up from right behind him. The girl had taken a liking to Simon and she was sitting as close as possible without being up on the bench beside him. "We've been going every year since I can remember. People come from all over. There are even caravans from as far away as Iondar. You'll see the most amazing things for sale. There will be traveling jugglers, and dancers, and bards. It's like a big trading festival and a carnival in one."

"They'll have candies you can't get anywhere else," Martin spoke up from somewhere in the depths of the wagon.

"Over the winter months I trap some furs, Cinda weaves rugs, and the children weave heavy mats out of grass. The 'vanners buy our goods to sell up north where it gets cold enough that people have more need of such things. We use the money to supplement our income from farming, and we buy a few luxuries as well."

"Mostly it's a fun way to spend a week after a long winter when it's still too wet to plow," Cinda said with a laugh.

They traveled on chatting idly for the rest of the morning before Rufus called for a rest. Cinda and Tina set lunch and Simon went with Rufus while they allowed their prisoner to stretch his legs and relieve himself. The man looked everywhere for the dragon. Simon wasn't sure if he was more afraid because he didn't know where she was, or because he might actually find her.

"A score of men are approaching from the south, Simon. I can't be sure, but I think they are all wearing uniforms."

"Keep a watch and see if they appear hostile. They are most likely a regular patrol, but be ready to move quickly if the need arises. Horne and Trent aren't the closest of allies, but they may have no problem sending me back if they know I am wanted." To Rufus, he said, "Sienna has spotted a group of armed men in uniform heading toward us."

Rufus shook his head, "Soldiers patrol out this way fairly regular. With any luck, we can turn the prisoner over to them."

The bandit began looking around like a scared rabbit about to be caught by hounds and started begging to be set free.

"Shut your trap," Rufus said sharply. "We could have killed you outright; if the soldiers take you, you only face a few years of hard labor repairing roads."

He looked like he might bolt, so Simon said, "If you try and run, I will have the dragon hunt you down and bring back what is left when she's finished."

The man hung his head totally defeated and walked placidly back to the wagon.

A quarter of an hour later the soldiers approached and a young lieutenant and one sergeant rode forward to greet them. Simon had Sienna circle close overhead.

"I can see the dragon is alone up there; where is her Rider?" the lieutenant asked.

"I am the Rider. My name is Simon and my Bond-mate's name is Sienna."

"I had expected someone older. Anyway, while the people of Horne often greet Riders with contempt, we bear no animosity toward your kind here, young sir. You don't have to keep her circling protectively. She can land if she likes."

Simon's eyes appeared to go slightly out of focus as he relayed the message to Sienna.

"Suppose they are simply trying to put us off guard? I am more effective up here."

"Suppose your attitude makes them suspicious and leads to me being discovered? I think you should come down far enough away so you don't spook the horses, and close enough to do so easily if the need arises."

"Good plan, Love, I will land."

Simon smiled at the young officer and said, "I'm having her land over there so she doesn't frighten your mounts."

"Thank you, Rider, that is most courteous of you." Then he turned to Rufus and said, "I take it you are going to gather?" At Rufus's nod, he continued, "How is it you find yourself in the company of a Dragon Rider who prefers to ride in a wagon instead of flying with his partner?"

Rufus quickly told the story of being waylaid by bandits and saved by Simon and Sienna. Simon had to admire that the man didn't embellish on the tale. Then Rufus finished by saying, "We have a prisoner, if you'd like to take custody of him."

The lieutenant had been looking at Simon with new respect. He looked at Rufus and replied, "I'd like to question the man, but I'm afraid we have no way of taking him into custody at this time. We have just set out on patrol and are going to be in the field for two weeks. We can't haul a prisoner around with us. You'll have to turn him over the constable in the village before you get to the ford."

As Rufus led the way to the prisoner, the soldiers stopped short when they saw the chestnut horse. The sergeant whistled and the lieutenant said, "I suppose that is one of the horses you took from the bandits?"

Simon answered first. "Yes, their leader was riding him. He's for sale if you would like to have him."

The sergeant nearly choked and the lieutenant shook his head and said, "Since you risked your life in a fight with the bandit who stole that horse, the law of Trent clearly says the animal belongs to you. However, that horse was the prized breeding stallion of a nobleman who lives in this part of the country, and he won't take kindly to someone else owning the stallion he raised from an unbroken foal. It seems that not only is the horse of superior stock, but that the man has quite an emotional attachment to him as well. While I would personally love to own a mount of that caliber, I wouldn't want the career problems that buying him from you would cause. The man is so attached to that horse he has offered a large reward for his return."

Simon smiled, "Then there is no problem. I have no personal need of a horse, and this animal is much too fine to turn into dragon food, so I will simply return him to his rightful owner and collect the reward for doing so. The nobleman gets his horse back, I am compensated for my time, and everyone wins."

The officer nodded, "You are a smart lad, but just remember not to make any mention of dragon food when talking about this horse to his owner. The man might be somewhat sensitive about the issue."

They all laughed and Simon agreed that he could be discreet when necessary. Then the lieutenant spent nearly a half an hour questioning the prisoner. Finally, after the officer agreed to write a letter pleading for leniency in exchange for cooperation, the bandit became quite helpful and provided a good deal of information regarding the location of several hideouts in the surrounding country. Once all of that business was concluded, letters had been written, and Simon had been given specific directions on how to find the former owner of the chestnut stallion, the soldiers moved on and they were able to get the wagon back on the road.

The remainder of the trip was more subdued. Everyone but Tina had been quiet since meeting the soldiers. The girl talked to Simon quite a bit and he tried to nod and make appropriate comments but, even though his newly maturing body told him to pay attention, he wanted nothing more than to be in the air with Sienna. It was nearly dark by the time they reached the village.

* * *

"We've had this discussion, Rufus," Simon said as he and the farmer walked toward the local jail. "I am the Dragon Rider, and the lieutenant gave the letters to me. I will take the prisoner to the constable and turn him over."

"I don't feel right about it. You may be a Dragon Rider, but you're still an eleven-year-old boy. I feel like I'm shirking my duty or some such."

"Rufus, think this through. If that bandit has friends in town and they see you turning him over to the authorities, you and your family become targets."

"What about you? You could become a target yourself."

"Yes, but I have a rather large, scaly friend who has a vested interest in keeping my hide intact. I will be fine."

Simon looked down at the new tunic and pants that Cinda had given him. They had been Rufus's but were a little small for the man. The clothes were too large for Simon, but they fit well enough to keep him from attracting attention like he would have in the tatters of what was left of his own clothing.

"You and Cinda have done more for me than I had a right to ask, but I am asking that you do one more thing. I will take the chestnut and find that nobleman; you take those other two nags and do with them as you will; either keep them or sell them. I will try to see you again before I leave the gather."

"What do you mean we've done more than you could expect? Oh, you didn't do much, just saved our lives! I can't take those horses."

"You and Cinda have shown me great kindness in a world that has been very unkind to me up until now. I did only what any person with an ounce of self-respect would have done when I saw those bandits on you. As for relieving me of the burden of those animals, I'm no good at horse trading. I'd be cheated out of what little they are worth. You get what you can and buy yourselves something nice with the money."

Rufus softened and shook his head, "You're a good man, Simon. Despite the fact that you're only eleven years old, you're still one of the best men it's been my pleasure to have met. Cinda and the kids will be very upset if you don't see us one more time before you go away, and so will I."

Simon blushed and said, "I'll look for you at the gather when I've finished my other business." Then he turned, and, taking the rope that was tied around the bandit's wrists in one hand and the lead on the chestnut stallion in the other, he headed off to find the constable.

At the door to the jailhouse, he stopped for a moment and spoke to the bandit. "I have no desire to ever see you again, but I want you to know this: that farmer and his family are under my protection, and the dragon knows your scent. If you have friends and they go looking for those people, I will hunt you down no matter where you go. When I find you, I will carry you off to Rorack territory and give you over to those foul beasts. They will eat you alive, and they will keep you alive as long as possible." He paused, looking hard at the man to be sure his threat was believed. "If you are smart, you will forget that those people exist."

The man's eyes were wide with fear as he asked, "What people, Rider?"

"Smart man," he said as he opened the door and led the prisoner inside.

CHAPTER 34

"I DIDN'T FIND YOUR horse, Sir. I recovered him from the bandit who stole him. However, according to the notice you posted at the constable's office, the reward for that animal is for his safe return. It makes no mention of any conditions. So, since I have indeed returned the animal to you, and you have verified that this is your prized stallion, if you will give me the reward I will stop wasting your valuable time and be on my way." Simon's words were courteous, but his tone implied that it was his own time that was being wasted.

Simon had found the estate of the horse's owner – Lord William Johnston – easily enough. He brought the animal right up to the front porch where the Lord was entertaining a large number of people. Since getting their attention he had been subjected to questioning by most of the men present as if he might have stolen the horse in the first place, and he was getting sick and tired of it.

A slightly drunken man who looked to be in his late thirties stepped forward and said, "Recovered him from the bandit who shtole him! I think you are the bandit who shtole him!" He turned to Lord Johnston and repeated himself, "He is the bandit who shtole him, Billy!"

Simon straightened in anger. "I had to kill a man to recover that horse, Lord Johnston. That man was a bandit. The law of this kingdom says that I am entitled to all of that bandit's possessions regardless of who he may have stolen them from. I could have sold that horse at the stock yards legally, and very likely gotten a good deal more than the twenty-five crowns you are offering as a reward. However, my sense of fair play has compelled me to bring the animal back to his previous owner. For my troubles, instead of your thanks and the reward you have advertised, I have received nothing but insult. The next man who accuses me of being a thief had better draw a blade as he does so."

Lord Johnston was taken aback, unsure what to say to this boy who stood speaking like a man. But the man who had just accused Simon of stealing the horse had been loosening his tongue with alcohol all evening, and he had more to say. "You little cur bastard, how dare you speak to your betters that way?"

The man grabbed the nearest thing he could reach—a small three-legged stool—and charged down off the porch. As he did, there was a horrendous cry from above them that sent the object of their discussion bolting toward the barn, and caused everyone except Simon to stop and stare stupidly up into the darkness.

Sienna landed so hard that the people on the porch could feel the impact. This was no young dragon child attempting to look as if she were mature. This was, for all intents and purposes, a fully grown, fully enraged dragon. While the change in her overall color due to her anger wasn't as noticeable in the darkness as it would have been otherwise, her eyes nearly glowed with red malice. Her teeth were bared and she hissed dangerously.

"If anyone here tries to strike my Rider, there will be much blood spilled on this ground tonight!"

Two of the women on the porch screamed, and one man actually fainted.

Simon quickly stepped in front of her and said, "Peace, Sienna. I don't want any blood shed here. These people pose no threat to either of us." He looked directly back at the man who had, just seconds before, been charging at him in a half-drunken rage.

The man was frozen in his tracks. He opened his hand limply

and let the wooden stool fall from his grasp. Then, unable to speak, he simply smiled at Simon and nodded.

The dragon relaxed, but only a little. She allowed her wings, which had been fully extended, to retract as she bent her knees slightly and settled a little lower to the ground. The overall effect made it seem as if she had actually shrunken a bit. Then she closed her mouth, hiding those formidable teeth.

Simon turned to Lord Johnston and said, "You have my apologies. While I am not wine besotted, I am tired from my travels, and that has made me irritable. I had a right to take offense, but I should have considered the source and chosen my own words more carefully."

The man stood staring for so long Simon wasn't sure he would accept the apology. Then he spoke up, "No real harm done, Rider. Harry here," he pointed at the drunk who had threatened the boy, "tends to over do at these parties. He is really quite harmless and none of us take offense, but he forgets that strangers may not be so forgiving of his insults. I'm just glad this didn't get completely out of hand. One day Harry's sharp tongue is likely to get him into real trouble."

"Well," Harry spoke up, playing to the crowd. "Now we know how a boy defeated a desperate bandit. He stood back and watched while this colossal beast squashed the man like an insect."

Sienna growled dangerously and said, "Simon defeated that man without my help, and you are very lucky that I chose to intervene before he dealt with you."

Harry tried to step back when the dragon growled, and, tripping over his own feet, sat down hard enough to leave himself breathless.

"Sienna," Simon said out loud. "You can't reason with someone who has had that much to drink. Ignore him."

Lord Johnston spoke, "You're right of course, Rider. And wise beyond your apparent years. I will go and fetch your reward money. In the meantime, there are refreshments laid out on the veranda, please help yourself." He hauled Harry to his feet and dragged him along as he went.

Simon wasn't used to deferential treatment from someone like Lord Johnston, so he didn't move. After a moment, a young woman, in her late teens—perhaps as old as twenty—stepped down from the porch and shyly held a plate of finger sandwiches and a glass of fruit punch for him. He took a sandwich and the drink and thanked her. She stood about five-foot-four, and Simon was surprised to find that he was looking down at her. He quickly estimated his own height to be about five-nine.

A woman on the porch poked her friend and pointed, mistaking Simon's prolonged stare into the young lady's eyes to mean that he was smitten with her. The two women giggled like young girls and watched intently.

Sienna didn't miss what was happening and became a bit jealous. "We should finish our business and leave as quickly as possible!"

"I am only waiting for the Lord of this estate to return with the money. I have no desire to stay here any longer than necessary."

The women on the porch mistook Simon's now dreamy expression as further confirmation that he was thoroughly infatuated, not knowing that he was in silent communication with the dragon.

"Then you should stop staring at that young woman and pay attention to other concerns."

Simon hadn't even realized that he was staring. He quickly thanked the young lady for the food and drink again, and turned back to his Bond-mate.

"You are jealous," he teased.

"I am not jealous! I am being protective. Despite your size, you are still a young boy. That woman is nearly twice your age. She has no right to make advances on you like she is doing."

"She brought me a sandwich and something to drink. She was only being courteous."

"Courtesy doesn't require that she stand there ogling you while you eat. You are obviously not ready for such a relationship! Therefore, I feel it is my duty, as your Bond-mate, to protect you from her feminine wiles."

Simon nearly laughed out loud. He was about to mention that such *'protection'* looked amazingly like jealousy to him, but Johnston returned at that moment with Harry following in his wake.

"Ah, here you are. And I see you have been given refreshment." He smiled and turned to the young woman, "Thank you for seeing to our guest, Sharon," he said to her as he subtly shooed her back onto the porch. Then he handed Simon a small jeweled, silken purse: the bag itself was easily worth several gold. "Twenty-five gold crowns, Rider, as promised."

Simon began fumbling for his own pouch to put the money in and Johnston said quickly, "Keep the purse, Rider. Consider it a small gift to make up for how badly you were treated when you first arrived."

"Thank you, Sir. I won't take up any more of your time." He looked around for a convenient place to set his glass and there was none. Before the situation could turn awkward, a servant stepped forward and relieved him of the burden. The slight interlude gave Harry a chance to finish the contents of his own glass and find his voice.

"I find it odd that a Dragon Rider, so virtuous, and elevated above the rest of us common folk," Harry was nearly shouting, and there was much whispering and even some laughter among the people still standing on the veranda. The man looked back and smiled at his audience nearly forgetting what he was doing. He started again. "I find it odd that one sush as you would shtoop to sush depths and accept money for sush noble deeds." He bowed so low to Simon that he lost his balance and had to take two steps forward to catch himself. Lord Johnston grabbed him by the arm and tried to shush him, but Harry would have none of it. He pulled his arm free and said, "Tell us, Rider." He made the title an insult. "Why would one so high and noble need something as commonplace as money?"

Simon had been about to ignore the idiot and leave, but the looks from some of those watching told him that they thought it was a valid question. He had lived on an estate for several years and had heard Lord Bastian make such asinine observations; first about

Warrick's riders, and then even more so about the honest Riders who replaced Warrick at the old fort. Something inside him just snapped.

"Why would a Dragon Rider need money?" he asked sarcastically. "Your tongue may be sharp, but that stuff in your glass has dulled your wit to the point of stupidity." Anger flashed across the drunken man's face, but Johnston grabbed him and held him back. Simon wasn't finished, though. "What would you have a Rider do? Would you condone him taking the clothing and other supplies that he needs without compensating the honest merchant who sells the goods? Are you suggesting that cattlemen shouldn't be paid if a dragon eats one of their herd? I have heard tales of Riders who do those things, and those tales are usually ended with curses on all Dragon Riders for the excess of a few."

Johnston started to speak up, but Simon didn't give him a chance. "Yesterday Sienna and I saw a family set upon by four bandits. We could have ignored it and kept flying with no one the wiser, but we felt compelled to help those people. During the fight, I was forced to kill one of them with my own blade, and Sienna killed another. A third bandit died, dragged by his own horse when it bolted trying to get away from the dragon. The fourth man we took as a prisoner. Then we helped those people by giving them one of the bandit's horses to replace their animal that had been killed. Sienna and I didn't save those people because we expected compensation; we did it because it was the right thing to do. Returning Lord Johnston's horse wasn't required of us, and has put me to some considerable amount of trouble. And now I am being treated like a beggar because I have accepted this money for going out of my way to return this man's property."

None of the guests would meet Simon's gaze. Lord Johnston cleared his throat and said, "You have done right by me, Rider, and have received little but insult for your trouble. You have my apologies."

The man held out his hand and Simon grasped wrists with him and shook. Then he turned without another word and walked back to Sienna. Once he was in place, she launched skyward and Simon instructed her to find a nice place to sleep. He leaned forward and laid his body against her neck and they flew in silence.

Chapter 35

THEY HAD SPENT the night in the open near the river that flowed through the center of town, and were just southeast of the village of Ford. The village itself had been named for the obvious reason of being situated on the shallow crossing of the waterway. The small community received a stipend from the Crown for maintaining the crossing on the most important trade route through the territory.

They were upstream from the town, and Simon could see no one nearby. Once he finished with morning necessities, he stripped out of his tunic and trousers and waded into the river. It wasn't as nice as a hot bath would be, and he didn't have soap and sponge – a situation he intended to rectify soon – but he was able to wash away yesterday's dirt.

"You were preoccupied last night after dealing with those people, Dearest. Are you better now?" Sienna asked.

"I believe so. I was upset at the attitude concerning Riders. It's like I'm damned if I do and damned if I don't. If I take compensation for our troubles, it makes us ignoble. If I don't take compensation and ask for the supplies we need without paying, we become parasites. If we simply take what we need, we are thieves. It's as if we are not only expected to protect the lands from evil, but also take up a trade." He made a rude noise and added, "I wonder how well they would think of us if I opened a smithy and fell behind in my work because I was busy chasing bandits while you depleted the area of game."

"My understanding of such human interactions is very limited. I'm afraid I have no answers for you, my love."

"I wasn't looking for answers, Sienna. I was merely voicing my frustration. I'm afraid that you and I will both grow old and die together without ever achieving universal approval. That, my love, is why we have each other."

The dragon nodded and said, "If you wish to retain your modesty I suggest that you don some clothing. There are several people about to emerge over the hill behind us."

He barely had time to slip into his pants before four mounted individuals came into view. "*Why didn't you tell me sooner?*"

"Don't be upset, I would have warned you if I thought they were dangerous. And while I see no reason to be concerned with such things, I could have shielded you from view if you hadn't gotten your pants on. I didn't want to interrupt your bath."

"We've found you," one of the men exclaimed unnecessarily.

Simon recognized him as one of Lord Johnston's servants. Two of the other riders were also male, but the fourth was the young woman, Sharon. Sienna bristled and he *cautioned* her against scaring these people.

"I didn't realize that I had gotten lost," he responded to the initial remark.

Sharon giggled prettily as she dismounted. Fortunately, no one but Simon heard Sienna's soft growl or noticed that her color had gone more red.

"You have a sharp wit, Rider," she said.

"You have a sharp wit, Rider," Sienna mimicked the girl unkindly. "And I just can't take my huge doe eyes off of your muscular chest."

Simon *said* nothing, but shot her a look that left no doubt that he wanted her to behave. Sienna snorted her contempt and stared back rebelliously.

He tried to ignore her and turned his attention back to the young woman. "If I may be blunt..." He realized that Sienna had been right.

The girl was staring at his chest, and it confused him. The dragon had been right last night also: a woman like this shouldn't be showing such interest in a boy his age. Of course, he had always been bigger and more physically mature than other boys of his own age, and, because of the magic, he had been growing at an increased rate since bonding. He could easily be mistaken for fifteen, and would probably be believed if he claimed to be seventeen. In Horne, sixteen would make him old enough to marry, and the law was probably similar in Trent. The two countries were closely related even if they weren't close allies.

"That is more than idle curiosity I see in those overly large eyes of hers," Sienna said. "Perhaps you should stop stammering and see what she wants so she will go away."

Again he gave that look to his Bond-mate, and again her look told him she would not be dismissed.

"If I may be so bold as to come directly to the point," he continued, "What has brought you out looking for me this morning?"

"If I don't like the answer to that question I am going to eat her horse and make her walk back to the estate," Sienna purred maliciously.

Simon ignored the dragon completely.

"My father, Lord Johnston, would like you to join us for supper this evening. I, that is to say, we all feel badly about how you were treated by our other guests and would like to make it up to you."

"I have much to do in town today. What time would I be expected to come?"

"We will dine at six. My father will be expecting you then." She reached out and laid her hand on his arm and added, "You may come earlier if you like. I could show you around the estate."

"If she bats those eyes at you one more time I am going to throw her in the river!"

"Sienna, please! There is nothing happening between me and this young woman."

"Really? The last time your heart was beating this fast we were fleeing for our lives from beast-men. Of course, that predatory look she is giving you does put me in mind of those creatures.

He shook his head as if to clear it and said to Sharon, "Tell your father I will be there." Then, almost as an afterthought, he added, "For supper."

Sharon smiled and turned to mount her horse. One of the men moved to help her, but she didn't wait for him. She grabbed the reins and a significant hank of mane in her left hand while she lifted her skirt and raised her left foot high up to the stirrup. As she did, her skirt slipped further up her leg showing off quite a bit of her thigh almost to her buttocks. She stood for a moment as if she needed extra time to make the climb before smiling back at him and mounting.

"She shouldn't show off her haunch like that to a dragon. I'll bet she tastes a lot like wild pig."

"You have no reason to be jealous, Love." Then he added mischievously, "I didn't even notice that long expanse of shapely thigh, or how wonderfully smooth the skin was under her dress."

It was over an hour before Sienna would even speak to him again.

CHAPTER 36

I T DIDN'T TAKE long for Simon to find the blacksmith's shop. He could feel his stomach knotting and his throat tightening at the familiarity of the place. While this shop wasn't the one where he studied under Boron, it was very much akin to it, right down to the smell of the coal fired forge. It took several moments for him to fight down the wave of homesickness that threatened to actually make him physically ill. He waited until he had his emotions under control before he approached the smith.

"What is it, lad? I don't have time for nonsense, and I have no small tasks that need doing. If you've come looking for work of that sort to earn money for the gather, you might do better sweeping out one of the merchant's shops." The smith did not even glance up from his work.

"I am not looking for work," Simon said as if addressing an equal rather than an elder. It hadn't taken him long to figure out that addressing someone as if he were an equal, whether that person liked him speaking to them that way or not, tended to get the person's full attention. "I am looking to commission some work I need done, and I have money to pay for it."

The smith stopped what he was doing and really looked at Simon.

The boy pulled out the silk purse and rattled the coins inside. "As I said, I can pay you for your time."

The man's eyes widened and then he shook his head sadly. "Well son, as much as I'd like to help you lighten that purse, I'm swamped right now. This is my busiest time of year. Folks from all over the kingdom come to this gather, and most of them on the outlying farms save up the work they need me to do for the year and bring it with them. Then there's the caravans as well; this is almost the halfway point for many of them coming and going, and they can only do so much of their work themselves while traveling. I have more to do right now than I can handle."

Just then two men walked in. One was fair skinned, and the other was so dark that his skin was nearly black as jet. They walked up to the smith and the light-skinned man said, "We need to speak with you, smith. We have work that can't wait."

Before the smith could say a word, Simon spoke up. "Excuse me. While I would normally be courteous, especially since your business appears urgent, today I have much to accomplish, and little time to do it all. I was here first."

The light-skinned man said, "You obnoxious little pup!" and grabbed Simon by the shirt.

Simon, startled by the sudden ferocity, reacted on instincts honed by his training with Boron. He twisted around and threw his shoulder into the man's midsection while he grabbed his attacker's arm and threw forward with all of his might. The man flipped over Simon's back and landed hard on his own. Unfortunately, he also held onto the boy's shirt and ripped it open almost all the way down the front.

"Damn it, Ted," the smith shouted at the dark-skinned man, "I've told you often enough that you vanners get no special attention from me. This boy is a paying customer and has as much privilege in my shop as you do. If you can't keep your hired hands under control, leave 'em in camp. Don't bring 'em here!"

His words were completely lost on Ted. The man was staring wide-eyed at Simon. More specifically, he was staring wide-eyed at Simon's dragon mark.

The light-skinned man had gotten to his hands and knees, and Ted shoved him so hard he ended up on his back again. "You've done it this time, Derrick. I've told you before to keep your man-parts in their proper place when dealing town folks. Now you've left them out for the world to see, and you'll be lucky if they don't get ripped off by this Rider's dragon!"

He looked back out in the morning light and then turned his gaze skyward as if expecting the dragon to swoop down on them at any second. When no attack came he turned to Simon and said, "I'm sorry, Rider. Derrick is one of the best teamsters there is, but he's not much for social graces."

Simon, who had instinctively drawn his long knife, and was now still holding it, didn't say anything. He was already getting damn tired of hearing "I'm sorry, Rider" after some idiot had simply assumed he was a street urchin who could be either ignored or bullied into compliance. He had only been back in the company of humans for a little more than two days, and he was beginning to wonder if he had been better off when he was being chased by beast-men.

"Fine," he finally replied, looking down at his torn garment. "But he owes me a new shirt."

Derrick sat up and said incredulously, "Dragon or no dragon, I won't be manhandled and then talked down to by some whelp."

Ted kicked him hard enough to elicit a yelp of pain. "You damn fool! Don't you see that skewer he's holding?" As Derrick looked where Ted was pointing, the caravan master spoke with awe in his voice. "That's a Dragon Blade in his hand. I've traveled most of the known world for more than twenty years and in all of that time I've seen one other in my life. The only way a new Rider earns one of those is by proving his bravery in service to his dragon's mother."

The smith looked at Simon with new respect, and even Derrick shut up and paid attention to Ted.

"I'd be willing to bet, Derrick, that this 'boy' has seen and done more in his life than you will ever do. In fact, I'd lay money on two things." He ticked the points off on his fingers. "One: that he's seen and done more than you would believe if he were twenty years older and twice as large. Two: even half of what this lad has been through would have you peeing in your britches just thinking about it." He paused before adding, "As for paying for the shirt you ruined, you'll do it or you can find a new job! I can't have someone in my employ creating bad blood between me and a Dragon Rider."

"I wouldn't hold this man's bad behavior against you, Sir."

"Doesn't matter, Son, I've been in a rough spot or two and had a Rider and his partner come to my rescue without thought of reward or even his own safety. I won't repay that by letting someone in my employ give insult to one of you."

Derrick was on his feet and he handed Simon three silver coins. "That should cover the cost of a new shirt, Rider. Ted's right; I need to control my temper. I apologize for what I've done, and thank you for not skewering me with that blade."

"We'll stand over here and let the Rider finish his business, Tom," Ted said to the smith.

Tom turned to his young customer. "You obviously don't need to have a horse shod, and you have a blade that is better than any I could make for you. So, Rider, what is it you need from me?"

"Well, it's about my blades actually," Simon responded. Then he pulled out his other Dragon Blade. As all three of the men in the shop gasped, he continued, "I need to have both of them fitted with guards and hilts."

Tom finally found his voice, "How is it that you came by two of these blades?"

"I don't know. When my dragon's mother etched them onto the egg, even she was surprised. She said she didn't think that there had ever been two blades etched onto a single egg before."

"I've never heard of such," Ted assured all of them, and Derrick nodded in agreement with him.

"Whatever we make for them will have to be pressed on. I've never personally worked on one of these, but I do know that no drill will penetrate that material to make a rivet hole."

"I was thinking we could sand cast the pieces in bronze and then drive them on hot. When they cool, they should shrink enough to hold fast."

Tom was impressed. "You know a bit about metal work."

"I spent nearly a year working in a blacksmith's shop. I'm not a journeyman, but I know my way around a forge."

The smith was obviously eager to work on the Dragon Blades, but he shook his head and said, "It's still no good. I'd like to help you, lad, but I'm working like two just trying to keep up with what I've already taken in."

Simon brightened, "I'll make you a deal. I'll come back tomorrow and start helping you with your work. I'll work for you for three days. When we catch up a bit, you can help me make the pieces for my blades. That way you get the help you need, and I get to keep my coins in my purse."

Tom considered his offer carefully before saying, "All right. Mind you, I mean no offense. I just don't know you. But if you aren't as handy in the shop as you think you are, I have the right to put a halt to this deal."

Simon smiled and held out his hand. "Done. I'll be back bright and early tomorrow."

After sealing the deal with the smith, he went in search of some new clothes. He bought three new shirts, two pairs of pants, and a set of light slippers, as well as new boots, and four pairs of stockings. The merchant looked at him strangely when he asked for a sweater, a heavy coat, and some gloves, but his money was still good even if the man thought his mind might not be sound. He spent quite a bit more than three silvers buying the garments.

He knew he would need a proper saddle soon. Flying without one that first day had left him a bit chafed by Sienna's scales. However, he decided to get some food before looking for a leather worker. He found a shop that sold pastries and decided to treat himself to something sweet. On the counter, he saw large rolled pastries filled with cinnamon and nuts and drizzled with honey. He bought one of those and a mug of milk. He didn't want to be bothered with coming back just to return the mug, so he found a space under the stairs that ran behind the counter and sat down.

He was thoroughly enjoying the decadence of the sweet roll when the conversation of two new patrons caught his attention.

"I'm telling you, except for the kid's height, the description of the boy is exactly the same," one voice said as if the argument had been made before.

"That may be, or it may be that this lad is older and just looks like that runaway from Horne. Also, and this is the most important thing, the description of the boy we're looking for said nothing about a dragon mark on his chest," the second voice countered. "That's a pretty big distinction, if you ask me."

"So he grew a bit and found a dragon egg since he escaped from up north. What's the difference? There's still a two-hundred-fifty gold piece reward for returning him to that Lord Bastian fellow."

"What's the difference? You idiot, you don't get a dragon mark unless you're bonded to a dragon. So even if it is the same one, he is now traveling with a dragon."

"So? Who cares about that? We don't have to take the dragon back, just the boy."

The man sighed heavily and asked, "How can you be so stupid and live? Do you think that dragon is just going to sit on her haunches and let us take that kid back to Horne?"

"I'm not afraid of that beast. From what I know of them critters, she can't be old enough to breathe fire yet. What's the problem?"

The man snorted and replied, "There must be some god who looks after morons, because the only way you could have survived this long is by divine intervention. Have you ever seen a dragon? I'm not talking about pictures, or off flying in the distance. I mean, have you ever been close to the real thing?"

"No, but what's that got to do with anything?" The second man started to answer, but the first cut him off and continued, "Look, working as guards on that trade caravan from home is a good paying job, but it won't make us rich. We could make this run twice a year for the next five years, and both of us together couldn't save up half as much gold as we can make for taking one kid back to Horne.

I'm doing this, and if that dragon tries to stop me, it will just be too damn bad for her."

It took several moments for the other man to get control of his laughter enough to respond. "Too bad for her is it? Let me explain something to you, little brother. Dragons are not stupid beasts that can be easily dealt with by tossing them a bone as a distraction. I'd dare say they are much smarter than you." He paused and drew a deep breath. "I fought in the army of Horne against Warrick and his beast-men. I was there the day those dragons fired that plain around the old fort and killed those monsters by the thousands. Even I, as much as I hate those creatures, couldn't help but feel a bit sorry for them as I watched them burn."

"As I said, this one is too young to breathe fire."

"So, she'll have to tear you limb from limb instead!" the older brother nearly shouted. "I stayed on for almost a year after the war was over. I've seen those creatures up close. I once saw a baby dragon, less than a week old, eat half a steer. Its teeth cut through the thickest bones like a hot knife through butter. A dragon as large as the one we've been told about could kill both of us as easily as we could swat a fly. You can't sneak up on them either; they'd know you were there before you got within half a mile. If your divine luck holds long enough for you to get the boy and sneak out of town, you'd never make it to the border, much less all the way back to collect that reward before she tracked you down and rescued him."

"There must be some way to do this. This kingdom can't harbor a criminal like this."

"We've already discussed that with the local constable. If we had an actual warrant, signed by the king of Horne, they might allow us to take the boy back if he were just some kid. But even if we had such a warrant, they would never condone us going against a Rider. The Riders are treated like royalty in these parts. If we somehow neutralized the threat of the dragon, the soldiers of Trent would stop us from taking the kid back. You need to give up this madness, little brother. You can't collect that reward if you're dead."

"I'm going to do this, brother, whether you help me or not."

"That's fine. You're seventeen and an adult now. I can't stop you if you put your mind to it, but do me one favor first."

Simon sneaked a peek around the counter and saw the younger man—a gangly youth—nod his head at his older sibling, who Simon couldn't quite get a look at.

"Sit down and write a letter to our mother," the older brother continued. "Explain to her why her youngest son is dead and I'm an only child. Make sure you tell her that I spent all this time trying to talk you out of this madness, so that I don't have to try and convince her it wasn't my fault that there weren't even any pieces of you left that were big enough to take home and bury in the family graveyard."

The younger brother said nothing as the two took their purchases and left the bakery.

Simon wasn't sure what emotion was the strongest concerning the conversation he'd just overheard. He was surprised to hear that Bastian had survived. To some extent, he was amused by the argument between the pair. It appeared that the older brother clearly had no intention of helping his younger sibling go against a dragon, while the younger brother was mostly just fantasizing and would do nothing without the other's approval and help. However, he had just barely gotten back to civilization and already Bastian's offer of a reward had found him out. He was angry because he didn't want to have to go back into hiding any time soon.

As he left the shop, he reached out for Sienna. She was still a bit miffed at him, but the jealousy issue was completely driven from her mind once Simon had relayed the conversation he'd overheard.

"I know that we had agreed that I might cause a panic among the local livestock if I actually came into the town, but circumstances have changed. I will not allow you to be so far away from me knowing that there is someone, even an idiot like the younger of the pair you described, who wants to capture you and take you back to Horne. I am coming to you."

Instead of arguing with her he said, "That might even work out, Dear Heart. We need to see about having a saddle made anyway.

Meet me at the tannery that is near the river on the edge of town."

"Very well, I will finish eating and meet you there."

Simon had the uneasy feeling that he was being watched as he went to meet Sienna. He frequently glanced over his shoulder as he moved along. He couldn't obviously see anyone following, but he couldn't shake the feeling either. He rested one hand on his sword as he walked.

There were no people in the yard of the tannery. Simon could understand why as he got a whiff of the place. Turning hides into leather was a smelly business. As he headed for the door to the leather worker who kept a shop right at the source of his trade, a voice he recognized as the younger of the two brothers spoke up.

"Going somewhere important, Dragon Boy?"

Simon had *known* they were there, so he wasn't surprised to see both brothers standing less than thirty feet away from him as he turned around. What the brothers hadn't expected were his quick reflexes: by the time he was facing them, both Dragon Blades were in his hands at the ready.

The older brother became wary, but the younger was unconcerned that his quarry was well-armed and appeared capable. The older one was holding back, more like he was just there to observe.

"Where's your dragon, boy?" the younger man asked.

"Right above you," came Sienna's angry voice as her shadow blocked out the sun.

The older brother turned the color of bleached linen and backed up several paces as the dragon settled to earth between her Bondmate and his antagonists. The younger brother paled as well, but seemed unable to move a muscle. Apparently, in the presence of the real thing, his earlier bluster concerning dragons dissipated like a wisp of steam.

Simon stepped up beside Sienna as several people came out of the tannery to see the dragon. "Now then," he said. "I was in the bakery and heard your earlier conversation about me, and I can assure you that I will return to Horne when I am ready. Trent will honor no warrant from Lord Bastian for my return, and if you try and force me to go now, this meeting will end very badly for you. In Horne, I may be considered a wanted criminal, but here I am a respected Dragon Rider. The local authorities will not be upset if we kill two men who are trying to kidnap me."

The older brother found his voice and yelled nearly hysterically at his sibling, "I told you, Gordon! This is way beyond you. Now that you have seen a dragon up close, maybe you'll forget this insane idea and come along." He looked at Simon and said, "I only came along on this so my baby brother could see her up close and realize how stupid he's being."

The younger man shook his head, backed nearer to his brother and said, "I didn't believe you, Jordan, but she's huge."

Sienna showed her teeth and Simon said, "Now that you fully understand the foolishness of this venture, I do not expect to see either of you again. Leave quickly, before she decides that you are too much of a threat to be left alive."

Jordan grabbed his brother by the scruff of the neck and back-peddled. "You won't see us again, Rider. We'll be leaving for Horne with a caravan soon."

"Good," Sienna shot back. "See that you stick to that plan. I will always be close to my Bond-mate, and I will kill you both if I catch your scent near us again!"

The two turned to run and Simon shouted, "Tell Bastian that I will be back! But on my terms! Not his! Tell him that anyone he sends looking for me will die if they find me!"

"I don't think they heard you, Dearest. They were running so fast that I doubt they heard anything other than the sound of their own feet on the ground."

"It doesn't matter, everyone else near us heard, and the story will spread." Then he remembered the business at hand. "I have to go inside and see about having a saddle made, Sienna. If you wait here, it will be more convenient to find you when the leatherworker needs to take measurements."

"You do what you need to do, Simon. I am not going anywhere. As long as we are still this close to Horne, I have no intention of letting you get farther away than I can jump in one leap."

A few minutes later, he came back out of the building followed by a tall, gaunt, middle-aged man.

"How long the saddle will take depends somewhat on your need," the man said as they approached Sienna. He showed no fear of the dragon whatsoever. "The most common design of saddle is large enough for two riders and requires more material and time to complete. It is more comfortable on a long flight and has a greater area to tie on your personal belongings. Of course, the more you carry, the more the load will fatigue your partner. A smaller saddle can be made comfortable enough for normal use, but if you carry a passenger, that person will be sitting directly on the dragon's scales and be subject to abrasion as the dragon flies. And, of course, you will have to be creative, as well as more frugal, when packing your belongings."

"I need to get into the air soon, within a week if possible. Also, I have some money, but I am far from rich. I have seventeen gold sovereigns from Horne to spend if it takes that much. I trust that since gold is still gold, there will be no problem using those coins to settle my debt." He didn't add that he also had twenty-four gold coins in local currency since he wanted to divest himself of the money from his homeland.

"We are situated at the junction of two major trade routes; north/south, and east/west. I regularly trade with merchants from Horne; the exchange rate is no problem. I believe I can accommodate you without completely depleting your resources, and I also believe I have just the design for your needs. There is a set of drawings for a saddle that my father designed when I was a boy. I can't even remember the Rider's name. However, that saddle is large enough to be comfortable but lighter than most saddles I have seen in more recent years. There is a flap of leather that can be unfolded to keep a passenger's legs and buttocks from being abraded by the dragons scales or used to roll your belongings in if you are alone. I believe it will be quite adequate for your needs and still be less weight for your partner to carry."

"How long will it take to complete?"

"Five days, maybe six." The man moved closer to Sienna and spoke directly to her. "If you don't mind, my dear, I would like to take some measurements."

Sienna was surprised to be spoken to so directly, but pleased by the man's courteous manner. "You may do so," she replied pleasantly.

He pulled a rolled up cord out of the pocket of his apron and walked along her side and stopped where her ribs ended. Then he said, "Just hold still, please. This won't be uncomfortable at all." Speaking like a teacher to Simon, he added, "This area just where the rib cage ends is where the belly strap of the rig rides. The elongated indentation here," he pointed to what looked like a small rut that ran from Sienna's backbone to her underbelly, "works as if it were specifically made for the purpose of keeping the belt stable. The band that rides here is used to hold other straps that help keep the saddle from moving side to side or slipping forward on her neck."

He paused a moment before turning to Simon. "There is, now that I think about it, a design for a small saddle that uses only two straps that cross over the dragon's back between her wings that is less cumbersome, but it has no provision for a passenger, and doesn't facilitate carrying much in the way of supplies at all. Such a rig is sometimes kept by Riders who remain in residence at one place for extended periods. It's cheaper and easier to make and much easier to secure into place, but isn't suited to your need to travel unless you are very adept at living off the land. By converting a standard horse saddle, I could have one of that type made by the day after tomorrow."

"Let me talk it over with Sienna. After all, she will have to deal with the extra weight." He turned to his bond-mate. "What do you think, Love? I'd like to have room for some supplies, but I'll go with whatever you say, since your comfort is more important in this matter."

"You know that I love you, Simon, so don't be offended at what I'm about to say. I don't find your scent unpleasant when you are clean, but I have had occasion to smell you when you have been working hard with no opportunity to bathe and wash your clothing. The smell of human sweat after it has had some time to ripen is unpleasant. I would prefer that you be able to bring soap and a couple of changes of clothes. Also, humans thrive better if they have more than just meat in their diet, so having room for some dried fruit and vegetables would be beneficial."

"Alright, Love, I understand." He turned back to the craftsman and said, "We'll take the larger saddle that you first mentioned, please."

The tanner nodded and threw the cord over the dragon's back and asked her to stand. When she obliged, he bent low and stepped under to grab the far end of the cord and used it to measure the circumference. Then he measured the circumference of her neck, and the distance from the edge of the depression where the saddle would sit to where the belly strap would ride. With Simon's help, he measured from the seat area to the belly strap along her spine. He also measured the distance from the edge of one side of the seat depression to the other, explaining that the saddle itself needed to set against the edges and not fill the entire space because there needed to be room for the flame bladder to expand when she filled it in preparation for breathing fire. Simon was actually quite impressed with the man's knowledge of draconic anatomy.

It took over an hour before the craftsman was satisfied. Then he again spoke directly to Sienna. "I'm sorry for any inconvenience, dear lady, but I have always said that if you measure twice you only need to cut once. I would rather err on the side of caution now than make a mistake in the actual production, especially since a failure of equipment could be so devastating."

"Not at all," she responded equally polite. "I understand completely. You have been most courteous, and I haven't been inconvenienced in the least."

He turned to Simon and said, "I will start on this immediately. Check back with me in four days. I will be almost finished and we can do a fitting and make any final adjustments." Then he walked back into the shop without another word.

CHAPTER 37

"IT HAS BEEN exactly six hours since noon, so by my reckoning you are right on time," Sienna said as she landed about ten yards from the Johnston manor house.

"It would have been courteous to be a few minutes early," he responded irritably. "You deliberately circled for a quarter of an hour waiting for the exact time of our invitation. Since it is now at least two full minutes after the sixth hour, you have made me late."

He wasn't sure why he was so upset at her. It wasn't just that he thought her jealousy was foolish, especially since he had no intention of giving himself over to Sharon's advances. However, he had to admit, at least to himself, that he found it surprisingly stimulating to have a beautiful young woman so interested in him. He was willing to play along up to a point.

"You only wanted to take that girl up on her offer to show you around the estate. Since she has intentions of showing you much more than the surrounding countryside, I did what is best for you."

"I can't believe that you not only don't deny your motives but that you are still trying to delude me into believing you are acting out concern for me and not out of jealousy. I believe it is the denial that upsets me the most."

"I am not in denial!" She growled as she spoke. "I admit that I resent having another female get between us, even though I know that such feelings are ungrounded. But I do think that the girl is much too old and mature for you. You are not ready for the kind of relationship she is seeking, especially considering your past."

Simon leaped down and rounded on her. "What has my past got to do with Sharon?"

"Your past has everything to do with it. You were badly used, and that will affect how you interact with another human in the future."

"What happened was not under my control, and I have put it behind me. I will have to go over it yet again when we do return to Horne to settle the matter, but until that time I refuse to allow Broderick to overshadow the rest of my life. I have spent more than a year taking that power away from him. I don't intend to give it back now!"

"Very well," she said dejectedly. "I will stop interfering, but I hope you are not making a mistake."

"Sienna," he said softly. "I can't let what has happened ruin the rest of my life. It would be bad enough to allow it to consume me for eighty or ninety years when I could put it behind me and move on. I certainly can't allow it to do so for the next three millennia or possibly more. Past experiences may shape us, but they don't have to rule our lives."

"You are right, Simon. You have to move on. I just hope you know what you are doing in this instance."

He smiled and hugged her. "Don't worry about it. While I find that I am flattered by this young woman's advances, I have no intention of accepting her offers, and she is only offering because she has no idea of how young I actually am."

Before the dragon could respond, a servant appeared to lead him into the house.

The conversation during the main course of supper was nothing more than idle chit-chat. Lord Johnston told Simon about raising horses while trying to keep up with his cattle interests. Simon tried to make occasional appropriate responses while remembering to keep his lips pressed together as he chewed his food, and not to talk with his mouth full. Fortunately for the boy, Sharon had found out his real age, and had done nothing more provocative than smile prettily at him since his arrival.

Once they were finished with dessert and were reduced to picking at small fruits while sipping wine-laced fruit punch, Lord Johnston moved to meatier subjects.

"Tell me, Simon. What was that whole scene at the leather works this afternoon about? I know that those two youngsters from Horne have been talking about nothing but you all over town since you delivered that bandit to the constabulary. They even tried to get the locals to arrest you for them. What could a boy so young have done to become a wanted criminal with such a high price on his head?"

Simon couldn't respond. Johnston's wife, Marie, mistaking Simon's shock for offense, chided her husband. "William, you've upset our guest. Perhaps he doesn't want his personal business aired in public like dirty linen."

Johnston was about to reply when Simon found his voice. "I'm not upset with the question. I was just surprised that His Lordship seems to know so much about it."

The man smiled and replied, "First, you may call me Bill. Second, I know everything that happens in Ford, especially when it happens on my property." At the boy's puzzled look, he added, "I own the tannery. Since our family holds the largest cattle ranch in this region, my father had it built, as well as the large smokehouse on the other end of town to process the steers we don't send out with the drovers. I heard about that little bit of drama from the foreman."

Simon sipped his drink to give himself time to collect his thoughts and decide just how much of the tale to tell.

"My father died owing Lord Bastian a large amount of money. I was indentured to pay that debt. During my time on the estate, I got on the wrong side of Bastian's son. Broderick, nearly six years older than me, attacked me, and I'm afraid I injured him rather badly. I knew that I would most likely be killed for what I had done, so I fled. Bastian caught up with me at the edge of Rorack territory."

At the mention of the beast-men, both women gasped. "I was alone, armed only with a dagger, and outnumbered by Bastian and the men he led to hunt me down. I had no choice but to cause a rock slide to prevent them from catching up to me. Several of the men were killed, and, at the time, I thought Bastian had died in the avalanche as well. After that, I escaped into the mountains and began to work my way south."

"I know of this Lord Bastian. I sent cattle to the Dragon Riders in the north of Horne. His lands cover both sides of the route, and both times he charged a high price for allowing my drovers to water our herds while on his property. Because he makes it so expensive to get our steers there, I have had to refuse the Riders' requests for more cattle. I think he does that to make sure that he is the only one who can make a profit selling his stock to the Riders. I have no idea how much he gouges them for the animals he sells."

Simon nodded his head and said, "Yes, I see that you understand the man."

"I believe you have kept some details of the events to yourself, but I will respect your privacy and accept that you are truly the injured party in this. We do allow reasonable indenture in this country, but we don't condone holding a child responsible for a parent's debt. Also, even the King of Horne himself couldn't sway Trent to extradite a Dragon Rider back to Horne, so you are safe here."

"I thank you for your assurances, Bill. But even so, I won't be staying long. I have to travel south anyway, and what happened today has only reinforced that. I will be leaving soon."

Sharon did pout at that news, but only a little. No one other than Simon noticed, and he silently chided himself for what could be nothing more than wishful thinking on his part.

Johnston was thoughtful for a moment and then spoke up. "Let me see if I understand the matter. You escaped from Bastian's estate with little more than a dagger and the clothes on your back into the heart of the beast-men's territory. You not only, by some miracle, survived, but you emerged more than two months later with a dragon. That's a story I want to hear. Where did you find your bond-mate, and how did you manage to avoid the Roracks?"

Simon could see no reason not to tell the story, so he did, trying not to make himself sound too heroic in the process. "So you see," he said finishing the tale, "it was really more luck than any skill on my part that allowed Sienna and me to survive as long as we did."

"I am not calling you a liar, Simon," Bill said. "But you have to admit that it sounds pretty incredible that an eleven-year-old boy could survive an encounter with a pack of beast-men, even with the help of a fully-grown dragon."

"Well, the only things I have to prove my story are the Dragon Mark on my chest, and these." He pulled back his long hair to fully reveal the four scars from the beast-man's claws that started up under his hairline and continued diagonally down his face in front of his left ear to his lower jaw.

While Marie gasped and Sharon nearly cooed, Bill said, "Women love battle scars, so long as they aren't truly disfiguring. Marks of manhood!" Then he traced the scar on his own cheek and added, "I got this one fighting bandits while on a cattle drive when I was younger. A certain young lady found it irresistible and married me." He looked at Marie, and she blushed.

An easy silence fell on the room for several minutes before Bill said, "While I did want to make up for how you were treated last night, I also wanted to offer you a business proposition."

Simon wasn't surprised. He had been expecting something like this. He smiled and inclined his head to indicate he was willing to listen.

The man subtly suggested that the women see to shutting down the house for the night. Simon was relieved that Sharon, showing much less interest in him since learning his age, didn't balk at her father's request for privacy.

Once he and Simon were alone, he got down to business. "I have a small herd and some trade goods that I need to send south to Meer, the capital of Iondar. This is more a favor than a real trade mission, and I am not really earning enough to make it worthwhile.

I've made arrangements to send my goods with a group of local 'vanners with whom I regularly deal. The convoy will be large enough to attract the attention of bandits, but won't be so big as to deter the brigands from attacking. However, it's not profitable enough to hire sufficient guards to ensure it gets through unscathed; if I have to do so anything I make will be spent hiring enough men. I would like to pay you to accompany them. Even a large group of bandits wouldn't be stupid enough to attack if they thought they would have to face a dragon. I will give you fifteen gold crowns for what is essentially lazing along for ten days or so babysitting a few wagons and a bunch of steers. Since you have already stated your intention to go that way..."

Simon chose his words carefully trying not to offend his host. "I can see two problems. One: I am meeting another Dragon Rider who is heading north, and I will not make it all the way to the capital of Iondar before I will be turning in whatever direction that Rider wants to go. Two: Sienna may be large enough to be scary, but she is too young to breathe fire. Without her fire, she is not an effective deterrent against a large group of men."

"But they won't know she is too young to flame them. It's like having a big dog in your house. It can be the gentlest animal in the world, but burglars will stay out because they won't take a chance that the beast might try and kill them." He leaned forward and added, "I'm not being untruthful when I say that I will make very little from on this venture. It really does have more to do with returning a past favor than business, but I'll sweeten the deal a bit for you. I'll send along ten more steers. You can either feed them to your dragon or sell them yourself when you reach Meer."

"I am tempted by your offer, but I still have the prior commitment. This Rider and his partner have offered to train Sienna and me. We need that training. I can't turn aside from that to line my purse. I'm sorry, Bill, as much as I'd like to say yes, I must decline your offer."

"My group won't leave for a week, about the same time your new saddle will be ready. A lot can happen in that time. You think about it, and if your situation changes in my favor, come back and let me know."

"Very well, I will think about it, and if things change, I will return."

CHAPTER 38

LORD JOHNSTON HAD offered Simon a room, but, even though he liked the nobleman, he didn't want to be obligated to him. He had given the excuse that he not only slept better under the stars with Sienna, but that he didn't want to wake the others in the house when he rose early to go to the blacksmith's shop to start work in the morning. He had Sienna fly to the same spot they camped the previous night and settled down to sleep. He found himself standing among the shifting clouds and changing hues of the dream state.

"Someone wishes to speak with you, my love. He is Leera's Bondmate. His name is Brock."

"Where is he? Is he close?" He looked around for the man but saw no one.

"He and Leera are still in Falen, which is a village near the capital city of Iondar. He is in the Dream State with Leera, and I will allow them to make contact if you agree to see him."

"I would certainly like to meet them. Please allow the communication."

"Very well, but I have to caution you about something. While you can talk with this Rider, you do so at the indulgence of the other dragons here. They come to this place for peaceful companionship. If you and this man let your emotions run high, you could be ejected. No matter what is said, make sure you don't' get too excited, and especially keep any anger in check."

"I will remember, Dear Heart. Let them come."

Suddenly a dark-skinned man and a blue dragon with an orange starburst mark on her face coalesced into view. The man stood only a little taller than Simon and looked to be in his early thirties.

He extended his hand and said, "I am Brock Ard and this is my Bond-mate, Leera."

"I am Simon," the boy replied grasping the man's wrist. "And this is Sienna."

They stood for a moment just watching the swirling colors in the clouds before Brock visibly shook himself and said, "I don't come here often. I have a tendency to get caught up in the place and forget why I came. In the five centuries that Leera and I have been bonded, I could have counted the number of times on my fingers." He turned to Simon and smiled before adding, "That was before the Legion of Riders starting using the place to stay in contact with each other, of course. I've spent more time in the Dream State since the war ended than I did in the five centuries before it began."

"I hadn't thought about that. I have been coming here with Sienna regularly since we bonded. I knew she was in contact with other dragons, I should have thought to ask if we could talk with other Riders. It might have saved us some trouble earlier on."

"I wouldn't worry too much about it, Simon. No one thought about it until a rather remarkable fellow named Delno tried it out of desperation as a way for our scattered forces to keep in contact during the war." Again he shook his head as if to clear it. "I don't know how Delno can stay so focused here. The place muddles my brain and makes me want to simply lie down and watch the clouds. We had better keep this brief. I agreed to meet you on the road, and we should have met up by now. However, I find myself delayed by family business. One of my relatives has died."

At Simon's look of concern, he held up his hand to forestall any comment. "It was natural causes and we weren't that close; I really didn't even know the man. However, his daughter is scheduled to get married soon after the funeral, and the family has asked me to present the bride at the wedding. I actually would like to refuse but, to their way of thinking, having a Dragon Rider present the bride will offset the bad luck of having her father die so close to the wedding date. I'm afraid that this whole business will delay my departure for at least a fortnight. If you intend to continue south, you will most likely get to Iondar before I can leave."

"Well, I have been delayed here. I have to have a saddle made and I have taken a temporary job with the local blacksmith so that I can get guards and hilts made for my Dragon Blades."

"Dragon Blades?" The plural wasn't lost on Brock. "Son, as much as I'd like to conclude our discussion and get out of this place, I think you had better tell me your whole story."

Simon decided that he liked Brock and set about telling him the entire tale. Several times during the oration Brock became upset and the landscape wavered as if they were looking through imperfect glass and the glass had moved. Each time Leera cautioned her Partner to control his emotions, and both dragons communed with and placated the others who had picked up on the Brock's feelings.

"That's quite a tale, Simon. I must say that if I didn't have the dragons verifying your truthfulness, I'd think you had heavily embellished it."

"If I heard this from someone else, I'd be hard pressed to believe it even with the dragons," Simon replied. "Sometimes I look back at all of it and think it must have happened to another person."

"I don't see your life getting simple anytime soon, but with two of us to keep an eye out it might get easier. You're right, though; you will most likely have to deal with this sooner than later. Leera and I will just have to make sure that you and Sienna are up to the task. However, I'm a bit worried about the people you left behind. If it's all right with you, I'll have Nassari check on them and make sure this Lord Bastian doesn't get it into his head that he can take his anger against you out on your mother or this fellow Boron. Now that you've sent two of his people back with that message, I'd rather be safe than sorry."

"I didn't think about that before I opened my mouth. I've been a bit worried ever since then. I appreciate whatever help the Riders in Horne can do."

"So, do you feel that you can trust this Lord Johnston? I'm sure I met his grandfather once, and if the two are alike he should be honorable. Also, it seems like an awful lot of trouble to go to just to lure you into the wilds to capture you."

"I think his offer is genuine, though I do believe there is more going on than simply returning a favor. I believe he is sending something more precious than cattle and trade goods. But if he needs to ship a valuable cargo in secret, the job is still the same. I have no need to know what I'm guarding."

"You're right of course. I'm impressed that you saw the subterfuge. There are no commodities that someone from there would be smuggling into Meer. He is probably shipping gold or jewels, most likely gold to buy jewels since Iondar has so many prosperous mines. But that doesn't matter. You should take the job. Not all we do earns us money, and we still need to replenish supplies now and again. Just remember to stay close to the caravan and land often to talk with the head man. Make regular reports on what you see from the air. But even if there is nothing to report, land and talk about the weather or something. Being seen as much as possible is what will keep the bandits from accosting your group. It's better to scare them off before they attack than it is to wait and fight them off later."

"I will go and tell Lord Johnston the good news tomorrow evening."

"Good; if all goes well, I will see you here in Iondar in less than three weeks. Now I have to go. I want to try and contact Nassari, and I need to get out of the Dream State."

As Brock and Leera faded from view, Sienna reminded Simon both he and she needed sleep and should do so. Then his surroundings went black and his subconscious mind took over as he slipped into normal sleep. He dreamed of his mother. She was looking for him, and no matter how much he shouted she couldn't hear him calling back. Though he walked for a long time toward the sound of her voice, she seemed to always be just out of sight. It wasn't a nightmare, but it was disturbing.

CHAPTER 39

THERE WAS A commotion, but Sheena continued working. She wasn't particularly interested in what went on outside these days. She knew it wasn't Simon returning home. She couldn't bring herself to believe that he had been lost in the beast-men's territory. He was smart, quick, and strong. She felt in her heart that he was still alive, but she longed for some proof.

Boron came in the door and said, "You had better come out and see this."

When she stepped out onto the porch, the first thing she saw was a tall, handsome man with a swarthy complexion and a girl in her mid-teens. There was something funny about the girl. Looking again, Sheena realized that she was a very petite woman. Most people would have probably guessed her age at about fifteen. Sheena, though, wasn't so easily fooled. She estimated early twenties.

"I am Nassari, and this is my spouse, Nadia. Are you Sheena Harding?"

She started to answer, but the words stuck in her throat when she noticed the two dragons waiting patiently on the street. Then she saw that there were several other dragons circling in the sky over the village.

Boron stepped protectively in front of Sheena as he politely asked, in a tone that implied he would get an answer before this went any further, "What is this about, Rider?"

"If this is Sheena Harding," Nassari said in a silken voice, "we have a message for her from Simon."

Sheena nearly fainted and leaned heavily on Boron who replied, "We should go inside."

Once they were all seated inside the house, they waited until Roland Fine poured refreshments for everyone. When that was done, it took more than a quarter of an hour for Nassari to relay what Brock had told him.

"I knew he was still alive," Sheena whispered as tears flowed down her cheeks.

Nadia put her arm around her and said, "He's not only alive, he is thriving. And now he is under the watchful eye of one of our most respected Riders. Brock will take good care of him."

Sheena leaned into the embrace for a moment, grateful for the support, before sitting up straight and asking, "But how did this happen? How could he have become a Dragon Rider?"

"It was late when Leera was finally able to contact Wanda. By the time Wanda had gotten me to the meeting, we didn't have much time if we were to get here early. We know that we have a lead on this information since any news coming to Lord Bastian will have to travel by more conventional means." Nassari sounded as if he were biting into something extremely bitter when he said the noble's name. "But Brock and I both agreed that we should use our advance warning to our best advantage. Consequently, he didn't have time to tell me everything he knows. All I know is that Simon met Sienna's mother in beast-men territory. She was dying and he took charge of the egg she had laid there. He mentioned that the boy was rewarded with a Dragon Blade, so it's obvious he did more than just bond with Sienna. But I don't know the full story."

"As his mother, you probably don't want to hear the whole tale until he is safely back in your arms and you can feel the proof that he is all right. Dragons don't bestow the honor of a blade on someone frivolously."

Nassari turned to Boron. "Brock also told me that while Simon believes he's had a run of good luck, he owes his survival to the fact that you took him in and taught him—against Bastian's wishes."

Boron's pride showed, but Nassari got the definite feeling that it was pride in the boy's accomplishments and not in his own contribution. Walker Longleaf of the elven Hunters had mentioned that the man had distinguished himself several times in battle during the last days of the war, but Nassari had been too busy with the Riders' affairs to take the time to meet the captain. Now he wished he had done so and said as much.

"Well, I had problems of my own at the time and didn't get a chance to visit the Riders' camp after Warrick was defeated, either," Boron responded.

"The only thing left to do now," Nadia interjected, "is to get these two to the Fort and under full Dragon Rider protection."

"To the fort?' I can't leave," Sheena protested. "I have my work and my studies."

"It's all right, Sheena," Roland said. "Your safety must take priority over my convenience, or your training." He turned to Nassari. "You see, this lady is much more than my housekeeper. She has such an affinity for the healing arts that I have taken her on as my apprentice."

"I wouldn't want to interfere in the relationship between an apprentice and her master, but until we are sure that she is in no danger, I'm afraid I must insist. We can't have Simon distracted from his training because he is worried about his mother's welfare," Nassari replied. "Nathaniel flew in last night and he is planning on staying at least until the Council of Riders meets at summer solstice. Perhaps he could be persuaded to help with your studies."

Sheena didn't have any idea who Nathaniel was, but Roland Fine did. "Nathaniel the half-elven Dragon Rider!" he exclaimed. "He's here?" When Nassari nodded in confirmation he turned to Sheena. "My dear, if this man would be willing to teach you then you must go. There is no finer healer outside the Elven lands, and I would be willing to accept that there is no finer healer there either. If you can learn even a fraction of his technique for judging the condition of the body by the pulse our positions may be reversed and I will be your apprentice!"

Boron considered the situation. "I'm happy that Sheena will be safe, but I think I will decline your offer and stay closer to Bastian's estate for the time being."

Nassari drew a breath to respond, but it was Nadia who spoke first. "I know about your history, Boron. I've talked with the soldiers of the post at the Fort. I understand that you can take care of yourself, but you are not immune to assassination. We can, and will, station Riders here to watch over the physician. However, Simon has never met the man, and his part in this is minor. We have assessed the danger to our good healer as minimal. You and Sheena are a different matter. Bastian is dangerous, his son even more so. A person like that is not opposed to using dishonorable means, and even illegal ones, to get his revenge for what Simon did to him. Those who are close to Simon are in danger. Not because you have helped the boy, but because harming you will hurt him deeply. There are always those who will do just about anything for money. That worthless mongrel would take great pleasure in harming either one of you, and he has control of enough of his father's assets to hire the help he needs to do so."

Sheena laid her hand on Boron's arm and looked into his eyes. "I would feel safer knowing you are nearby."

He smiled back at her and said, "That's not fair. You know I can't refuse you."

"As you have pointed out so often in recent weeks, my love, the politics of the situation have nothing to do with being fair."

"Well, that's settled," Nassari said as he saluted all those present with his glass before placing it to his lips and draining it. When he finished the contents he politely waved Roland off before the man could refill it and continued talking. "Brock and Leera will actively train Simon and Sienna as they make their way back to Horne at a leisurely pace. They are planning to arrive as others are gathering for the Council of Riders' meeting. Once they are here Simon will be able to confront Bastian and his son, but he will do so as a full-fledged Rider with a large contingent from the Legion of Riders backing him up. We intend to put paid to this account decisively."

Boron was puzzled. "I know the boy is now a Rider and you take care of your own. However, you speak of Simon as if he is more than just another member of your ranks. I'm not complaining. I had high hopes that the lad would do well and I'm pleased to see he has up to this point. But why the special treatment? Despite all he's done, he's still an eleven-year-old boy."

"I suppose we didn't make it clear. Simon is now bonded to a Lineage Holder. Sienna's position gives her great authority among her kind. Most other dragons will obey her without question and, because of the bond he has with her, most Riders will do the same with Simon. He may be an eleven-year-old boy, but he has suddenly been elevated to the status of royalty. That lad could walk into a council of kings and bow to no man!"

Chapter 40

"YOU'VE BEEN TRUE to your word, Simon, and I have to admit that I'll miss you tomorrow," Tom said as the boy drove the hot bronze guard onto his long knife.

Simon had worked hard the last three days but found that, despite some new blisters, he had enjoyed being back in the shop. Tom wasn't Boron, but he was a good man, and Simon had enjoyed the easy companionship that the two shared. He would be sad to move on.

"I'll miss you and the shop, too. But I have commitments I have to live up to," he replied as the guard seated against the blade. "As soon as I set the pommel on this blade I will be done here, I'm afraid. I do hope to get back this way and see you again."

Tom used the tongs he was holding to pull the hot piece from the fire. He set it carefully and held it in place while Simon drove it home with the hammer.

"You've done a lot more than I bargained for, lad, and I know you refuse to accept payment…" Simon started to speak up and the smith held up his hand to silence him. "I'm not going to offer you money again, so save your breath; I know a lost cause when I see one. Still, you've done a lot more than that bit of bronze is worth, especially when you did the work on that yourself. Since you insist on sticking to the bargain and won't take further payment, I took the liberty of making you something as a going away present." He handed Simon a bundle.

Simon started to object and then simply took it rather than risk offending the smith. Inside were a leather belt and two fine scabbards for his Dragon Blades. The scabbards were made of the expensive black hardwood from the southern region of Iondar, and a stylized dragon had been burned into the surface of each, while a similar pattern was tooled into the belt.

"I took the measurements for them while you weren't looking. I know I shouldn't have touched those Dragon Blades without your permission, but I figured you'd forgive me handling your weapons for such a purpose."

Simon shook his head. "Tom, I don't know what to say. These are so beautiful I am almost afraid to use them out of fear of harming them."

"Well, that's some of the hardest wood there is, and I put three thick coats of lacquer on them. That and the metal reinforcement on the edges should protect them from normal wear. I just hope they serve you well."

Simon suddenly found it hard to speak around the lump in his throat. "It seems I no sooner make a friend than I have to move on these days." It wasn't puberty that was making his voice crack as he spoke.

"I've heard that's the way it is with Dragon Riders sometimes," Tom responded sadly. "Fate has dealt you a hard lot of tiles to play at such a young age, son. I wish you could stay here and be my apprentice, but that's impossible. So think kindly of me when you look at those scabbards, and if you find yourself back this way, stop in and say hello. You'll always be welcome."

Simon didn't want to leave, but there was nothing more to be said, and he didn't want to stand there until he started crying like a baby. He walked away into the evening gloom. He thought of his mother and Boron while he walked, and tears flowed down his cheeks. Leera had told Sienna that the two of them were safe and under the protection of the Riders at the old fort, and he wanted nothing more than to go there and be held in his mother's arms while being lulled to sleep by the sound of both of their voices.

It took nearly an hour to get his emotions under control. By that time, it was completely dark, and he wanted a bath and some food. There was an inn nearby that was also a public bath house, and for a little extra, they would fetch him some food from the local pub. He settled into the hot water and let the penetrating warmth soak away his cares as well as the minor aches from his exertions. A young boy, actually about his own age but much smaller than he, brought him the food. He dried his hands and took the tray. The boy stared openly at his chest in awe of the Dragon Mark he saw there. Simon quelled his irritation and let the boy get an eye-full. He had figured out that it was best to let people get a good look and get it over with up front rather than be distracted by them trying to sneak a peek down his shirt.

As he dug into the plate of food, he heard the rough voice of a man asking for bathing accommodations for himself and his two companions. The bath tubs were arranged in a large room, curtained off for privacy. Simon couldn't see the men, but he would have had no trouble hearing them even without his senses being magically enhanced. At least one of them was speaking with the loud, slurred manners of someone who should have stopped drinking and gone to bed, and that man called for distilled wine as he was led to a tub. Simon tried to ignore them and enjoy his meal but he couldn't help overhearing their conversation.

"I tell you," the drunken man said. "Those two idiots are better off hightailing it back to Horne. They should have left such business to real men."

"Huh, I supposed you'd have fared better against a dragon," one of the other two snorted.

Simon *reached out* to Sienna and she assured him that she was only a few hundred yards away and could take the roof off the building he was in if it was necessary to come to his aid.

The man who had done the talking when they first entered spoke up. "The weak link in the chain is the boy. Get control of him and you get control of the dragon. She won't do anything to jeopardize his life. All we have to do is hold a knife to that whelp's throat and the dragon will do as she's told. Remember, if he dies, she dies, so I imagine there's a bit of self-preservation that comes into play as well as concern for the brat."

"You can have my share of the reward," the man who wasn't drunk said. "I want no part of this."

"You're a coward," sneered the drunk.

"That may be, but I have a wife and babe at home, and I intend to see them both again. That won't happen if I follow you and run afoul of a dragon. I've seen what those creatures are capable of, and I'd rather face bandits and beast-men."

Simon set his tray aside and moved his Dragon Blades closer. He hadn't had time to wrap the hilts yet, but he could still use them if the need arose. A woman walked by and looked to see if he needed anything and he motioned for her to come over. He took a towel from her and silently indicated that she should take the tray.

"Very good, young sir…" she began but he placed his finger to his lips in a shushing gesture.

The three men ceased talking. He shook his head, rolled his eyes, and put his pants on without bothering to use the towel first. Getting out of the bath house was top priority; he could dry his clothing later.

He listened for a moment and heard no sounds of movement, so he hitched on his belt, grabbed up his dirty clothes and boots, as well as his small pack, and began walking toward the front door.

Just when he thought he might get out without any trouble, the first man's voice said, "Well, now. It seems our quarry has come to us."

At the sound of the man's voice, Simon dropped everything in his hands and drew both Dragon Blades as he turned to face them. He heard the front door of the bath house slam shut behind him and silently *called* for Sienna.

The man who ran the place shouted, "I've sent one of the lads for the constables. I suggest you gentlemen take it outside. I'll have no fighting here."

"There's not going to be a fight," the first man said. "This boy is going to drop those blades before he cuts himself, and then he's going to go with us nice and quiet like."

Simon smiled maliciously and responded, "You've obviously had more to drink than I first thought, and it has clouded your judgment badly. I have no intention of lowering my weapons, and anyone who tries to take them from me will die." Sienna screamed in rage just outside and Simon motioned with his head. "That is the sound of a very angry dragon who has no intention of letting you take me back to Horne. Your plan of controlling her by controlling me won't be as easy to implement as you had thought. Talking about it while lounging in a bathtub drinking distilled spirits is one thing. Making it happen while facing an enraged dragon is quite another."

Two of the men were on their feet, but the man who had taunted the drunk was still seated in his tub. He looked at Simon and said, "They're just my traveling companions, Rider. If this goes from bad to worse, remember that I don't have any part in it." The first man looked at him harshly, but he wasn't moved by the gesture. He looked the other in the eye and added, "This is your foolhardy plan Tanner; I never agreed to it. I have no intention of dying for this. If you want to commit suicide, you're not taking me with you. As far as I'm concerned, I agree with the hosteller. Take it outside so I can finish my bath in peace."

Sienna said, "There are several constables out here requesting that I move and let them in. Do want me to keep them away?"

"No! Let them in, they are here to help."

The door behind Simon opened and he heard heavy footsteps on the wooden floor behind him. The constables took stock of the situation and positioned themselves between Simon and the three men. "What's the problem here, Rider?" the duty officer asked.

"These men were attempting to kidnap me," he replied while pointing in the general direction of the tubs.

One of the guardsmen laughed out loud and the other three shook their heads in disbelief.

"Trying to kidnap you?" the officer asked as he looked at the two naked men standing empty handed in the tubs. "I don't see that their weapons look all that large and dangerous." All four guardsmen men laughed out loud.

"I suppose that they were hoping, because of my youth, that I could be easily frightened into compliance. Also, I confronted them before they had a chance to retrieve the belt knives that are with their clothes just out of reach."

The officer looked at the men and asked, "How did you think you were going to convince that dragon outside to comply? Or have you had so much to drink that you forgot about her?" Before anyone could answer, he held up his hand and said, "Never mind, I don't even want to know. All three of you get up and put your clothes on. We'll escort you back to your caravan master and tell him to keep you out of the village for the rest of the time you're camped here."

The man still seated looked to Simon and the boy spoke up in his defense, "That man came in with the others, but he wasn't a party to the trouble. In fact, he tried to talk some sense into the other two, but they refused to listen."

"Very well. You two can either put your clothes on now and lead us to your employer, or you can spend some time in our jail."

Simon pulled a clean shirt out of his pack and pulled it over his head as he stepped out onto the wooden sidewalk where Sienna could see him. The duty officer accompanied him through the door.

"Your presence here is no secret, Rider. I dare say that every 'vanner within a hundred miles of Ford knows you're here."

"Are you telling me that I should leave town?"

"I'm simply saying that two hundred and fifty gold is a large amount of money. A lot of people are going to put a few drinks into their gullets and suddenly feel brave enough to take on a dragon. So far, facing the real thing has sobered them up enough to stop them. But it's only a matter of time before real blood is spilled. What you do with that information is up to you. I have to tell you, though, those men didn't actually do anything bad enough for me to arrest them." At Simon's look he added, "Not that I have any problem with taking them back to their employer and keeping them out of town, but if I arrest every man who gets a few drinks in him and makes a threat, I'll have to start holding them in the animal pens at the stockyard because the jail isn't big enough."

"I know you're right," Simon replied. "But I still have business here in Ford. I will be leaving soon. Until then, I will stay out of town as much as possible."

"I didn't want to ask it, Rider," the watch commander said regretfully. "However, it is better for all concerned."

He turned to accompany his men as they brought the caravan guards out. Sienna suddenly moved closer and put her nose nearly against the man who had formed the grand plan to return him to Horne.

"What's she doing?" the startled man asked in a shaky voice.

"I am getting your scent. If I get wind of you near us again, I will kill you and anyone with you!"

The man paled visibly and allowed himself to be guided away by the town watch.

Sienna and Simon walked away side by side despite the fact that there was barely enough room for her to do so on the main street.

"We have to get clear of this place, Dearest. I know you don't want to go back on the run, but at least in the wilderness, we have less trouble picking friend from foe."

"You're right. In the wilderness, they are all foes. I had started to like having the occasional friend."

"We have friends, but they are farther south."

"I know, Sienna, but the saddle won't be ready for another two days at least. Then we will travel with that group Lord Johnston is sending to Meer. Once we meet up with Brock and Leera, we will have two more pairs of eyes to watch for trouble."

Simon heard a familiar female voice, and she was obviously in distress. He rounded the next corner and found Tina being accosted by three boys. He estimated them to be in their late teens. One of them held Tina by the arm, and she was struggling to get free.

"Let go of her!" Simon said in a dangerous voice. He had had all he was going to take this day.

"The older boy looked at him and scoffed. "What are you going to do if I don't?"

"If you don't take your hand off of her, I will take your hand off of your arm!" He drew his long blade.

The boy looked like he was about to say something stupid when Sienna's head appeared around the corner and she growled, "My Bond-mate has told you to let go of this girl. I suggest that you do it."

All three of the boys backed up several paces before they turned and ran into the night.

"Tina, what are you doing out after dark? And in the company of boys like that? Where are your parents?"

"Simon, thank you. I came to town to look in some stores and lost track of time. The next thing I knew it was dark, and then I got lost trying to find my way back to camp."

Simon was rapidly becoming cynical in his old age. He looked at the girl skeptically and said, "I'm sure there is more to the story than that. But I'm not your father, so I don't need to hear it. For now, your parents must be frantic; let's get you back to them."

"Do you have enough room to take off, Dear Heart?"

"I can get airborne without damaging myself or the surrounding structures," the dragon replied.

"*Good, we have a passenger this time.*" He led Tina forward and helped her climb into place, and then climbed up in front of her. She put her arms around him as if frightened. It only took a second for the fright to give way to some other instinct and she snuggled against his back a bit seductively. Sienna had been looking back, but if she noticed she showed no sign of jealousy. "*Circle the gather and see if you can see Rufus and Cinda's camp, Love.*"

"It shouldn't take long. The locals are all camped in one area. I will go there first."

Tina was more interested in being close to Simon than she was in flying, so she was disappointed when Sienna landed near her parents' wagon only a few minutes later.

Rufus had just returned to the camp from searching for his daughter, so both parents were there when Simon arrived with Tina. He simply told them that he had found the girl in town and knew they would be worried, so he had Sienna fly her back to them. He left out the part about chasing off the boys who were accosting her and let her tell her own story.

There was much shouting and crying, as well as threats of dire consequences if it ever happened again. After all of the emotions had played out, as he had not been able to finish his earlier meal, Simon joined the family for a late supper. Then he and Rufus stayed up talking well into the early morning hours.

CHAPTER 41

"HERE WE ARE in Meer, Rider. As soon as I break out the strong box you can collect your fifteen gold, and take your ten steers. Nice bit of bargaining on your part with the price of beef in this country. Are you sure you won't be available to run escort on the trip back? While we won't be working for Lord Johnston we could still use the help once we pick up a cargo here. We saw signs of bandits on the way down, but the sight of your dragon was enough to keep them away. It would be nice to have the same when we head back north, and it will save me some of the expense of hiring more guards."

"I'm meeting another Dragon Rider here and he and I will travel together for a time. It would be easy money, and the coins would be nice to have, but I can't make a commitment to you under the circumstances."

The Trail Boss, Martin, turned and shouted to the man who was rummaging through the wagon. "Damn it, Arnie! What's taking you so long? Just give me the box so I can settle up with the Rider and pay the toll the locals charge for camping."

Simon looked at the three men who had come out of the city to collect the toll. All three were dark skinned and average height. They were handsome with finely chiseled features, and they acted pleasantly enough, especially to him. Lord Johnston had told him that, as a people, the Iondarians were shrewd in their business dealings, but honorable, and as honest as the day is long. While it was likely these people had their bad apples just like every other society, in general, if one of the dark-skinned fellows said something, you could believe him. And if he made a commitment he'd stick to it or die trying. The Iondarians also idolized Dragon Riders as much as the people of Trent.

Arnie produced the lock-box and Martin tried to keep his broad back between it and everyone else. Simon could see the gold inside, but there was something wrapped in several layers of cloth that he couldn't discern. He looked away, figuring that it had something to do with why this trade excursion was sent. It was none of his business, and idle curiosity would do nothing to either get his account settled or further his own plans.

Martin counted out fifteen gold crowns and handed them to Simon before handing the same number of silver coins to one of the Iondarians. The functionaries from Meer thanked him and bowed to Simon before heading back inside the city. One of them said something in an unfamiliar language as they walked away, and they all laughed.

"Only madmen and northerners conduct business under this brutal sun," Martin translated.

Simon smiled and responded, "He's got a point. I didn't realize that a couple of hundred miles could make such a difference. It was warm for late spring when we left Ford, but this is downright uncomfortable."

Martin laughed outright. "If you think this is bad, you had best not stick around for summer. That time of year, people spend half of the day sleeping, if they can, and conduct their business at night wearing heavy cloaks. This is a harsh land, Rider, and most of it is desert. The summer sun will broil you alive, and the temperature can drop so low and so fast after sundown that the sweat on your body almost freezes to your skin. It doesn't rain here for months, and most of the locally grown vegetables have to be watered by hand from the wells. There's some good farmland to the southeast, near the elven lands, and that eventually runs into a large rainforest where that wood comes from." He pointed at Simon's scabbards. "That's what I hear, anyway; never been that far myself. Not terribly interested in dealing with the elves, even if they could be persuaded to deal with me."

"What little I've heard of the elves has led me to believe they are decent, honorable people," Simon observed.

"Oh, I suppose they are, Rider, but they have some strange customs, and they are mighty picky about those they trade with. Most 'vanners who don't come from these lands let the locals deal with them, and then buy the elven goods second hand. That's why elven wares are so rare and expensive; well, that and the fact that the elves don't tend to make much more than what they can use themselves."

Simon only nodded.

He looked around as he wiped his brow with a kerchief before adding, "Glad I only have the one trade run down here this year. I'll take my chances on making my profit up north this summer, and be glad not to put up with the sand and heat."

"I suppose this is an extension of the desert that covers the southernmost portion of Horne as you get near the sea," Simon replied. "I've never been there either, but my mother told me of it."

"That's another thing, Rider. Don't go around volunteering that you're from Horne." At Simon's quizzical look he explained. "The King of Iondar sent two hundred of his best troops to help with the war. Those weren't just regular infantrymen. The man actually sent his own personal guard, his best fighters, to help out. It seems that the King of Horne didn't see that as much of a gesture, and when the war was over what was left of those men were sent home without so much as a nod in thanks. The King of this land, and most of his subjects, took that as a direct insult and cut off trade relations with your homeland. Trade has finally opened back up, but the two sides are barely civil to each other. Mentioning that you come from Horne could get you a whole pack full of trouble. If anyone asks, just tell them you came in from Ford and let them draw their own conclusions. It's not a lie, and it might keep you from having to get those pretty blades of yours all bloody."

"That's good to know. I didn't leave Horne under pleasant circumstances anyway, so not telling anyone about my country of origin fits into my plans. Thank you for the warning."

Simon's past was a subject that had been discussed much by the men of the small caravan during the trip. They all knew about the price on his head and wondered what he had done at his age to deserve such. Martin looked at the boy expectantly in hopes that he would divulge more, but Simon held his peace.

Finally, Martin shrugged and said, "I suppose we need to get to the cattle buyer and see how much we can get for these beasts. If you like, I'll negotiate for the lot of them and then pay you for your ten after the deal is sealed."

"Thank you, Martin. I have never traded livestock and would be easy game for anyone wanting to take advantage of the situation. I'll let you handle the whole affair."

They were quiet as they walked. Simon looked around so much that his head appeared to be too loosely attached to his shoulders. There was so much to see. For such a drab country, there was color everywhere. At first, all of the man-made hangings looked to be a jumble of differing hues and designs. Awnings were striped, while the circular canopies were covered in swirls like pinwheels. The buildings themselves were painted brightly in mostly yellows and oranges, while the clay paving stones beneath his feet were two shades of reddish brown laid out in a checkerboard pattern. There were so many merchants crowded into the main plaza that it looked like one big, outdoor store. At first glance, he thought it was just a big hodgepodge, but, as he walked among the shops and stalls, the place blended into a cohesive whole.

"What is that?" he asked Martin as they strolled by what looked like dried mud patties piled next to a stall selling cheese.

"That's dung," Martin replied with a laugh. "While that man's sons tend to his farm, his wives and daughters spend part of their day collecting the dung from the animals, mostly milk goats and maybe a few cows, I'd guess, and mix it into a paste. Then they roll the dung into balls and throw it against a wall, which is what gives it that shape. They let the patties dry in the sun and then scrape them off the wall and load them in the cart for the man to sell in town to supplement the income they get from selling the cheese they make from the milk the animals produce." At Simon's doubtful look he added, "I told you it's a harsh land, Rider. The man can't get enough fodder to feed enough cows and goats to support his family selling cheese. So they do whatever else they can to make a living."

"What is the stuff used for?" Simon asked.

Again the Trail Boss laughed. "Fuel for their fires!" He stopped and looked Simon in the eye. "Rider, we've been on the trail a fortnight getting here. In the last week, have you seen even one single tree?"

Simon thought about it and realized the man was right. He hadn't seen a tree in at least six or seven days. The lush lands of southern Trent had given way to scrub, and that had finally given way to barren sand. The closest he had come to seeing an actual tree were the tall slender things that grew around the oasis that the large city was built around.

"You see," Martin continued, "in this country what little wood they have is a scarce and valuable commodity. It's worth too much to burn, so they make do with something they have in more abundance. You have to admire such frugal ingenuity." He paused a moment as he looked around. "Ah, we're here. This building houses the livestock merchant I am going to sell the cattle to. The thing is, these people don't like to have anyone who isn't directly involved in the negotiations watching, so it would be best if I do this alone. There's a little place over there where you can get something to eat and drink. I have to warn you, though, if you ask for coffee make sure you tell them you want it light, or it will be so strong you can't choke it down." He shook his head and added, "I don't know why the locals bother to brew the stuff. The way they drink it they might as well just chew the beans into paste and swallow them."

Simon moved on as the 'vanner entered the building. He stood near the food vendor hesitating. "I'm not sure I'm ready to eat food that has been cooked over smoldering dung!" he muttered under his breath.

"That sounds strange coming from someone who will wear clothing that has been soaked in urine," Sienna observed dryly, breaking into his thoughts.

"I only did that to cure those hides. I washed them thoroughly before I put them next to my skin!"

"It's not like the dung is going to touch the food, Love. You should eat while you can. Brock and Leera are on their way and will be here soon."

"How soon?" he asked excitedly.

"Leera reached out to me a short time ago while I was eating. They have left Falin and will be here in less than half an hour." Then she added, "You should have kept one of those cows. All I could catch this morning was one of the scrawny lizards that afflict this land, and I am still hungry. The hunting in this place is terrible."

Simon shook his head. The scrawny lizards she was speaking of were about ten feet long and weighed around twenty stone. The things plagued the local goat herders and, according to Martin, were even known to occasionally kill and eat full-grown men unwary enough to wander into their territory unarmed. He marveled that, even though her growth seemed to have slowed somewhat, her appetite hadn't diminished significantly.

"Had I known you would be lacking I would have let you have one of the steers, Love. But it is too late now. The animals have all been sold," he said as Martin came out of the building and waved to him. "If you cannot find more food I will see about buying one of them back."

"Thirty silvers each, Rider," Martin said with a smile as he joined Simon. "With so few traders making the trip from Horne supply is low and demand is high. His Lordship wouldn't have had to worry about his profit if he'd sent more livestock." He counted out Simon's share and handed it over.

Several people in the square started speaking in their own language and pointing at the gate. This time, Simon didn't need Martin to translate. There was a blue dragon with an orange starburst mark on her face just outside the city, and Brock was walking across the plaza toward them.

Simon extended his hand and smiled as the older Rider approached, saying, "Brock, it's good to finally meet you in the flesh." After clasping wrists, Simon introduced Martin.

Brock wasn't discourteous to Martin, but he pulled Simon away as quickly as possible. "I trust you have completed all of your business and are now ready to move on," he said. At Simon's nod, he continued, "We will be heading northeast as soon as possible; the king of this country is a relative, and if we don't get away quickly we will be held for at least a day feasting and being shown off. Also, my son, Connor, has turned sixteen and will be taking the Oath of Allegiance to the Legion of Riders this year. Since the Legion headquarters is our ultimate destination, he will travel with us from Orlean."

"I had assumed we would be traveling directly to Horne," Simon said in confusion.

"Never assume anything, especially when dealing with dragons or their riders," Brock answered as if speaking to a particularly hard-headed student. "Look, Simon, I know that you have accomplished a great deal on your own, but you still have much to learn. Leera and I have agreed to teach you and Sienna, but we need to understand the ground rules right up front if this is to work."

Simon looked into the man's eyes to see if he could detect any duplicity. When he was satisfied that Brock was just being honest with him, he nodded.

"Good," Brock said. "Even though Sienna is a Lineage Holder and technically has more authority than Leera, she must do as Leera tells her for now if she is to learn. The same goes for you and me. You may feel the urge to take charge because of your bond to Sienna but you have to agree that, until you are fully trained, I am in charge. You are the student and I am the master. If we can't agree on this, we may as well go our separate ways now."

Simon nodded and replied, "You have already done much for me, and I am grateful. I realize that I have much to learn from you. However, you need to remember, before you accept me as your student, that the reward on my head is large enough that two attempts to abduct me have already been made. I am willing to accept your terms, but you may be placing yourself and Leera in danger by taking this responsibility." They looked at each other for a moment and Simon added, "I just think it's a good idea if all of us enter into this agreement with our eyes wide open, fully aware of the entire situation."

Brock smiled openly and held out his hand, "I think we have a deal, Simon."

CHAPTER 42

BROCK SAID THEY would be training as they traveled, but Simon hadn't thought he would be so true to his word. The four of them weren't making nearly as much headway as Simon expected because of the schedule Brock had established.

After they woke early every morning, he and Brock would spar with practice swords while Sienna hunted and ate lightly. Then, after a couple of hours, Leera put Sienna through aerobatic maneuvers while they traveled in a general northeasterly direction. Once the dragons were exhausted for the day, usually several hours after noon, Sienna would hunt and eat a bigger meal while Brock taught lessons on magical theory and practice, and the principles of supporting a draconic partner in aerial combat.

Simon had thought he was good with a blade, but Brock put an end to any false pride he may have had their first day. He was good, but Brock was better; and by more than just a little bit. Simon didn't want to think that it was possible, but he was pretty sure that Brock was even better than Boron. Brock told him that after he'd had a few decades of practice he would be just as proficient.

When it came to teaching him to work with his partner, he had thought about Sienna being able to use flame against enemies, but hadn't worked through the mechanics. His ideas of diving down while flaming an enemy straight on were certainly romantic, but not based in any kind of reality. While the dragon's flame might have some magical component to it that caused it to ignite on contact with air, once it left her mouth it became subject to the normal laws governing gasses. On the ground, a dragon could breathe fire directly to the front, as Brock had Leera show him in an impressive display. However, if she breathed fire straight ahead in the air while flying at more than twice the speed of a galloping horse, as the flame slowed down she would fly right into it and burn herself and her partner.

He soon found out that if a dragon becomes involved in such combat she aims her flame down and back to avoid getting caught up in her own breath. Against ground troops, it was a pretty standard maneuver for the dragon to lower her head and aim back as she passed slowly — still faster than even the swiftest horse - over the target, with her rider watching forward while maintaining shields to protect her, especially her wings and eyes, from enemy missiles.

He and Sienna learned that while there were no standard maneuvers in aerial combat against another dragon, the principles of the actual flame attack were still the same. She must aim below and behind to make sure that it would not blow back in their own faces. While doing that, she also had to be careful to not allow her enemy to get above and ahead of her. The Rider's job was not only to maintain shielding, but also help keep track of enemy movement to prevent them from getting an advantage, all the while using magic to attack the pair, mostly concentrating on the rider because of the dragon's natural resistance to such an assault.

The subject of fighting another bonded pair caught Simon off guard, and he told Brock that he didn't think he would find himself in such a conflict. Brock stated that he had thought the same, and then reminded the young man of the war for control of the known territories of the world that had recently taken place. That war might have been called the War Against the Roracks in Horne, and the War of the Blades in Palamore, but it was actually the War Against Warrick. While Warrick had been in control of thousands of beastmen, in the end, the outcome had been decided in the air on dragonback.

After two weeks of their routine, they were finally within a day's flight of Orlean. Brock had purposely avoided any other human habitation up to this point to skirt any possible bounty hunters. Simon was looking forward to eating a meal that wasn't cooked over a camp fire and contained more vegetables than the few roots and tubers they had managed to find. It wasn't that he had any moral difficulty with sharing the flesh of the animals Sienna killed, or even hunting for himself. He simply wanted something besides a steady diet of fire-roasted meat. He didn't mention it because he didn't want to sound childish, but the first thing he wanted to find was a bakery where he could buy something yeasty and sweet.

"I wish we could carry more supplies when flying like this, but we have to be so careful about weight—especially with all of the fancy maneuvers we're doing. Even hard bread, though, would be a nice change to an almost all-meat diet," Brock said, mirroring Simon's own thoughts. "You know, in Iondar, most people don't get meat more than a few times a month, if that often. It's a harsh land and not suited for raising cattle, sheep, or pigs. Most of the animals raised there are used for the milk they give, and the hair they shed; much too valuable to be eaten until they are too old to produce. The desert has expanded over the centuries and there just isn't enough grassland left for large herds. The average Iondarian eats a diet of grain and rough greens, with a little cheese thrown in for good measure. The only other things they get regularly are the small melons like those six I brought along that we ate the first two days. Of course, those grow no bigger than a man's fist, are mostly water, and are eaten to quench the thirst rather than fill the belly. The meat that is eaten in my homeland is nearly all imported, and is much too expensive for the average person to buy on a regular basis."

"I hadn't realized that," Simon replied. "The culture of Iondar is so different from where I grew up. It seems almost as if it is another world entirely. Not that I have a great deal of knowledge about such things. I think, when my other considerations are behind me, I would like to return to your homeland and learn more of the people there. Then I would like to spend some time traveling and doing the same in other parts of the world as well. It's one thing to live out a normal life in one place, but I think Dragon Riders should broaden their view of the world. I can't be expected to help someone off in some foreign land if I don't have any idea of the culture I am dealing with."

Brock stared at him for a moment and then just smiled broadly.

"What? Did I say something funny, or do you think I'm just being childish?"

"No," Brock said seriously, "I definitely do not think you are being childish. In fact, that statement shows a maturity far beyond your years. I smiled because you are not the first Rider I have heard make that speech."

"So that is a common sentiment among Riders, then?"

"Unfortunately not; it isn't as common as some of us would like." Brock drew a deep breath and sighed before continuing. "Simon, you have to understand that despite our enhanced magical abilities, our longevity, and our elevated position in society, Riders are just men. A lot of them come from a commoner background, and they have no idea about the world outside the one they were born into. Some of them have little or no desire to learn. It's not that they are bad men. They simply don't have the long-term vision to see past their ingrained teachings and prejudices. You have told me of the way that Bastian talks about the Riders, and we both know that he has no justification for doing so against those who watch over his lands now. However, there have been Riders in the past who did fit those descriptions. As I have heard many times, the truth usually lies somewhere in the middle." He paused for a moment, again just looking at Simon, before going on. "The first time I heard a similar sentiment to the one you just made was from a Rider named Corolan. Others have spoken similar words over the centuries, but until recently none truly understood them. Then a couple of years ago, it was my honor and great pleasure to train Corolan's grandson, Delno. He, too, understands his role as a Dragon Rider in this world."

"I thought the role of a Dragon Rider was pretty simple: do our best to do the right thing for all concerned. Help where and when we can while not allowing ourselves to be used by others for their own selfish gain."

"You, my young pupil, are way ahead of the learning curve. It can take decades for some Riders to understand that much. There's even more to it, but that is not for me to explain to you. I'll leave that to the Riders of other Lineage Holders."

"I don't understand all the fuss about Lineage Holders. I know that being one makes Sienna special, but she would be special to me regardless. How does her birth right make me more than just another Rider?"

Brock shook his head, "I was afraid of this." At Simon's puzzled look, he held up his hand before the boy could interrupt with questions. "You have asked the one question I don't want to answer for you. I have five centuries of experience as a Rider, but Leera is not a Lineage Holder. It is not for us to teach you and Sienna of such things. Those lessons are for Delno and Nassari to teach. Unfortunately, Delno is off in Llorne, and Nassari is in Horne. That leaves you stuck with me."

He put his canteen to his lips and drank to give himself time to gather his thoughts. "I will tell you this much, Simon. Lineage Holders are not just privileged because they have a connection to the past. They are leaders. Most humans think of dragons as wild beasts. As Riders, we know they are intelligent and have feelings just like we do. What even many Riders know, but don't understand is that dragons have their own society that is completely independent of ours. It's the Lineage Holders who watch over and guide that society. They hold councils when necessary, they guide young dragons in their early years, and they try to settle territorial disputes before blood can be shed. They are like the queens of the countries of men. It was the Lineage Holders, including Geneva, who convinced so many unbonded dragons to aid our cause. I've told you of the war. Why do you think that Warrick couldn't get more Riders to follow him, and was completely unable to enlist the aid of the un-bonded dragons?" Before Simon could form an answer to the question, Brock said, "Partly because he was an insane megalomaniac who couldn't be trusted. However, he would have had more success, at least initially, if he had the authority of being bonded to a Lineage Holder. Then the other bonded pairs and un-bonded dragons would have felt compelled to come to his call, at least until they realized how insane Warrick and Hella were. A dragon can resist the influence of a Lineage Holder if that Lineage Holder is obviously wrong, but it is hard for them to do so. It's like rising up in rebellion against your king."

"Then why me? I'm nothing special. Or are you saying that my bonding to Sienna was not just an accident? That I was somehow brought to that place to help her mother and become bonded to the unhatched dragon? That's a bit of a stretch when you look at what had to happen in the right sequence for the whole set of events to be more than happenstance."

"Remember what I said: take nothing for granted when dealing with magic, and be doubly alert when dragons are involved. Sienna's mother was old and might not have been able to care for her even if she hadn't been attacked. However, her mother was determined that Sienna would be her last daughter, and carry on her unbroken lineage. It is possible that she could have been killed and Sienna lost before she hatched. That type of thing has happened a few times to other lineage holders in the past." Simon started to speak up, but Brock held up his hand for silence. "I'm not saying that her mother contrived this—somehow divining that you would be there at the right time. What I am saying is that the magic of dragons is deep and mysterious. Jhren is one of the smartest and most powerful mages in the world, and he admits that he has almost no understanding of the hidden workings of the magic that surrounds the creatures. The strangest part is that neither do the dragons themselves. So, it is possible that the magic at work had a great deal to do with your being in the right place at the right time because you were the right person to take on the job of helping to ensure that Sienna's line went on unbroken."

"That doesn't answer the question. Why me, then, if not by accident? While I am very happy with the way this has worked out,

I have no special qualities that make me the obvious choice. It had to be an accident."

"Really? You have no special qualities? Simon, you look like you are at least fifteen, and if you claimed to be older it would probably be believed. Some of that is simply that you are growing faster than normal because of the bond you share with Sienna, but some of it is how you carry yourself, and that has nothing to do with magical enhancement. You are more mature than many boys who are five years older than you. There are two young Riders you will meet in Orlean who have been training under my son, Connor, since before the war ended. Both of those boys are bit older than you are, and while they are good people and will make fine Riders once they mature a bit, neither of them could have done what you have done. If one of those boys had found himself in your situation, trying to raise a baby dragon deep inside Rorack territory without help or guidance, both Dragon and new Rider would have died. I don't want what I'm about to say to go to your head, so don't get cocky, but there is more to you than you realize. You are not just an eleven-year-old boy."

Once he finished speaking, Brock rose to his feet. "I have to take care of personal needs. I suggest that you do the same. Sienna has eaten herself nearly into a stupor this evening, and even Leera hunted today. I've set a grueling pace with the training and we're all tired. Tomorrow we will be in Orlean, so any more questions you have can wait. Get some sleep.

*   *   *

"Is Sienna here tonight?" Delno asked Geneva later that night as he and Brock stared into the swirling reddish clouds.

Brock nearly missed the question and shook his head to clear it. Delno laughed.

"It's easy for you here," Brock protested. "There's a reason I didn't spend much time in the Dream State before I met you. I feel the peace of the place and can't seem to keep from getting caught up in it."

"If you open yourself up more, you can actually hear the dragons talking quietly in the background - at least, the dragons who aren't trying to hold private communion. It's almost like sitting in a large dining hall and being able to overhear bits of whispered conversation around you. It soothes the nerves."

"It would soothe my nerves to the point of catatonia. If you want me to report on this young Rider's training, I'd best not open myself up any further." Brock paused for a moment while Geneva reported back to Delno that she couldn't find Sienna. "Simon is a good boy. He's eleven going on seventy. Sienna is a typical dragon when it comes to the training. She sees it more as a game than something that will save her life one day. But it's a game she enjoys playing, so she practices hard. On an instinctual level she understands that even if she never finds herself in actual combat, the maneuvers she's practicing will serve her well in mating competition. The pair will be trained by the time we get back to Horne. Speaking of mating flights, by the way, Leera competed but didn't win, so she won't clutch this year."

Delno nodded to the comment about Leera and remarked, "Well, it may be that Simon being more mature than his years should allow is a good thing, since he's bonded to a Lineage Holder."

"That's all well and good, but I'm not sure I like it so much. A boy should have the chance to be a boy. I'm not training him so that you and Nassari can lay the weight of command on him before he's even a man," Brock responded, hotly enough that the landscape wavered slightly.

"Peace, my friend," Delno said as he held both hands up with the palms forward to show he meant no harm. "The only plans Nassari and I have for this lad are to guide him as he grows so that we don't end up with another Warrick in the future. We all agreed that Riders of Lineage Holders should receive more careful handling. Warrick and Hella came too damn close to achieving their goals for my liking. If Geneva hadn't been a Lineage Holder, Hella would have swayed her early on. It was only due to the fact that Hella didn't have privileged status in draconic society that Warrick couldn't get more Riders to follow him in the six years he spent recruiting. We don't have the manpower to do more than basic training with most new riders and hatchlings, but it is imperative that we keep a very close eye on pairs like Simon and Sienna while guiding them in the right direction." He smiled broadly before adding, "Besides, do you think my spouse would allow us to put the boy in a position that would bring about even a remote possibility of putting him in harm's way?"

Brock laughed and said, "How is Rita taking all of this about Simon?"

"It's only because Geneva ordered Fahwn not to take her to Horne, and the fact that our three children are with us, that she didn't go and tear that estate apart brick by brick looking for this Bastian and his bastard son."

"I've heard him called that on several occasions now; is it fact, or just a derogatory term?"

"Oh, it's true. When the news of what happened in Trent finally got back to Bastian, he and Broderick led a large group of men to town to 'arrest' Boron and Sheena on a trumped up charge of helping the boy escape. They were surprised to find two bonded pairs watching the physician's house. His Lordship had just about whipped his men into enough of a frenzy to try and muscle their way past the two dragons to search the place when Nassari, Nadia, and five other pairs arrived as backup. Nassari spoke with Bastian and Broderick about the whole affair, and during that time, Wanda, having heard the accusations about the boy, took it on herself to smell both men and declare openly that Broderick bears none of Bastian's scent. Bastian denied it rather forcefully and called Wanda a liar. Fortunately for the man, Nassari has worked so long in politics that he isn't easily moved to anger. He told Lord Bastian that he should watch his tongue if he didn't want to find himself in a duel, and the older man backed down. The whole scene would have been comical if the subject matter weren't so serious. It ended with Bastian doubling the bounty and saying that it is payable dead or alive. Then he said he was going to petition the King of Horne directly."

Brock shook his head sadly and said, "That's not good. Horne is the one southern kingdom that never accepted parliamentary rule on any level. The King's word is law and the Dragon Riders are there with his permission. If Bastian actually convinces the man that the Riders are in league with a wanted criminal, he could rescind that permission and we'd lose the Legion Headquarters."

"I wouldn't worry about that, Brock. That fort and the surrounding lands are ours by written treaty thanks to Nassari's machinations. I have no intention of letting that be taken away from us. We will hold that by force if necessary. We've put too damn much into it to let it go. The thing we have to worry about now is that bounty. It was one thing for it to be two hundred-fifty gold for the boy's return. Now, since it is five hundred, and dead or alive, the possibility of assassination is just too high to be ignored. Someone will try and collect that money. That is why Rita and I are leaving Llorne this morning. We will be in Palamore shortly before noon. The queen will insist that we stay over at least one night, but we should be able to meet you in Orlean the day after. Then all of us, including Connor's young protégées, will head to Corice together once the boys have completed their duties for the garrison in about a week. We will stop in Corice briefly and meet up with Will before continuing to Horne. I want enough Dragons and Riders around that boy to ensure that a mean-spirited field mouse couldn't get close to him undetected."

"I'm glad you have a plan, Delno. When you mentioned the change in the reward I started to worry. With Connor's help, I should be able to keep him safe until you arrive."

"I'm sure you could, my friend, but you're going to have even more assistance. Working through Connor, I've made arrangements with Robby. While he's in Orlean, that boy won't go to the privy without four armed guards escorting him. You and he will stay with Pierce, and Robby will station as many men outside the house as it takes to keep Simon safe."

Brock noticed that he was again losing focus and said, "Since we have everything as much under control as we can, I need to get out of this place." Delno smiled as Brock added, "I'll see you in a few days, my friend. Kiss the kids for me," before he faded from view.

"There is something you held back from Brock, Dear One, Geneva said. "What is it? I know you and that old conjurer have discussed this. What did Jhren tell you?"

"Only that he has used magical means to look over the situation, and the boy is somehow deeply connected to the magic of the dragons, though whether that connection has come about because of his bond to Sienna or was there beforehand is still a mystery."

Geneva snorted and replied, "Nothing earth-shattering there. That's no more than he says about you and Nassari. The bond between Lineage Holder and Rider runs much deeper than the bond between other pairs. Sometimes I wonder if that old man really knows anything or just likes to appear as if he does." She said this as if speaking of a favored uncle who is prone to spinning tall tales.

Delno laughed and responded, "I'm never sure of that myself, Dear Heart. Now we have others to speak to about different matters that will come before the council, and the sun will rise soon."

Chapter 43

"I JUST WANT TO go and find a bakery," Simon complained bitterly when Brock told him that he was restricted to the house and the garrison until further notice.

It was bad enough that he couldn't take a bath without an armed guard first checking the room. He simply wanted to take a bit of time to himself and get a sweet roll.

"I've explained the reasoning behind all of this, Simon," Brock replied. "You know that there's been plenty of time for assassins to get word of that reward and come looking to collect."

"No one even knows we are in Orlean," the boy protested. "We didn't tell anyone our travel plans, and you avoided towns and villages to throw off any pursuit. Besides, it's not like I'm incapable of defending myself, and I won't be alone. I can't even have a pee without an armed escort!"

"This really is for your protection," Pierce, the physician whose home they were staying in said. "If you want something specific from the local bakery Missus Gentry can have it brought over."

"Look, Simon, I know that you would like to get out. When the reward for you was lower, and only good if you were returned alive, it attracted idiots who didn't understand about dealing with a dragon. Now the offer is as much as the average man can earn for ten years of hard work and all he has to do is put an arrow through you at a distance. There will be men who will forget that Sienna will seek vengeance even if they can kill you," Brock spoke roughly. He lowered his voice and softened his tone. "It should be a crime that Bastian can do this to you, especially considering what's already been done in the past. But you and Sienna aren't quite ready to deal with it yet, and you have to survive long enough to get there. The kind of money we're talking about could bring out people who know enough magic to be really dangerous, and not just to you, but to the innocent people around you as well. Wait until Delno arrives tomorrow. Then perhaps he and I will go with you if you want to wander around town."

Just then Pierce's housekeeper, Missus Gentry, came into the sitting room with a huge plate of assorted fruits and breads, including small, sticky sweet rolls. "You folks get started on these and I'll get something to drink." She looked at the soldiers who stood around the room and shook her head, tsking at them, then added, "You boys can relax enough to have a bite to eat, too. If your captain questions the action, tell him you were tasting the food to make sure I didn't poison the lad!"

Even Simon laughed as the woman went to get drinks. As he bit into one of the sweet rolls, he had to admit that he might be in a cage, but it was a gilded cage, and his keepers kept it well stocked.

Just as everyone in the room started to relax someone knocked on the front door. Pierce excused himself, explaining that it was probably a patient, as he went to answer it.

"Delno wants to begin making his way to Corice in about a week-" Brock said.

"Sooner if possible," Delno said from the doorway.

A small, pretty, darkly tanned woman with black hair pulled back on one side and held in place by a mother of pearl comb stepped into the room. A pair of blonde girls followed. About five years old and identical to each other, they came running in yelling, "Uncle Brock!" and threw themselves at the older Rider's legs. Brock, smiling broadly, stooped down to hug them both.

"Gwendolyn, Gillian, you two have grown so much I almost didn't recognize you," he said, holding the two young girls.

Both girls giggled and Gwendolyn said, "We've just turned four, Uncle Brock. Of course we are growing!"

"I've grown a bit, too, Uncle Brock," said a boy, obviously the girls' older brother, as he stepped out from behind the pretty woman.

The boy looked to be about seven, but his eyes were strangely older, like he had already seen so much in his young life that it had aged him beyond his years.

Brock looked at the boy and said, "Well, Marcus, don't you have a hug and kiss for me, too? Or have you grown so big that I have to settle for a handshake?"

Marcus grinned. "I guess six isn't too old for a hug," he said and stepped into Brock's embrace.

The girls made way for their older brother, but it wasn't because they were shrugged aside. They parted and allowed the boy to step into the group. Simon couldn't quite catch what was going on between the three children, but he could sense a subtle communication that required no words. He realized that these children shared a bond that almost rivaled that of Dragon to Rider.

Missus Gentry came in with glasses and two pitchers of fruit juice. She almost dropped the tray as she squealed like a young girl and threw herself at the dark-haired woman. "Rita! It's wonderful to see you! And you still have that silly comb."

Rita kissed the woman on the cheek and replied as the two hugged, "This comb is not silly! It was given to me by a dear friend."

"Well, I'm glad you like it. The man who gave it to me was special, but it never stayed in my thin hair very well." Missus Gentry had tears in her eyes as she spoke.

"This must be Simon," Delno stated as he stepped farther into the sitting room and extended his hand. "I'm Delno Okonan, and I'm very pleased to finally meet you, son."

"I thought you would be delayed in Palamore," Brock said as Simon shook hands with Delno.

"We thought so, too, but the queen was busy with an envoy from Horne, of all places, so we dropped off our diplomatic package from Llorne and got back into the air before she had time to waylay us."

"Horne?" Brock asked in surprise. "Does this have anything to do with our business?"

"Yes, and no," Rita responded. "The King of Horne is asking for troops from his old allies. It seems that trouble is again brewing down there, only this time, it's disgruntled nobles, not beast-men."

"Civil war? How'd that come about?"

It was Delno who answered. "As you know, most of the import and export business in Horne is run by the noble families. The trade embargo from Iondar hurt them badly."

"The Iondarians were provoked, and that embargo was lifted almost a year ago," Brock replied hotly.

Delno held up his hand to silence further comment and continued, "I know all of that. The whole thing was brought on by Thomas Horne's refusal to acknowledge the troops sent from Iondar. Even though every Rider who was down there gave testimonial to the bravery and dedication of your nephew's command, and despite the fact that I personally told the king the Iondarians were the cutting head of the spear we drove into Warrick's beast-men, the man refused to make the effort to thank Iondar for their contribution. He even went so far as to insult them by pointing out that Corice, with whom Horne has no diplomatic ties, sent over half a thousand regardless of being embroiled in a bitter war of their own. Because of the man's pompous attitude it took all our effort to get the two countries to pull back from the brink of armed conflict. The merchants who traded with Iondar suffered large losses during the trade embargo."

Brock started to come to his countrymen's defense but Delno once again stopped him. "I know, Brock, they brought it on themselves, and it was Iondar that relented. However, Iondar imports much of the goods its citizens use, and they had to have those commodities regardless of the posturing of kings. Many of Horne's merchant nobles now find themselves bidding for trade contracts that had been in place previously for generations. Since the only viable trade routes go through Trent, it is simply cheaper and easier to buy from the merchants there now that new relationships have been established. Entire industries sprung up in Trent to fill the void left by the trade embargo, and those people are now fighting hard on the business front to stay in the markets it's taken them years to get into. Added to all of that is the anger at the crown that has built up for generations among the nobility of Horne for the kings' propensity to rule with an iron hand, and in general, stifle trade, and you can see that what was a breeding ground for dissension has become a hotbed of rebellion. At least, that is what Thomas fears."

"Sounds just like the kind of political situation the Dragon Riders should avoid getting involved in," Brock replied. "We don't let ourselves get drawn into real civil wars, and in this case, I don't have too much problem letting this one run its course and even helping the rebellion if it comes down to it. Horne is the only one of the southern lands that has not embraced a more parliamentary form of government. The kings of that country have ruled, often as tyrants, since before the first Riders bonded eight generations of dragons ago. Maybe its time has finally come."

Delno shook his head. "I agree in principle, but it may not work out in practice. According to Nassari, Bastian is one of the dissenters against the king. He's a minor player now, but if a rebellion takes hold he could be elevated rapidly, and become a force that the Dragon Riders will have to reckon with."

Rita interjected. "I don't see how the nobles think they can win this. The king still has complete control of the armies, and it is the king's line that has kept the country safe from the beast-men for so long that most people don't fully understand how much time that has really been."

"It's because of keeping the country safe from beast-men that a rebellion could win," Delno replied. "The war against Warrick depleted the resources of Horne, especially the number of her armies. In the two years since the war, Horne hasn't had the manpower to rebuild its armies to even half of its former strength. We killed ninety percent of the Roracks in that conflict, but that still leaves a lot of those monsters around. The beast-men had reached such numbers that they almost completely depleted the resources in their territories. Those resources haven't recovered, so the beast-men who are left are still quite a threat, especially along the borders. Raids are still common, and the bulk of the army is occupied with keeping that in check. The Riders help, but it's actually harder to fight small numbers of them from the air because they are cunning enough to hide from the dragons, and they stick to terrain that would force us to land to fight while they are in their own territories. Those that we killed in the war were the least cunning and most easily controlled, and that may yet come back to haunt us. What all of this means in the current situation is that the king can't pull troops from the borders to hold his capital against rebels without leaving the population at large undefended. If he does that, the population is likely to side with the rebellion. At the very least, he will have large numbers of refugees converging on the capital. If that happens, then starvation and disease will run rampant, and that again will fuel the fires of dissent."

"Are you saying we have to help Thomas put down this rebellion?" Brock asked, incredulous.

"No, I'm not saying that at all. What I'm saying is that if we don't act fast to deal with Simon's problem we could find ourselves with a great deal more trouble than we have now. We have to get to Horne as soon as possible and deal with Bastian and his son. Connor and the two boys here won't be ready to travel for at least another week. Will and Saadia are in Karne visiting our mother and will meet us on the trip. We will leave in the morning."

Just then Simon jumped to his feet and drew both of his blades. "Sienna!" he shouted as he bounded for the doorway.

At the same time, Geneva nearly screamed in Delno's mind, "Assassins! They have attacked Sienna! We are holding them, but one is a powerful mage."

"*I'm coming, Love, hold them as long as you can!*" Delno responded as he drew his own blades and bounded out after Simon.

Apparently every Rider in the area got the same message. Brock was one step behind Delno and Rita was hot on their heels, and the soldiers assigned to protection detail were right behind them. Connor, Tim, and Jim—just back from patrol—were running out of the garrison toward the city gates where the dragons were resting. They all saw the bright flash of more fire than one lone dragon could breathe. For just an instant they heard the hideous screams of men in extreme pain before the cries were mercifully cut short.

Even with his longer legs, Delno was several paces behind Simon when they reached the gate. What he saw nearly brought him to a halt. Sienna was on the ground not moving. Geneva and Leera were standing between her and a lone, middle-aged man: both dragons were bristling with anger and ready to kill. The other four dragons had just finished turning an indeterminable number of men into ash and were rounding on the stranger.

The man looked at the people approaching, and when he saw Simon it was obvious he recognized the boy. Simon didn't wait to talk, he ran directly at him obviously intent on cutting him down with his blades: before he could get another six feet a visible bolt of energy shot out of the man's hand directly at him. Simon, in his concern and rage over Sienna, realized too late that he hadn't even bothered to shield himself. He braced for what he knew would be a deadly blast. Just before the bolt of energy hit him it broke against the shield that Delno had erected.

Geneva and Leera both roared as they breathed fire at the mage. The man's screams were drowned out by the noise of the dragons. He was engulfed in twin cones of flame for close to twelve seconds. When the flames stopped, the man was still standing, but what was left of his clothing was still smoldering, his hair was mostly gone, and he was burned so badly that everyone watching stared in amazement that he hadn't yet fallen. He staggered forward a step and collapsed.

Simon, too shaken with concern for his bond-mate to be either impressed by the display or appalled by the carnage, ran to Sienna. He put his head against her and listened. He could hear her breath and felt some relief that she was alive. He turned to Delno with tears running unchecked down his cheeks.

"Geneva says that she is just unconscious. Between Sienna's own natural resistance to magic, and the shield that Geneva managed to get up in front of her, the blast she took didn't do any real damage," Delno said kindly.

Rita wrapped her arms around him and said, "She's going to be all right, Simon."

Sienna's eyes fluttered open and she said, "It's all right, Dearest. I am a bit disoriented, but I am unharmed. Fortunately, Geneva felt the attack in time and was able to protect me."

Brock, standing next to the fallen mage, shouted disgustedly, "He's alive. Barely."

Delno moved to Brock's side.

Simon gripped his blades tighter and tried to go with Delno, but Rita held him in place. "See to Sienna with me. Delno and Brock can handle the mage," she said, and eased his sword out of his hand. Simon reluctantly allowed her to take the blade. He turned back to Sienna and knelt beside her.

"What do you need, Sienna?" he asked.

"Just you near me until my head stops spinning."

Delno knelt down next to the mage. He examined the man's wounds and shook his head. The injuries were so severe he had no doubt the man would die, and even his own considerable skills were not enough to save him.

The mage looked at him with the one eye that could still focus; the look was pure hatred. "There were only supposed to be two dragons," the mage coughed. "If the rest of you hadn't been here, I'd have killed that beast."

"Perhaps," Delno replied, "Or you may have found two dragons more than a match for you. Doesn't matter now, though. You lost."

The mage actually laughed, but the laugh ended in a fit of coughing. Apparently, he had tried to breathe while he was engulfed in flame and burned his lungs as well. "There'll be others. When Broderick finds out I'm dead, he'll find one to take my place; I'm not the only one in the world who hates Dragon Riders...." Another fit of coughing choked off anything else he had to say. This time, the fit left the charred remnants of his tunic flecked with blood. Then he died, gasping for breath.

Delno stood up and looked at Brock. "Kill the dragon, kill the boy. We should have planned for this. He was apparently ready for Leera; if Geneva hadn't been here he might have succeeded."

Brock nodded, "We could have lost two Dragons and Riders today. We'll have to be on our guard."

"It also looks like Nadia's prediction about Broderick acting on his own has come true as well. This man was sent directly by him. He probably figured on collecting from the son, and then collecting the reward from the father, as well. That kind of money will bring more of them out. He's right; our kind have made enemies over the years, and a chance to settle old scores coupled with such a reward will draw attention. You said it yourself a long time ago; there are those who hate us and those who would kill us simply for the bragging rights. Getting paid only sweetens the pot."

"What do you want to do?" Brock asked.

"We move. The best way to stop this is to deal with the source of the trouble. I would have liked to give Geneva and Fahwn a rest, but given this, as soon as Sienna can travel, we get into the air. I want to get to Horne before the news of this mage's failure does."

CHAPTER 44

"IT NEVER WORKS out, does it?" Robby asked. "We keep hoping you and Brock will come back and stay with us for a while like before, but you're no sooner here than circumstances force you to leave."

"I wish it could be different," Delno replied as he tightened the straps on Geneva's saddle. "That first couple of weeks I spent here was the closest to a normal life I've had since I bonded with Geneva."

"That's what you get for being a Good Samaritan, Dear One. If you hadn't gone to help a lady in distress, you'd be a fat, happy politician in Larimar now," Geneva said playfully.

Robby laughed. "Well, I just wish you and Geneva could stay. Jennie and I are thinking about having you and her named godparents to our son, you know."

"I don't know how well that will go over here in Ondar," Rita replied as she came over to double check Delno's work. She trusted Delno more than anyone else in the world, but they both always double-checked each other's rigs now that failure could cause the death of one or more of their adopted children.

"There is precedent," Brock stated flatly. "Leera's ready; are you sure you don't want Marcus or one of the girls to ride with me? As much flying as Geneva and Fahwn have already done today, even a small reduction in weight would be a help to them."

"There's precedent?" Robby asked. "I wasn't entirely joking, but Jennie and I thought we would be the first to name a dragon as godmother to our child."

"Oh, no, you definitely wouldn't be the first. Geneva's mother had many godchildren among the royal houses over the years. Leera has two godchildren in the royal house of Iondar now."

"Ahem," Rita coughed and feigned indignation, "you seem to be forgetting her other three godchildren. I realize they aren't officially royalty, nothing but a bunch of vagabonds living on the road with their parents, really. But they look to you and Leera just the same."

Brock held his hands up palms out in mock surrender. "I didn't mean to slight your family, Rita. However, we are so close to those three we tend to think of them as our own, and you and Delno as well."

"That settles it then," Robby said. "Jennie and I were going to talk to you and Geneva about it. We wanted to discuss it formally, but your stay here seems to be cut rather short. We want you and Geneva to be officially named as little Robert Delno's godparents." He held up a hand and added, "Before you accept, think about it for a moment. If we do this officially, it means that if something happens to us, you and Geneva will be named as the boy's guardians, even ahead of his grandparents."

"I don't have to think about it," Geneva replied. "I accept this honor."

"Well, it would be a shame to have to send her to Ondar by herself to see a child who is named after me." Delno turned and extended his hand to the Captain, saying, "I also accept this honor, my friend."

Robby grasped Delno wrist and shook. "I'll tell Jennie as soon I get home: she'll be thrilled. We wanted to have a picnic for the occasion since it would be rather hard to have Geneva sit down at the dinner table, but that will have to wait until you visit our town again. Hopefully, you won't be in such a hurry to leave the next time you stop by. We have to get the papers filed making this official. The boy is three months old and my family is after me to get it done."

Rita pronounced Delno's rig safe for the children. Robby wished them all a pleasant journey and headed back into the city. Brock offered one more time to take one of the kids but both Rita and Delno declined, saying that their own saddles were specifically designed for the purpose and his wasn't.

Delno turned to Connor. "You make sure those boys are damn careful about crossing Rorack territory. If you weren't pledging allegiance this year, I'd just tell the three of you to stay put. Don't do anything foolish."

"I'm sixteen, Delno; I may have more maturing to do, but I'm not the young boy you hunted down over two years ago. As far as not being reckless, are you sure you're the one to give me that speech? It's not me who has trouble keeping my buttocks firmly planted on the seat of that saddle when I'm a couple of thousand feet off the ground."

"He's got you there, Handsome," Rita cooed.

Delno shot her a look before responding to Connor. "You know what I mean! Those two boys with you are barely more than babes themselves, and this will be the first time they have really been away from home. I don't want them getting the idea that they are all grown up but don't have to behave like it."

"Delno, we'll be fine. Even if the boys want to get a little headstrong, their partners are nearly as old as Geneva and are both very sensible. They won't let the boys get into trouble, and I know enough about Roracks not to let either of them stray out of my sight while we're near the beast-men's territory." He looked so much like Brock when he smiled that the reply Delno had formed was stopped in his throat, and Connor ended the discussion. "I'll watch out for Jim and Tim, you take care of this new boy. We'll see you at the Fort in a couple of weeks."

Connor hugged his father fiercely and said, "One of these days maybe fate will give us a break and let us travel together again."

"That would be nice," Brock said, returning his son's embrace.

Brock and Connor helped Rita strap the children into place, and Delno took the opportunity to have a word with Simon.

"You've been pretty quiet since what happened earlier." They both looked toward the charred patch of ground where the mage had died. Robby had a detail carry the body off and bury it, but the spot still stood out as a reminder of how much they nearly lost. "Are you all right?"

"Yes…no…I don't know." He shook his head and forced himself to turn away from the blackened ground. "I almost lost her today. I was so scared that all of the fluids in my body just dried up. I had no spit, and could barely breathe. I've never been so frightened in my life." Then he looked hard into Delno's eyes and added, "Brock says that the magic may have been guiding me for a long time to get me to be there for Sienna. If what I went through is the price I had to pay for that, then it was worth it. If anything happened to Sienna I wouldn't want to live. Then when it came down to her being attacked I forgot all of my training and acted like a frightened little boy. I was so scared! If there'd been any water left in my body I probably would have peed myself. It's easy for you to say it's all right. It's a bit different when you're the one who is frightened out of his wits."

Delno snorted, "Do you think you're the only one to ever doubt your own courage? I don't know how much Brock has told you about me, Simon…"

Simon cut him off before he could complete his thought. "He said you were a war hero before he met you. He also told me about you in the war against Warrick."

"Did he tell you that every time I did something heroic I was so afraid I nearly soiled my trousers?" Delno paused while Simon contemplated the implications of the question. "Of course you were scared, son." He put his hand on Simon's shoulder. "Being brave is overcoming your fear, which you did. Not having fear is called insanity. Don't beat yourself up over this. You've been thrust into an adult world at the ripe old age of eleven. Give yourself a little time to get used to it. Remember, dragons are powerful creatures, but they aren't invulnerable. What makes the Dragon Riders so strong is that we work as a team. We watch out for and protect each other: that's what makes us the strongest force on the planet."

"What if, the next time, I get her killed?" Simon whispered.

"We're not rushing into this trip because the dragons like to travel so much. We hope to prevent a next time." Then Delno smiled, "You may have momentarily forgotten your magic lessons, but that's why we drill them into you until they become a part of you. I'm a soldier, Simon. I was watching you, and you didn't forget how to use those blades in your hands. As far as the rest, well, it takes a little more than a couple of weeks of training for any skill to become automatic. If there is a next time, we'll all face it together, and Brock and I will work hard to make sure you're ready for it."

Simon smiled back. He still felt a little like he had let Sienna down, but intellectually he knew Delno was right. He couldn't think of anything else to add to the conversation so he simply said, "Thank you."

Delno ruffled his hair and replied, "No problem."

The sun hung low on the horizon and they would be traveling in darkness inside of an hour. Delno gave the signal to get airborne and the four dragons beat down as they pushed off with their back legs. Even the day's earlier events couldn't dampen Simon's elation at the thrill of flying. Sienna climbed high behind Geneva and the two dragons seemed to be racing. Simon looked back and realized that Brock and Leera were lagging, and even Fahwn, who was a big dragon, was falling behind. Once they were about three thousand feet off the ground Geneva slowed the pace to let the others catch up. Sienna flew just behind and to the left of the other Lineage Holder. Brock and Leera settled in on Geneva's right, with Fahwn and Rita to the right and behind the blue dragon.

"Geneva has relayed that we are flying in the Second's position, and that, by right of experience, Brock and Leera should be here. Brock has stated he doesn't mind since I am a Lineage Holder. However, he has also stated that if anything happens we are to drop back and let them take our place. Since they have much more experience and are our teachers, I have no problem with that," Sienna said.

"Perhaps we should give Brock and Leera this position as a matter of courtesy," Simon responded.

"We can, soon. I would like to fly here for a while. I didn't think it was possible, but I have grown accustomed to the company of other dragons, and I like Leera very much. However, I am a Lineage Holder, and a lead position is mine by Dragon Custom. Since Geneva is the older Lineage Holder, and a proven leader I don't expect her to relinquish her place, so I will stay where I am for now."

Simon was surprised by Sienna's attitude: he still had a lot to learn about dragons, especially his own partner. "Very well, Dear Heart. You seem to understand. I'll defer to your judgment, though I don't see what the position has to do with our trip."

"That's simple, the air currents," she stated flatly. "You see, by flying here I benefit from Geneva flying in front of me. Those on the other side get that same benefit. Geneva has to work a little harder than the rest of us because we are using her lift to aid our flight. Leera only has one dragon on her right and doesn't lose as much to Fahwn as Geneva does to having two dragons trailing. The Second position takes over if the Lead becomes too tired, and the entire group can continue to fly longer that way. It's the same reason birds fly in a V-formation. Of course, in our case, when Geneva tires we will most likely land for the night. It is my understanding that Delno only wishes to get far enough away from civilization to ensure our safety this evening. Geneva and Fahwn have already flown much today and wish to rest."

"I had no idea that there was an actual reason for it. I don't understand it, but I don't have to," Simon replied. "I know you are extremely large for a dragon your age, and you are very strong. Shouldn't we give this position to Leera, who is smaller than you?"

"Leera is a small dragon, but she is very strong. Flying Third won't overtax her, so indulging my compulsion to fly Second is doing no harm," she said, almost petulantly.

Simon realized that he would not win this argument, so he let it drop and settled into the flight. Once again he found her attitudes amazing. She had nearly been killed less than four hours ago, but now she was more worried about her position in the formation than her brush with death. He marveled at the draconic ability to leave the past behind and get on with her life. He hoped that his close association with her would cause more of that to rub off on him!

Delno called a halt about two hours after dark. Geneva had been setting a tough pace and all of the dragons were tired. The humans did little more than divest their partners of the gear, eat a cold supper, and settle down to sleep. The youngest three members of their party took it all in stride. Marcus, Gillian, and Gwendolyn were exhausted and fell asleep the minute they laid their heads down on their bedrolls. The adults weren't far behind.

*　*　*

"We're about three hours' flight north of Orlean," Delno said to his brother in the Dream State.

"I will leave Karne in the morning and angle my flight to intercept you. We should get to you before you reach the mountains. I'll tell Mother why you won't be coming home for a visit. She'll be disappointed that she won't see you, but she'd be more disappointed if you did anything other than deal with this mess immediately," he said angrily.

The landscape shimmered and Delno replied, "Careful, little brother. I know it's an emotionally charged issue, but you have to keep it under control here."

The two men stood side by side watching the clouds swirl for a few moments. Other than their height they didn't look much like brothers. Delno had short dark hair, with brown eyes, and his features were classically handsome. Will sported blonde hair that he had taken to tying in a ponytail. His eyes were an almost perfect match for the sky blue color of his draconic partner, and though he certainly wasn't ugly, he had the rougher features of his father's people.

Will looked at his half-brother and said, "I will inform Nassari of everything. You need to rest. Go and get some sleep."

Delno laughed and replied, "I am asleep, Brother, and so are you."

"Delno," Will said seriously, "I know that you are getting the rest your body needs, but your mind needs a break now and again also. Even the dragons say that you can't spend all of your sleep time in the Dream State. It's starting to show around your eyes, even in here. It's not good to spend every waking hour working, and all of your sleep time dealing with everything else when you should be resting. When are you going to learn to delegate some of your tasks?"

Delno sighed, "I wouldn't mind, but the world seems to have other ideas. I no sooner get one thing settled than two more crop up."

Will turned to Geneva, "Are you going to let him keep doing this to himself?"

"I watch him closely," she replied stiffly. Then she softened and added, "You are right, though. He has been spending too much time here. I think we will let you talk with Nassari and he will sleep."

"Don't you two start ganging up on me…" Delno said sharply, and the landscape once again wavered.

"Delno, I'm your brother; I worry about you. Get some sleep and take care of that new Rider. I'll contact Nassari tonight and then set out to meet you in the morning. Geneva has given Saadia the route you will be taking and we will be close enough to feel your presence by the day after tomorrow. Which reminds me: has Jhren had any luck figuring out a magical way for us to keep track of each other?"

"Several, actually. But the problem is that we can't do any of them and be absolutely sure that no other mage can use our own tracking system to find us. I'd still be interested in his opinion about how that mage managed to find Sienna so quickly. I should talk with him and…"

"No!" Will held up his hand to stop further comment. "I'm sorry I brought it up. You get some sleep. We'll all be face to face soon enough and we can talk about it then." Delno looked like he was about to protest, so Will quickly added, "Besides, if Jhren had anything he would have contacted you. Since he hasn't he won't take kindly to having you contact him on the matter." Will screwed up his face and elevated the pitch of his voice in a passable imitation of the mage. "Always have been impatient. Did you think I'd come up with a solution and was keeping it secret out of spite?"

Delno laughed out loud and said, "You're right of course. It doesn't do any good to push the old man for answers. Very well, since you have everything under control, I will delegate to you and get some real sleep. Tell Mother I love her, and that we will try and bring the children up as soon as the annual meeting is over."

Will nodded and waved as Delno faded from site.

CHAPTER 45

SIMON WATCHED THE sky-blue dragon land. He always found the grace of the creatures amazing, especially considering their size. Her wings barely kicked up any dust as she settled to the ground so gently that her rider barely felt the touchdown. She was larger than Leera, but not by much, and her color was the same as a clear blue winter sky with no other markings at all.

"She's beautiful," he remarked out loud to no one in particular as she and her partner walked nearer.

"Thank you," the tall blonde Rider shouted and waved at Simon before turning to the task of removing the saddle and other gear from the dragon.

Simon turned to Brock and asked, "How did he hear me say that?"

It was Rita who answered. "Saadia is probably the one who heard it and relayed it to Will. Either that, or he's learned some new magic trick from Jhren that allows him to eavesdrop on other people's conversations."

The girls and Marcus bolted toward Will shouting "Uncle Will! Saadia! You're here!" as they ran.

When they reached the pair, all three of them hugged, first their uncle, and then the dragon as if doing so was simply the most natural thing in the world. Once again, Simon marveled that the children not only showed no fear of the dragons, but simply accepted them as people, the same as their Riders. He remarked on that to Rita.

Rita smiled and gave him a quick, motherly, one armed hug and said, "The dragons are people; just really big."

Delno clapped him on the shoulder and added, "It takes time to get used to that idea, even for those of us bonded to them. The children have spent two years in the close company of dozens of dragons. For the girls, that's half their lives. Also, the dragons say the little ones all have strong magic about them and will make good Riders if we don't do anything to ruin them."

"How can we ruin them?" Simon looked at him in confusion.

"Children, if you'll let your Uncle Will get his gear taken care of, he will be able to give you more attention. Marcus, either help Will get that stuff off of Saadia's back, or get the girls out of the way, please!" Rita called out sternly, though she was almost laughing at what had become a rather comical scene of Will trying to actually accomplish his task while entangled in a mass of small arms and legs.

Saadia was laughing openly at the antics going on around her front feet.

"Geneva says that almost all of the very young children she has met have some connection to magic. Though not all of them are strong enough to become Riders, a good deal more would be good candidates if the adults in their lives didn't stifle that connection." At Simon's perplexed look, he explained. "Many adults refuse to indulge a child's fantasies, especially when they get over the age of five or six. They tell the child that their toys aren't really alive, and they don't accept such things as imaginary playmates. They push the child to be serious and 'keep his feet on the ground' when they should be encouraging him to sprout wings and fly. Eventually, the child is pressured into cutting himself off from the part of his mind where the magic dwells the strongest and loses the connection. That's Geneva's theory, and I tend to agree with it."

"I had an imaginary playmate," Simon admitted sheepishly. "My mother used to set a place for him at the dinner table," he added turning a bit pink at the admission.

"So did I," Delno responded with a laugh, "and Will wanted a dog and we couldn't have one because my father gets so stuffed up he can't breathe around the animals."

"So your brother had an imaginary dog?"

"Nope," Will responded, "I tried that and dad said it made his nose itch, so I had to give it away. Then I got myself an imaginary pet bear!"

The blonde Rider was trying to step close enough to extend his hand to Simon but the process was being hindered by the girls who had each firmly attached themselves to one of his legs and were now riding on his feet.

"Girls, let your uncle walk," Rita spoke around her laughter. "He's been riding all day, and he's tired."

"He's had his butt parked in a saddle; the exercise is good for him," Marcus replied.

Will looked with wide eyes at Marcus, and then turned on his brother. "You've been coaching the boy!" he accused, and they all laughed more.

Will had brought candy and cookies from his mother, so it was nearly an hour before the bedlam settled down, and the adults could actually talk without constant interruption.

"Why can't I be part of this?" Marcus asked. "He's only eleven and he's allowed."

"Because this is about him," Delno replied. "If it were about you, we might let you sit in and have a say. Now, why don't you join the girls over by Geneva and Fahwn and tell them a story? It's getting late, and we all need to rest soon."

Marcus shook his head and responded, "When I'm a Rider..."

"But you're not a Rider, yet," Rita said kindly, but firmly. "Now do as we ask, please." She hugged him briefly before giving him a gentle push in the right direction.

"We'll be over beast-man territory by mid-morning tomorrow,

earlier if the wind is still with us. That's why I had us make camp before sundown and meet up with you here," Delno said to Will.

"You've made good time. Even pushing the dragons as hard as you've been doing, I figured it would be one more day before we made the mountains. It's a good thing Saadia didn't rise to mate this year, or she would have been too exhausted to keep up the pace I had to set to catch up with you."

"Well, I'm sorry about that, but I definitely want to get to Horne before word gets back to Broderick that his assassin failed. If he sends someone else I want to be sure that Sienna is safe in the Fort before another attempt can be made."

"Getting in shouldn't be a problem - getting out again may be something else entirely," Will declared. "I spoke with Nassari. And before you get upset that we didn't contact you I only found out last night, so don't get in a fit. I couldn't have told you before we met up anyway." Delno relaxed a little and Will continued, "Nassari told me that Bastian has directly petitioned the King. Thomas was about to sign an order for the return of Simon—dead or alive—when Nassari's messenger got wind of it. The King was a bit miffed at Lord Bastian when he found out the man had left out the 'small de-tail' about Simon being a Dragon Rider."

"I'll bet that went over well," Brock interjected. "Even if the com-moners aren't our biggest fans, the royalty of Horne has always held us in high regard, though not so much as some others."

"Flew like a brick!" Will replied. "Thomas spent nearly an hour 'educating' Bastian on the position of Riders in society, and then told him in no uncertain terms to go home, lick his wounds, and forget about it; even ordered him outright to withdraw any reward for the boy."

"So that means this is over?" Simon asked hopefully.

"I wish it did, Son," Will said sadly. "Unfortunately, a lot of the other nobles see this as one more depredation in a long list of of-fenses against the loyal nobility of Horne. Now that the beast-men have been relegated back to a minor threat on the borders, the old complaint about Riders indulging themselves at the expense of honest men has moved back to the forefront of their minds."

Delno nearly shot to his feet in his anger. "Indulging themselves at the expense of honest men? Requesting food and lodging for dedicating their lives to the protection of the country is too much to ask? Perhaps we should stop patrolling the borders of Horne and let the beast-men have a go at them again!"

His outburst upset the dragons, who growled at the thought of giving the Roracks any quarter.

Will held up his hands for peace. "Delno, we're not going to settle this tonight, and we're all too tired to fly off and deal with it before morning, so settle down and I'll finish telling you what I know." Delno leaned back against the log behind him to listen and Will continued. "The nobles have been under the iron rule of the Kings of Horne since before the first Riders. They want change and are using this perceived slight against one of their own as a rallying cry. They have even raised an army and are making noises about moving against the king if he won't abdicate some of the Crown's power to a parliamentary council. Thomas has flatly refused for now, but the country is a tinderbox and Simon's situation is a smoldering ember. All it needs is one fresh wind to blow and the whole thing will erupt into civil war. Nassari says that if the nobles win, there are those who are already calling to eject the Dragon Riders once and for all."

"Don't those fools see that it's we Riders who protect them?" Brock demanded.

"Nassari says that when he has pointed that out, the response has been that it was a Rider who, working with the beast-men, instigated the last war and nearly bankrupted not only the economy, but the manpower of Horne, which is what brought about the current situation. They say that if it weren't for the Riders, they would not now be facing the harsh choices they have to make."

"So now they imply that all Riders are in league with the Roracks," Delno said, shaking his head. "Well, there's nothing we can do about it now. We will have to face it when we get to the Fort, but for the time being, we all do need to rest. I don't intend to lessen the pace of our travel."

He got up and headed off into the brush. Brock walked off in a different direction with similar purpose.

Simon sat for several minutes just staring into the fire. "I should have killed Broderick!" Simon said as anger burned in his eyes.

"Not killing a man is a mistake that is easy to rectify, Simon," Will answered softly. "However, once the deed is done, if you killed him for the wrong reason, you can't take it back; best to err to the side of caution in such a circumstance."

"How do you know that leaving him alive won't just give him the opportunity to cause more harm?" The boy asked.

"You don't!" Delno replied as he stepped back into the firelight. He knelt down and gripped Simon's shoulders almost painfully, then shook him once, gently. "Simon, I want you to understand one thing. No matter what happens, none of this is your fault! Broderick and Bastian make their own decisions. The one thing no one can ever completely take away from a human being is the freedom to choose. The choices may not be pleasant, but there are always choices. Some time ago, as we were just beginning to get involved in the war, I made the decision not to kill a Rider who had tried to murder me. I had him helpless and no one could have legally faulted me for doing so. Killing him in that situation would have also killed his dragon, and it simply felt too much like murder to do it. Because of that decision, the man went on to attack us again and the battle resulted in his death and the deaths of two of his followers. We lost three dragons and Riders because that man was allowed to live, but it was his decision to continue with his plans, not my decision to spare his life that got him and the others killed. You did the right thing at the time, and that's all anyone can ever expect of you."

Simon smiled weakly. "I understand here," he touched his forehead, "that this isn't my fault. But it's here," he moved his hand to his gut, "that isn't convinced. Leaving Broderick alive almost got Sienna killed, and Leera could have been next. When does my gut strengthen up and let me have some peace?"

"With luck it never will," Delno replied. "Son, the pain in your gut is your conscience. You have to listen to it, but you don't have to be crippled by it. You're upset because you feel responsible that what you did or didn't do might get your friends and family hurt. That's normal; you eventually make friends with it, but it's what helps to keep leaders honest. I still feel that at least two of the Dragons and their Riders we lost that day over Palamore could have been saved if I had done things differently. I don't let my sense of right and wrong stop me from defending myself and others if necessary, but I won't let how events played out turn me into a cold-blooded murderer either. I did what was right at the time, and so did you. Every situation is different, and we have to keep reminding ourselves that the only man beyond redemption is a dead man." Simon shook his head, but he smiled, and Delno finished with, "You think that over. I have to go and get the kids while Rita lays out their bedding. The girls have fallen asleep on the dragons' legs." Then he looked at his brother and added, "Come on Will, you can carry one of them and I'll carry the other."

Rita hummed in sweet clear tones as she worked, the way his own mother used to do. Marcus walked over and kissed Rita good night before sinking into his bedroll. Simon moved to his own blanket and slid in. He listened to the woman humming and thought about times when his mother would sing him to sleep. He found it strange that now he was so close, and would be seeing her again soon that he was nearly overwhelmed with homesickness. Tears sprang to his eyes, and for the first time in a long while, he cried himself to sleep.

CHAPTER 46

THE SUN RODE low on the western horizon and would soon disappear over the mountains. Already it would not be visible to someone on the ground. Delno had been true to his word. The last leg of the trip had been no easy flight. They had taken off before sunrise the first day and only stopped three times before making camp each night while flying over beast-men territory—once to eat, and twice again to give the children and anyone else who needed the break a chance to relieve themselves. Geneva set a grueling pace, only relenting and allowing them to simply ride the air currents when they reached the downhill slopes of the western side of the mountain range. After four days in the saddle, they were all exhausted.

"There is the Fort, My Love. Geneva has contacted Wanda, who is bonded to Nassari, and we have been instructed to land inside the walls of the structure. I am very hungry and would like to hunt, but Geneva says a steer will be brought for me. I would prefer to be alone when eating, but the precaution is wise considering what happened in Orlean."

Simon watched the fort grow larger as he and Sienna got closer. Boron had told him once that this was the oldest man-made structure in the world; possibly built during the mage wars that nearly destroyed everything tens of thousands of years ago.

"I love to fly with you, Sienna, but after this trip, it will be good to be on solid ground for a while."

"It will also be good to see your mother. I told you once some time ago that you would see her again."

"Yes, you did, Dear Heart, and I'm sorry I doubted you."

"I understand why you did, Simon. I doubted myself back then. Hang on, we're going down. There's only room enough for two dragons and one already occupies the place. This is going to be a bit tight."

Sienna came to a stop and hovered for a second over the courtyard. Simon thought there would be more room for the dragons if it weren't for the huge rock formation in the middle of the space. Then he remembered Brock telling him about what happened to Warrick and his dragon. The structure was what remained of Hella and Warrick after they were killed. The magic of the place had coupled to the magic of the compelling stone that Warrick wore around his neck, and they were turned to stone when they hit the ground. This was Rider's Mound, where the Riders took the oath of allegiance to the Legion.

The orange dragon in the courtyard pressed herself against the wall as much as possible to make room for Sienna to land. Sienna set down lightly to one side of the Rock and stooped so that Simon could dismount easily. A group of people approached and Simon knew he should control himself and make introductions before anything else, but thoughts of courtesy drained away as soon as he saw his mother's face. He forgot about everything and ran headlong into her arms.

Sheena cried and kept repeating "I thought I lost you, I thought I lost you…"

All of the others present stood quietly, waiting until the two of them had time to recover from their reunion. Nassari took the liberty of ordering two younger Riders to remove Sienna's gear.

Finally, after almost a quarter of an hour, Sheena held Simon at arm's length and said, "Let me take a look at you. You're as tall as I am now. You've grown so much I almost didn't recognize you. You look so very much like your father."

"You haven't changed a bit, Mother," Simon replied. "I'm sorry I had to sneak off into the night like that. I wanted to come to you, but I knew that would put you in danger."

Both mother and son looked around and noticed that they were now standing in the middle of quite a crowd. Delno and the rest of the group had joined them, as well as many faces Simon had never seen before. He found Boron among the throng. His old mentor was standing next to the biggest man Simon had ever seen in his life. Boron just smiled and nodded in approval at him.

Introductions were made all around and then Simon, his mother, and Boron were invited to join the leaders of the Riders for dinner and conversation. Since Riders sometimes came and went at all hours the Fort usually kept some type of stew hot so that anyone could get a good meal no matter the time. Nadia had several younger Riders bring food for all of them.

After eating, it took over an hour for Simon to tell his whole tale. Nadia had been right; Sheena was very happy she had not heard the entire story of her son's adventures in the wilds until she could see and touch him. She brushed his hair with her fingers and couldn't help but trace the scars on his face where the Rorack had clawed him. If the injury had happened after he had been bonded for some time, it would have healed without a trace. When Simon finished his story, he handed his Dragon Blades to Nassari, who examined them and then passed them around the room for everyone else to see.

"Not bad work," the giant smith of the Fort, Elom, said about the guards and hilts. "A bit plain, but serviceable. You did the work yourself?"

"Mostly," Simon replied. "I worked out a deal with the smith at Ford so that he let me use his forge and equipment. He watched over my shoulder and made suggestions, as well as holding the pieces with tongs while I drove them on hot, but I just felt I should do as much as I could on my own since they were my Dragon Blades."

Elom looked at Boron. "You taught the lad well. This may not have the artistic complexity of the guard I made for Delno's Blade, but it should hold just fine." Turning back to Simon he added, "When all of this other business is handled, come and see me if you'd like a stint in the smithy here. Boron is working with me, and between the two of us, we'll make a fine craftsman out of you."

"Coming from Elom, that's extremely high praise," Nassari interjected. "Men who have been working the trade for several years send letters requesting to train under our good Mastersmith. It's pure luck that he is here at all. He was only going to come to the fort long enough to set up the metal shop before returning home to Corice. If he hadn't inadvertently met and bonded to Nora on the plain outside Larimar shortly before we left, he probably wouldn't have stayed on. As it is, you've just been offered a stint in the best metal shop anywhere under a master smith who is arguably the most highly skilled in the business."

Simon could see the pride in the looks of both Boron and his mother. He started to let it go to his head for a moment. Brock smiled indulgently at him and Simon's pride deflated just a little. He remembered his mentor's words, "*Take pride in your accomplishments, but don't get cocky: there's always going to be somebody who can do it better.*" He smiled back at Brock in understanding and Brock gave him the barest nod of approval.

"Now then," Nassari spoke up. "What's to be done with our current situation?"

Delno shook his head and replied, "I was hoping that you would have some good ideas on the matter. How close to boiling over is this whole affair?"

"Very close, Del. But, since Boron was one of the King's elite and knows the situation best I'll let him explain."

All eyes turned to Boron, and he cleared his throat before speaking. "The major noble houses, twenty-two of them, have always kept their own guard. Usually close to forty well-trained, well-equipped men at arms. The guards' families have been linked to their respective houses for generations, and the officers are members of the house itself, so loyalty to their own faction isn't in question. The reason they haven't overthrown the king, or at least severely limited the Crown's power, before now is that there is so much bickering among the greater houses. They all want to be the one in charge, and none of them have been willing to take second place. Since the Crown normally keeps about three hundred elite fighters, and has control of the rest of the standing army, the major players haven't been able to come up with enough cohesive strength under a single banner to force capitulation from the King."

Boron paused for questions, but no one asked anything and Delno politely signaled him to continue.

"I've spoken to some of my old friends in the military, and I've learned that Thomas is grossly overextended. He lost almost half of his elite guard in the war, and then he had to send a good many of those left, especially the officers, back to the regular ranks to keep the borders safe. About two thousand Roracks got away from our combined forces the day you defeated Warrick. They ran off into their old territories. They found those territories nearly stripped clean. It didn't take them long to meet up with who knows how many of their kindred who weren't under Warrick's control and go back to their old ways: small bands of twenty to sixty making regular raids on our lands. The army, depleted in both manpower and equipment by the war, has its hands full just keeping those monsters at bay. Thomas has fewer than a hundred elite guards at the capital, and no more than two hundred fifty regulars near to hand. The King is damned if he does and damned if he doesn't. If he pulls troops back to guard his capital, he weakens the border. Doing that will not only hurt his economic base, it will create so much dissent among the towns and villages that are left undefended that those people are likely to join the rebellion. Even if they don't openly oppose him, his capital will swell with refugees who will need food and medical attention. Those refugees will use resources and not contribute to anything but the Crown's downfall."

"So let's be generous and say that the Great Houses have forty men each. That's less than a thousand soldiers. Surely the Crown can withstand such a force?" Delno asked.

"Less than a thousand, but all of them seasoned veterans. And don't forget the more than thirty minor houses, plus the outlying nobles like Bastian," Boron responded. "At one time in this country's history, Awards of Arms were handed out like party favors to keep money flowing into the king's coffers to pay for expansion of the realm. Now, on an average day in Fallon, you can hardly spit outside without risk of hitting some nobleman or another. Having so many titled families is one reason the king has never wanted to share any power for fear of losing too much." He paused to collect his thoughts.

"After dealing with many of those same families while getting the Legion established, I can, to some extent, sympathize with Thomas on that point," Nassari said.

Boron cleared his throat and continued before a side discussion about the size of the peerage roster could get going. "Those lesser nobles don't normally keep a formal standing guard, but they have retainers who owe their livelihood to the local lords. Those retainers could easily swell the numbers to as many as fifteen hundred, perhaps even two thousand. Granted, most of them are farm hands and laborers, but put them up front as arrow fodder to cover the well-trained troops, and they become a real threat."

"That's a despicable use of men," Delno stated flatly.

"I agree, Rider," Boron nodded. "But this isn't a popular rebellion we're talking about here. This is the Noble Houses railing against the King. Those highborn merchants don't give a tinker's damn about how many commoners get slaughtered."

Delno got up and walked away from the table. Boron started to rise, but Nassari signaled him to wait. Delno paced for several minutes until he had his anger under control before sitting back down.

"I'm sorry about that. I was an officer in Corice, but that was because I was elevated from common soldier to the rank for my actions. I was born and raised a commoner, and I didn't learn of my blood connection the royal family until after I bonded with Geneva. It strikes too damn close to home when I see nobles use people so callously. Men die in war, but they shouldn't die simply to further the profit of those who should, by right, be concerned with their welfare."

"I understand, Delno," Boron replied. "I am the bastard son of a noble father and a common mother. My father helped me get my rank as a junior officer, but everything else I've ever achieved I've done by working twice as hard as the next man in line. I'm not saying I approve of this whole thing, I'm just reporting the facts as I see them."

Delno nodded and changed the subject. "So how does Simon fit into all of this? Surely there are better ways to rally the nobles to the cause than persecuting one boy?"

"I'd like to say you're right, but that's not the case. It seems that using Simon kills two birds with one stone. They can not only say that the King has sided with a commoner who has caused serious injury and grievous insult to a noble, but that he has also sided with the Dragon Riders against the nobility." He shook his head and grimaced, "If it weren't for the current situation, with the Dragons to verify which boy is lying, we could probably have Broderick convicted for his crimes and sent off to spend a few years *apprenticing* in his majesty's mines. However, the Great Houses are terrified that you all will come to the aid of the Crown, so they are crying that one of the main reasons Horne hasn't regained its former prosperity since the war is that the Legion of Riders is quartered here using up resources. It's a blatant falsehood, but people like to have someone besides themselves to blame for their troubles."

"I've seen chamber pots filled with sweeter smelling stuff than that rot," Nassari said disgustedly. "I negotiated the treaty that gave us this Fort and the surrounding plain after Warrick was defeated. We agreed that the Riders would pay their own way, and we have done so. These same nobles overlook that it is due to the fact that I house several Riders at the capital and make them available to carry messages that they are able to communicate in a matter of hours with trading partners when such communication would have previously taken days or weeks. We may charge them a small fee for the service, but our contribution is the most vital part of why they have been so successful at getting their own contracts signed ahead of their competition. They forget the fact that it was the Riders, especially Brock," he nodded to the dark-skinned man, "who headed off a costly war with Iondar and reopened trade routes with that country. All of these things were done more to support them, and the country at large than for the king of Horne." He threw up his hands and said hotly, "Perhaps we should quit this place and return to the northeast and let these idiots swing in the breeze!"

"I have no intention of abandoning this place, Delno stated hotly. "Corice may have helped greatly in outfitting this Fort, but their debt to us is paid and I don't fancy the idea of returning to them with my hat in my hands. Besides, we've put too much into this Fort, and still have too much to learn about it to turn it back over to Horne and leave it for some non-bonded magic user to discover its secrets, especially since those secrets are so closely tied to the dragons and the magic surrounding them. I'll be damned if someone who is a potential enemy of all dragons and riders will get a chance to use knowledge gleaned from this place's connection to the world magic against us." He slammed his open palm on the table hard enough to rattle the glasses, "This entire plain is ours, and we will not be driven from it!"

Boron snorted with ironic laughter. "None of the other nobles like Bastian. The man is a miser and cheat. If they didn't need this as a rallying cry, they'd probably thank us mightily if we killed him and Broderick outright."

Nassari saw the expression on Delno's face and knew that his oldest and best friend had the beginnings of a plan. "I know that look well, Del. What do you have in mind?"

"Nothing solid yet, but I have an idea. We're all tired and need rest, so I won't go into any detail until I've had a chance to sleep on it. What I need you to do, Nassari, is use all of your contacts. Make sure that all of the Houses of Horne know we have no intention of being forced out of this Fort. We will defend our position here with every means at our disposal. If they successfully move against the King and are then foolhardy enough to send the remainder of their forces against us, this plain will once again be littered with burned corpses. If, on the other hand, they are willing to negotiate peacefully, we may be able to work out an agreement that is to everyone's benefit."

Nassari said, "You can't drop something like that into this fire and just walk away, Del. You have to let us in on the rest of it."

Just as Delno was about to refuse, a young, dark-haired girl of about twelve came bursting into the room. "Nassari, you have to come quick."

"You had better get down here to the clutch, Love. You need to see this, and bring the children's parents," Wanda said as the novice Rider was gasping out her message.

"Geneva says we need to get to the courtyard," Delno stated.

He and Rita were already half way to the door as Nassari and Nadia moved to join them.

The girl who interrupted the meeting added, "We didn't realize what the children were doing until it was too late. They've always been allowed to play around the dragons, so we weren't watching them closely."

CHAPTER 47

BOTH NASSARI'S AND Nadia's partners had risen to mate in the spring, and both had conceived. Wanda laid one egg, and Pina laid two. Not being novice mothers, they had agreed that combining the clutch into one would facilitate care while the humans looked for suitable candidates.

Gwendolyn, Gillian, and Marcus were indeed there with the joint clutch. Marcus had rolled one egg a little away from the 'nest': the twins kept the others close together. Each of the children was fondling the egg nearest to him or her. It was obvious to all of the Riders present that all three children had bonded to the baby dragons inside the shells.

Rita shook her head and turned on the girl who had delivered the message to Nassari. "Who was supposed to be watching them?" she demanded.

The girl stared at her, unable to utter a word.

Delno put his hand on Rita's shoulder and said, "The dragons were watching them, if you will remember. If you want to yell at someone, yell at Wanda. This poor, terrified girl isn't to blame. It's our fault for not taking precautions to prevent this."

Always able to see the bright side of any problem, Nassari spoke up, "Well, we figured they'd be Riders some day, and this does solve the problem of finding suitable candidates for the young dragons."

Rita rounded on him. "We had hoped that they wouldn't bond for at least another six to ten years. It's hard enough to raise a baby dragon with a more mature Rider. Do you know how difficult it will be trying to get the pair to behave when the human child is four?"

A lesser man would have backed off from Rita in a full-blown fury, especially when she was being a protective mother. Nassari, however, smiled and used his silken voice in a soothing tone. "Don't yell at me. I was upstairs with the rest of you when the children bonded. I am merely saying that, now bonding has occurred and can't be undone, we should look for the good, and deal with the situation."

Rita's stance softened and she managed to smile. "It's going to be a big job keeping up with three hatchlings who are bonded to children so young. This is going to take a coordinated effort from everyone."

"My people say it takes a village to raise a child," Nadia intoned fondly.

"It only takes one five-year-old on a dragon to raze an entire city," Delno replied. "We've definitely got our work cut out for us." He shook his head and added, "Why can't we get one problem solved before more crop up?"

Marcus looked up at the adults and said, "Sonja says she won't be ready to come out for several more days. She also says that she is tired and the sound of your voices is keeping her awake."

Gwendolyn chimed in. "Bridget says she is not tired but would rather not listen, too."

Gillian nodded in agreement, but said nothing. She simply turned back to the egg and continued communing with the dragon-child inside.

Delno shook his head and stared at all three for a moment before saying, "All we can do is play the tiles we've been dealt. We'll leave the kids where they are for now, and if they decide to sleep with the eggs we'll bring their bedrolls out. Nassari, have a couple of the novices watch over them and see that they don't get into any more trouble. In the mean time, I want a bath and some more food, and wine."

Nadia volunteered to stay with the children for a while until Nassari could make arrangements to have the novices watch in shifts. Simon and the rest of the party were led to quarters so they could bathe and rest.

CHAPTER 48

"THE NOBLES HAVE moved against the King," Nassari said without formality as Delno and Brock walked into the main room of the Legion Headquarters. "They have gathered almost two thousand troops and the capital is under siege. So far no blood has been shed, but Thomas refuses to negotiate. What's worse is that he's named all of the leaders as traitors and decreed they are no longer members of the peerage."

"What was he thinking?" Delno asked in amazement. "By declaring the leaders outlaws with no titles, he has left them with little choice other than to see this through. Does the man actually want civil war?"

"Thomas isn't far-sighted under the best of circumstances," Boron interjected. "He's also pig-headed. He won't back down until they've got a knife to his throat. The man actually believes that the Horne family rules this land by some kind of divine right."

Delno looked back at Nassari, "What about the Riders at the capital?"

"All of them are little more than novices sent to be messengers. They're last year's crop who've completed training but were still too young and immature to release into the world without supervision. Thomas demanded that they fly out and destroy the nobles' army, but they had the good sense to simply come home once they were airborne. They're actually still an hour out, but close enough to re-lay the situation through the dragons."

"Why didn't they contact Geneva?" he accused.

"Del, I'm in charge here for a reason, and they did contact the one Lineage Holder they knew would be here," Nassari gently re-buked his old friend.

Delno smiled sheepishly, "I'm sorry, Nassari, you're absolutely right. I keep forgetting that I'm not the only one in charge anymore." He looked around at Boron, Will, Sheena, Nat, and Simon. "You could have informed me first."

"We all just kind of showed up here, and had just settled down to coffee and biscuits when Nassari received the message, Brother," Will said, coming to his old squad leader's defense. "The first thing Nassari did was have Geneva contact you."

"Again, my apologies; so much is happening at once that I fear losing control of everything. You did well, Nassari. It's good that the youngsters pulled back here, but we do need to keep track of what's going on. Will, it's been three days since we arrived after that intense pace I set getting here. Are you and Saadia up to a long morning flight?"

"I thought this was coming and asked Saadia; she says she's ready. We can be in the air in half an hour."

"Good. When you get there you are to observe and stay out of trouble. I don't need you to stay cloaked." At Will's look of surprise, Delno explained. "It won't hurt our cause if you are seen, especially since you have dealt with Thomas in the past and he responds well to you. In fact, I would prefer that you take a little extra time and get at least two other Riders you can trust to obey your commands and take them with you. Circle the en-tire area regularly, and stay out of bow range of either group. I want both sides to know that the Dragon Riders are interested in the outcome, but remaining neutral as long as our welfare isn't at risk."

Will wasn't sure what exactly Delno and Nassari had planned, but he saluted and marched out of the room.

Delno turned back to Nassari. "Looks like we're in the thick of it whether we want to be or not. Any word on Lord Bastian?"

It was Nat who answered. "Roland Fine, the physician who moved here from Larimar, came in yesterday to speak with me. He told me that Bastian had left with a large group of men the day before, and that Broderick was in charge of the estate. He also mentioned that he has seen several unsavory types in the village in the last few days, and he's sure they went to visit the estate shortly after Bastian's departure." The half-elf gave him a sheepish look and added, "I'm sorry, Delno, I suppose I should have reported this, but I was preoccupied with all of the healers who have been coming to get supplies and advice from me."

"Damn!" Boron swore. "I wish I had known that before now."

He scowled and Sheena stepped in front of the half-elf and said sternly, "Don't blame Nat; he's a doctor, not a politician or warrior. You can't expect him to keep track of these doings and train the novice Riders in the healing arts at the same time."

Boron calmed himself and apologized, "I'm sorry, Nathaniel, you did nothing wrong. I'm just worried about Simon, and those men Roland spoke of are probably more assassins. It's just like that selfish little twerp, Broderick, to put his own concerns ahead of everything and everyone. He wants revenge, and not even being caught up in a civil war will deter him. The rest of the country can fall to ruin as long as he gets his way."

Delno's eyes took on the distant, almost vacant expression of a Rider in mental contact with his partner for a few seconds. When they cleared he said, "Geneva has just been contacted by Carra. Jhren is less than two hours out. If Broderick has hired another mage, the man will be in for quite a surprise."

"That's the first good news we've heard this morning," Rita responded. "We were expecting Jhren at least two days ago. I was beginning to get worried he wouldn't make it in time to help."

"Actually, everything we've heard this morning is good news. The nobles are pretty much playing right into our hands, and Thomas's stubborn pride will aid us as well. The fact that Broderick is most likely bankrupting Bastian's estate in his quest for vengeance gives us more than enough excuse to put an end to his schemes any way we have to." Nassari spoke in a voice that Delno recognized as him at his most devious.

"Yes," Delno said. "I believe that, for now, at least, we will watch the capital and not interfere. Jhren is late arriving because I spoke to him in the Dream State and had him delay his departure to do a bit of research. He is carrying notes that should be helpful in negotiating a peaceful solution between the Crown of Horne and the nobles. With a little luck, when this is over, Horne will have a more parliamentary government as my Grandfather had planned, and we will be even more secure in our position here at the Fort."

Nassari stood up suddenly, "Wanda says that the egg she laid is hatching and that the other two won't be far behind. She has already sent for two steers to feed the new dragons. If we wish to attend the births, we had best get down there quickly."

Delno was first out the door followed closely by Nassari while Rita yelled for them to wait up for her. Boron could have easily kept up with the two men, but politely held back and escorted Sheena. Simon, being eleven, forgot all courtesy and ran pell-mell to catch up with the older Riders.

Marcus sat cat-like, watching as the shell containing his Bond-mate rocked faster and faster. Faint tapping noises were coming from inside. A crack appeared and the tapping became almost frantic. The crack widened and the egg tooth and nose of the baby appeared. The rocking stopped and the shell nearly vibrated as the little dragon spread all six of her limbs against the weakened casing until it almost exploded. She stood there glaring around as if offended that so many had watched her hatching.

"No one thinks that you were undignified," Marcus said out loud to Sonja. "They have seen dragons hatch before so they know that you did well."

The dragon's overall color was light gold, but there was an orange stripe down the middle of her back and the leading edges of her wings were orange as well. She took one look at Sienna across the courtyard and growled.

Marcus turned to Simon and said, "She doesn't like Sienna being here. She had expected her mother, and wasn't too happy about that, but she wants Sienna to leave so that she can eat without another dragon nearby."

Delno stepped forward, "Tell her that she will have to get used to it. Sienna could be in mortal danger if she leaves right now. There is more than enough food for all of the dragons in and around this Fort, so there is no reason to be territorial."

Simon had been alarmed at the ferocity of the gesture aimed at Sienna, and Delno whispered, "Geneva and Wanda are both telling her to settle down. She will be able to overcome her instinctual impulses and accept Sienna being present. If it becomes a problem, we can actually move Sonja and Marcus."

"I wouldn't mind flying off for a while," Sienna said softly. "I have been stuck here on the ground since we arrived, and I would love to stretch my wings."

Delno patted her neck and replied, "I know it's a hardship, Sienna, but we have to keep you out of sight until we have full control of the situation. You'll be in the air again soon. I promise."

Both of the twins squealed and everyone moved to watch the remaining eggs. The babies hatched almost simultaneously.

Bridget's body and leading wing edges were solid, hunter green. The color lightened on her wing membranes due to the thinner skin. She had no other markings. She didn't complain about other dragons in the vicinity, but she immediately looked for food.

The last dragon-child was a deep, dark blue, the color of the sky just before darkness falls. Her wing membranes lightened to purple, and she had a red stripe on either side of her face that ran from the front corners over her eyes to the back like the makeup won by some noble women. Then the stripe continued from there to her ear openings.

Gillian looked up at the adults and said, "Linden says that she is very hungry, and that if we do not give her some of the meat that is being cut she will simply help herself."

CHAPTER 49

BRODERICK OPENED THE door slowly, careful not to make the slightest sound. He knew he was in the right room because the same pendant that rendered him invisible also made his vision work better in darkness. The thing had been hideously expensive, but since the mage who had come to the estate four days ago had absolutely refused to act against Simon here at the old Fort with so many dragons and riders present, he had had no choice but to buy the amulet and do the job himself. The mage was a coward. Broderick had snuck into the place without so much as a twitched nose from any of those colossal beasts. Finding Simon's room had not been hard either, thanks to his own ability to be stealthy. He had looked in other rooms, but no one would ever know he was there. He would have killed Simon's mother if the whore hadn't been sleeping with that big oaf. Even if he had killed the smith first, the woman would probably have woken up and raised an alarm.

He crept closer to the bed. His prey was asleep, lying on his stomach. Broderick briefly thought of pouncing on the boy and tormenting him before killing him painfully. However, one noise from Simon and the whole place would be up in arms. Invisibility might allow him to escape, but the possibility of someone accidently bumping into and discovering him was too great. It had to be one quick stab to the kidney. That way it would be excruciatingly painful, and he could watch the little bastard die before he slipped away. He wished he could stay and see the looks on their faces when they found the body in the morning. Leaving her son dead would actually be better than killing the woman, anyway.

He took his time crossing from the door to the bed; savoring every second of this. Finally, he stood directly over the boy. The dagger in his hand was nearly a foot long and a hand wide. It was double edged, so that it would cut in both directions when he swung it back and forth once he had plunged it into Simon's back. Weaver had instructed him just how to do it, told him exactly how to judge where the kidney is. He said that stabbing the boy in the kidney would cause so much pain that Simon wouldn't be able to move air in either direction, so it would prevent the boy from screaming while he died in agony. He raised the blade high, aiming carefully.

"Time to die, Little Mouse," he said as he drove the blade down with all of his strength.

He felt the knife penetrate, but there was less resistance than he had expected. Also, the body didn't move or show any sign of pain.

Broderick's eyes were momentarily blinded as a bright globe of silvery-white light suddenly burst into being directly over his head. As his eyes adjusted he stared down at the mound of pillows he had stabbed. Simon was not in the bed.

"Think you're the only one who can play with magic, boy?" a high-pitched man's voice asked from the corner of the room.

Broderick had the presence of mind to hang onto the knife as he rounded on the speaker. The man who had spoken was a little over six feet tall and had hair the color of jet.

"Where's the boy?" Broderick demanded; menacing the man with his blade.

"Right here, Little Kitten," came Simon's voice from behind him.

Broderick spun around, and there was his quarry, standing next to a dark-haired man Broderick had never seen before. Simon had his short Dragon Blade in his hand.

"Put the weapon down, boy," Delno ordered Broderick. "You don't have a chance here. Even if you manage to get past all four of us, there are at least five more armed Riders in the hallway, and that trinket around your neck isn't fooling anyone."

"It won't hurt my feelings if you try to use that blade," Boron said from yet another corner of the room.

Broderick stood staring for several moments, completely dumbfounded. "I just saw you in his mother's room. How…"

"You didn't see him," Jhren stated in a matter of fact tone. "Or his mother, for that matter. You saw Nassari and Nadia, the leaders of this Fort, disguised by a glamour. Lucky for you that you didn't get stupid and try to hurt them. Nassari might have been in a playful mood, but Nadia is all business when it comes to assassins creeping about in the dead of night."

Broderick reached up and touched the amulet, concentrated on becoming invisible and said, "Hide me."

The black-haired man let out a shrill, piercing laugh. "You didn't pay good money for that thing, did you? I penetrated the glamour on it before you got within a hundred yards of the gates." Broderick stared at the man blankly, and Jhren added, "Charms like that can be useful if you want to spy on a cheating spouse, or escape from unwanted visitors without appearing to be rude, but you should never have believed that it would get you in here. First time I made one of those was about ninety years ago. I was seven."

"You see, Broderick," Simon spoke up. "We let you get this far so that there could be no doubt of your guilt. We have caught you trying to assassinate a Dragon Rider on our land. Once you came here, you left Horne and are now subject to our laws, and our justice. Now drop the blade!"

Broderick was so shaken by the change in Simon and the air of authority he projected he almost complied. Then something inside of him snapped, and he lunged. The attack was vicious, and would have been successful against an untrained opponent, but Simon was far from untrained. He turned the attack aside with his left hand and reflexively brought his own blade up into his attacker's midsection. The force of his thrust combined with the forward momentum of the attack caused the long knife to penetrate so deeply that over an inch came out of Broderick's back.

Broderick's eyes opened wide in shock and he fell to the floor in a heap with Simon's Dragon Blade still in his body. Delno knelt next to the young man and examined the wound while he had Geneva relay to Marlo that he needed Nat—immediately.

CHAPTER 50

"IT'S BEEN NEARLY an hour," Delno complained. "Where is the old wizard?"

He asked his question out loud but his answer came from Geneva. "Jhren has returned, Dear One. He wants you to meet him in the courtyard."

The sun was just coming over the mountains so there was enough light to see that Carra was carrying a man who was firmly encased in her front claws. The look on the man's face was a mixture of pain, terror, and indignation.

"Don't get directly under us," Jhren yelled unnecessarily. Everyone present knew better than get into the dragon's blind spot while she was landing. "I think he may have soiled himself on the way here and I wouldn't want you to be under him if any falls out of his trousers." He had obviously made the statement more to cause the man embarrassment than to warn the bystanders.

Carra landed harder than she needed to because Jhren wanted to further shake up his captive. She put the man down with enough force to knock him to the ground and lowered herself to facilitate her partner's dismount. Jhren immediately walked over and kicked the prostrate man in the ribs.

"Get up, you sack of offal!" he shouted.

The man grunted in pain and got slowly to his feet.

"So, this is the great mage who sold that idiot the talisman?" Delno asked Jhren.

"The very same. I found him in the local inn, and Carra helped me persuade him to come and have a chat with us."

"I-I have done n-nothing wrong. You have n-no right t-to abduct me like this," the man stammered.

Jhren slapped him on the back of the head and snarled, "When we want you to speak, you'll know it. Until then, keep it shut, or I'll shut it."

"You know that the Dragon Riders cannot let this go unpunished. You have willfully aided a young man in an assassination attempt," Delno said menacingly. "By the look of you, you haven't yet reached your twenty-fifth birthday, and if I don't like the answers you give to my questions, your longevity could be in serious jeopardy."

"You have no evidence that I had any part in such a plot."

Jhren slapped the young man again. "Don't try and lie your way out of this, youngster. I was practicing real magic before your daddy was more than a wicked thought in your grandpa's mind. I traced this little ditty," he held up the amulet they had taken from Broderick, "back to you. You didn't even have sense enough to remove your magical signature. Now stop being stupid and wait until you're told to talk before you open your mouth, and when you do talk, tell the truth."

The young magic user looked at the ground as if he was a child caught with his hand the cookie jar.

"I see we are starting to come to an understanding," Delno said. He raised his hand as a signal and Boron and Nassari led Broderick into the courtyard. "This boy certainly wouldn't lie to protect you, so don't think you owe him any favors. He snuck into a Rider's bedroom and tried to kill him. You sold him this amulet so that he could get in here and kill a Dragon Rider, am I right?"

Broderick looked as though he would rip the mage's heart out if he hadn't been bound and held by two large men.

"Yes. He offered me a thousand gold to do the job myself. I'm no assassin! I was lured here by a man named Weaver with the promise of a reward to help apprehend a criminal, not to kill a boy so that some over-privileged young bastard can get revenge for something I know almost nothing about. Besides, I know what a dragon is capable of, and the boy he wanted dead was surrounded by more than a dozen of them. I would have refused regardless, but even if I had been willing to commit murder, I knew I couldn't get in, do the job, and get out alive. For that matter, if by some miracle I managed to escape the fort, the boy's bond-mate would surely spend her final days hunting me down and ending my life in some extremely painful and messy fashion."

Delno nodded, "What happened when you refused?"

The young man took a couple of deep breaths before he spoke. "He offered me more and told me that he simply wanted me to bring the boy to him, not make the kill myself." Looking Delno squarely in the eye he continued, "He had no proof that the boy was even wanted other than a warrant signed by Lord Bastian. Being from Fallon, and having friends in the royal court, I know that warrant was vacated by the king himself. Not only did I have no legal reason to do what he wanted, I wouldn't do what amounts to treason by going against the wishes of the crown." He paused for a moment and then pointed at Broderick, adding, "He got irate and told me I wouldn't leave his lands alive if I didn't help him, so I sold him an amulet of shadows I keep for my own use for two-hundred-fifty gold pieces."

Jhren almost choked. "Two-fifty? You may not be much of a mage, but you're one heck of a con-man. Sneak thieves don't pay more than twenty gold for those things in any big city in the south." He laughed in that peculiar high-pitched tone of his. "Tell me, how did you expect him to get out if he actually got the job done?"

The younger mage smiled maliciously and said, "I didn't. He and those two goons with him threatened me. They literally had their hands on me, so I couldn't use the amulet to get away. I had to come up with something quickly, or try and fight my way out of there. I figured if he was so intent on suicide, and I'd never see him again, why not take his money? Then I showed him how to use the amulet before going back to my room at the inn, which is why I didn't have the time or opportunity to clear away any magical signature that could be traced back to me. I was going to take my gold and get out of here this morning. I didn't see any harm in turning a profit, since he wouldn't need the money once he was dead." He turned to Delno and added, "If I had actually thought he might get past your dragons, I would have come and told you of the plot. But I saw no point in doing so since I expected him to be ashes before he got to the gate. I don't have any desire to get on the wrong side of the Dragon Riders."

Jhren laughed again, "I might have misjudged you, boy. Maybe you do have some common sense after all." He put his arm around the young mage's shoulder and led him toward inner buildings, "He didn't get past the dragons, though. We saw him coming from way off. We allowed him to get into the Rider's bedroom so that we could catch him in the act. It was all we could do to keep from laughing and giving the whole charade away when he was skulking around opening doors looking for the right room." Then he added, as he showed the younger man through the main door, "Now let's get some lunch and you can write all of this down as an official statement. Once all of this business is done, you'll be allowed to take your two hundred and fifty gold and leave."

CHAPTER 51

"THIS COLLAR WILL hold him," Elom stated to Boron. "Jhren and I both worked magic into it, and Nora lent me her power when she used her fire to heat the metal. I put as much into that as I've put into any blade I've made in the last two years. No one is going to remove it without mine or Jhren's say so."

"You can't put that thing on me," Broderick protested. "I am the son of a Lord of this land. I have rights."

"You'll wear it, boy," Jhren said with a menacing smile, "or I'll cut you so badly that none of the healers here will be able to save your life. As far as I'm concerned, they should have left you to bleed to death when you tried to kill Simon a week ago. However, I'm just an old mage. I'm not in charge here and don't want to be. Delno and Nassari say you're to be kept alive, at least for now."

"Be glad it's the Riders who are deciding your fate," Boron said. "If it were up to me, I'd hang you and be done with it."

Elom reached out with one massive hand and grabbed Broderick, pushing him to his knees. The youth tried to struggle, but he would have been no match for Elom even if the huge smith's strength weren't magically enhanced by his connection to his dragon. Elom put the collar around Broderick's neck and forced him down to the anvil so that he could set the rivet that would hold the thing in place.

Broderick stared wide-eyed as Jhren reached into the forge fire with his bare hand and pulled out the red hot piece. Then the wizard brought the metal stud to his mouth and said several words before dropping it into a bucket of water. The water hissed and green steam rose into the air. Jhren nodded. Elom retrieved the piece from the bucket and put it through the holes in the open end of the collar.

"I've never missed my mark with a hammer yet, boy, so just don't move. It's probably best if you close your eyes so you don't flinch." Elom said without any trace of emotion.

The hammer looked large even in Elom's hand. He had to use his biggest hammer because the rivet was not only made of his best steel, but Jhren had also worked his enchantment to harden it. The thing would have been easier to set hot, but that might have burned the wearer and no one was interested in torturing Broderick. He raised his arm and Broderick closed his eyes, crying silently. The hammer fell and the sound of steel on steel was like a thunderclap in his ears. The smith had to hit the rivet three times with the twelve-pound hammer to set it.

Elom hoisted Broderick to his feet as easily as someone else might lift a small child. "It's done, he pronounced as he examined the collar closely. That's not coming off any time soon."

"We can put this one away until the meeting then," Jhren said to Elom. "I know you and Boron have work to do, so I'll take him back inside."

"You can't put me on a leash like some mongrel dog," Broderick said with more bluster than any of the men would have thought him still capable of. "My father and the other Lords will soon put an end to this outrage."

Elom shook his head sadly and turned away. "My part is done. Get him out of my shop, and out of my hearing, before I shut his mouth permanently."

Jhren led Broderick out of the smithy and back toward the fort. "You don't know the nature of that collar, boy. We have no intention of attaching a tether to it. The collar is the leash."

"What are you talking about?"

"It's quite simple really. The magic our gentle giant there worked into the metal makes it nearly indestructible by normal means. The magic I worked into it is a bit more complex. The collar measures your intent. If you don't behave yourself, it will tighten until you either behave or die of strangulation. At this point, we don't even have to watch you anymore."

"What's to keep me from leaving and going directly to my father and the Council of Lords?"

Jhren chuckled. "Go ahead, take off. I'm just an old man. I'm probably too weak to stop you anyway."

The boy looked at Jhren suspiciously. This was no old man, too frail to be a threat. He couldn't be more than forty. It had to be some kind of trick.

Just then a shadow passed overhead and Jhren was distracted by three dragons landing. Broderick saw his opportunity and took off at a dead run toward the open plain. If he could put enough distance between himself and the Fort, he might actually make it. However, with every step, the collar got tighter. He hadn't made it thirty paces before the thing was so tight he couldn't breathe, and the lack of fresh blood going to his brain was causing stars to blink in and out of view in front of his eyes. The world seemed to swim for a moment, and then everything went black.

"No, he's alive." Broderick heard someone very close to him say. He opened his eyes and a blonde-haired, blue-eyed man with roughly handsome features was kneeling next to him.

"Didn't Jhren tell you that collar would choke you if tried to run away?" Will asked.

"I mentioned that he had to behave, but I might not have been specific," Jhren answered from several feet away. "You know I'm getting senile in my old age."

Will looked at his friend and mentor. "Old age my foot! You've been getting steadily younger since we met, you old fraud. It's a side effect of bonding with a dragon. You may have been ninety-four and on death's door before you met Carra, but your body's in no worse shape now than any man in his late thirties. That ancient and feeble act might have worked when your hair was still white."

Jhren's face split into a huge grin. "Get that idiot on his feet and let's get back inside the Fort. It's nearly noon and I want lunch. Besides, I'm sure you have a report on doings in the capital for Nassari and your brother."

Several hours later Delno, Brock, and Nassari sat in Nassari's private office.

"You're certain all of the Lords will come as requested?" Delno asked.

"The leaders of the rebellion will be here. Many of the minor nobles are not coming, and will take charge of the troops besieging the capital. The problem is going to be Thomas. He has flatly refused to come here, or even negotiate at all. We'll have to fetch him by force."

"I don't like the idea of kidnapping the sovereign ruler of a country," Brock said hotly. "It sets a precedent that could lead us places we've pledged not to go. In fact, we specifically pledged not to do what we are discussing."

"We pledged not to 'participate in any attempt to usurp power from the rightful and just rulers of any sovereign nation in an effort to gain power for ourselves or any master'. We are not trying to usurp power for that reason. We are simply trying to head off a civil war that could not only bring about the ruin of this country, but give the Roracks open ground in which to breed and become an even bigger threat to the rest of the world. We aren't planning to kidnap Thomas to dethrone him, but he not only refuses to speak with the rebels, he has recalled his troops to the capital, which will leave the borders undefended."

"He has to know that those men will refuse to leave their homelands and families to the depredations of the beast-men," Brock responded.

"Thomas may be self-centered, egotistical, and even a bit slow on the uptake, but he's not completely stupid. It has always been the policy of the army of Horne to not station their soldiers close to home, and to move them around regularly to prevent the troops from becoming too friendly with the locals. That way, if things go badly the men are much less likely to disobey orders and not answer a recall to Fallon," Delno replied. "About two-thirds of the troops are marching back to the aid of the Crown now. We are watching the border towns as best we can, but we can't protect all of the people without sufficient ground troops. If we don't act now a whole lot of people are going to die at the hands of the Roracks while more die in a bloody civil war. There will be conflict on two fronts with us caught in the middle."

"Brock, you haven't been living here like I have," Nassari said. "I've had the Riders keep tabs on the beast-men. Conservative estimates say there are at least five thousand of them in those mountains, and Jhren thinks the number is closer to seven thousand. As the troops pull back from the borders the Roracks sense the weakness and begin making raids. They're not coordinated like they were under Warrick, but that actually works in their favor. We have about half the Legion here now, less two dozen seasoned Riders. Add a dozen of the children who've been trained but haven't seen real conflict and it's an impressive amount of firepower. However, the beast-men are coming across the border at all points in groups of twenty to sixty. There's so much area to patrol that we can't keep up with it all. If we step up patrols in one area those monsters are clever enough to move to another. It's like trying to hold back a small stream with your hands. It simply flows around and continues on its way. Without the troops Thomas has recalled, this entire country could fall into chaos."

"We don't want to oust Thomas completely," Delno added. "It's not like we're trying to establish open elections of commoners and put everything under complete democracy. This country has existed in a state of war since its inception, and that was more than eight generations of bonded dragons ago; about thirty thousand years. They need strong centralized leadership to survive, but there's no reason the Crown can't share some of its power with the rest of the nobility." He paused and sipped his drink before explaining. "There have been times when the beast-men were quiet for so long every-one thought they were all dead. There have been times, like now, when they were a threat looming large on the horizon. In fact, it was at a time, long ago, when the beast-men were overrunning the country that the first Riders met and bonded with their partners. Through it all, though, Horne has been the main buffer between the Roracks and the rest of the civilized world. The mountains to the east are a natural barrier for the most part. Even though a few of the more adventurous members of the species are found and killed in Trent or Tyler from time to time, all of them have been younger males. The creatures seem reluctant to risk their females trying to climb down the treacherous eastern crags, so the monsters continually test the lands to the west. If Horne falls, the next logi-cal step for the beast-men will be to move south and east. Without the mountains in their way, and enough food to allow their num-bers to increase they will spread across the known world like lo-custs. That is why the elves continue to send Hunters north year after year to cull the species."

Delno sat back and Nassari took over. "We don't like abducting Thomas any more than you do, Brock, but the man is being com-pletely unreasonable. Therefore, Will, Jhren and I are going to the capital to bring him back here. We will lock him in a room with the leaders of the rebellion and force them to talk until they reach an agreement. With Thomas here his troops will not move against the rebels, and, hopefully, we can keep the Roracks at bay until some semblance of normalcy is restored. If, in the end, he still won't see reason, we will return him to his capital and let this civil war run its course while we fortify our own position and salvage what we can after the contest is decided."

"I have trusted both of you with my life many times in the past. I hope you are right this time, also," was Brock's only comment.

Chapter 52

"First you kidnap me, then you compound your crimes by handing me over to these traitors. You'll pay for this. Horne has been tolerant of the Dragon Riders up until now, but this action will be your ruin. When I am free and this rebellion is crushed, I will wipe this land clear of you and level this place to the ground!"

"Sit down, Thomas," Delno said tiredly. "You are in no position to make threats. Even if you had enough manpower and money to move an army against us here, we would simply burn them to cinders before they could establish a foothold on this plain. So please stop making asinine threats."

"We were told the King would be here to talk, but I see no evidence that he is here to do more than continue his posturing," Count Larran said in a nasal whine that grated on Delno's nerves.

Everyone in the room began trying to speak at once. The volume continued to rise as each person tried to outshout the next. Suddenly there was a tremendous bellow from one of the dragons in the courtyard and total silence followed in its wake.

"Now that I have your attention," Nassari said, "it's time to get down to business." Thomas started to speak, but Nassari glared at him and held up his hand for silence. "We have heard all of the posturing and threats we will listen to. This kingdom is in real trouble.

While all of you sit here bickering, the majority of Horne's soldiers are languishing in and around the capital when they should be defending your borders from the beast-men. If we do not stop this nonsense and settle the issues that are in question here, you will all have damn little to return to."

"I thought the Dragon Riders were watching the borders." Thomas made the statement an accusation.

"The Riders can only do so much," Delno responded. "There are leagues of border to watch and only so many dragons to watch it all. Also, the beast-men are moving in groups that are no larger than fifty to sixty strong. We cannot do it all from the air. We have to have ground troops in place, and you have pulled those troops from their assigned positions."

"I wouldn't have had to pull those troops back to the capital if it weren't for the traitorous actions of the nobles."

"We wouldn't have been compelled to act in open revolt if you had listened to our complaints and tried to help us with our needs rather than telling us that your word is law and we have no right to demand a say in foreign affairs and trade. It is we who do the trading and pay the taxes that support this kingdom." Larran shot back.

"You have been lucky up to this point that We have allowed you to operate within Our borders," Thomas responded.

Larran and the other nobles present were nearly beside themselves with rage at the king's use of the royal plural. It was a mannerism Thomas adopted as a dismissal, and they had no intentions of being put off.

"You're lucky that the Riders have taken away our belt knives, Your Majesty," Larran made the title sound like an insult. "Or I would give you several inches of cold steel between your ribs to think about." He turned to Delno and Nassari and said, "This is pointless! The only way this will be settled is on the field. This man will never see reason. Either let us kill him here and now, or return us all to our camps and we will see if this tyrant's army can withstand our forces."

"Our forefathers," Thomas said pompously, "have been ruling this land by the will of all gods down through time beyond memory. We will continue to hold what is Ours..."

"Enough!" Delno shouted, so loudly that he was actually heard out in the courtyard, and Geneva roared in defiance of anything that was upsetting her Bond-mate. "I have tolerated all of the pomposity and outright threats I am willing to put up with." He looked squarely at the King and said, "Thomas, I know of you and your family. The memory of the elves is much longer than that of humans, and their libraries are extensive. Your forefathers carved out a small country here long ago, and it was only through the tolerance of the Dragons and, later, the Dragon Riders, that you have been able to hold it. During the Clan Wars it was House Horne, your ancestors, who could not accept being ruled by others and kidnapped a son from House Bourne, and another from House Corice—my family – and used foul magics to corrupt their minds and turn them into assassins. It was because of that act those two ruling houses were so devastated that they were forced from their ancestral lands into the inhospitable north. That brought about three more decades of the bloodiest fighting of the Clan Wars here in the south. In the end, several of the Houses in control of city-states were wiped out entirely. Horne, which had long before consolidated itself into a country by allying itself with House Larran, House Brand, and House Sellars, to name the chief players, was then able to more than triple its size by claiming all of the territory from the mountains in the north to the sea in the south and west, and to the borders of Trent and Iondar to the east, much of which had formerly been owned by House Bourne. Because of your family's malicious deeds, my family lost its territory when it was divided up between House Ondar and House Palamore. Since that time, House Horne has ruled these lands as tyrants and made frequent war against its neighbors. That has come to an end! You will either treat with these men, or we will return you to your capital and let them bring you down by military force. Your claim of total sovereignty over these lands is not yours by divine right as you would have others believe." He paused for a moment to let that sink in before continuing.

When Delno was certain he had everyone's undivided attention, he added, "Horne is yours by the machinations of your ancestors and the actions of corrupt mages, as well as the loyalty of the forefathers of the nobles you are so callously ready to cast aside. And through it all, for more than twenty-five hundred years since the Clan Wars, and ten times that long since the original bonded pairs of Dragons and Riders first came to the aid of your forefathers, it has always been protected by the Riders and their Bond-mates who have worked to keep the Roracks at bay. It is for these reasons that the Royal House of Horne has flourished and expanded Horne's borders to where they are now. However, at this time, there are more beast-men and fewer Riders, and we cannot now accomplish our task without the complete cooperation of Horne's military. If you do not soon learn to work with your nobles and end this current strife, Horne will cease to exist!"

Nassari was the only one who noticed, but Thomas's demeanor changed almost imperceptibly. For the first time, he began to understand that he would either have to kill all of his nobility or die at their hands if these negotiations failed. If either of those things came to pass, the country would still be laid to ruin by the Roracks. The realization was a blow, but he held it in well. He did, however, sit down and shut up for the moment.

"I believe," Nassari said, "that we can now begin to listen to each other. Count Larran, if you will read your list of grievances, the king will at least sit quietly and pay attention. Then we can begin to hammer out the basics of a compromise."

Larran looked at him like he had lost his mind, but the King nodded. The Count was surprised at the sudden change, but he shrugged his shoulders and picked up a small stack of papers off of the table directly in front of his chair.

At first, Thomas got in a snit over everything on the list, nit-picking each single point until the nobles were once again beginning to believe that bloodshed would be the only answer. It took all of Nassari's skill, as well as his magical talent of persuasion, to keep the talks going without violence erupting, but by day's end, both sides were beginning to see that an agreement could be reached.

Before they closed for the day, though, Delno had one last thing to attend to. "Gentlemen, before we adjourn for the night, I have to bring up some unpleasant business that must be finished." He went to the door and opened it.

Bastian was one of the few minor nobles who had been allowed to come from the capital, and he was ushered into the room. Shortly after Bastian strutted in, Simon, Sheena, and Boron joined them. Bastian was obviously distressed to see them, but Count Larran put a restraining hand on him before he could make any comment. Even Larran couldn't control the man when Broderick was brought in wearing the collar that Jhren and Elom had fashioned.

"This is an outrage!" Bastian yelled and leaped to his son's side. "Remove this thing from my son at once. I'll see you all dead for this insult!"

"You'll hold your tongue and listen to what is said, or you could find yourself sharing this boy's fate," Delno replied.

Larran looked at Delno and said, "Get on with it, Rider. Our group has been indulgent so far, but our patience has it limits. There's no need to rub this nobleman's nose in it any more than necessary."

Delno nodded. "This young man purchased a talisman that rendered him invisible and used that talisman to try and get into this Fort to assassinate a Dragon Rider. In the past, he committed grievous insult and injury to the same person he tried to kill here. He committed rape…"

Bastian tried to protest, but Larran stopped him. "Your son is to be turned over to the Council of Lords. Let them present their evidence. If the boy is innocent, he will be allowed to go free; if he is guilty we will decide his fate."

Delno waited for a moment and when Bastian made no further objection, he continued. "Broderick repeatedly raped the young indentured servant, Simon. He used force, and threats of violence against the boy's mother to do this. When Simon finally managed to get out of his control, he turned his attention to another boy on the estate. Simon caught him in the act of trying to rape that boy and the two fought. Knowing he couldn't stay at the estate once he had fought with Broderick, and not willing to leave Broderick to continue to prey on the other boy after he had gone, he castrated the Lord's son before running off into hiding."

"Then he killed four of my men and four of my horses while escaping, and nearly killed me as well," Bastian spoke up vehemently.

"It could be argued," Nassari said in a silky tone, "that since the boy had committed no crime by coming to the defense of the younger boy, you had no right to pursue him, especially beyond the boundaries of your own lands. It is arguable that he was within his rights to use any means to escape."

"That's preposterous…" Bastian began, but he was cut off by Larran.

"Bastian, if you don't keep quiet we'll never get through this. I told you that the Riders have agreed to accept the judgment of the Council of Lords on this matter. Since there are more than enough Lords present to speak for the whole Council, let us handle it."

Delno cleared his throat and continued. "I will dispense with what occurred between the time Simon left Horne and the time he returned, since the Lords of this kingdom have no jurisdiction over events that transpired in Trent and Ondar. I will restate what happened here since our arrival. Broderick attempted to hire a young mage to sneak into this place and capture Simon. When the mage refused, Broderick then used threats of violence to force the mage to sell him a talisman of invisibility known among sneak-thieves as an amulet of shadows. He then used that talisman to attempt to sneak past the dragons and make his way to Simon's room. The dragons, of course, weren't fooled by such simple magic, and we laid a trap for him. He crept into Simon's room and thrust a large dagger into what he thought was the sleeping Rider. That we were aware of his plot and foiled his attempt does not, in any way, mitigate the fact that he tried to commit murder here. At this time, if the Council wishes, we can bring in the other boy to present testimony about the assaults he endured before the night Simon escaped, as well as the mage Broderick coerced in this matter."

"We've all read the written testimony," Larran said. "There's no need to put the young boy through the ordeal of doing so in person, and the mage was quite thorough when he wrote down his account of events."

"This is starting to sound rehearsed," Bastian said. Then he looked at Larran and accused, "By all of you!"

"Well, then, that leaves this in the hands of the Council of Lords," Delno said before that track could go farther. "There is one last bit of evidence I would like to submit to the Council for consideration, though." He hauled up a cloth bag and set it on the table. "In this bag are both the official and unofficial ledgers from Lord Bastian's estate."

Bastian jumped to his feet and yelled, "Those are my private property! You had no right to seize them!"

"Oh, we had the right," Nassari said silkily. "As you well know, the wealth of a minor noble is not entirely his to do with as he pleases. Said noble is bound by law to ensure that his holdings are kept viable so that his proper share of taxes can be paid to the crown. When your son and heir illegally used large amounts of the funds available to try and enforce a warrant that had already been vacated by the King, he placed the security of your estate in question. The governor of this territory, out of concern for the welfare of Horne, felt he had no choice but to issue a warrant for the seizure of all records regarding your lands and other holdings. That document was viewed and approved by all of the Lords on this council who are present. It seems they've had their eyes on you for a while now, Lord Bastian." Nassari held up the warrant for all to see.

All of the color drained from Bastian's face and he sank into a chair without another word.

"We will examine the documents and give you our decision in the morning, Riders," Larran said. He then turned to the King and addressed him most courteously. "Your Majesty, speaking for all of the Lords, I can say that we have made great strides in reaching an equitable compromise. I will bid you good night, and the Council will be happy to resume our meeting at your earliest convenience tomorrow."

The King nodded, and Larran added, "If you Riders will be so kind and let us have the use of this hall for a bit, we will now meet in closed session and decide the fate of this pair." He indicated Bastian and Broderick.

CHAPTER 53

"WHY HAVEN'T THEY let us know what is going on?" Rita asked.

Sheena, Simon, and Boron looked up in anticipation of Delno's answer.

"They aren't even dealing with Broderick and Bastian right now. According to what Nassari has relayed through the dragons, the King was up all night thinking this over. It appears that he has come to the full realization that his only option is to share power with the Council of Lords. He called a meeting early this morning. Both sides have asked Nassari to mediate."

"I don't get it," Rita responded. "Those stuffed shirts spent several hours behind locked doors last night to settle the matter concerning justice for Simon, and then they refuse to tell us what was decided?"

"They aren't refusing, Dear; the issue has taken on less importance in their eyes since Thomas called them this morning so intent on working out the business of state. To their minds, Simon's issues are a minor affair."

Rita started to make a heated reply but Sheena laid her hand on the woman's arm and said, "It's all right Rita, we understand. It's not as though Simon is still in danger. The King and the Council of Lords have reiterated the decree that any reward formerly offered is rescinded. Bastian is locked in quarters, and Broderick can't use harsh language without risk of activating that collar. We can wait until the business of setting the country right is handled before we deal with more personal problems."

"Besides," Nadia said with a malevolent look in her eye, "I don't mind having Broderick stuck in the collar for a little longer."

Finally, at nearly four hours past noon, the door to the council room opened and Nassari came out. He walked straight to Delno. "I'll tell you what, Del; that was one intense political session. I'm glad it's over. We did, however, get an agreement signed by both sides. The King has ceded certain powers to the Council of Lords, and they have agreed that their authority to veto the Crown's decisions should be limited, as well. It took all of my talent of persuasion to keep them from coming to blows at times, but it's finally over. There will be a formal re-signing of the charter once all parties are back at the capital, but what we have is binding. Also, I got our security reiterated in the By-Laws. This plain is officially outside of the jurisdiction of Horne and is ruled by the Riders. We are also to be paid a stipend for patrols from now on, and we have retained all the rights of our original charter."

"Ahem," Rita and Nadia both cleared their throats at the same time.

"Oh yes, sorry ladies; I don't know what was decided about Bastian and his son. The subject didn't come up."

Count Larran overheard the last comment as he walked toward them, and said, "We have come to a decision and will make an announcement as soon as the Lords have had a chance to take care of necessities and get some refreshment. If you will all meet back here in one hour?" He turned to Nassari. "And have the accused brought, too."

Nassari nodded and Larran moved quickly in the direction of the privies.

"Damn that man," Nadia swore softly at the retreating nobleman.

"You can hardly blame him, my love," Nassari responded. "After all, we've been stuck in that room since before sun-up with nothing more than a biscuit, a piece of fruit, and a couple of cups of tea. It was an exhausting session."

Simon shrugged his shoulders. "I guess we'll find out in an hour. That gives me time to have a quick flight with Sienna before the Lords give us their decision." He saluted Delno and Nassari before he turned and left to find his Bond-mate.

Boron shook his head and said, "I suppose for him it's pretty much over any way you look at it. He's beaten Broderick, and he and Sienna are safe. It would be nice to see him start acting like an eleven-year-old boy for a while."

"You can be sure that he will get the chance," Rita said while she glared at both Delno and Nassari. "I won't allow that boy to be pushed too hard in his training. I don't care if he is bonded to a Lineage Holder; he's not to have the responsibility of leadership laid on his shoulders before he's at least sixteen!"

Both leaders made a gesture of surrender.

*   *   *

Simon barely made it back to the conference hall in time. He found his place at his mother's side just as Count Larran had stepped up to the front of the room to announce the Council's ruling.

Broderick and Bastian were both seated to one side of the room, and both were miserable. Bastian looked as though he hadn't slept in days instead of just the one night he had spent under house arrest. Broderick looked like a small animal caught in a trap searching for an escape route.

"The Council has deliberated on the facts in the cases of both of the accused. Since their crimes are not the same, we will deal with them as separate cases even though they claim to be father and son. First, Bastian, formerly Lord Bastian Waverly, has been found to have cheated the crown out of at least five thousand gold crowns over the last ten years that his personal ledgers cover. He is hereby stripped of his title, and his lands are ordered to be surrendered to Horne. He may keep one horse, which is to be chosen for him from those animals in his possession, one pair of trousers, two shirts, one pair of boots or shoes, one blanket, one piece of rope not to exceed fifty feet, one piece of canvas suitable for making a shelter, and one water skin. Further, he is to be escorted to the border, given one week's hard rations, a small plain belt knife, and banished from Horne for all time to come."

Bastian made no effort to protest. He was probably glad to get away without being condemned to hard labor to pay off his debt to the crown; a punishment that, at his age, would be a death sentence. His skin was the color of parchment, but he stood stoically and followed his escort out the door. He wasn't allowed to even be present for his son's sentencing.

Larran stood staring at Broderick so long that people were beginning to wonder if he would say anything at all. When he finally spoke, he had to fight to keep his emotions in check. "Broderick, I will not read the list of your crimes here in front of the ladies who are present, though I suspect that they have already heard of them. If you had simply kept yourself in check once Simon left, we might have had some very small measure of compassion and only sentenced you to a few years in the iron mines for what you did to those two boys. However, you have not shown the slightest remorse or willingness to redeem yourself in any way. Your lust for vengeance has driven you to greater and greater depths of depravity and fouler and fouler deeds. It is, therefore, the decision of the Council of Lords that your life is forfeit. You are to be taken from this place and executed without ceremony. The last and only dignity we offer you is to choose between hanging or having your throat cut. You have one minute to decide."

Simon jumped to his feet. He could barely believe it when he heard his own voice say, "I object to the Council's decision!"

Count Larran looked at Simon and smiled. "I understand that this young man's crimes against you are serious, lad, but this is about justice, not vengeance. I'm afraid we cannot allow for a more painful or gruesome death."

"I'm not objecting to the method, Sir. I'm objecting to the sentence. I don't want him killed."

Now everyone stared in surprise.

Simon spoke quickly; he wanted to say what was on his mind before it changed. "I've met a lot of people in my young life. Some of them have been bad, like Broderick. Most have just been folks who are doing their best to get along the world. Some of them, though, are great men and women, people I've come to respect. Right now, two things that I've learned in recent months have come back to me. One man told me that not killing someone is an easy mistake to fix, but killing can't be taken back once the deed is done. The other thing that was said is that the only person beyond redemption is a dead person. It's highly possible that this man will never redeem himself, but I can't be positive of that. The only way to be sure is to wait and see. If we kill him now, we'll never know. If the Council of Lords doesn't want the responsibility, then leave him with us. That collar is linked to this Fort. As long as he is wearing it he can neither leave nor cause harm to anyone else. I'm only eleven, and I already have enough deaths on my conscience. Killing Broderick won't change what's been done, and it will only add to the burden I already carry."

Larran was thoughtful for a moment before he looked to Nassari and asked, "Will the Riders accept the responsibility of this prisoner?"

Nassari would have answered yes anyway, but he glanced to see if Delno approved. At Delno's nod, he spoke, "We have taken similar action in the past. We will accept the responsibility of Broderick's incarceration here if it will ease Simon's burden. As the boy has said, if it proves to be a mistake, we can always carry out the original sentence."

Larran nodded. "Very well; Broderick's crimes were not an affair of state, meaning we do not need the King's approval to change the sentence, so, if there are no objections from the Council of Lords…."

he paused to give the other nobles a chance to speak up. When no one did he said, "So be it. The prisoner Broderick is to be transferred back to the custody of the Dragon Riders."

Later, Broderick approached Simon in the courtyard. Even if the boy hadn't been wearing the collar, Simon wouldn't have worried. Sienna growled and Broderick stopped about ten feet away.

"Sienna, he can't hurt us," Simon said softly to her.

"That collar doesn't mean I have to like him."

"I don't like him either, but I see no reason to taunt or torment him at this point. I have put the past behind me for the most part."

"The other night you drove a dagger into me and nearly ended my life; this afternoon you spoke up and saved me. Why would you do that for me?" The former nobleman's speech came out in a rush, as if he were afraid that his courage would fail before he could say what he wanted.

"I don't know if you will ever understand all of it, Broderick. I wonder if you can even comprehend the concept of compassion. So let me try and put this in terms you will understand. I didn't do this just for you. I did it, in large part, for me. Make no mistake; if you attacked me again, I would kill you without a second thought. Perhaps, one day, I will stop hating you. For now, I don't like you, but I do believe that you can become a good person if you work hard enough at it. Perhaps then you'll know what was going through my mind in that room."

CHAPTER 54

"ONE OF THE junior Riders found him this morning," Will said. "The poor girl is only fifteen and had never seen a dead body before. She was half asleep and almost walked right into him on her way out to commune with her dragon. Shook her up pretty badly; Nadia is with her now."

"Judging from the condition of the body, I'd say he died about midnight, or shortly after," Nat said as he examined the corpse.

"Did he do this to himself?" Simon asked.

"One set of tracks leading up to the spot," Brock replied. "The bark on the tree is disturbed here where he climbed up and tied the rope; most likely swung out from the same place once the line was secure and his head was in the noose. Besides that, Broderick was not huge, but the only one tall enough hoist him up there and reach the limb to tie the rope is Elom, and if Elom had wanted him dead, he would have just broken his neck with his bare hands and been done with it. No one had any reason to murder him once he'd been sentenced. It's suicide."

"Aye, thanks for the vote of confidence, Brock," Elom responded.

Simon's mother tried to guide him away from Broderick's body, but the boy stood his ground. "I think I might have been the last to see him alive. He asked me why I spoke up for him, and I'm afraid I wasn't extremely nice when I answered."

"Don't blame yourself for this, Son," Delno spoke up. "Broderick made his own choice."

"I'm not blaming myself. I'm just wondering if he did this out of remorse, or as the only way he could strike out at me for ruining his life. He might have felt some guilt, but he also knew that I didn't want another death on my conscience. I guess we'll never know for sure."

Delno shook his head and drew his belt knife. He reached up and cut the rope as Elom caught the body.

"We'll wrap the body in a shroud and Nora and I will carry it off the plain to bury it," Elom said. "No human should be simply left to rot, but this plain has been hallowed by the blood of our own—he doesn't deserve a plot here."

Delno nodded and the big man turned without further comment and walked away carrying Broderick's corpse. Everyone else headed back inside the Fort.

CHAPTER 55

A COUPLE OF HOURS after Broderick's body had been found and disposed of, the leaders of the Dragon Riders met with Sheena and Simon in Nassari's private office.

"I wanted to talk with you all about Simon," Sheena stated. She held Simon's hand, and Boron stood by her side as she spoke to Delno, Brock, Nassari, Rita, and Nadia. Nat, Will, and Jhren all sat on a couch listening intently. "I know that he is the Rider of a Lineage Holder, and that position has been explained to me, but he is still my son."

Before she could continue, Rita spoke up. "Simon is young enough that no responsibilities will be laid on him for a few years, Sheena. If he wants to stay and live with you, we certainly have no objections. That will work out much better for all concerned if you continue to live here at the Fort, but even the village is plenty close enough for us to keep an eye on Simon until he is old enough to take on the responsibilities of his position." She emphasized the words "old enough" more for Nassari and Delno than for Sheena. She was adamant that the boy would be allowed to grow up without the burden of his station being heaped on his shoulders.

Sheena smiled gratefully at the woman. "Thank you, Rita. I have come to trust you all more than I ever thought would be possible. You felt you had an obligation to Simon due to his bond, but you had no obligation to me. In spite of that, you all took me in and treated me as one of your own. Not once have I been made to feel as if I owe any of you anything, and I owe all of you everything." Delno and Nassari both opened their mouths to speak, but Sheena held up her hand to stop them. "I know you will say that you simply did what is right, and that I owe no debt to you, but I feel differently. And you aren't going to change my mind, so don't try."

The men settled back into their chairs and waited patiently while Sheena gathered her thoughts before continuing.

"I saw something in my son this morning that every mother anticipates with dread and delight. I saw the clear indications that my little boy has grown up. That gruesome scene out there would have had a child hiding in fear behind his mother's skirts. But my son stood with the rest of the men and tried to make sense of it. Being mature beyond his years is more than just a byproduct of his bond with Sienna. He is only eleven, but he has seen so much. Not even counting the crimes that were committed against him, his life has been hard, and he was forced to mature early and take on the responsibilities that were left when his father died. No child can go through what Simon has without being forced to mature. I had already suspected it before, but the events of this morning have crystallized it in my mind. He still has a lot of growing to do, like all of us, but he has moved beyond my parenting. Simon can make his own decisions about his future. I'm just glad that he has so many wonderful people he looks up to from whom he can get guidance. If he wants to stay with the Riders here at the Fort, or even move on with Brock or one of the other instructors, it's not for me to stop him."

"I understand what you are saying, Sheena," Rita replied. "But I still insist that Simon, or any other youngster, is not grown enough for full Rider's responsibilities—not before the age of sixteen, at least. The boy should stay close to his mother, and not go off into the world with little or no guidance."

"He's done pretty well by himself so far," Nassari argued. "He didn't need guidance to survive for more than two months in Rorack territory."

"Don't pull that on me, Nassari Orrin. You know damned well that was different. There's no one chasing him now. There are more choices available to him, and I say he's to be given the time to grow into his position."

"I think you should all stop trying to decide his fate for him," Will said from across the room.

The argument that was about to boil over went back down to a simmer as they all looked at Delno's half-brother.

"I've learned in recent years that the best way to find out what someone wants is to ask him. Have any of you even bothered to see what Simon thinks his next move should be? After all, he's proved that he's pretty level-headed."

"I guess," Nassari said chuckling, "that we were so caught up in deciding his future that we never thought to check and see if he had any preferences."

Everyone in the room looked at Simon. He stepped forward a bit and said, "I actually have given it a great deal of thought. I want to be the best Rider I can be. To that end, I need to train under the best teachers. Brock has taught me much, and he is a good man, as well as a great Rider. But he admits that I need to be trained by the Riders of Lineage Holders. So, while I would like to travel with him and learn about the world at some point, now is not the time. Delno is a fine man and can teach me much, but he and Rita have their hands full with three very precocious children who have unexpectedly bonded. They will be around for a while, and I will learn from them. And I can help them keep up with the kids. Nassari has more to do than most men, but following a mentor and watching him in his day-to-day duties can be very instructive. Also, Dragon Riders aren't independently wealthy, so I want to take Master Elom up on his offer to have me learn from him and Boron. Staying at the Fort for now not only gives me a chance to study under all of them; it allows me to remain close to my mother." He turned to Sheena and added, "I know I'm growing up, but sometimes I just want to be your little boy again for a while."

The Dragon Riders all nodded, and Boron clapped Simon on the back. Tears flowed down Sheena's cheeks as she hugged her son tightly.

ABOUT THE AUTHOR

J.D. HALLOWELL, AUTHOR OF the popular *War of the Blades* and *Legion of Riders* series, is a 60-ish father and husband who is blessed to have lived an interesting and active life. His varied experiences include such diverse occupations as automotive mechanic, photographer, bouncer, paralegal, and massage therapist. He has been a soldier and an EMT, and has served as the chief of a volunteer ambulance squad. At one time, he was a diamond courier, and later owned a working kennel, and he has trained law enforcement dogs as well as personal protection and assistance dogs. He studied martial arts for over 30 years. Although he is now disabled  by the cumulative result of injuries sustained both in and out of the military (he has been shot, stabbed, blown up, bludgeoned, poisoned, and has even had harsh language directed toward him), he writes whenever he can, and has had four fantasy novels, *Dragon Fate, Dragon Blade, Dragon Home*, and *Dragon Justice* published, and has several other fantasy and science fiction projects underway. His other interests include but are not limited to history, archery, cooking, and making jewelry. He currently lives on the Space Coast of Florida with his wife, his son, and his Great Dane service dog.

A Portrait of the Author with Indie the Wonder Dog and a Hawk

ALSO BY J.D. HALLOWELL

War of the Blades Series

Book 1: *Dragon Fate*
Book 2: *Dragon Blade*

Legion of Riders Series

Book 1: *Dragon Home*

JOIN THE CONVERSATION

If you enjoyed this book, please consider taking the time to leave a rating or review at the retailer where you purchased it and/or on Goodreads, LibraryThing or other book discussion and review site.

www.ingramcontent.com/pod-product-compliance
Lightning Source LLC
Chambersburg PA
CBHW020252120726
47904CB00001B/174